Critic ... **...** of ...

Th

"A wry, street-smart, bare-knuckles, behind-bars brawl that bears up under a thick plot and a large cast of dirty denizens. . . . It's difficult to tell the schemers from the scammed as Orin Boyd, a proud Vietnam vet blessed with equal helpings of brains and brawn, takes on all comers. . . . Fans of the police procedurals of early Wambaugh and late McBain will delight in the gruff sensibilities of Westermann's heroes and the unregenerate sleaziness of his villains."
— *Kirkus Reviews*

"Westermann delivers another gripping police thriller."
— *Chicago Tribune*

"Orin Boyd, Jon Westermann's Long Island cop-hero, has been convincing from the first, a complex character, at once maddening and sympathetic, who struggles as much with his own contradictions as with the villains he pursues. Orin is a victim of his own ironic humor, a man bent on devouring himself. . . ."
— Stephen Solomita

"Westermann, who worked twenty years as a Long Island cop, brings plenty of colorful detail to the novela and to Boyd, who's smart, funny and not above taking the law into his own hands. The pacing is relentless, and the uncovering of secrets old and new will keep readers glued as they're plunged into a Long Island that's way beyond Levittown."
— *Publishers Weekly*

"Westermann is a talented storyteller. . . . Cop novel fans need to put Westermann's books on their required reading list."

—Thomas Gaughan, *Booklist*

"[A] fine police procedural. . . . well plotted, well written and consistently absorbing. . . . The image of people usually perceived as the good guys now filling the role of the bad guys is one that catches the imagination. These are complex characters. . . ."

—Joan Kotker, *The Armchair Detective*

"A fast-moving, mordantly funny look at cops gone bad."

—*The Hartford Courant* (CT)

"The pace is truly relentless—it moves so fast you are absolutely glued to the pages, and the hero is smart and funny."

—*Ellenville Press* (NY)

"Police procedural fans will like Westermann's forceful prose, natural wit, and constant action."

—*Library Journal*

Books by John Westermann

High Crimes
The Honor Farm
Exit Wounds
Sweet Deal

Published by POCKET BOOKS

THE HONOR FARM

JOHN WESTERMANN

POCKET BOOKS

New York   London   Toronto   Sydney   Tokyo   Singapore

This book is a work of fiction. Names, characters, places and incidents are products of the author's imagination or are used fictitiously. Any resemblance to actual events or locales or persons, living or dead, is entirely coincidental.

POCKET BOOKS, a division of Simon & Schuster Inc.
1230 Avenue of the Americas, New York, NY 10020

Copyright © 1996 by John Westermann

All rights reserved, including the right to reproduce this book or portions thereof in any form whatsoever. For information address Pocket Books, 1230 Avenue of the Americas, New York, NY 10020

ISBN: 0-671-87123-4

First Pocket Books paperback printing January 1998

10 9 8 7 6 5 4 3 2 1

POCKET and colophon are registered trademarks of Simon and Schuster Inc.

Front cover photo illustration by Joe Perez

Printed in the U.S.A.

For my mother and my father

Acknowledgments

Usually the author will express in this space his gratitude for the people who helped him write the book. This time out I have to thank the people who helped me live to see its publication: Dr. Steve O'Brien of The Hospital for Special Surgery in New York; Dr. Yuman Fong and staff and volunteers at Memorial Sloan-Kettering; my friends and my family; but most of all my brother David. In the midst of disaster, he was a rock.

THE
HONOR
FARM

1

SATURDAY, JUNE 25, 1:00 A.M.

IT BEGAN ON A NIGHT WHEN HE THOUGHT HE WAS finished, when all he wanted was peace.

"Here comes another one," the eager rookie sitting next to him said. "That makes five."

Orin Boyd lowered his *Newsday* and watched the 1976 Cutlass roar by on Northern Boulevard. "But who's counting?"

Between them—where gung ho cops kept designer briefcases—Orin had wedged his Igloo minicooler, that night packed with a ham sandwich and a container of Quik, a few loose Tic-Tacs, firecrackers, and coffee-stained felony complaints.

Probationary Officer Meyers had brought nothing, said he was too nervous to eat. He flipped through his virgin summons pad.

Another marriage made in heaven, thought Orin, wondering again how they paired men off at the precinct, what data were employed to match impressionable rookies with burned-out hairbags. Orin had not the time nor the inclination to share his police experience with this twerp. He wanted to read the sports section and catch a nap next to a Dumpster, continue in solitude his cruise into the safe harbor of municipal retirement. Both men were wearing mourning bands over their silver shields to honor a fallen comrade, the police commissioner's son. What they had in common ended there.

They were on routine motor patrol, meaning they were responsible for the safety—if not the sales receipts—of Manhasset's Miracle Mile, the shopper's slice of the Gold Coast.

Orin dropped the gearshift into low, started singing softly, "Rolling, rolling, rolling . . ." Ten miles an hour, since midnight. Rolling. Trolling. Marking time, checking storefronts for breaks, bistro parking lots for damsels in distress. All the while Arnold Meyers was biting his fingernails, spitting them out, making sure he still had his handcuffs and gun, checking his look in the sideview mirror.

Orin said, "Hey, Barney, I ever tell you—"

"Arnie," said Arnold Meyers.

"Did I call you Barney again? I don't know why the fuck I keep doing that."

Then a duct-tape Caddy with fins swooped past them at warp speed and Meyers cried out, "Jesus Christ! What's it take for you to write a ticket?"

"Whoa, baby. Chill. Those are city cops, bugging out from four-by-twelves, most of them shit-faced. Now, if you want to meet a few and show them your brand-new gun and badge, we can flip on the old roof rack here . . ."

Orin reached slowly for the plastic knob.

Meyers held up his summons book and said, "We don't burn other cops?"

"Of course not. What the fuck are they teaching you guys?"

Meyers pulled his cap down low. "Sorry. I didn't know."

"And stop apologizing."

Orin had not liked this spit-and-polish new kid from day one, which had been yesterday, last night—too many dumb remarks, too many personal questions, as if some departmental historians had already prepped the kid on Orin's colorful past. A pimple-faced probie with a boot-camp haircut, just out from behind the counter of a Suffolk County deli, the poor chump looked the way Orin had when he was marched off to Vietnam.

To make things worse, this goofy kid was supposed to be his partner for the next six months, the last six months of Orin's twenty-year obligation, before Orin took his pissant pension and became a ward of his wife.

Twenty years without advancement, thought Orin, was hard to manage in a scandalously top-heavy police department that had somebody officially in charge of everything, whether it needed it or not. Only the truly independent or the crazy escaped promotion and spent their careers outside, in the elements, scorned like dogs. Orin's lack of advancement had never been a concern until it came time to compute his pension benefits.

And now Barney Fife here wanted Action and Adventure, because he had obviously never seen any; while it sometimes seemed to Orin as if Action and Adventure were all he had ever seen, from his years with the Walking Dead of the Ninth Marines, to the armpits of Nassau County. He had long ago stopped counting the men whose deaths he had caused, directly or otherwise: NVA regulars, Cong, a crooked Belmont cop and the scumbags who had owned him, a punk kid who had ambushed an honest cop, an innocent chain-gang wino named Batman. Five sober years had passed since the last awkward funeral.

The radio squawked, and the 911 dispatcher assigned a neighboring patrol car to an aided case, a possible miscarriage.

Meyers looked at Orin. "Back them up?"

"Arnie, Arnie," said Orin, "you're not making good decisions. I'm gonna have to include that in my field evaluation."

"But—"

Orin held up an instructive finger. "For God's sake, think, Arnie. That's all that poor woman needs right now is extra cops trooping through her house. These people are not geeks, you know, here to *amuse* you."

Meyers's neck burned red above his navy blue collar. "You feel like running some warrant checks, then? We got a long night ahead of us."

"Dark one, too," Orin added.

"How can you just circle all night long?"

"You don't dig circles, you're in the wrong line of work."

"It can't all be like this."

"No," allowed Orin, "most of it is worse, which reminds me: We still got to get you qualified mouth-to-mouth."

Meyers chucked him an especially sour mug, given his scrawny physique and Orin's fact-backed reputation for brutality. And then Orin recalled that several other people had given him that look lately, usually after he had said something cruel. He lit up a Carlton, his only concession to the surgeon general's shocking numbers for Marlboros.

Meyers looked at him sheepishly, and said, "Would you mind putting that out?"

"I told you kid, I don't smoke, I get cranky as hell."

"But I checked the *patrol manual,* like you said I should, and Commissioner Trimble's orders say that when two men are assigned to one car——"

Orin held up a second instructive finger. "Dave Trimble just buried his only son. He don't care if I smoke and you die."

"But that's not fair."

Orin took a deep drag and looked at his black rubber runner's watch, blew the smoke out the window. "You hungry, kid?"

"I could probably hold down some tea."

"I knew we'd get together on something." Orin whipped the steering wheel hard right and bounced the blue-and-white patrol car into the brightly lit Dunkin' Donuts parking lot, screeched to a halt near the side door. Meyers got out of the car. Orin shifted to reverse and backed away. "Pick you up in ten," he yelled.

"But——"

Orin held up a third instructive finger, and when he could

see in the rearview mirror that Meyers had given up his foot pursuit, he cut back on the gas and resumed his slow patrol of the post, happily alone with his addictions, lounging and lurking outside stores he could not afford to shop in on what the police department paid him.

Orin was forty-five years old, with short-cropped reddish blond hair, thick neck and chest, and muscular arms and legs. The pale green tattoo on his right biceps showed a skull wearing dogtags. The inscription read KHE SANH 1968; his left arm bore a skull awash in red roses, the phrase, WHAT A LONG STRANGE TRIP IT'S BEEN. The one on his ass said U.S. GRADE A PRIME. He was sick of them, as he was sick of most of the colorful mistakes of his life. The medals he was entitled to wear above his shrouded police shield were in the bottom drawer of his dresser at home. Unless Judy had thrown them out or his daughter Dawn had pinned them to one of her G.I. Joe dolls.

No one knew where his cash was stashed, which was just the way he liked it. Not that folks hadn't pried and spied from almost the moment Orin had gotten his meaty hands on those two hundred and eighty-seven thousand unfettered bucks. He would sense guys watching him, tracking his movements, rifling his station-house mail. Sometimes it was tax snoops, sometimes Nassau cops. He heard about every business opportunity, every stock tip, every fast horse, every scatterbrained scam, as that much loot that could not be reported stolen was always worthy of a sting. He suffered through every bad-break and hard-luck story, then reached into his pocket and handed over tens, same as always.

Rumors abounded, died, revived. Yet Orin lived his life as if the money did not exist, which he figured was the only way he would get to keep it. It was enough he was sober. A father to his daughter.

It did, however, gall him that that musty pile of pirate's treasure was not earning interest, nor dividends, nor frequent flier miles, not even bonus points in a Christmas club. Orin felt sure Arnold Meyers would have had that kind of money in stocks, bonds, and pork bellies, looking long-term. Then he realized his hatred for this kid was nearing the pathological.

Orin tossed his butt out the window and made a right onto Northern Boulevard, cruised past a black-tie dinner letting out, the guests lined up in front of Leonard's, awaiting valets. Halfway down the block he spotted a black stretch limo with extra chrome double-parked in the bus stop, a limo he suspected came complete with condoms, intoxicants, and a girl who took credit cards. Orin flashed his roof lights, pulled up broadside, closing down the eastbound lanes completely.

The elderly black driver lowered his tinted window six inches, said out of the side of his mouth, "You know whose car this is?"

"Pretty sure it ain't yours," said Orin. "Now move it, before I feed you my quota."

"Yassuh, boss."

"Asshole," Orin said under his breath, and then it occurred to him that he was prejudiced, that he had a bug up his ass when it came to chauffeurs, because when Orin rode in limousines it was always to weddings or funerals, occasions where only the chauffeurs went home unscathed and well tipped.

On his next pass around the block (four right turns again, as opposed to more difficult left-hand turns), Orin saw that the limo had not moved. Its curbside rear door was now open, and its passengers—two yuppie white men in tuxedos—were arguing with a well-dressed young black woman at the head of the alley, then clutching at her, then roughing her up.

While the taller gentleman pressed her face against the wall, the shorter man turned his back on them and opened her gold purse, dumping her cosmetics, her cash, digging deeper.

Orin slammed on his brakes and goosed his siren, reasonably sure he had a package deal gone bad. The penguins looked up, squawked, caucused for a moment, almost as if they were unconcerned, then ditched the purse and waddled into the alley.

"Six-oh-two to headquarters," said Orin, "I'm out of the car, near Leonard's, investigating a possible assault."

Orin charged past the startled black woman and knocked down the first tux at the end of the alley, grabbed him by the back of his collar, slammed him face-first into the chain-link fence, then spun him around and hooked him hard in the cummerbund, finished him with a hard right cross that launched a thick black toupee into orbit. Orin cuffed his lifeless arm to the base of the chain-link fence, and said, "Sit tight, maestro."

Orin sprinted into the near-empty rear parking lot after the other creep, past an overflowing Dumpster, hither and yon from circle of light to circle of light, and finally gave up at the dark woods at the edge of the lot. Hoping his quarry had not doubled back and lost himself in a sea of tuxedos, Orin put his hands on his hips and yelled, "Hey, Shithead. Come on out of there. Your boy already gave you up. . . . Why not save us both some time and trouble."

No one answered. Nothing moved. A siren broke the silence. Help on the way.

"Okay, later, dude. Watch out for the ticks and dogs and Hanta-virus mice."

Orin could feel the man watching him, hating him, and he reveled in it. He stepped forward ten paces, found darkness, and slipped silently next to a large evergreen tree, smelling the woods, thinking of Christmas, faraway places, high school girlfriends, but always listening hard to the present, knowing how excruciatingly slowly time was passing for his quarry.

Three minutes later, thirty yards away, the leaves rustled.

Thirty seconds after that, the quarry was unconscious and Orin was fighting off a powerful urge to waste him, forcing himself to walk away. The most this yuppie slob had done was bitch-slap a hooker, probably digging for her dope. Hardly a capital offense. Maybe nothing at all by the time the Sixth Precinct dicks were done shirking their duty. He lit a cigarette, then stubbed it out, coughing.

Orin gathered himself and then dragged this second prisoner out of the woods by his ankles, all the way across the asphalt parking lot, back to his first prisoner.

"What happened?" Meyers yelled from the mouth of the alley, fumbling for his flashlight and gun and anything else he might need. "Why'd you dump me?"

Orin dropped the second man's ankles, pushed past Meyers to the street, saw that the limo was gone. The woman, too. A less than promising start to any pending prosecution, making it *his* word against the word of these two no-doubt illustrious citizens.

Back in the alley, Meyers was examining the bloody bald head of the body cuffed to the fence.

"You didn't happen to order all the black folks out of the area, did you?" asked Orin.

Meyers shook his head. "What did you hit this guy with? I think he might be dead."

Orin squatted next to the maestro, found the carotid artery throbbing nicely, shook his head in disgust. Then the second prisoner gurgled and grunted into the pavement, turned his head sideways, and belched. Red wine and linguine sluiced from his mouth like the guts of a shark onto a dock.

Orin said, "By, George, we've found it, your chance at mouth-to-mouth."

Meyers grimaced, backed away. "I'm filing a complaint."

"No. Really. Get the Tic-Tacs from my cooler."

Meyers stayed where he was, shook his head in horror.

"Up to you. Anyway, first we clear the airway. Actually, you clear the airway. With your fingers."

The groggy man lifted his face from his own vomit. His long black hair was lacquered to his skull and he had the swept-back ears of a Doberman. "That's Senator Thomas Cotton, you fucking assholes."

Arnold Meyers took a moment to examine the maestro's face more closely. "It doesn't look like him."

"It did before you beat the dog shit out of him."

Orin found the soiled toupee, splattered against the fence like roadkill, and patted it back into place, framing the victim's face.

Meyers blanched in recognition.

"Senator Sewer?" asked Orin.

"It wasn't me," Meyers cried. "I was having herbal tea. This is only my second night. I—"

Two flashing squad cars swerved to the curb at the end of the alley, discharged their uniformed occupants. A big gray Plymouth brought big gray detectives. Surrounded by brother officers, Orin patted Meyers on the back, felt his bulletproof vest, and knew it wouldn't save him.

2

SATURDAY, JUNE 25, 2:00 A.M.

THEY NEVER EVEN MADE IT TO THE SQUAD ROOM.
The street sergeant called a lieutenant who woke a captain
who called County Executive Gil Otto, who angrily interrupted the furtive lovemaking of Chief of Patrol Anthony
Malone and his secretary.

Police Officers Boyd and Meyers were ordered to respond to the Sixth Precinct desk officer to await further
instructions while those big gray detectives ferried the senator and his executive assistant, Townsend Tripp, to the
Nassau County Medical Center for massive overtreatment
of a variety of minor injuries.

The next sign that things were going badly for the street
cops was when the desk officer refused to hear Orin's side
of the story, insisting that as long as he knew nothing, he
couldn't be involved.

Meanwhile at headquarters, over coffee and ring cakes, a
rapidly sobering senator had ample opportunity to build his
version of the case, with Tripp applying topspin where
needed.

This was craziness, said the heavily bandaged senator through puffy purple lips, for the police to suggest that either he or his assistant would ever rough up a black woman. They had just come from a charity function down the street; therefore this patently illegal detention was an assault upon all decent Americans. . . .

"Wait," said Malone, "until the boss arrives and sorts this out."

"I'm a busy man," said Senator Cotton.

"So am I," said Malone, "since you voted with the NRA."

"I *knew* that was it. I said this was politics. Right, Towny? When I'm right, I'm right. And I'm never wrong."

"Maybe just this once," said Malone.

Townsend Tripp slapped his calamine-coated palm on the desk, slopping coffee onto the blotter. "Picture this: I declare publicly that Officer Boyd beat you up to intimidate you, that Officer Boyd dropped his partner off without authorization so there wouldn't be any witnesses. That he told us to change our minds on gun control or this was just the beginning."

"Only one problem," said Malone. "Officer Boyd's an ex-Marine Corps weapons expert. He loves fucking guns."

"A crazed veteran, then," said Cotton, "a ticking time bomb, tucked away on the graveyard shift by superiors who should have known better."

"Sir, I am extending a courtesy to you," said Malone. "You want me to stop, I will; you want us to go ahead with Officer Boyd's version, I can tell Trimble to go back to bed. Then Public Information can tell *Newsday* what's happening."

"Don't be a wise guy, Chief. I'm the fucking wise guy around here."

SATURDAY, JUNE 25, 4:35 A.M.

POLICE COMMISSIONER DAVID TRIMBLE, THOUGH dressed in tan chinos and a blue NYPD sweatshirt, did not look as though he had been roused from his bed. His thinning blond hair was neatly combed and his eyes were haggard, not puffy from sleep. He met with the night shift gathered on the top floor, then alone with Senator Cotton in his private office, where he promptly told the senator to shut up and stop whining, that he was sick and tired of cleaning up after his no longer so tiny indiscretions.

"Don't be a hard-ass, Davey. You've done your share of catting around."

"You think you got law-and-order problems now, Tommy? Keep fucking with me and my men."

"Davey, Davey. Remember when we used to address each other with respect?"

Dave Trimble glared at the senator. "Quite a long time ago, wasn't it? Before the sewer district kickbacks, and the county bandstand for your birthday party, and the drunk driving, and the complaints from cops you've embarrassed."

Tommy Cotton wasn't listening. "I want this man fired," Tommy Cotton was saying, "immediately. Then arrested, the old-fashioned way, then thrown in goddamn Attica."

"Sorry, Tommy. That won't wash."

" 'Sorry, Tommy'?"

"The facts don't support that resolution."

"Are you actually telling me no?"

"I'm saying you're not making mileage off this. You want last night buried, you throw in the first dirt. Just like the sewer district, only nobody's cutting any ribbons this time."

Tommy Cotton bowed his head dramatically, and Trimble noticed the sand still trapped in his black toupee. "If you said that to be funny," said the senator, "I'm not fucking laughing."

"I said that to remind you that you don't need any of this shit in the worst way."

Cotton inflated like a blowfish, slowly let the air out his ears. "My fucking jaw is killing me, Davey. I want some satisfaction. You can understand that."

Trimble picked up Orin Boyd's personnel folder and flipped through the first few pages, thinking that this was the opportunity he had been praying for, handed to him on a platter: the perfect off-the-wall mole for a difficult penetration. "Tell you what," he said to Cotton. "I got something else I can hang on Boyd, an old beef worth a short trip to the Honor Farm. Settle for that and walk away."

"The man's a dangerous public nuisance—"

"Six months mired in cow shit and blood. And your wife never knows what a bastard she married."

"Done," said the senator. "Done and done."

Then Thomas Cotton shook Trimble's hand and happily signed a release that stated he had not been beaten or abused while in custody of the police following a routine traffic investigation.

Tommy Cotton found Townsend Tripp asleep in the conference room, kicked his chair, explained the deal he had made, without, he added, any assistance from anyone. "Not bad, right?" said Cotton, reattaching his cummerbund. "Given the circumstances."

"Given your wife, you mean."

"And the good news is, we got people in their jail, too."

Saturday, June 25, 6:00 a.m.

ON THE FRONT LAWN, NEAR THE POLICE MEMORial, an elderly white janitor was raising the American flag to half-staff as the sun was rising over Mineola. Orin saluted Old Glory as he rode by, then parked his black-and-silver Harley in the half-filled headquarters parking lot.

He locked the handlebars, opened his saddlebags, and pulled out a magnetic decal (Property Of The Fucking Pagans), which he slapped on the fuel tank, rendering his bike safe from all but illiterates.

Orin had been told to change to civvies and report to the commissioner's office. Arnold Meyers had been relieved of his duties and sent home by the chief of patrol. Neither development was encouraging. As a rookie, Meyers enjoyed the job security of a black man on a loading dock; and Orin figured if they planned on taking him out of headquarters later in handcuffs and leg irons, they would rather he not be wearing the proud navy blue of the Nassau County Police Department.

Commissioner David Trimble's office was in a corner on the top floor of the honeycomb building, with a commanding view of The Dale Carnegie Institute, but no angle on Orin's Harley. Orin made his way through layers of high-ranking lackeys, then entered the dark, wood-paneled office reverently.

David Trimble sat stone still behind his desk, and Orin realized that his son's death had already aged him viciously, cutting jagged lines in his face, bleaching his skin and bones.

"Commissioner."

"Boyd."

Orin folded his hands below his waist, and said, "Sir, I haven't had a chance to tell you how sorry I am about Skip. If there's anything—"

Trimble said, "I was rather surprised when your name came up again in controversy. I would have figured you for a desk by now."

"I'd be home at night, on weekends."

Trimble smiled knowingly and nodded.

"Sorry about all this," said Orin. "Want to hear my side?"

"Not particularly. I want to ask a favor."

Orin felt a familiar flutter in his stomach, a sense that he was already a link in some unfortunate chain. One did not slap a senator silly, no matter what the circumstances.

"I want to pull you off the street," said Trimble.

"Hey, Commissioner, I wasn't off-base out there. I hit him maybe once too often, in the heat of battle. And I'm willing to go public if they are."

"I'm not asking you to quit, Orin. I'm asking you to find out what happened to Skip."

Orin felt the air rush from his chest. He sat down on the

commissioner's couch, recalling the press coverage. "I was led to believe he committed suicide."

"So was everyone else," said Trimble.

"You don't buy it?"

"I'm not sure anymore. And now I don't know if it's me, or the case, or what."

Dave Trimble walked around from behind his desk and dropped a photograph on the couch next to Orin. Orin picked it up and studied the handsome face of the commissioner's son as it had looked on the day he had graduated from the police academy. His happy father had his arm wrapped around his son's slender shoulders, yet Skip was bearing up well under the weight. Did Skip Trimble look as satisfied and pleased as the old man? Orin wondered. Was this the face of a man who would later hang himself in his jail cell? Orin recalled vaguely that young Skip Trimble had smashed an ashtray over someone's head, at a night-club, caused injuries too severe to be swept under anybody's rug. "You want to give me the details? You want someone else to—"

"Skip was my only child, twenty-six years old, in good health, recently married, a graduate of Adelphi University, a cop for two years before his arrest. He . . . allegedly hanged himself with a day to go on his sentence, after eighteen months without a complaint."

"Like someone didn't want him coming out?"

"Who knows. Up until then he had been a model prisoner, at least according to Warden Barthwell and his staff. No problems with the guards or other inmates."

"Or maybe a message to you?"

Dave Trimble's eyes flared angrily, then he gathered his rage and nodded. "The timing suggests it."

"You talk to the prison shrink?"

"According to Dr. Marvin Robbins, Skip went through his periods of depression at the Farm, just like anybody else, nothing major or indicative of suicide; but of course he has to say that to cover his ass. Skip did his chores and read his books and played his tennis and golf."

"Did his wife go to see him?"

"Not that much."

"Why?"

"Why," Trimble repeated wearily. "A while back Maureen told me Skip wouldn't sleep with her anymore. They hardly talked, and when they did, they fought. He started staying out all night, sometimes with an excuse, sometimes not. He was like any young cop, probably just like you were. I told him fun is fun, but keep it under control."

"Honest, if not terribly moral, advice," said Orin.

The commissioner frowned.

Orin stood and walked to the window, smothering a grin. Across the street a highway cop was shagging three white bums from the Lord & Taylor bus stop, perhaps pointing out Orin's Harley to them, suggesting they ride it out of town. "I'm not here for my tact, right?"

"Right." Trimble's pale face began to crack. "And now my detectives tell me he killed himself, with a day to go—"

Orin swallowed hard. "Did Skip leave a note?"

"No."

"Any previous attempts?"

"Never once in his life was Skip suicidal."

"Jail can change people," said Orin.

"That cop-zoo didn't change Skip. Or steal his will to live."

"You're absolutely sure? In your heart of hearts?"

"Come on, Boyd. The Honor Farm is a fucking country club."

"Unless you happen to be a member."

The commissioner snorted dismissively, opened a desk drawer, and pulled out some files.

"I have friends on that farm," said Orin. "And there's no such thing as easy time."

"Whatever. You'll be a one-man task force, reporting directly to me, with access to any resources you need. And I want you to think big. We've got electronics you wouldn't believe. Cameras. Weapons. I saw what you did the last time with no resources."

"Different situation here, boss. I was immersed in that mess and I was drowning."

"Please. Here's a copy of the case jacket. I've also prepared a list of primary suspects of my own . . . from my conversations with Skip over the last few weeks of his life."

"Were there many?" asked Orin, accepting the file. "I mean, did you visit him often?"

"At least three times a week."

"He talked to you . . . man to man? Life in jail, making big ones into little ones, all that shit?"

"Why does that surprise you? I was his father."

Orin shrugged.

"I loved my son, more than anything. I didn't care that he lost his cool exactly once. . . . Now, the other problem is that the first of these suspects, a former aide of mine named Prank Dinostra, gets out in less than ten days. Most of the rest, within the next few months. Once they scatter, which they will, any chance at developing new leads is gone."

"I see," said Orin, though he did not see how he was going to investigate a gaggle of crooked ex-cops who were locked away at some swanky Gold Coast mansion, playing golf and tennis.

"So you've got to be sentenced immediately."

"You mean infiltrate?"

"I'm afraid it's the only way."

"It's almost never the only way."

"I can't send you in there openly. I'd look pathetic, like I was using the department for my personal ends. I'd undercut my own homicide squad, and no one would tell you the truth anyway."

Orin said, "It's just that working undercover you can't ask too many questions. You're all the time protecting your flanks."

"So find another way."

Orin saw that the commissioner had already made up his mind, a negative response was unacceptable. "You sure Barney Meyers can be trusted?"

David Trimble frowned and checked papers on his desk. "We've already found Officer *Arnold* Meyers less challenging duty."

"Why me?"

"I'm looking for a killer. I figure it takes one to know one."

Orin's throat tightened around a response he would have regretted. David Trimble was a father who had lost his only son, maybe his last living relative. If his manners suffered temporarily, who was Orin to complain?

"Dominick Ril is in there," said Orin. "So is George Clarke. You really think we can fool them twice?"

Trimble said, "Neither one's exactly a criminal genius."

Orin did not defend his old mates, merely said, "Didn't Shakespeare once say something about tragedy and farce that might apply to—"

Trimble smiled. "It wasn't Shakespeare. And actually, I believe your old friends will be so busy trying to find where you hid all that money, they wouldn't notice if you collared the warden."

Orin ignored the reference to his money. "And if not?"

"You're a pretty tough cookie. I'm not worried."

An attitude similar to one Orin had encountered in Nam in sixty-eight, when everybody back home was getting drunk and stoned, fighting for pussy and peace over the dinner table, while Orin and all those future homeboys huddled in thunderous bunkers. He was not shocked to discover the boss considered him expendable.

"On the plus side," said Trimble, "think of a life with no more midnight tours, no more lousy weather, no more punks with attitudes and Uzis. A gold shield, and any squad you want. Stick around a few years and pad your pension."

Orin nodded dumbly as the realization struck that for this plan to work, his already tarnished name would have to be thoroughly, if temporarily, destroyed. His daughter's father would be in jail. Judy's husband. And then there was that long list of those who would gloat. "The Marine Bureau," Orin said. "I want the boats."

Commissioner Trimble agreed, told Boyd that if he actually found out what had happened to his son, he'd make Orin an admiral. If the case was a bust, they would go public, restore his reputation, say he was sent in to protect Judge Kane, the only non-cop serving time on the Farm.

"Judge Kane gonna go along with that?"

"He will when we let him out early."

"We can do that?"

"You'd be amazed."

"Then my old partner George leaves the Farm when I leave. No parole or nothing."

"Done."

"What if I find out Skip really killed himself? We got a plan for peace with honor?"

"I'll deal with the truth as it comes."

Orin stared at his hands, considering his future, what skills he might retain from his past. "I'll need a contact I can trust."

"We'll use your wife."

"I'm liking this less and less already."

Commissioner Trimble then produced two signed copies of an order outlining their agreement. Orin read one quickly, saw that it already included the George Clarke provision. Orin signed both without comment, handed one back.

"Put it in a safe place," said Trimble. "I'll do the same, like the glove compartment of my car. Not that I don't trust my staff, but . . ." Dave Trimble stood up and held out his hand apologetically. "I'm afraid I'll need that badge and those guns now. Obviously, you're under arrest."

"Obviously."

"Come on, now. Cheer up. Didn't you once tell me it was only a matter of time before someone locked you away."

"It's been a while since then. I've changed."

"Pray not too much."

3

SATURDAY, JUNE 25, 8:50 A.M.

"A TEMPORARY ARRANGEMENT?" JUDY BOYD cried. "After your picture is in the newspaper? Who do you think you're kidding?"

Orin set the Trimble files on the knotty-pine dining room table and smiled down at his pretty wife of fifteen years. "So they'll fix it with a bigger picture," he said. "And all your friends think I'm a criminal anyway."

Her blue eyes flashed and her cheeks colored. She was frosting her hair these days, wearing it in a loose ponytail held together by a black velvet bow. "You don't fool me for one second, Orin. This is not about Commissioner Trimble and this is definitely not about George Clarke."

"So we'll call this my midlife crisis."

"In addition to your boat and your motorcycle? No way," said Judy. "This is above and beyond the call."

She needs more time, he thought, to get behind the mission, get a different perspective. "Don't you always tell me problems are opportunities?"

"For someone on the way up, not out. You're short, remember, you *don't* volunteer."

She was dead right, he knew, as was so frequently the case. Her levelheadedness and compassion had steered their small family through more than one stretch of rocky road.

She said, "Don't think this is that fourth-quarter comeback you always thought you'd make."

"And didn't," he said softly. "Please, Judy. Help me with this. While Dawn's away at camp. The timing couldn't be better."

"For me to spend a summer by myself?"

"It won't take more than two weeks."

She stared hard at him. "Then you prepare for this, Orin, like you've never prepared for anything. Half-cocked is how you get embarrassed. And let's face it, tough guy, you're not as young as you used to be."

"I will. I promise."

"Two weeks is a long time for me to play the humble wife," she said. "I'm no actress, never was, never will be."

"Let *me* be the judge of that," he said.

SATURDAY, JUNE 25, 12:30 P.M.

ORIN SAT IN CLOGGED TRAFFIC, SLOUCHED FORward on his motorcycle, his head spinning with legal documents and witness depositions, thinking that perhaps he had been lucky to get out of trouble so easily, with an undercover assignment as a bonus. He had fully expected Senator Cotton to do everything in his considerable power to punish him. And he had not. The brash young turk had cut his losses and backed off. Man, thought Orin, if people only knew. What a gaggle of goons they all were, practitioners of selective enforcement and revisionist history.

The signal light changed again.

The IKEA furniture truck in front of Orin belched a black noxious cloud, and a couple of jerks leaned on their horns. Orin had WFAN Sports Radio on his handlebar stereo at the moment, and some whack-job named Ira from Sands Point was on a call-in, raging about yesterday's Mets' loss. The Mad Duck was telling him to deal with it, turn the page, not to let the losses tear him up.

Orin lost his patience with everyone and everything and jumped the Harley out of the line of traffic, onto the sidewalk. He loudly blasted around the tie-up, the cause of which seemed to be two black girls kicking the crap out of a single black boy in the middle of Guy Lombardo Avenue. Orin buzzed them. "Assholes!" he cried. "Be gone!"

The combatants froze for a moment, united against a common enemy, and Orin heard the word "motherfucker" ring out behind him.

He considered prolonging the encounter with multiple arrests, then remembered that he was unarmed, without his shield, an accidental civilian.

He flexed his wrist, roared south to the Freeport waterfront, and parked the noisy hog at the dock.

The *Grunt* was a 21-foot Superboat with a 200 Merc shoved up its ass, a nautical version of the Harley. Orin kept her tied up behind Blotto's Fish Market, lost among larger commercial tenants, a cheap if unfashionable seaside address.

He stepped lightly on the deck and checked the sky to the southwest, over Baldwin Harbor and Long Beach, because he longed for one last wave-dance around Randall Bay. But mountainous thunderheads were chasing bigger boats in, and soon the waterfront saloons would fill with laughter and lust, making Woodcleft Avenue no place for a perpetually recovering drunk. He peeled back the canvas cover, ducked inside the small cabin, and locked his copy of the commissioner's special order inside his tackle box, where it would be safe.

SUNDAY, JUNE 26, 4:00 P.M.

THEY SPENT THAT LAST, HOT, MUGGY SUNDAY afternoon at home, in their centrally air-conditioned Cape.

Orin and Dawn, packing for their separate adventures, made a game out of colliding in the hallway between their bedrooms, falling to the carpet like clowns.

Dawn was leaving for four weeks upstate at the PAL Camp, just like last summer, eager to see old friends, eager that they see her. Orin seemed to remember a Daniel being mentioned rather often upon her return, and he felt the ache of her growing pains collide with his own excitement. He followed her into her cozy room and sat at her desk, picking the opening bars of "Satisfaction" on her guitar, watching her decide among her shorts, enjoying her sense of organization and purpose. She was at ten, he thought, many things that he was not now and never would be. Hopeful, studious, sensitive, reliable. The women on Judy's side of the family were already lobbying for her to babysit younger cousins, that they might enjoy more economical evenings out. Orin had thus far delayed his daughter's descent into slavery, at least until those younger cousins finished throwing food and wetting beds.

"Daddy, if I don't like sleepover this year, can I come home?"

"Sure," he said, leaning her guitar in the corner. "You can always come home. What made you ask that?"

"How about you?" she asked. "If you don't like the Farm?"

"Sure," he said. "Any time I want."

Dawn, who did not quite yet understand prison hangings and undercover police work, had only been told that her father had been picked to work at a special farm, probably what he would have said if his conviction were genuine. She hugged him around his neck and kissed his cheek three times, then tried to shoo him out of her room; he was holding up progress, as usual.

"Before I go," he said, holding up a plain white envelope. "I'm putting this in your suitcase, for the monsignor. Don't forget to give it to him. You know he loves to get letters from his boys."

Dawn saluted smartly, and Orin patted her on the head, then stepped out her door and into Judy, whose arms were filled with warm, clean laundry and whose eyes were filled with tears.

"What?" he said. "What's the matter now?"

"Sometimes," she said, "it just kills me to see how close you let her."

"Why?" he said.

"Because it shows you can do it."

MONDAY, JUNE 27, 2:00 A.M.

ORIN STUDIED UNTIL TWO IN THE MORNING ON his last night at home, familiarizing himself with the following information:

The Nassau County Correctional Facility at Sands Point—the Honor Farm—covered two hundred and ninety rolling north-shore waterfront acres. The forty-room main building had been erected of mammoth gray fieldstones in the Georgian style between 1903 and 1906 by Long Island shipping mogul Cyrus Kreeling during the early heyday of the Gold Coast mansions. Its cavernous chambers, ball rooms, and solariums were once opulently furnished with contents from bankrupt castles in Europe. Kreeling called his home Soundview for its unmatched command of the coastline. Larger homes, such as Guggenheim's Falaise, were built nearby afterward, but none enjoyed such lovely cliffs and beachfront. Two generations of Kreelings and their servants lived there more or less happily until bad business decisions coupled with rising real estate taxes forced the family to vacate the homestead.

In a Nassau County Public Works pamphlet, Orin read that the main house had a slate roof festooned with gargoyle rainspouts and a widow's watch, and currently housed the administrative offices of the prison, the library, classrooms, the infirmary, the commissary, and the cafeteria. Four basement cells were rarely used.

Aerial photographs showed, scattered around the main

house, the more modern tractor garages, maintenance sheds, and a power plant. The stables were original construction, built into the side of a gentle hill, a combination of wood and stone and iron; the insides had been gutted and modernized into a slaughterhouse, at taxpayer expense. The produce barn was shiny new aluminum. A satellite dish sat on the roof of the thirty-room dormitory, once the servants' quarters. Nearby were Har-Tru tennis courts, an Olympic-size swimming pool, boccie courts, and a weight-lifting pit under a green plastic awning. Planting fields ringed the buildings in all directions. Bridle paths dissected apple orchards and rose gardens. A Vita-Course jogging track ringed the planting fields. Then dense woods, stone walls, and high razor-wire fences.

Directly to the north lay marshlands, the beach, the Long Island Sound; in all other directions, the peaks of other Gold Coast hills, the roofs of other mansions, most more happily employed. A two-hole golf course was tucked away in a corner of the property, first a dogleg right, then a dogleg left, nine laps to make an eighteen-hole match. Balls hit out-of-bounds, Orin supposed, remained out-of-bounds.

The Kreeling boathouse was the only original structure situated outside the fences, yet the signs posted on the thin beach-entrance road would lead one to believe it was off-limits to the general public. This was not true, Orin knew. Anyone with the courage to drive past armed guards was not so much welcomed as tolerated.

Soundview had been deeded to Nassau County in 1944—when Cy Kreeling III failed to cough up the municipal vig—and came with the fifty-year stipulation that Soundview be used as a minimum-security prison, largely because Mr. Kreeling wanted to screw his snooty neighbors. This condition had been frequently challenged by a cash-starved county over the years, never quite overturned. To mitigate the neighborhood uproar, the Honor Farm prisoners had always been former police officers, serving time safely segregated from the truly dangerous in East Meadow or the upstate hellholes at Clinton or Attica.

Real estate wolves were circling, ready to storm the walls, aware the stipulation on the use of the property expired in December.

The group of prisoners Orin was joining had pleaded to or been convicted of a garden variety of crimes, some committed on duty, some off. There were twenty prisoners at present, Orin was given to believe. He would make twenty-one.

The Honor Farm was under the supervision of Warden Jack Barthwell, winner of the New York State Police Olympics powerlifting gold medal for the last six years and, according to Commissioner Trimble, a decent man, the father of six with a fat, happy wife. Warden Barthwell commanded a staff of one captain, sixteen guards, one doctor, and six clerks and, it was rumored, one ghost. Inmate labor picked up the slack.

A Captain Smith was responsible for security and operations, the alleged *correction* of the hearts and minds of the prisoners. He oversaw everything from sick time to telephone abuse, smoking in restricted areas to curfew violations. His résumé indicated that he held a degree in criminal justice. To ensure Orin's safety, neither official would be briefed on Orin's mission. He would be treated just like all the other scum.

Orin set aside his background research and picked up the case file again, noting that Detective Lieutenant Thomas Kruger had certainly covered his ass with reams of paper and scores of expert opinions. His final report was a thorough if unimaginative argument for suicide, all the science piled up on one sad side.

There had been no signs of a struggle. No signs of foul play. No other wounds or bruises to the body. A publicly ruined man had hanged himself rather than face his life in shame. Common as dirt.

Orin checked over the crime-scene photographs. The color shots of Skip dangling in the air, the sneakered feet scant inches from the concrete floor. The surprisingly frail body laid out on the naked mattress. The black-and-white autopsy shots.

Something was wrong here, Orin thought. Who the fuck took a picture before cutting down a friend? Orin checked the initials on the back of the photos, found them illegible. He read further, saw that Kruger's follow-up efforts had only hardened his original position: on the morning of his death, Inmate David Trimble, Jr., willfully tied one end of his twisted bedsheet around his neck and the other around the sprinkler head in his dormitory room and stepped off a chair. An interpretation, Orin knew, the commissioner could not abide.

David Trimble, Jr., was found dead at approximately eleven A.M. by Inmate Luther Bailey, who stated he entered Skip Trimble's room to borrow some toothpaste. Inmate Bailey, per Honor Farm rules and regulations, immediately notified correction department personnel (Officer Oliver Bridges), who immediately notified Lieutenant Owen Kirby of the Sands Point Village Police Department, who immediately notified Nassau County detectives. Captain Roger Smith ordered an immediate lockdown of the Farm. All other inmates were present and accounted for. The same was true for the prison staff.

Warden Barthwell, who was on vacation, was notified at home and responded. Monsignor O'Rourke was notified and responded to administer last rites. Dr. Marvin Robbins, head of Honor Farm Medical Services, was on the grounds and responded immediately to the scene. He described the cause of death as cardiac arrest, preceded by strangulation, possibly self-inflicted. Tox screens proved negative for drugs or alcohol.

The Nassau County Police Department sent a police-woman and a priest to Skip's house to inform his young wife of the tragedy. According to their report, Maureen Trimble fainted upon hearing the news.

Big fucking deal, Orin thought. Everybody got notified. Everybody responded. Everybody reacted. Now it was his turn.

He set aside the case file and opened the notebook the commissioner had prepared for him on the current Honor Farm inmates—a roster of familiar faces and cases, a

Who's Who of felons and fuckups, some friends, some enemies—sure he would learn far more about both than he had ever wanted to know. Then Orin felt a gentle hand on his shoulder, smelled a breath of perfume.

"It's my last night, too," said Judy.

"Coming."

4

MONDAY, JUNE 27, 6:30 A.M.

HONOR FARM INMATE NICK MORELLI LAY ON HIS
bed in his single room in the prisoners' dormitory, his legs
propped up by extra pillows, sipping coffee, smoking a De
Nobili cigar. The walls were white brick, like the hallway
and every other room in the former servants' quarters, the
floor naked concrete. Outside his open window trucks were
shaking to life, men calling insults to each other, tractors
rumbling into the fields. His door was ajar, and he was talking on the pay phone, which was on the wall outside his
room, which was why the room was his.

Nick Morelli was a former PBA president and the third
most highly decorated cop in Nassau County history—due
more to juice than heart. If Nick had been in the precinct
basement hoisting barbells when a caper rolled in, Nick
went on the list for citations. And if Nick was on the list,
bars were in the bag. So many guys placed him at scenes he
never graced, Nick got fat from testimonial dinners. A man
who had once negotiated contracts for three thousand cops,

29

Nick Morelli had been nailed draining beer money from the Kiddie Print program.

David Trimble had called him in that Friday three years ago, asked him to explain several odd transactions. Nick had misjudged the situation, eschewed the suggestion of his own vice president that he retain counsel. He tried to laugh the scam off as something easily fixed, laundry best washed inside the job. Trimble heard him out, then explained regretfully that things were not that simple. Then IAD detectives walked into the office and slapped the cuffs on Nick, using evidence his soon-to-be-ex-wife had gleefully provided. He would be out by Thanksgiving if he continued his record of excellent behavior.

Nick was speaking on the pay phone that lazy summer morning with his old friend Townsend Tripp, who wanted to tell him a story about a rotten cop named Orin Boyd, who was headed to the Farm.

Nick told Tripp to save his breath, that he knew Boyd personally, having defended his minor scrapes from time to time. "He's a scumbag, all right. Made me look bad more than once."

"Really?"

"Hard-on won't play ball, even when he's wrong. What'd he do?"

"Enough."

"I don't get to hear?"

"He crossed a line that can't be crossed. Okay, Nick? Or do I offer someone else the chance to be of service to the senator?"

Nick laughed, sat up, and fluffed up his pillows, saw by his alarm clock it was almost time to stroll on over to the mansion for breakfast. "How the mighty have fallen, eh, Towny?"

"Excuse me?"

"I'm talking you calling me, in here. What's going on, kid?"

Tripp said, "Tommy still hits the clubs a tad too hard. Other than that we're okay."

"So what do you want?"

"This punk gets six months of hell," said Tripp. "Nothing less. You get paroled first shot out, then a tit-job."

"White collar?" asked Nick.

"If we hear the howls."

"Boyd must have really frosted Tommy's balls."

"Cracked a fucking molar, to be precise."

Nick Morelli struggled off his bed and hung up the phone, wrapped a Velcro back brace around his thick, hairy gut, and swaggered down the cool concrete hallway to Artie Tobin's room. He knocked loudly on the thick wooden door, as if he had a warrant. "Hey, hard-on," Nick yelled. "Hike up your shorts."

Morelli and Tobin had been partners in the street, partners off duty, in everything, before Nick became the PBA president. They had lived in identical white Cape Cods, two blocks apart in Baldwin. They had fixed cars together, dug clams, hung Sheetrock, and landscaped, passed around a plethora of business cards that described the pair variously as exterminators, underwater salvage divers, and unlicensed electricians and owned corresponding magnetic signs that they interchanged on the side of Nick Morelli's black van, the bumper of which always bore the sticker: MY KID BEATS UP YOUR HONOR STUDENT. Anything anybody asked them to do, they were experts for the bottom dollar.

Artie Tobin was serving a year for selling illegal cable television boxes to people in his patrol sector and for possession of marijuana. He was pale and angular, with braces on his small teeth, and when he opened his door, he was wearing what was left of his ash-blond hair slicked back in a ponytail.

Nick Morelli was swarthy and thick, a man who had planned no personal improvements during his time out of the public eye. "Guess who's coming to spend some time with us?"

"Who?"

"That space-shot Orin Boyd."

"Really?" said Tobin. He started to grin and nod. "Great addition. Once I saw him grab this guy's—"

"I fucking hate Orin Boyd."

MONDAY, JUNE 27, 4:30 P.M.

THE NASSAU COUNTY SHERIFF'S DIRTY WHITE Econoline van descended a narrow road through the thick forests of the Sands Point peninsula. Two armed corrections officers rode in the front, their eyes looking straight ahead, bored.

Inmate Orin Boyd sat on the bouncing wooden bench in the pen and stared out through the screened windows, mentally recording his last glimpses of freedom. They had his duffel bag, his Walkman, his tennis racket and golf clubs, somewhere up front.

Orin didn't know the older hack driving, but the partner with the sidearm was Sally Miles, a smart, blonde hard-body in her forties. An old friend from her days as a court officer, a woman who could take a joke, Sally had so far avoided any mention of their prior association—not at his house when they had picked him up, not during his intake processing at the Nassau County Jail. He was grateful for her tact.

All Judy would have needed to see was him climbing into the sheriff's van with a pretty woman from his past. How quickly a palm-slapping, butt-pinching reunion with Sally Miles would have soured those farewell embraces.

Orin caught Sally looking at him in the bouncing rearview mirror, and said, "I suppose it's okay to say hello to me now."

Sally faced him through the screen. "Hey," she said. "How you doing? You want one of your cigarettes?"

Orin slid closer on the bench. "I was thinking now might be a good time to quit."

The driver belly-laughed. "I'll bet you're gonna get in shape, too. Maybe pick up a master's degree."

Orin asked Sally when she had switched to corrections.

"Two years ago," she said.

"You like it? Inside with the scum?"

"Ten times better than wiping some crooked judge's ass all day. And the cops are cake. Plus I get to spend more time with Kevin. He's in high school now."

"How is old Jack these days?"

"As far as Kevin's concerned, he might as well be dead."

Captain Jack Miles had been an ice-hearted robbery squadder with a grudge against the world. Retired to Kentucky with a former topless dancer. Sally was better off. Kevin, too.

"Three more years and he goes to college," she said.

"Ah, but you'll always be his mother."

Orin knew missing his own daughter, Dawn, would be the toughest part of his stretch on the Farm. The little things, like watching her make them both breakfast after Judy left for work, shooting Hogan's Alley at the range, kissing her rosy cheeks good night. And he would miss his speedboat, slicing through magenta sunsets on the Great South Bay. The sandy taste of fried clams at Kismet. Buffalo wings anywhere. The Harley hot between his legs.

"I was surprised you took a plea," Sally said.

"They had a videotape I didn't want my kid to see."

"Six months and out?" she said.

"Four, if I behave."

Sally said, "Orin, this is Vito Kelly."

Vito held up the peace sign, and said, "Peace through vegetables."

The narrow road dipped into a golden valley, then ran straight down a hill to the jagged shoreline. To the north the Long Island Sound glistened green and blue. Across Hempstead Bay, the roofs of other Gold Coast mansions pierced the lush green canopy, lending to the neighborhood a sense of nostalgia for a time that came and went so fast. For Orin knew this shoreline was steeped in the legends and scandals of wealth beyond measure, the glittering hills crowded with family vendettas and ghosts. From his crash course he had learned that Woolworth's daughter, denied her lover, haunted a castle whose dining room floor was paved with the headstones of children. Down the winding coastal road once lived a grieving mother who made a wax dummy of her son after he hanged himself in a water tower. The dummy often joined family and guests for dinner.

"It's not like you won't know anybody," Sally was saying. "Your buddy George Clarke is so happy you're coming he's been pissing in his pants."

"Nice of old George."

They were now running along the twelve-foot high razor-wire fence, on their right. Just up the hill, visible above the interior stone wall, two men in traffic-cone orange jump-suits leaned on a tractor, smoking cigarettes. Near them a uniformed guard sat in a golf cart, reading a paperback. He waved to the van. Vito Kelly goosed the siren.

A radio-controlled model airplane, of the sort the Red Baron flew, buzzed the van, then swooped up over the lawns and fields. A gaunt, bald jogger loped along a path inside the fence, wearing yellow headphones and a glazed look that said he might have been anywhere. Vito Kelly goosed him too, and the runner flinched, then held up a friendly third finger.

"Billy Masters," said Sally. "Zen."

"Nice guy who killed one too many people," added Kelly.

Orin almost lost his balance as the van slowed and turned into the main driveway of crushed bluestone. It lurched over two speed bumps and squealed to a halt at a sign that said Nassau County Correctional Facility at Sands Point— All Vehicles Must Stop.

Ten feet inside the second fence was the ivy-covered for-mer carriage house, built of limestone, which now housed the guards' dormitory, lounge, and locker room. A modern concrete security compound had been constructed beside it at great public expense.

A correction officer inside the command post hung up a wall phone. Another stepped into the no-man's-land be-tween fences. Another stepped through the pedestrian gate, to check the occupants of the van. The guard found Orin's name on his clipboard, which pleased him enormously. He slid a mirror on wheels under the chassis of the van, as if some idiot might try to break in, and then the gates rolled open on the scene of the crime, if indeed a crime had been committed—which Homicide had just disproved to nearly everyone's satisfaction.

These were Khe Sanh odds, Orin thought, beginning a

follow-up investigation compromised by the passing of time, the deterioration of physical evidence, and the unhappy fact that he had to be discreet in his inquiries.

Sure, all the suspects were still gathered at the scene, but there had been ample time to shore up alibis. Not that he would be able to question them directly. Lieutenant Kruger had already handled that, and timidly, from Orin's reading of the case and his subsequent discussions with Commissioner Trimble. Detective Kruger had been rather willing to accept the word of the inmates as gospel, as if they were still sworn officers. And then again maybe Skip Trimble really did skip out, and the inconsistencies could be blamed on the variables of human memory.

Perhaps Commissioner Trimble was sliding into a black hole of grief, dragging Orin in after him, and who knew who else, like angry soldiers taking it out on innocent villagers, cops beating shackled prisoners. He had told the commissioner he knew Skip, but meant "only in passing," that he knew who he was, as any moron would. There are generations within the police department, and different castes. Skip Trimble would not have known Orin Boyd.

Orin looked down at his high, black Chuck Taylor All Star sneakers, whose eyelets were backed with tiny self-adhesive Giordano microphones, and he realized that he should have been flounder fishing with his daughter or hacking up the Red Course at Bethpage State Park.

He slid forward on the bench and banged his cuffs against the cage. "Hey, Sally," he said. "Anybody ever escape from here?"

Vito Kelly laughed again. "What the fuck for?"

"Just one more question. What the hell is that smell?"

MONDAY, JUNE 27, 5:00 P.M.

THE SOLITARY MAN OF SIXTY-FIVE WAS EATING breakfast during the dinner rush at the counter of the Spartacus Diner. He sipped his black coffee and opened his

Newsday from the back, read first the sports, the comics, his horoscope, then flipped to the front.

HI, I'M HELEN—the middle-aged but still buxom waitress refilled his mug, asked if he wanted anything else.

He held his tongue, swallowed his smart remark, lit a cigarette to hide behind. Watched her.

She left him to his newspaper, the color cover of which promised articles inside attacking monstrous pay raises for the chairman of the Long Island Lighting Company and his son, a sex scandal in a Massapequa synagogue, multiple drug murders in Roosevelt.

On page 3 the lonely man at the counter read with some pleasure that one of his least favorite politicians, that young punk Nazi Thomas Cotton, had been injured. According to spokeswoman Sherri Sawchuck, the always combative state senator took an accidental elbow in the jaw during a "particularly brutal basketball game" with members of his Albany staff. The accompanying photograph showed Cotton holding his raincoat over his face like a felon.

The old man wiped his mouth with his napkin and grinned. He scanned Liz Smith's column, saw that none of his favorite celebrities were mentioned, flipped to the local news.

The smile vanished from his weatherbeaten face when he read on page 21 that recently fired Nassau County Police Officer Orin Boyd had pled guilty to third-degree assault upon an unidentified participant in the Federal Witness Protection Program.

He blinked and read the story again—carefully this time, to get the details right—saw that Officer Boyd was to be remanded that very day to the Nassau County Correctional Facility at Sands Point to begin serving a sentence of six months to one year.

Which the man knew from personal experience meant four months inside if he behaved, which meant for the next four months Officer Boyd's family would be living alone, unprotected.

And him, with all this time on his hands.

He shoved aside his corn muffin, called for more coffee,

and could he borrow a pen, please, Helen. He would need a plan for this job, once he honestly defined his objectives, separated the possible from the pipe dream.

Twenty minutes later he collected his notes-on-napkins, then tucked three dollars under the saucer and slid off his stool. He waited for Helen to favor him with a smile of gratitude, then left, a wink hanging in the air.

When he had paid and was gone, Helen told the busboy that good tips or not, she wished he would eat an occasional meal somewhere else, that he seemed so sad and lost he sometimes gave her the creeps.

"Who? Robert? He's harmless."

5

WARDEN JACK BARTHWELL SAT BEHIND HIS GRAY
metal desk in the large oval office whose balcony overlooked the sloping front lawns of the estate. He was a
gnarled mound of muscle with a deep tan, short blond hair,
and blue eyes, wearing a torn Gold's Gym T-shirt and black
spandex bike shorts. His beefy left arm was presently extended to an elderly man in a lab coat who was holding a
hypodermic needle.

"My vitamin shot," Barthwell said to Orin.

"Do what ya gotta do," said Orin.

"Say hello to Doc Robbins, our own little HMO."

Orin blinked.

"Health maintenance organization," said Barthwell. "The
company doctor."

Dr. Robbins said, "Boyd, right? We have a ten o'clock
tomorrow."

Orin said, "I'll pencil you in."

Dr. Robbins grunted, shot up the warden, and packed up
his bag. After the doctor was gone, Warden Barthwell said,

38

"The boys have turned that HMO into Homo, but don't you pay them any mind."

"Say no more."

"Anyway, here's the deal, right up front: It is a privilege to serve a sentence here, one which can be easily forfeited. You and I know the difference between time on the Farm and time in the joint. For a cop it can be life and death, or at least his virginity."

Orin squirmed in his chair, looked up at the elk head mounted high on one wall, turned to check out the moose on the other side.

Barthwell tried not to smile, and said, "You ask any one of your new buds out there what they fear most—other than their wives boffing their friends—it's me kicking their butts off this farm."

"I'm no troublemaker."

"Spare me the horseshit, Boyd. I read your case," said Barthwell, swinging the tractor-tread soles of his Nike cross-trainers up on the desk. "And the probation report. I think you got a lousy deal. Unfortunately, that's eyewash. You ain't the first innocent man to do time, and you won't be the last. Don't make me the target of your anger and we'll get along fine."

"Sounds fair enough."

"Take a couple of days to look around, pick a job you think you might like. We got plenty of openings. You're not a masseuse, are you?"

"Negative."

"We just lost one of the best."

Orin nodded sorrowfully.

"Now, I know the line between the jailers and the jailed ain't much, so you won't find my guys lording it over you or breaking your balls. Just as I won't stand for any bullshit from you. Point is, this doesn't have to be a waste of time. Do your stretch smart, you add years to your life and life to your years."

Orin smiled slyly.

"You know what I'm saying."

"And appreciate it."

"You get unlimited collect phone calls, three square meals and one snack—but no one ever counts—a newspaper, last year's paperbacks, a clean room with cable TV, and clean clothes. Visitors on Tuesdays, Thursdays, and Saturdays, but we'll work with you there. When your chores are done, your time is your own. You can roam the grounds or brood in your room. We got job counseling; we got holy men. A model airplane club. Pen pals. Basketball, swimming, tennis, golf. Last fall the guys did *Camelot*. I understand there's a boccie court around here somewhere, and if that doesn't fill your days, lots of guys just sleep."

"You've got it all."

"You get depressed in here, you tell someone. I'm serious."

"Check."

Barthwell nodded. "You look like you've pumped some iron. We hit the pit around two-thirty, and you're welcome to join us. It's my favorite way to make the clock spin."

"Yes, I see that. Thanks. Could I make a phone call now? I imagine the wife is kind of worried about me."

"Sure. Take a freebie. Marion Whithers will fix you up. Then go back downstairs and get your blues from the laundry, then wander on over to the dorm and get settled. You're in room number one, I believe, a corner suite with a view."

MONDAY, JUNE 27, 5:10 P.M.

MARION WHITHERS LOOKED AS IF SHE CAME with the house, but she was pleasant enough. In a faint English accent she told Orin she was sorry for his recent bad luck and of course he could use a phone. "Take the captain's office. He likely won't be back for another hour or so."

"He won't mind?" asked Orin.

"Actually, it would bloody kill him."

Orin smiled, sensing a possible ally in a strategic location, a fellow pawn awaiting word of the rebellion.

Marion said, "Captain Smith thinks he's a people person, but he's the only one." She giggled at her own joke. "Close the door if you like. First one's usually the toughest."

"Thank you," he said, gratefully. "You don't know . . ."

Orin sat behind the highly polished cherrywood desk and dialed home. Judy Boyd picked up on the second ring.

"Hey," Orin said.

"Hey, yourself."

"Got myself a corner suite."

"Terrific. Seen anybody you know yet?"

"Nope."

"Why are you calling? I just got rid of you."

"I feel like I forgot something."

"Don't annoy me, darling."

Orin grunted, lit a cigarette, spun around in the captain's studded leather chair, and pulled aside a blue velvet drape. A tennis match was in progress down below, the level of play surprisingly high. On the adjacent concrete basketball court a very tall black man was dribbling the ball off his feet and tossing up bricks, losing to a short, skinny white guy with frizzy red hair.

While Judy caught him up on her many tasks for the next few days, Orin got busy snooping. He rattled the locked desk drawers, then picked up from the credenza a very expensive Nikon camera fitted with a lens that looked like a megaphone. He held the phone on his shoulder and used the fold-down tripod to sight in the Soundview Yacht Club, focused on several happy members clutching umbrella drinks on the veranda.

He carefully replaced the camera and memorized the file cabinet labels, not sure which might turn out to be important. He opened the door to a closet full of cleaning supplies, a second door to a large private bathroom, stocked to the rafters with toiletries and beauty tools.

Orin sat on the edge of the captain's desk and peeled a Giordano mike from his sneaker, then stood on the captain's big windowsill and secured the sophisticated little bug inside the open end of the curtain rod.

Satisfied with his opening salvo, the ease of target penetration, he sat behind the desk again and looked across the room at himself in the biggest mirror he had ever seen. On the wall by the door was an oddly familiar oil portrait, no doubt of the captain himself, his Smokey cap worn low, as if he was the bad guy, Barthwell the good.

"Are you still there?" asked Judy.

Orin exhaled a plume of Carlton smoke, fouling the captain's air. "Where else would I be?"

"I thought you were gonna quit."

"Friday, I think. We get a lecture."

"You're such a jerk."

He laughed. "Gotta run, babe. My turn for electroshock."

MONDAY, JUNE 27, 5:30 P.M.

DOMINICK RIL, NICK MORELLI, AND ARTIE TOBIN stood by the casement window of their air-conditioned conference room, watching a laundry-laden Orin Boyd walk the stone path bordered by yews from the mansion to the dormitory. On the long table against the wall an electronic pen was hard at work signing Nick Morelli's name to the many useless forms required to manage the Farm with strict accountability.

"Great to see old friends, ain't it, Dom?" said Nick.

"Sometimes yes," said Ril. "Right now, no."

Dom Ril had richly deserved to do hard time at an institution more severe than the Nassau County Honor Farm. That he was not some crazed killer's love-slave at Clinton or Attica was due entirely to the speed and depth of his confessions when scandal rocked the Thirteenth Precinct, a scandal set in motion by one Officer Orin Boyd. Ril was the Honor Farm senior office manager, as he was the inmate—other than Gramps McKay—currently imprisoned the longest.

In reality a monkey could run the place, and everybody who worked upstairs pretty much did what they liked. By eleven A.M. the clerical unit was usually finished with the daily counts and free to manage their own affairs. These jobs were prime assignments, requiring addition and subtraction, providing ample opportunities for personal initiative and growth—patronage positions, so to speak.

"So Boyd was a crook?" Morelli asked, leaning his short forehead against the glass. "What really happened in Belmont, Dom? He didn't ask for my help on that one, and I sure didn't offer."

"A loose cannon. As one of the guys put it 'a frog with hand grenades.'" Ril moved from the window and sat down behind his empty desk, started opening the drawers. "It all began so innocently, too, just another bum transferred to Belmont. His partner was dying and he was drinking his face off, so then this do-gooder spade Alonzo Daniels dried him out at Camp Cope. We got him just as Blogg was taking over for Jimmy Donnelly. Then Donnelly overestimated Blogg and underestimated Boyd. He picked a fight he couldn't win."

"Why not?" asked Tobin.

"Boyd don't fight fair. Ask George. He started locking up everybody in sight. When Blogg wouldn't back him, the crazy fuck went to war."

"And won that war, as I recall," said Morelli. "Hands down. Hard-on even kept his job, after everything. Which you gotta admit is totally amazing."

Ril gave up searching his desk and opened up a file cabinet behind him. "Where's my Maalox?" said Ril.

Nick cracked his knuckles and grinned. Tobin picked at orange pulp caught in his braces. The twenty-four-hour clock on the wall ticked twice. Then Tobin finally said, "He's so smart, how come he wound up here?"

"I couldn't care less."

Nick pressed his nose against the glass, stared out at the surrounding Gold Coast hills, the billion-dollar coastline. "You really think he's still got your money?"

"*Donnelly's* money. The motherlode. I'm sure of it."

"How much?" said Tobin. "Round numbers."

"I got caught with a hundred thousand bucks."

Nick gave Ril as sincere a look as he could fake. "I still

say that's one of the saddest stories I ever heard on the job."

"*I've* always felt that way. And the thing of it was, my PBA president all of a sudden didn't know me."

"You were sending my constituents to jail, Dom. Let's not forget that." Nick wagged his finger. "It was me, I'd be trying to get back some of that gelt for my old age," said Nick, "even if I had to hire help."

"You don't know this guy," said Ril.

"Sure I do. I saved his sorry ass when he was drinking. I covered his questionable shoots. I know exactly what we're dealing with here. Believe me."

"I want my peace of mind," said Ril.

"For half the take, we'll do all the worrying."

Ril sat back and raised his eyebrows. "Get out of here."

"I'm fucking serious, Dom. This hard-on ain't no one to me no more. Just another meal in the jungle, babe."

Ril looked at Nick as if he were seriously considering the deal. Then Ril made the mousy face he always made in response to lowball offers. "Half, huh? I can find lawyers work for less."

"Not in here you can't. And not with my connections."

Ril knew Nick was right, that the former PBA president continued to exercise a considerable remnant of his power on the local and statewide levels, was still an active player from behind the walls. He was also the owner and operator of a very cruel temper, a man used to throwing unpunished tantrums. Ril said warily, "What do you have in mind?"

"Nothing yet. Don't know that we got the job."

"Suppose you did."

"We'd need to know what you know."

"Yeah. And?"

"Then you could forget what you know," said Nick, returning his attention to the great outdoors.

Tobin snapped his fingers to draw Ril's attention, and said, "George Clarke really came away with nothing?"

Ril said, "Less than nothing, to hear him tell it."

"What a fucking asshole."

6

GEORGE CLARKE HAD JUST LAST WEEK CELE-
brated behind bars his forty-ninth birthday, if one considered the fences that circled Soundview bars. He owed the
state four more months on a bigamy conviction, a crime he
insisted was clerical oversight, a technicality of love. Wife
number five, whom he had married in New York, learned
that George was not divorced from wife number four,
whom he had married in Florida. Then Speedrack George,
ever the cheapskate, retained shopping-center lawyers and
didn't take their advice. He insisted upon a trial, taking the
stand in his own behalf to set the story straight. Shmeckle
and Shmeckle had grown so sick of him they allowed it.
Judge Conchetta Rodriguez sat mesmerized throughout his
testimony, then, with jowls wobbling and hands shaking,
sentenced George to a year of real time, as if he were actually a danger to society.

George was presently in the locker room adjacent to the
pool, fresh from a short dip and a long shower, priorities he
knew he should reverse as he checked his look in the mir-

ror. Pretty freaking sad, he conceded. Twenty pounds over-weight and growing boobs like a big, hairy mama bear. He made a mental note to prepare for Orin's first wisecrack and was rapidly pulling on his shirt and muttering possibilities to himself when big Luther Bailey, a six-foot-six-inch, jet-black beanpole, came in breathless and sweaty from shoot-ing hoops.

"Make any today?" asked George.

Luther Bailey was the worst tall black basketball player in the world, bar none. There were African ambassadors new to America who could take Luther to the bucket.

"I mean other than dunks, which any fool can do."

"Except you," Luther pointed out.

Which was true. George couldn't touch the net. George played basketball the way he played everything, generally tripping and holding, and waiting for his more athletic op-ponents to go airborne so he could cut their legs out from under them.

Luther Bailey stunk at basketball, but he could play the hell out of a clarinet. A band nerd when his growth spurt struck, Luther had henceforth borne the black man's burden of athletic expectations, a thousand times forced to explain that no, he was not a slam-dunking, backboard-sweeping credit to his race. Luther was using his three-year forgery stretch to right that wrong.

Formerly of the art squad, and a nationally known forgery expert, Luther Bailey had been busted selling phony Chagalls, Miros, and Dalis in California, copies made in a cousin's lithography shop in Wyandanch. He had used the money to help a sister raise twin boys, sophomores at Dartmouth now, who would graduate around the same time Uncle Luther walked.

Luther, as always, had adapted, put the time to good use and earned a buck, giving haircuts to inmates and guards, painting portraits of the inmates and their visitors. "Why you got to be such a prick, George?" Luther said. "Instead of mocking me, come play with me and Genghis. Rough me up in the paint, make me pay for my points."

George allowed a hangdog look to cross his face. "I don't know, Luther. Today's been one of them real slow days."

"A day for the blues," said Luther as he peeled off his shirt, revealing a meatless rack of ribs. "Yes, indeed. That's right where I'm headed. Well, cheer up, homes. Your man got here about an hour ago."

"Orin Boyd?"

"Saw the hacks march him in to Happy Jack."

George grinned widely. "Well, all right, all right."

Luther patted him on the back. "Nice mood swing, George. Make sure you share it with Doc."

MONDAY, JUNE 27, 5:57 P.M.

INMATE RICHARD PETTIBONE, A FORMER LIEUtenant in the sleepy Seventh Precinct, was lying on the rumpled bed in room 1, watching *Live at Five*, munching Ritz crackers and Cheez Whiz.

Orin stepped through the narrow doorway and said, "Hey, yo."

Pettibone jumped up, snapped off the tube, and said nervously, "Hey, guy, who are you?"

Pettibone was slightly built, short for a cop, and balding, with features bordering on the feminine and thick black-rimmed glasses. His jeans were soiled at the knee and his white T-shirt was streaked with mud and processed cheese spread. Orin glared over his shiny head at the mess on his bed. "You think my room is your fucking den? Clean that shit up. Now."

Pettibone brushed the crumbs from the bed into his hand and dumped them into the wastepaper basket. "Sorry, guy. This room's been empty . . . Pettibone's my name. I'm the gardener here." He held out his hand in friendship.

Orin's nearly extended hand flew up to scratch behind his ear. "Sick Dick Pets-his-bone?"

"Richard. Please."

47

Orin scowled. "Where can I get me some clean fucking sheets?"

"You only read the headlines," said Pettibone. "That's not fair."

"Wrong, pal. I saw the shithouse cartoon."

Pettibone put his hands together in prayer. "Please. Give me a chance to tell the story. Before anyone slanders me. I haven't had a friend—"

Orin's golf clubs and duffel bag landed with a bang on the hard stone floor. Orin put his hand on his hip. "You got thirty seconds."

"Thank you. Bless you."

"Twenty," said Orin.

"I was on meal. It's two-thirty in the morning and I'm horny. I go to my chick's house and toss a pebble off her window, climb a tree, next to the house, with a branch that puts me up close to the bathroom window . . . She dances for me."

"What?"

"You know, exotically."

"While you're hanging in the tree? I think I got the picture."

"She leans out for a gobble, right? And I got my eyes closed, so I don't see her husband slip up behind her. He grabs her ankles, lifts. She falls on her head."

"Thank God she let go," said Orin.

"The next thing I know, he's barking up the tree with a meat cleaver. I had to put one in his shoulder."

"Quite a night."

"But sick? Clinically? The God's honest truth."

Orin made him wait. "Na."

"Thank you," said Pettibone. He pulled off his bifocals and wiped them on his filthy T-shirt. "You don't know what that means to me."

"Nobody likes you?" asked Orin.

"Not even the shrink . . . and they pay him to like me."

Orin opened the single narrow casement window, took a gust of foul air in the face, rolled the window shut. He remembered the Pettibone dossier: Divorced, more than once.

Three kids by two former wives. As a sergeant he once accepted a three-day suspension for suggesting to a female prisoner that things would go easier if she "licked his lolly-column." Eligible for parole at the end of December 1996. Commissioner Trimble had said Skip never mentioned him, not to waste time on the pervers.

"But she did let go," Orin said to Pettibone. "She could have taken you with her."

Pettibone bowed his head sadly. "It's been a long time since anyone told me to count my blessings."

"Glad I could help."

Orin got busy then, opening the dresser drawers, the tiny closet, a signal for Pettibone to leave.

Pettibone said, "This was Skip Trimble's room. They tell you that?"

Orin shook his head and shuddered dramatically. "Well, ain't that fucking creepy. He hang himself from that busted sprinkler head?"

Pettibone nodded without looking up, as if he had already examined the scene too many times.

"Hope what he had ain't contagious," said Orin.

"I wouldn't worry. Skip was—"

Before Pettibone could elaborate further, the burly body of George Clarke darkened Orin's doorway, and his hooded brown eyes flashed with hatred when they set upon Pettibone. "I swear to Christ, Orin, you go straight to the bottom of the barrel, every freaking time."

"Hey, partner. Fancy meeting you here, but probably inevitable."

"Ya think?"

They had not seen each other much since Belmont. During the first months following their misadventure and a successful reconciliation with his wife, Orin had stayed home while George had stayed out. A short while later they were banished to different precincts. Then George fell in love with some lucky girl and entered another epoch during which he failed to return phone calls from males.

Orin didn't need a dossier for this bum. He remembered the first time he ever saw George Clarke, in the locker room of the Thirteenth Precinct in Belmont, wearing a flowered shirt, Bermuda shorts, and Beatle boots, his iron gray hair combed forward like an altar boy's, knee-deep in scandal, as always. Orin liked George because George was truly clueless, and funny about it, because he never stood a chance in a world that had changed.

"Hey, Dickhead!" George said to Pettibone. "Take a hike."

Pettibone blinked at Orin through his glasses. "Your room, you make the call."

"Sorry, dude. Me and George go back to original sin. I'll talk to you later, okay?"

"No you won't. But that don't matter."

Pettibone gathered his noshes, his *TV Guide,* and left. George slammed the door behind him for effect.

"Bully," said Orin.

"Freaking loser," said George. "Goddamn lowlife."

George was still the slob of the outfit, Orin could see, no matter that everybody was given clean clothes every day: work shirt untucked, buttoned to the neck, fly half open, the cheapest sneakers made in Asia. His gut had grown some since he came to the Farm. His hair was whiter and his tan was dark.

"Even hardened convicts hate sex offenders," said George.

"He explained all that. Coulda happened to anyone."

"Not to mention he's a fucking rat, always running to Captain Smith when someone messes with his mind."

Orin threw the last of his labeled socks and underwear into the drawers, then kicked back on his bed while George sat down on the single plastic chair and lit a cigarette.

"Orin, my man, this is the Rancho Mirage of America's prisons. Like a college campus without the sororities, and we're working on those. Until then, most guys have binoculars for scoping pussy at the beach. We eat good, sleep good; ain't nobody ever trying to pork you in the buns. We get plenty of rest, conjugal visits, cable TV, and stall showers. You'll appreciate those babies in a day or two. And have Judy send up a pair of shower thongs."

"You should write a brochure. Folks could apply for fellowships."

"Let 'em find their own utopias."

"How's the staff?"

"We pretend to be inmates, and they pretend to be guards."

"So then the only problem is, what the fuck is that smell?"

George cocked his head and wrinkled his brow. "Actually, that's two smells. The moist smell is fresh chicken shit. The other, kinda tangy smell is fertilizer, which is basically cow shit that ain't so fresh."

"I heard they're thinking of closing it down, that I might not finish my sentence here."

"Every new guy says that. Even I said that."

"Persistent rumors have a way of coming true." Orin slipped off his All Stars and shoved them under the bed.

"As long as Barthwell's here, the Farm is ours."

"How tough are the chores? I never worked on a farm."

"Farm work is like everything you ever wanted to do as a kid. We drive tractors. We play in the mud. Work with our shirts off. Fuck up animals."

"You're giving me a chubby."

"I'd quit talking like that. Image is everything here," said George. "Trust me."

"Trust you?"

"I'll see what I can do about getting you on my crew. Right now it's just me and Luther, in the transportation end of things. He does the bull work and I do the thinking. We probably got room for one more level of management."

"What's the danger factor?" asked Orin.

"Zippo."

"Skip Trimble died right here in this room."

"Skip Trimble was a fucked-up dude."

"I think Pettibone was just gonna tell me that, too, when you busted him."

"Skippy Trimble was royalty, man. Like a little prince. Even in here, he acted like he was freaking running for office . . . Not our kind of guy at all," said George. "Dom Ril's here, speaking of danger. He still hates you, and *he's* alive."

"First, tell me how someone goes to jail for bigamy."

George slouched in the chair and rolled his eyes. "You're not gonna believe this: My own big mouth. I'm sitting with Mary, she was wife number five. You never met her. We're in a restaurant, just back from our honeymoon in Vegas, during which time, I assure you, I banged the freaking balls off her. You've never seen a bitch so happy. I was happy, too, tell you the truth. So anyway we're in this swanky waterfront restaurant, and I'm shit-faced on martinis, and she asks what went wrong with Sue, wife number four."

"Yes?" said Orin.

"So for once I'm all sincere and everything, and I tell her . . . I thought Sue was cheating on me. I had a watchman's job at a boatyard in Lauderdale right after I retired, so she had every opportunity. The signs were there. I've seen them before."

"I believe you."

"I left work early one night, to check her out. I bust into the bedroom with my gun out, sure I'm gonna catch some trailer-park scumbag humping her brains out."

George stopped speaking for a moment and studied his hands as if they were monsters with minds of their own.

"What?" said Orin. "Don't tell me this is painful."

George shook his head. "Here's where I frigged up."

"In the bedroom?" asked Orin.

"In the restaurant."

"What did you do in the bedroom?"

"Played a little Russian roulette until I found out who was who. Then I went after the guy. When I got back, she was gone."

Orin lay his head back on the thin, starched pillow and closed his eyes. "You told this to Mary? Of your own free will?"

"Orin, her freaking jaw dropped into her soup. So I says, 'Does this disturb you?' "

George, who now looked as hapless as he must have looked that fateful evening, shrugged like Atlas.

"Her you saw again," Orin said.

"In family court, where her lawyer had a ball proving that me and Sue never got divorced. And get this: When I get out, I gotta do five hundred hours of community service at a mammography center, at night, when it's closed."

"Talk about shooting yourself in the dick."

"Really," George said. "I finally open up to a broad and look what freaking happens."

7

MONDAY, JUNE 27, 7:00 P.M.

THE MAIN DINING ROOM OF THE GREAT MANOR
house was like many of its other rooms, drafty and high-
ceilinged, with rich wood paneling and tall casement windows. The tables and chairs, however, were Nixonian white
Formica and molded orange plastic, the original furniture
having long since been carted away to other estates in
private hands. It was a noisy room, Orin noticed, full of
echoes and laughter—with little tension, if his long-
dormant antennae were working. The inmates were eating
in small groups, apparently engaged in lighthearted banter
and good-natured grousing. Some kept entirely to themselves, avoiding the intrapersonal flashpoints so prevalent
in prison.

There was a seating of four night-shift bakers having
their breakfasts and a table of the stunned—Team Tho-
razine, George called them as he and Orin stood in front of
the sumptuous steam tables—high all day, sleep all night,
with wake-up calls waiting down the road. One of them was

Stephen Gomas, a former narc who got bagged stealing beepers from drug dealers and selling them in Brooklyn.

Allan Kelly and Barry Comstock, an infamous pair of frequently bribed highway cops, sat facing each other, playing palm-slapping games. (Comstock was famous for retiring a day before Internal Affairs got him and was one of two inmates receiving state pension checks while serving time at the Farm. Nick Morelli was the other.)

Not quite heaven, Orin judged, but certainly no hell. An atmosphere more like high school than college.

He loaded his plate with a well-done steak, baked potato, salad, a cup of coffee, and a chocolate doughnut, then walked behind George to the crowded table next to a bay window at the rear of the tiny room, where the in-crowd dined. Management, as it were. Dominick Ril saw them coming, and cried out, "Hey! There he is. Welcome to jail, Boyd-brain."

"Hard to believe, ain't it?" said Orin, bowing and smiling, acknowledging several choruses of "Him, him, fuck him."

"What comes around goes around," said Ril.

"My God, you are original," said Orin.

Dom Ril had aged some, but he was still every inch the dapper little thief he had been at the One-Three. His denims were the bluest, his T-shirt the whitest.

"Any room there next to you, little buddy?" asked Orin.

"We might break fucking bread together."

"Come on, Dom. Let's let bygones be bygones."

Ril turned pale, most likely remembering those bygones, the night when everything he hoped for and saved for disappeared: his wealth, his reputation, and his freedom.

Orin felt a nudge at his thigh. "Kinda pushy for a new guy, ain't you?"

Orin looked down at the sallow-faced Italian-American with dark hair and a thick gray mustache who so obviously spent his free time in the weight pit. "It's my first night in jail, Nick, and I don't know how to act."

"How you act is," Nick said, "you don't sass your elders."

"Who says I did that?" Orin asked innocently. "I haven't done anything like that, have I? Where's my buddy Dickie Pettibone? He'll eat with me, I bet."

George Clarke said, "Fellas, fellas, this here's my old partner, the guy I was telling you about."

Artie Tobin said, "The guy you stole all that money with that you didn't get to keep?"

"Fucking A," said Ril.

"Come on, Dom," said Orin. "Tell the boys the truth. What I got was mad money. You're still sitting on the big enchilada, right?"

"Wrong." Ril pointed his finger at Orin. "I'm fifty-two years old and I don't got a fucking dime, thanks to you."

Orin's face showed first shock, then concern. "My God, you're serious. Dom, baby, I had no idea you'd be that dumb, to put all your eggs in one basket."

"I should have put a bullet in your head."

The audience grew silent, holding its breath.

Orin smiled broadly, and said, "Problem with that plan is, you didn't have the balls. Now move over. My steak is getting cold."

The other prisoners at the table gazed up at Orin, faces he recognized from headquarters or the commissioner's dossiers, or as the unfortunate result of gavel-to-gavel coverage: "Zen" Masters from Emergency Services, and vice cop Bobby Damato, the black guy Bailey, the commissioner's longtime lackey Prank Dinostra. Artie Tobin. Ira Cohen. Detective Greg Kaminsky, once chubby, now thin as a rail. Poor Mikie Hutchinson, in a wheelchair at one end of the table. Some guy dressed up like a chef. No one he could count on.

"Look, Dom, don't blame me for what happened to you in Belmont. You just sucked the wrong dick."

Ril looked as if he'd been slapped, as if he would trade the rest of his life for a weapon that would drop Boyd with one round, no chance of only wounding him.

The chef slid his tray aside to make room. "Why doesn't everybody just get along?"

"Stay out of this, Judge," said Ril.

The chef stood up at his end of the table, all six-foot-five of him. "I will not stay out of this, nor will I have my dinner ruined. Orin, my name is the formerly Honorable but still trustworthy Brendan Kane, and I'd be pleased to join you and George at another table."

"Why, thank you, Your Honor. And, Dominick? I think your anger is eating you up inside. It's unbecoming and counterproductive."

Before Ril could respond, Judge Kane, George, and Orin turned and carried their trays to an empty table in the far corner of the dining room, where they subsequently played several minutes of "departmental do you know?" with each other while Orin cut up his steak. Deputy Chief Moses, Inspector Joannie O'Meara, Inspector Jack Kilbride, Monsignor O'Rourke, and the rest of headquarter's windbreaker squad, all fucking pissers, no doubt at that moment dining well and on the arm, they agreed.

"They're not eating like this," said George.

"Nope," said Orin.

The judge, George volunteered, was the Honor Farm chef, not only because he was a freaking great cook, but because he was considered the inmate least likely to piss in the soup. And he always finished in time to join his mates for the meal, accepting praise and criticism where due, suggesting wines they might have ordered if they were free.

"How's everything been going, since Skip?"

"Same as it ever was," said George.

"Did you know Skip?" asked Kane.

"Not really."

Kane sighed as if he were actually feeling some pain. "His poor father must be devastated."

Orin remembered what he knew about Brendan Kane, the only non-cop doing time at the Farm. Wealthy by most measures, the judge was serving easy time on a semifraudulent medical dispensation for claustrophobia. Kane and a number of his political allies had induced their elderly parents to fall and injure themselves on Nassau County Health Department property, file suit, then settle their cases quickly at generous terms, all of which created immediate

wealth that might soon be passed along to future generations. The lawyer at Health who made those generous set-
tlements—and in turn received a healthy kickback—was
currently doing hard time at Attica. It was suggested but
never proven that the judge had needed the extra money to
support a mistress in the style to which she aspired after
watching thousands of hours of *Dallas*.

His good friend the police commissioner was made to
look bad, both in the eyes of the press and the rank-and-file.
Judge Kane had actually had his own parking spot behind
police headquarters, as well as keys to the pistol range and
the use of the police launch one allegedly wild night off
Fire Island Pines. David Trimble had arranged for his acceptance to the Honor Farm. "The men talk to him," Trimble had explained to Orin. "They retry their cases in his
movable court. We could learn things." If the situation
arose, Trimble said, where Orin needed help, he might consider Brendan, but only as a last resort.

"I don't suppose you know Dave personally," said Kane.

Orin grunted in the negative. "We move in different
circles."

George Clarke stopped cramming chow in his mouth
long enough to belly-laugh, while Kane continued, "A
shame, what's happened to that man. If Skip were here, I
swear I'd slap his silly face."

"You so sure he did it to himself?" asked Orin.

The judge raised his prominent eyebrows. "No reason to
suspect otherwise, that I know of."

"Over the wife?"

"As good a guess as any."

"That'd be my guess," said George, "if I gave a flying
fuck."

"George," said Orin, "likes to distance himself from anything so terminally unpleasant as death."

Judge Kane said, "Skip and I never talked the nitty-
gritty. He felt I was a pipeline to Pop. Which I suppose I
was."

Orin nodded, chewed, kept an eye on Ril and his buddies
over Kane's shoulder. Ril caught Orin staring at him and

sneered. Orin filled his tongue with a wad of steak and showed it to Ril. Half the guys at the long table laughed.

Kane said, "Forget Ril. His bark is worse than his bite."

"Then he ought not bark at all."

"How long did you get?" Kane asked Orin.

"Six months."

"I've done that and more." The judge sat back and lit a cigar. "In a way it's been the most valuable period of my life. A chance at perspective and a well-deserved rest. Sure, I'm ruined, but that's temporary. They'll find me a job at Off Track Betting when I get out. Or the Elections Commission. I'll get a big fat raise and a car, and piss on all of them."

George, who did not expect a cushy patronage job when he got out, told Kane he had put on another "good feed," then excused himself to refill his plate. When he was gone, Orin leaned forward and said to the judge, "I read about your case. You made quite a splash, Your Honor."

"My deal was dumb politics," said the judge, waving his hand. "A wind shift while my head was up my ass."

"Whose ass?"

Kane grinned rakishly, sat forward, and said, "George has told me something of the sting you pulled off in Belmont. A remarkable enterprise, if he can be believed."

"That's a big *if*." Orin recalled for the judge the time George saw a flying saucer, actually filed an incident report, then with his hair puffy and blown dry, sat at attention on the *Hard Copy* couch as if he were testifying in traffic court.

"He does tend to exaggerate, doesn't he," said Kane, "as well as eat like a fucking shark. Anyway, even though he lost his share of the proceeds, he seems to think you were ever so much more fortunate. Clearly, so does Dominick Ril."

Orin looked Kane in the eye. "George is nuts. Ril never knew what hit him, and still doesn't. Me, I'm lucky I'm alive."

"Be that as it may, should you actually be sitting on a chunk of cash and wish to invest wisely for the future, I am available for all manner of financial planning. That's all I wanted to say. I didn't mean to pry."

Orin sat back in his plastic chair. "You want to trade my vast portfolio?"

Kane looked around. "Running the kitchen is relatively undemanding, as long as George stays clear. One must somehow fill the other hours."

Orin looked over his shoulder at George, reloading as if he'd just walked in. "He really has put on weight."

"Orin, my civilian staff consists of two middle-aged Dominican women who don't speak English. Of course, as far as George is concerned, each possesses a rare and valuable commodity of which George is in tireless pursuit. Their husbands have already complained."

"What do you charge for your services?"

"Nothing. Really. There's a reason these guys like me, and it's not because I can glaze a duck."

Orin glanced around the dining room. "Fuck these guys."

"You say that now. We really are a family here."

Orin sopped up his Russian dressing with a roll that was still warm. "What a horrible thought."

"Now, about that money—"

"Judge, I wish I had a couple of bucks stashed away. My daughter goes to college in like eight more years."

"Then there's no time to lose."

"And not a nickel to invest."

"Really," said Kane. "I'm finding that hard to believe."

MONDAY, JUNE 27, 7:15 P.M.

DICK PETTIBONE DINED ALONE THAT EVENING, IN his own locked room in the dormitory, sitting in his chair in his best clean underwear, watching *Jeopardy!*

He was agitated, constantly checking his watch. Still full from his afternoon snack, he had barely picked at his steak.

Twice he called out answers that were so totally wrong he felt ashamed.

In the seemingly endless commercial break before Final Jeopardy, he dumped the remains of his meal in his wastebasket, then stared out his window at the haze shrouding the Sound, rubbing his hands along the damp white bricks. Aching. The way he had when he was young.

Alex Trebek returned and posed another smart-aleck answer. Dick Pettibone grew angry that he had no idea who or what the fuck a Maya Angelou was, and he punched off the set, spared himself the winner's smug celebration.

A bad day, he thought, about to get better.

He stepped close to the stainless-steel mirror bolted to the wall, examined several clogged pores on his nose, pinched them until they oozed, then slapped on cologne as though he was going somewhere, felt the burn. He sprayed his armpits with deodorant, humming a seagoing jingle, lit a cigarette, put it out, used Lavoris, left the cap off. On his bed next to his clean jeans and work shirt were a pair of ten-pound barbell plates connected by a six-foot length of rope. His counterbalance to gravity. His wings.

MONDAY, JUNE 27, 8:15 P.M.

ORIN TOLD GEORGE AND THE JUDGE HE HAD TO call home, to remind Judy to cancel his motorcycle insurance and ESPN. He scraped his plate into the garbage and left the dining room, made his way to the front of the house through darkened hallways, and ambled out into the dusk, trying to imagine what it would have been like to live in the mansion during its heyday. With servants seeing to every need, horses everywhere, and the rich blonde women who hang around horses. Cotillions. Yachts. Debutantes. Polo. Fox hunts. The sense that no one on the planet was more important than you and yours.

He lit a Carlton and strolled across worn cobblestones around to the back of the house, enjoying the breeze, upwind of the barn, trying to imagine Soundview as it had been, without anachronisms: the basketball court, with its three-point arc; the boccie court, its balls clustered around the tiny balleen like planets at rest around a dying star, their canvas sack crumpled in the dirt; the satellite dish on the dormitory roof; cash crops crowding out meadowland; razor wire, guards, and golf carts.

Mist off the Sound hugged the Honor Farm as Orin wandered into the woods along the golf course, remembering from other night patrols how to walk recon. How to wait, and listen, and look twice. How to do without. How to think on his feet.

He needed to know his way around, how long it took to get from place to place, on foot, on one of the many apparently donated bicycles lined up behind the house, perhaps on his belly.

Orin froze behind a birch tree and counted to thirty-five, then continued through knee-high grass up the gentle slope to the eastern boundary of the estate and the cliff where the Kreeling family cemetery lay overgrown in ivy behind a wrought-iron fence, six feet high.

He opened the gate, stepped among the dead, all long forgotten, their perpetual care abandoned to the tax man. In the dying light he found the patriarch and his brood under headstones covered with moss: Baby Constance, aged three, and Baby Abigail, aged two, taken from this earth within weeks of each other in February of 1928. Elizabeth Reed, aged six, died in 1933, perhaps the child of a maid. Later generations of Kreelings were housed in the mammoth family crypt, inside which the powerful smell of damp earth mingled with the brackish air of the marshlands below.

Back outside, in front of the freshly dug grave with the large bouquet of flowers and no headstone, Orin wondered if the Kreelings were Roman Catholics, if he was standing on consecrated ground, or if on the basis of Detective Lieutenant Tommy Kruger's investigation, the church had denied Skip Trimble and his father that comfort, consigned the corpse to this forgotten bluff. Orin knelt at Skip's grave and pulled from beneath the flowers a highly modified Walkman, wondering if the boss was watching him, which was likely, because the boss wanted updates at the fence behind the graveyard, in person. "Nightly, if possible."

"If practical," Orin had said. "I won't risk the mission because you're impatient sitting at home. If it's that big a deal, I'll send up flares."

"I'll be there anyway, most nights, to change tapes. And don't get too goddamned comfortable in there. Part of the problem with that place is you forget what you're doing there. You start to think you're a Kreeling."

Orin didn't feel like a Kreeling as he knelt among their dead. He made the short stroll to the stone fence, cocked his arm, and lobbed his old Walkman up the hill, where he supposed the commissioner was sitting, doing his own thinking, his own waiting, his own doing without.

Orin took the long way back to the dorm, on a perimeter path that led past the lower cornfield. Halfway home he heard something off to his left, amid the chest-high stalks. A man. Alone. With a flashlight. Not three hours in-country and they were on to him, Orin thought. If this were war, he'd be dead. He got down and lay still, flat on the ground, while the short hairs rose on the back of his neck. He smelled cigar smoke as the man moved closer.

Gramps McKay. A nice old man in jail for an ancient double manslaughter conviction. Orin let him pass unmolested and tried to delete from his muscle memory what it felt like to cut a man's throat.

8

THE LONG HALLWAY IN THE ONE-STORY DORM
was deserted. Orin leaned on the wall outside Nick
Morelli's locked bedroom and quickly bugged the earpiece
of the pay phone, then slipped into his own room, a man
with a great deal of work to do and a growing desire to
spend no longer with these losers than necessary.

His biggest problem was that he had no idea of how to
begin. His long list of combat medals and spectacular arrests had been won with bravery and last-minute hunches,
stupid, futile gestures that had somehow panned out. He
was not now, and had never been, a top-notch criminal in-
vestigator.

Nevertheless, he paced the small white room and considered a plan of action, deciding what research was absolutely necessary: learning the basic anthropology of the
crime scene, the social arrangements, the security lapses,
timing the rounds of the guards so that he might later move
about the Farm unseen. Orin was first, last, and always a
marine, trained on Parris Island, blooded in Nam. He would

find high ground to defend, which might have nothing to do with its elevation.

According to Commissioner Trimble, Zen Masters, Nick Morelli, Arthur Tobin, Luther Bailey, George Clarke, and Dom Ril were the most likely suspects who did not have what he considered iron-clad alibis. Skip had worked in the inmate office with some of them, had at times indicated to his father that none had been successfully rehabilitated. All were known to hold grudges against upper management in general, the police commissioner in particular.

"Separate Tobin and Morelli, if you can. They're useless without each other, not much better together. . . . Unless it was Zen Masters," said Trimble. "A beast we built ourselves."

William Masters, formerly of the precision firearms team, was simply and irretrievably a killer, one of the best.

Gramps McKay was the least likely suspect, said Trimble, a nice old man who liked where he was. Everybody else on the grounds that morning, including the prison staff, fell somewhere in between. Prank Dinostra was to be checked first.

"Isn't he a close friend?"

"We came on the job together. I carried him up the ladder."

"And then?"

"He got greedy. Incidentally, he's keeping a diary of his life on the Farm. To show me what he's gone through, that I can bear witness to his punishment. I get to read it when he gets out. He told Skip he was gonna stop by headquarters and shove it up my ass." Commissioner Trimble had nevertheless insisted that Prank be treated like all the others. "Maybe he hates me. Maybe he blames me for his troubles."

Yeah, and maybe not, Orin thought. Maybe it was Skip who had hated him. Orin got out his new, improved Walkman, opened his bedroom window, and peered out into the dark. He smelled bread baking and dung cooling, admired the glowing lights of the mansion looming over them, and hoped the boys upstairs were in a gabby mood as he tuned in the captain's office.

He fiddled with the dial until he was pleased with the re-

ception and was disappointed that all he could hear was
Lite-Rock wafting from the captain's radio. And then nothing from the pay phone. Lite. Nothing. Lite.

A heavy fist knocked on Orin's door.

Orin switched off the Walkman. "It's open."

Zen Masters, shirtless, in running shorts, leaned into the
room. "Want to burn dinner?" he said.

"Maybe another time."

"Maybe I won't ask another time."

Orin gave Zen a crooked look. "So I'll get over it."

MONDAY, JUNE 27, 9:50 P.M.

THE POLISHED MARBLE HALLS ON THE GROUND
floor were dark and quiet, though Orin could hear soft
voices coming from the front of the mansion. He knew
sound traveled easily within, at night even more so. Any
mistake would be amplified. All the fine draperies that had
once muffled and soothed life in these halls had been
yanked from their walls, as surely as Cyrus Kreeling had
yanked them from disintegrating castles in Europe. In their
place were now glossy, autographed, black-and-white publicity photos of Nassau County Executive Gil Otto and his
brother Tom, the U.S. senator. Also present were past potentates Fran Purcell and Eugene Nickerson, and wasn't it
nice, Orin thought, that Joe Margiotta could still get his
mug hung around the county.

Orin climbed the narrow servants' staircase at the back of
the house three steps at a time, froze like a rock on the
second-floor landing for sixty-five seconds. Moved on to
the third floor. Waited.

The library door was unlocked, the room dark, heavy
with the smell of dust and decay. Orin lit his Bic and
stepped carefully past the wing chairs and overstuffed
couches, the chest-high bookshelves and a glass display
case containing arrowheads, fertility beads, and a pair of
shrunken heads. Orin wondered if the two knew each other,

if they had died together, if they minded being locked up in a white man's castle.

Prank's little corner of the world, according to Trimble, was preserved by covenant, as it was when fortune smiled upon this house. Orin sat in Prank's chair and turned on Prank's terminal.

A phosphorescent green GOOD DAY appeared in the middle of the screen. In the righthand corner of the screen a digital display showed a ten-second countdown: 10, 9, 8, 7, 6.

Orin hit ENTER. The box began a countdown: 5, 4, 3, 2, 1, 0.

GOOD DAY disappeared, replaced by FUCK OFF, ASS-HOLE.

Orin shut off the power, rebooted the machine.

The computer would hear nothing of it. FUCK OFF, ASSHOLE.

"Asshole" was right, Orin thought.

MONDAY, JUNE 27, 10:45 P.M.

DICK PETTIBONE TOOK HIS THICK BLACK glasses off and tucked them into his shirt pocket, trusting the plan, his decision to carry through. In total silence and grateful submission, he accepted the loose-fitting canvas bag over his head as necessary to secrecy, to a repeat of this peak performance.

He turned himself clockwise four times, until he staggered, then he felt a reassuring hand on his arm, the small of his back, and stepped outside the ivy-covered dormitory into the night, the ground solid under his feet.

They were moving then, quickly, finally doing it, finally making for the tunnel.

The weights draped over his shoulders were the key. They made the whole thing work, this wild ride. What he had been dreaming about was now possible, scant seconds away.

His heart beat faster, and he had to admit it, he hadn't felt this good since they had stuck him in here, this alive.

MONDAY, JUNE 27, 10:52 P.M.

CAPTAIN ROGER SMITH SAT IN HIS OFFICE WITH his windows wide open, enjoying a glass of port from the Soundview cellar as the end of his working day drew near. He had spent the evening catching up on his chores after a weekend away in Atlantic City. He was presently listening to a Blood, Sweat and Tears tape and shining up his pocket change with Gorham's Antique Silver Polish, because he had already wiped down all the flat surfaces of the office with Fantastik, vacuumed his chair, and disinfected his phone, anything to conquer the stink of stale cigarette smoke, a stink that had no business in his office.

He made a note to speak harshly to Marion Whithers when he saw her tomorrow afternoon, then put away his cleaning tools and started through his In box. He checked the daily produce reports, the telephone records for both inmates and staff, the time sheets, and he entered the data into his computer. A stickler for records, Roger Smith could tell you who took what books from the prison library last week, who left the light on in the sauna last night. His résumé showed stints with the safety patrol, police cadets, volunteer fire departments, and his local Neighborhood Watch. He held an associate degree in criminal justice from Suffolk Community College, a B.S. from Hofstra. Roger Smith had planned all his life to be a cop. Only a pilonidal cyst had deflected him to Corrections.

Roger Smith took comfort in organization, a predictable sequence of events, men whose conduct was consistent. He believed in rewarding such men, allowing them liberties. That comfort in order evaporated when the new prisoner's name leaped out at him from the top of a seemingly innocuous form, flooding him with a terror he had not felt since childhood. He suddenly hated that his revolver was locked up at the command post. "BOYD, ORIN," the revised inmate roster screamed.

Knees jelly, hands shaking, he forced himself to remember that somehow, for some reason, the worm had turned and their situations had reversed, that he need not be afraid.

He was the jailer; Orin Boyd was the jailed.

Color slowly returned to his face, and he smiled at his reflection in the monstrous mirror across from his desk. There was a God, and He had been paying attention, because God didn't make mistakes like this. Injustice and indecency were punished in good time, diligence rewarded. Because God knew Roger Smith had worked hard and studied long, french-kissed many highly placed assholes to get where he was today. He had suffered gladly the humiliations reserved for toadies, until he was in a position to dish them out.

Orin Boyd had meanwhile violently despoiled everything he had ever touched; his sole reason for being the degradation of others. At last what goes around had come around for the meanest bully ever to stalk a public-school system.

Roger picked up his phone and called his house, never mind the late hour. "Hello, Mommy," he said. "He's here."

"Who's where, Roggie?" asked Elsie Smith. "What time is it?"

"My worst nightmare, my whole life, Mom. On the Farm."

"You mean Orin Boyd? From across the street?"

"Yes."

"You put in for a transfer immediately, Roggie. That boy—"

"I don't think so, Mom."

"Excuse me?"

"I think this time I get even."

"You've been drinking again, haven't you?"

Roger swallowed more of the exquisite vintage and considered dropping by the dorm right then to say hello, with a backup squad of guards armed with nightsticks. Maybe tear Boyd's cell apart. Kick in his TV and piss on his bed. Order the guards to give him a kung-fu cavity check. To what end? Happy Jack would want to know in the morning. To set the bastard on notice that he would soon be begging for the hellish tiers of East Meadow.

"Gotta get back to work now, Mom. I'll be home at the regular time."

"Roggie, you be careful."

MONDAY, JUNE 27, 11:05 P.M.

ORIN'S HEAD AND FEET HURT. HE STRETCHED OUT on his bed and changed channels again from the captain's office to the dormitory pay phone, overheard George Clarke begging a woman for a conjugal next Wednesday, promising historical splendors, the chance to boff where Gatsby did, if she would only sign the ledger as his fiancée.

"Gatsby was fiction," she said playfully. "He didn't exist."

"Tell that to the freaking people around here."

Back to the captain's office, where someone was whistling off-key along with "You've Got a Friend."

Back to the pay phone, where Ira Cohen was explaining to an unhappy young woman who wouldn't leave her name that Dick Pettibone wasn't in his room and no, Ira had no idea where he might be and no, he wouldn't "search the grounds for the little freak."

Orin shut off the Walkman and watched the local news for a while, then some of a West Coast baseball game on ESPN, stopped channel-surfing for "The Star-Spangled Banner" as PBS signed off the air. He was reminded of a junket he took to South Bend, Indiana, with the Emerald Society to watch Notre Dame play Miami, the Catholics versus the Convicts. Before the game the honor guard raised Old Glory into a cold gray sky, and everyone in the famous stadium sang with adoration first "America the Beautiful," then the national anthem. Orin remembered the lump in his throat and sting in his eyes, and then the profound sense of gratitude one knows when a lifelong quest ends. Orin had finally met the Americans he had fought for in Vietnam. They were real. They were grateful. They just didn't live on either coast. He flipped back to the baseball game. A pitcher's duel was now a blowout.

Life, he discovered, was going on without him.

Like it had when he was in Nam.

Like it had when he was drunk.

TUESDAY, JUNE 28, 1:20 A.M.

AN ALARM BELL CLANGED THREE TIMES IN THE hallway, waking Orin.

He stuck his head out the door, saw Zen Masters next door do the same. Down the hall: Comstock. Kelly. George. Morelli. Like a row of trophy kills for Barthwell's office.

Across the hall Artie Tobin was lighting a cigarette, coughing up a lugie.

"Fire drill?" asked Orin.

"Lockdown," said Zen. "Stay in your room for a head count. Maybe a shakedown, a search for contraband."

"They do this a lot?"

"No."

Orin closed his door and sat on the bed and waited, heard a soft knock at one-thirty. Then a short black guard with shocking gray hair and a name tag that said Oliver Bridges stuck his head in the door.

"I do something wrong?" asked Orin.

"We'll let you know."

There was another soft knock on his door at one-thirty-five.

"Hey, yo," said Orin. "Where do I complain about noise after curfew?"

"It's me," said George, walking in and sitting on the edge of the bed. "I think Sick Dick escaped."

"Good. Now you don't have to worry about my morals anymore. Go home."

TUESDAY, JUNE 28, 1:50 A.M.

"BOYD!" BARKED WARDEN BARTHWELL. "WE'RE coming in."

Orin had his bare feet on the concrete when they pushed in the oak door and turned on the overhead light, *they* being Warden Barthwell, Officer Bridges, a sun-wrinkled blond guy in a seersucker suit, and another prison official Orin could have sworn he'd seen someplace before.

The four big men crowded into his room, stared down at him and his aluminum ashtray filled with cigarettes, their distaste palpable.

"How long you been in your room?" asked Barthwell.

"Since after dinner."

"You never left? Not even to piss?"

"No, sir."

"Zen Masters said he saw you around nine," said Barthwell.

"He asked me to go jogging. I politely declined."

The blond asked, "You talk to Dick Pettibone today?"

Orin looked at him. "Exactly who the fuck are you?"

"Detective Lieutenant Kruger, Nassau County Homicide. And I asked if you talked to Dick Pettibone today."

Tommy Kruger was an angular fifty, with his hair worn long in the back. His tan suggested lifeguard rather than sleuth.

"Now that you mention it," said Orin, "he welcomed me warmly to the Honor Farm, even brought snacks." Orin pointed to the crumbs on his floor. "We had a delightful visit, although I'm sure he would have rather entertained me in the mansion."

"George Clarke says you threw him out, called him a pervert."

Orin shook his head sadly. "Some things never change."

"What's that mean?"

"The way two people can see things completely differently. Have you ever been married?"

Kruger said, "You calling Clarke a liar?"

Orin put his hand over his heart. "Goodness, no. The man's given so much for so long."

Kruger looked at Warden Barthwell, who nodded and said, "Clarke *is* totally full of shit."

Kruger made a note of this on his clipboard. Then wrote something else about George, then something else.

"Dick Pettibone among the missing, as they say?" asked Orin.

"Dick Pettibone's among the dead."

The air rushed out of Orin's gut. "How? Why?"

Kruger looked up from his clipboard. "Drowned in the swimming pool, sometime between dinner and midnight, weighed down with barbell plates like some kind of chick poet. And as far as I can tell, you and Clarke were the last ones to see him alive."

Orin looked over at the grinning face of the younger man he thought he knew, the guy who seemed to be enjoying the grilling. "You look familiar," said Orin. "Are you my lawyer or something?"

Roger Smith grinned. "Captain Roger Smith, most definitely not your lawyer."

Orin smiled, slapped his own forehead, offered his hand.

"Sissyboy Smith. Well, I'll be damned. Hey, your skin cleared up really nice. How you been?"

"Don't you call me that, ever."

"Well, I'll be damned," said Orin, "Sissyboy Smith. Hey, how's your mom? Is she still alive?"

Roger Smith grabbed Barthwell's sleeve. "He calls me that again, he goes in the hole."

"This is an honor farm, Roger. We don't have a hole. And Boyd, you call the Rog here Captain Smith."

TUESDAY, JUNE 28, 2:17 A.M.

THE INMATES WERE ROUSTED FROM THEIR BEDS, marched from the dorm, and lined up in the dark near the boccie court, far enough away from the pool to preserve the crime scene, close enough to watch the goings-on. "Good idea," was how Roger Smith put it to Barthwell. "Rub their noses in it. Why should they be asleep while we have to stay awake. Maybe one of them will confess."

"Actually, Rog, the detectives want to search their rooms."

"Right."

Richard Pettibone's corpse had already been hauled from the bottom of the pool and was laid out on a gurney by the diving board, his drowned face white in the harsh spot-lights, his clean, wet prison clothes clinging to a body that looked even shorter than it had when he was erect, alive. Pettibone had been discovered by an Officer Marshall, who had planned to swim laps on his break.

Three kids, thought Orin. And nothing to live for. So common these days. And drowning was too horrible to con-template, the roaring in the head, water pressing in. And tough to change your mind when you bring barbells along for the ride.

He was wondering if Pettibone had at any point changed his mind when Tommy Kruger found Orin, got in his face. "He seem at all despondent to you?"

"Oh, he seems way past that."

"I meant this evening, asshole."

"How the fuck do I know? I met him exactly once. He might have been feeling down. He might have been happy-ass."

Kruger growled and flipped through the pages on his clipboard, stalling, and Orin feared he was a fill-in-the-boxes dick, a favor to somebody Big, an empty suit.

"Any connection to Skip Trimble here, Lieu? Two guys in two weeks . . ." said Orin. "I don't fucking know."

Kruger turned to Warden Barthwell. "I can't believe he was only a uniform, talent like this."

Barthwell smiled half a grin and called Kruger aside for a chat. Orin and the other prisoners watched the morgue mutts trundle Pettibone into the meat wagon. Cops in jumpsuits crawled around the pool, collecting evidence; more scoured the lawn on hands and knees, hunting for reasons.

Orin tried to remember if Pettibone had ever made it to the dining room that evening, wondered if he had rejoined the flow of human events for so much as a moment after being tossed from Orin's room; or if he had sullenly, and alone, nursed this new and last affront, until it became a suitable reason to die.

"Lieutenant?" cried a detective.

Kruger spun like a top, marched off. Barthwell followed him. Captain Roger Smith crooked a finger at Orin, pulled him ten yards behind the lines. Before Roger could so much as open his mouth, Orin said, "Pettibone didn't drown himself. You realize that, don't you, Roger?"

"You shouldn't talk about things you don't know about."

"I know about things like this, Rog. Good Lord, you're still a fucking putz. Aren't you?"

"Maybe so. But you're in the slaughterhouse, mornings, starting tomorrow, just as soon as your bullshit session with Homo is over."

"The rehabilitative portion of my day, as it were."

"You got field work afternoons."

"When it's hottest?" said Orin.

"I think you're catching on."

TUESDAY, JUNE 28, 9:00 A.M.

WHEN ORIN ENTERED THE DINING ROOM FOR A cup of coffee, the few other prisoners without early chores and the stomach to eat kept their mouths shut, each perhaps assessing what part he might have played in the destruction of Richard Pettibone. Orin took his cup out to the still, blue, swimming pool, looking for clues the big guys might have missed in the dark, but the crime scene was already sanitized, even the boccie balls roped and tied inside their canvas bag, tucked under the spectator's bench.

Why Pettibone? Orin wondered, as he wandered back and forth on the flagstone deck, rubbed the grass with the toe of his sneaker, tried to peer through the clear blue water to the bottom. And why last night? And what did this have to do with Skip, if anything?

He sat down on the granite bench and stared at his sneakers, telling himself that things would happen that he could not control, that might have nothing to do with his mission or with him. He told himself to be patient. He had been on the Honor Farm less than seventeen hours. At least no one had made him for a cop.

At ten o'clock he trudged up the marble front stairs of the mansion for his meeting with Doc Homo, wondering how he was going to fool the little shrink into thinking he felt remorse for a crime he did not commit, or that he was fit to return to society, an entirely different proposition. Orin held out little hope for a therapeutic miracle as he entered the doctor's cluttered outpost of psychiatry.

"Ah, Boyd. How are you feeling this morning?" asked Dr. Robbins.

"Actually, I've been thinking of killing myself."

"Then you've come to the right place."

"Excuse me?" said Orin.

Doc Robbins folded his small white hands over his ample belly and smiled. "Gallows humor. To deal with the stress of serious situations. You should try it."

Marvin Robbins was in his late sixties, shiny bald on top with a thick fringe of white above his ears. His skin was pale and wrinkled, his accent Borchst Belt. Doc Robbins wholeheartedly believed that Orin Boyd was in his office for his intake interview, one small step along the rocky road to mental health. Orin knew better, that he was there to stick a Giordano minimike to the underside of the patients' couch.

"Now," said Robbins, "where to begin with someone like you."

Orin turned his head, saw his file from the police department on the doctor's desk, no doubt unread by this latest in his long line of publicly-funded shrinks. How he hated these first sessions, the core curriculum; his dad, who went walkabout, always took such a beating.

"You say this particular death upsets you?"

"Both of them. Skip Trimble, too."

"*These* deaths upset you?" Dr. Robbins corrected himself.

"Things happen in threes, no?"

"The deaths are unrelated. Believe me. For Richard Pettibone, it was only a matter of time—here, when he got out. A very self-destructive man. And Skip's problems ran deeper than anybody ever suspected. We tried and we failed."

"I just feel very sad, and tired, and, I don't know, tense," Orin said, as if he assumed he was supposed to catalogue his feelings at the moment.

"There is a great deal of shame and guilt associated with a prison sentence. For some it is overbearing. Let me ask you this: Have you ever tried to kill yourself?"

Orin recalled the night outside his house—during one of their separations, watching Judy make out with her boss—the cold gun in his ear, how far away the stars had seemed. "I punked out. I looked into the abyss and saw it didn't want me."

Dr. Robbins said nothing for a moment, then checked the form on his desk. "I was going to ask what sort of work you'd find rewarding here, but I see you've already been assigned duties. Any problem with that?"

"Blood and guts I can live with. USMC trained."

"Yes, I realize you were in combat. So the question naturally arises: Has Orin Boyd made it all the way home from the jungle?"

"The highlands," Orin corrected him. "Most of me made it home."

"Nightmares?"

"Subterranean homesick blues, none of them Dylanesque. I hate loud noises and superior officers."

"Many veterans still cry for their buddies."

"And lots of others have forgotten," said Orin. Why were they probing that wound, he wondered, making one more attempt to impose sense upon chaos? Orin folded his hands and stared at the cracks in the high plaster ceiling.

"You must have buried a great deal of guilt."

"Actually, Doc, what I buried was a great deal of money."

Tuesday, June 28, 10:46 a.m.

DR. MARVIN ROBBINS LOCKED HIS OFFICE DOOR and lifted his tape recorder from his desk drawer. He removed the tape of Orin Boyd's first session and threw it in the garbage pail, loaded a fresh cassette, then he slouched back in his swivel chair and dictated his session notes from memory, while his impressions were fresh.

"Inmate Orin Boyd presents a myriad of symptoms suggesting a highly unstable personality. Avoids eye-contact. Bristles when one suggests he may be wrong about something. Chain smoker. Seems terribly worried about a number of issues, almost all of which relate to his inability to connect on any meaningful level with other people. Has low self-esteem, a view of himself as an outcast. Consider hypnosis."

TUESDAY, JUNE 28, 11:00 A.M.

"HARMLESS" ROBERT LIMPED AROUND THE dusty potholes in the rear lot of AAA Auto Sales, a junkyard in a Bethpage industrial park where he knew one of the mechanics from jail.

Robert had six hundred dollars in the pocket of his jeans, the bulk of his liquid wealth. Sitting on old tires, Robert and his pal reminisced a while, like soldiers remembering a battle. Then Robert drove out of the lot in a gray 1988 Excel, for which he paid four hundred dollars. The heavily dented subcompact bore stolen New Jersey license plates, for which he had greased his friend an additional hundred.

Robert got himself a cup of coffee and a road map of Nassau County at the 7-Eleven on Old Country Road and sat in the hot little car sweating bullets onto the page that showed the Sands Point Peninsula, a seaside block of green labeled N.C. Corr. Fac.

Beautiful, he thought. So it didn't matter that Boyd's home telephone number was unlisted, his address a mystery—though there were ways he could get it, people in low places he could bribe. Unnecessary, he thought, and burdened with the chance of calling attention to himself.

The wife would go to see him; they almost all go once. Until they see what happens to their men in jail and can no longer bear to watch.

Once would be enough, thought Robert. Poor girl would flee the prison spilling tears, gulping fresh air, and head straight home to a shower that would never get her clean.

And he would follow, and hold her under his wing.

10

POLICE CHAPLAIN MONSIGNOR MARTIN O'ROURKE
heard Gramps McKay's confession first, and the oldest
Honor Farm inmate's sins, as always, were trivial. Monsignor O'Rourke dispensed absolution, then begged him
one more time to go home. Parole had found him a studio in
Hempstead, said the priest, near a Catholic church, an HIP
clinic. All he had to do was apply.

Gramps said, "Begging your pardon, Father, but I don't
plan to spend my sunset years in fucking Hempstead, thank
you."

"It's a place to start, Bill."

"Garden City's a place to start."

"But I don't know how much longer I can hold up your
release. And no one knows how much longer this place will
be a prison."

"As long as Barthwell's here, we're okay."

"Bill."

"What would I do all day? My doctor's here, my
records." Then Gramps added, rightly, that he was the only

inmate who knew a damn thing about farming. "I leave, who the hell's gonna run the farm? The Rog?"

"You've got to rejoin the world. It's part of your penance, don't you know."

Gramps said, "Everything I have left is here, in that produce barn and in those fields. The police department saw to that. The newspapers. If they want, I could commit a couple new crimes."

"It's a terrible shame, to settle for a fantasy."

"Mine's that much nuttier than yours?"

Outside the confessional, Orin patiently waited his turn in a hand-carved pew, reading the first bit of mail to reach him at the Farm, a short cheerful note from his daughter, mailed yesterday, the day he had surrendered himself. The second bit of mail to reach him was an offer of pen-palship from a sixteen-year-old girl at Westbury High, which began, "I imagine it must be hard to be all locked up." Who, he wondered, thought of introducing this legion of sociopaths to swarms of willing victims? Who was the program designed to benefit? If these sorry bastards didn't have their own correspondents, it was largely because they were scumbags.

Like Detective Lieutenant Kruger, Orin thought.

That morning Kruger had commandeered the conjugal trailer for use as a temporary command post. Squadrons of experts were meeting there now, perhaps minutes from breaking both cases.

The confessional curtain slid back. Gramps shuffled out; Orin shuffled in, hit his knees. The small screen in the dark booth slid open, admitting a waft of incense and a shaft of dim light. Neither man made any pretense that religion played a part in their business.

"I can't believe you wound up here," the monsignor said angrily. "Of all the men to come through my camp—"

"Believe it. How's my daughter?"

"As lovely as ever. Are you sober?"

"This ain't the Hard Rock Cafe."

"Some of the others stay high."

"I'm okay."

"What does, 'Don't believe everything you read,' mean? I hate cryptic messages."

"Sometimes innocent people go to jail."

The monsignor considered this a moment, perhaps gauging Orin's sanity, remembering a role he had played before. "You're telling me you were framed?"

"By the best."

"Is there anything I can do? Pull some strings?"

"Don't give 'em the satisfaction. I'll be home before the snow flies. Just answer me this, Father—Were the Kreelings Roman Catholic?"

"Lutheran, I think. Why?"

"So Skip is not buried in consecrated ground."

The priest coughed. "No."

"You couldn't do the old man that favor?"

"I offered. He declined." Monsignor O'Rourke went on to explain that Skip had loved the old cemetery, that he had spent many peaceful hours watching the Sound from its confines, that the moldy old headstones somehow placed his problems in perspective.

Orin said, "They might reopen Skip's case until they rule out any link to Richard Pettibone. That could give the old man some hope." He paused a second, then said, "How bad does that suck—you wish your kid had been murdered."

"The truth be told, Orin, I worry about him more than I worry about you."

"Amen."

O'Rourke mumbled some quick Latin over Orin's pitiful soul and then dismissed him without penance to perform, or hope of salvation. Outside the confessional, Orin felt no relief, none of the balm that might have come with cleansing his conscience.

TUESDAY, JUNE 28, 3:30 P.M.

THE HONOR FARM MEMORIAL SERVICE FOR RICHard Pettibone was held that afternoon in the chapel. Attendance was mandatory; the audience uniformly dressed in clean denims.

Luther Bailey played a Mozart fugue on the house organ,

and Allan Kelly, one of the slap-happy Highway cops, followed him up with "Amazing Grace" on his bagpipes. Everybody tried to look suitably downcast, but even so, Monsignor O'Rourke's benediction sounded silly, given what the prisoners knew of Pettibone's real life and predilections.

A soul saved through penance and service? An expanding love of his fellow man? Were we talking the same Dickster? Orin wondered.

It was amazing how fast death had improved his reputation and, for most in the audience, no doubt comforting. Orin made a note to watch for a similar situation in Skip Trimble's case, not to let death cloud the collective memory.

There was no casket to ponder, no fake farewells.

Some of the boys in the back row did quietly grumble that a perfectly good afternoon of weight lifting was ruined, a tennis tournament thrown off schedule. And only Gramps and Zen Masters took communion, which had all the lapsed Catholics joking about the jerk-off epidemic as they crowded out of the chapel.

TUESDAY, JUNE 28, 6:50 P.M.

TEN MINUTES BEFORE DINNER AND NICK MORELLI was still in the weight pit, doing preacher curls, topping off massive biceps when he should have been working on his gut.

Art Tobin sat on a stationary bicycle nearby, smoking, sipping a container of coffee.

Nick set the bar down and prowled the pit like a bear, rechalked his hands, then said, "You think Boyd's tough?"

"Other folks sure do."

"You know what? I don't fucking care. We're going for his money."

"Cool."

"Tommy Cotton wants blood, this'll do it. I mean, it

beats the hell out of pissing in his food and canceling his conjugals. And if it works, we make a fortune. What you call a win-win situation."

Artie Tobin cocked one eyebrow, looked around the pit at the other inmates heading for predinner showers. "How?"

"We wipe him out. His visible assets. His invisible assets. Force him to the cash."

Tobin's face was a blank. "Oh, yeah?"

"We steal or spend every cent he's got, then make him send his old lady for more. We have someone watching her take what's left."

Artie Tobin twirled his ponytail, thinking.

"What's wrong with it?"

"Would you tell a bitch where you hid your treasure?"

"If I had to."

"How we gonna do this?"

"With computers," said Morelli. "This is the nineties, hard-on. You can wipe somebody out in an hour, you know what you're doing."

"But we don't know what we're doing."

"That's never stopped us before."

Tobin grinned and fieldstripped his butt, tucked the filter in his pocket.

Nick said, "You know, we got a pretty goddamn good hacker right here on the Farm."

Artie tapped another cigarette up from his pocket, shook his head. "Prank's in the wind on Saturday. Ira's already collecting for his party."

"All the more reason to hire him now."

Tobin got it, started to pedal slowly. "What about Ril?"

"Fuck that hard-on. He had his chance."

"Fine with me."

"I wouldn't use Prank if I didn't have to."

"What do you think a share might be worth?" asked Tobin.

"The difference between a rooming house and a condo with a pool, when you get out."

"Sounds like a plan."

TUESDAY, JUNE 28, 8:00 P.M.

NEW YORK STATE SENATOR THOMAS COTTON'S hastily assembled Ad Hoc Committee for Corrections Reform gathered at the Honor Farm for an emergency meeting that evening, in response to frantic calls from area residents and realtors. The estate owners, both private and corporate, were concerned about the rise of violence in the neighborhood and had decided they wanted the Honor Farm closed. The value of their investments could shrink due to all the bad publicity. Formerly a vocal supporter of continuing the Honor Farm concept beyond the expiration of the fifty-year stipulation, the brash young senator was now reported to be having serious misgivings.

One accountant, a matrimonial lawyer, two lobbyists, and the obligatory insurance hack, all Republican committeemen, sat in the main conference room of Soundview, making cellular calls while they waited for the senator to arrive. No sense plunging into anything; they would follow his lead. These men enjoyed very comfortable lives by following orders, and they were not about to rock any yachts. Roger Smith felt his disdain for them grow by the minute as they talked around him, above him, as if he were a piece of furniture. He was almost ready to say something nasty when at last the senator and Townsend Tripp entered the conference room, followed by Warden Barthwell, who, thankfully, had ditched his workout clothes for a massive gray suit and tie.

"Good evening, Senator," everyone said as they pocketed their phones.

"Sorry to keep you waiting," Cotton said with some difficulty. His jaw was visibly swollen, his cheekbone discolored. He made himself as comfortable as possible in the chair at the head of the table, shoved a water glass aside. "So let's have it," he said. "What the fuck is going on? Inquiring minds want to know."

Jack Barthwell looked him straight in the eye, or as straight as someone can look at a man whose head is misshapen. "Senator, two prisoners with personal troubles sadly took their own lives."

"Something's going on here, Warden," Townsend Tripp corrected him. "Your ultraliberal procedures aren't working."

"Excuse me?"

"Coddling criminals has never worked," said the senator. "Letting them wander about the woods, contemplating their navels, playing tennis and golf—"

"We don't coddle criminals here. People who kill themselves haven't gotten away with something."

"We've got to instill a little discipline here," said Tripp. "We look bad on this, very bad. When the senator first threw his support behind this project—"

"We've got to break their fucking balls, is what we've got to do," said the senator. "The polls show it. The populace demands it. Now, I'd never recommend mixing these prisoners into the general population, but it's clear they've had it too damn easy."

"Never say never, boss," said Tripp, right on cue.

"It's either that or sell the place to the Park Service, make it accessible to all the people."

"You may be right, sir," said Smith, animated by the thought that his cushy office might soon be despoiled by park rangers, "about our liberal policies. Current research—"

"Excuse me, Roger," said Barthwell, looking at his watch, "but don't you have some vendors coming in this evening?"

Smith stared at his legal pad. "Yes, I do."

"I can handle things here."

TUESDAY, JUNE 28, 8:38 P.M.

THE REALLY BIG TEARS DIDN'T SPILL UNTIL Roger Smith was safe in his own office, with the door locked. He sat at his desk and stared at his mirror and repeatedly relived his humiliation, his dismissal as if he were nothing more than a troublesome lackey, recalling the frost in Barthwell's voice, how the committee members got busy with their briefcases during his ignominious exit. The smug pricks, with their political appointments, none of whom knew a damn thing about jails, about the men who run them and the animals they oversee. None of whom knew a thing about what he had gone through to rise through the ranks. Wait until Mom heard this.

The phone on his desk beeped.

His blood pressure soared. He slammed the intercom button and snarled, "I said I didn't want to be bothered, moron. Now, how many goddamn times—"

"Townsend Tripp to see you, sir."

"Yes, of course. Thank you. Send him in."

The handsome hatchet man swept into the office and closed the door as if he owned the place. Roger Smith stood behind his own desk, anxious to shake hands, tempted to salute, afraid that if he left his position, Townsend Tripp would sit down in his chair and never leave.

"Relax," Tripp said. "My boss told your boss what's what."

"Excuse me?"

"Happy Jack wants to run the Farm, playtime's fucking over."

Smith's eyes grew wide. "Does Barthwell know you're here, with me?"

"So what if he does," said Tripp. "The senator likes the way you think. I told you that the last time."

Smith blushed. "Where is the senator?"

"He wanted to spend a minute alone with Judge Kane, so I thought I'd drop by to see you."

"What can I do for you?"

Tripp cleared his throat, bent forward, and whispered, "There's sort of this idea the senator has; we want to test it out quietly. Without Warden Barthwell's involvement. If it works, he can take the credit. If it doesn't, no one will ever be the wiser."

"Go on."

"We're looking for a prisoner to make an example out of. Someone who maybe doesn't deserve the chance to be here at all. Tom figures if we hammer one guy hard, the others will get the message. We can give the homeowners' committee their pound of flesh and move on to bigger issues. Like pay raises and promotions for appropriate personnel. Maybe one of the new arrivals, someone who hasn't earned the loyalty of the other prisoners yet. Guy by the name of Orin Boyd."

Roger Smith smiled and remembered Orin at different stages of his youth: In junior high, giving everybody arm-numbing nuggies, dumping their books, never with any of his own—not that Smith would have tried to get even. Boyd puking on an opponent to gain advantage in a wrestling match. Smoking bales of marijuana behind the high school. Drunk at the college boards. The night, when he was captain of the high school football team, he gave an incoherent speech at a pep rally in response to the student body president's peacenik prattle about the joy of sport with our brothers from Brentwood. Orin had shoved the president aside and said, "You don't get it, do you? We want to wipe the fucking field with them; we want to kidnap their girlfriends and piss on their cars. I mean, we want to wreak such havoc on these no-good motherfuckers . . ." Roger Smith remembered two shop teachers marching Orin from the podium, the gym in an uproar. Then Boyd had sailed off to Vietnam, come back with scrambled eggs and shredded legs, and all, save prior victims, thought him a hero. But not anymore.

"I've already got him shoveling shit."

"Oh, come now, Rog, let's use our imaginations here." Townsend Tripp already had the door open, a man at the mercy of the minute hand, the call of weighty events.

TUESDAY, JUNE 28, 8:50 P.M.

"MY FUCKING MOLAR IS BROKEN," SAID TOMMY Cotton. "My fucking dentist says it has to be removed to save the others, *maybe*. I'm seeing a guy in the city on Thursday."

They were in Brendan Kane's small office behind the pantry, just the two of them, and they had just passed fifteen minutes remembering better days, Kane changing from his chef whites to a gray Champion sweat suit, Tommy Cotton smoking a cigar as he got around to the subject.

"So what the fuck's going on here, Judge? What's that stink in the air? and I don't mean the chicken shit."

Kane's face registered surprise. "Tragic coincidences, I'm afraid. Why are *you* concerned?"

"Drawn us a lot of heat, I'm afraid. Not sure we don't just turn the page on this place." Tommy Cotton went on to tell Kane he was thinking of forcing the closure of Soundview, for the good of all concerned.

"There is no mad cop-killer stalking these grounds. Believe me. I would know."

"The neighbors are sick of the ambulance traffic."

Brendan Kane walked to the door and gazed out upon the supplies and implements of his second craft. "I've grown to love it here," said Kane. "The sunrises are breathtaking, like from the deck of a large ship."

"I can't look weak on crime, Judge."

"Dave Trimble gonna go along with this?"

"Once we take the position that we're tough on all kinds of crime, white collar and blue. That we're not afraid to buck the big public unions. That the Honor Farm was wrongheaded from the start. Liberal lunacy, I call it. What's he gonna say? 'No'?"

"You know his boy is buried up the hill?"

"So I guarantee him a spot nearby."

Kane looked at the senator and shook his head in wonder at the younger, tougher generation. "Don't ever lose an election, Tommy. The dogs will fight for your gonads."

"One more thing," said Cotton. "You just got a guy named Boyd, right? It would be okay if you poisoned him, accidentally." Cotton punched the judge in the arm and left him laughing, managed to find his way through the house out to the limo. "Investigate the county selling us this place, for a dollar," he told Tripp. "Start now."

"We can't outright buy it and break it up."

"I don't want to buy it or sell it, or pay the fucking taxes. I want to live here and work here. Preserve its grand traditions. I was thinking we throw some battered women in the gatehouse if we have to, qualify for grants." Cotton leaned closer. "You take care of that piece of shit?"

"Done."

11

NICK MORELLI MET HIS COUSIN FREDDY DURING
the morning work session, at the service gate near the employee parking lot, under the eye of a fence guard who
couldn't have cared less.

Nick whispered through the chain links what he wanted
done. "You cover her, Freddy, like a blanket. You sleep in
the fucking car if you have to."

"Yeah?"

"This will happen fast, I'm telling you. Watch for signs
of uncertainty, then panic. When she goes for his money,
you ride up and take it from her. It's not like she'll be calling the cops."

Freddy groaned and examined the grime residing underneath his fingernails.

"What? You got a problem with ripping someone off?"

"It ain't that."

"How much you make a week, Freddy?"

"I take home six."

"Well, now you're taking home eight."

"If it works," said Freddy. "Right?"

"Every businessman exposes himself to risk."

"I don't know."

Nick said, "Forget I called. I'll get someone else. It ain't like this is brain surgery. I know you and Aunt Carla are kinda down on your luck, so I just wanted to give you first shot—"

"Okay," said Freddy. "Okay."

"Come here," said Nick. "Shake my fingers good-bye."

"Huh?"

"Come here."

Nick passed him the necessary information through the fence, Boyd's home address and phone number, Nick's written instructions.

Freddy waved good-bye to the guard and got in his red Mustang with the black windows. Nick watched him rev his engine, turn around in the driveway, and patch out, and he hoped against all reason the dopey hard-on could pull this off.

WEDNESDAY, JUNE 29, 10:30 A.M.

MORNING SUNLIGHT FELL THROUGH THE STAINED-glass windows of the Soundview library exactly as it had since it first illuminated the devil's-in-the-details paperwork of robber baron Cyrus Kreeling (1875–1936). Prank Dinostra (1943–   ) looked up from his own bedeviling work and took a break from his labors, after eighteen months on the Farm immune to the charms of the fine old room—the carved desks and wing chairs, the intricate stonework and Indian carpets—the only chamber of the house preserved intact by covenant except for the wine cellar.

This was harder than he had thought it would be, writing a book. Some of his memories were decidedly unpleasant and getting the words right seemed next to impossible.

Everybody had always said to him, Prank, baby, you've

seen it all, you've done it all, write a novel; people love this shit. So while Prank had been at home awaiting his first trial, he sent away to some place in Ohio for a fiction correspondence course, wherein on page 2 of the introductory pamphlet, it said that the novel was the most extensive web of interrelatedness ever devised by man.

It was obvious to Prank that the writer had never pulled off a four-part scam on a Hempstead town councilwoman, you want to talk about webs of interrelatedness. So Prank transferred to the nonfiction course, where he assumed it would be safe to pile whipped cream on bullshit. His autobiography, he figured. A cautionary tale, to get him on *Donahue*. Not enough to brand him a pussy. It sometimes brought tears to his eyes, this comeback he envisioned. "Just Desserts," he called it. To show remorse.

Start with a middle-class childhood that began in Freeport and ended in Vietnam. Join the police department. Get a good sweet wife. Three nice kids. A high-ranch in Seaford, two blocks from the Great South Bay. Make the commissioner's special squad. Rise to the rank of inspector. Get handed the keys to the county. The story was writing itself.

Prank balked only when it came time to tell about the underage girl, the backfired bribe, and the overdose. Which were followed by the arrest, the trial, the conviction, the divorce, and the bankruptcy. A writer's block the size of a gravestone stood between Prank and the meat of his book, the part where the lovable hero pisses everything away, and then gets sent to jail, even though he never meant anybody any harm.

So the autobiography became a prison diary.

A short and portly man with sparse silver hair, Prank had been spending these last days of his sentence alone in the library, looking for the Prank he had met in his abandoned autobiography: the young hero, the dashing rogue. He had but days left to wrap up his reporting, find his theme, his slant, and get the manuscript printed on a laser. And yet at that moment Prank shut down the diary, changed menus, and used the modem to log himself into the Nassau County

Police Department mainframe, wherein he accessed a hidden, backdoor password he had buried in the program more than two years prior.

The screen flashed, blipped. WELCOME, FATHER.

Prank typed: YOU CAN CALL ME DAD, and the backdoor swung wide open, or as Prank liked to think of it, the bitch spread her legs.

He posed his pointed questions, found the name *Boyd, Orin,* tap-danced across a few more keys, discovered that the Nassau County Police Department personnel information one would normally expect had been erased, replaced by a short paragraph: "Boyd, Orin, Police Officer, fired subsequent to Assault 3rd Degree conviction, Rockland County Criminal Court, Judge C. Frederick, presiding. All records sealed and confidential."

Interesting, thought Prank. Sealed records. And a judge from out of district. Far more interesting was that it sometimes took the police department two months to answer a simple vacation request. Six months to process dental forms. A year to change a tire. And yet a small-time street cop convicted of a small-time assault was off the books in days, as if the department couldn't wait to be rid of this particular bad apple.

Maybe Nick Morelli was right about a big score.

Maybe Prank Dinostra didn't need to write a book at all.

WEDNESDAY, JUNE 29, 10:45 A.M.

THE SHARP REPORT OF THE .22 ECHOED THROUGH the air-conditioned slaughterhouse half a second after the retractable punch slammed through the young calf's skull and into his brain.

Before the animal was dead, it was hoisted by its hind legs, its throat slit, its blood pouring into a trough.

Barry Comstock steadied the little fellow with tongs while Allan Kelly whacked off the head with a chainsaw.

The brain and other organs were visually checked for

parasites, the carcass stamped by the state agriculture inspector, who, like the inmates, was wearing a butcher's
apron and freezer boots. An assembly line of near-comatose
cons then scrubbed, gutted, and butchered the carcass and
stacked the meat in a large freezer from whence it would be
loaded onto trucks for East Meadow and the county-owned
rest home. Today it was veal. Tomorrow it could be chickens, turkeys, whatever headquarters bought cheap.

The prisoners who worked the slaughterhouse spent their
workdays mired in gore. Some loved it; some soon begged
for other assignments. Knives were counted in and out.

"Yo!" Kelly tried to hand the bloody gun to Orin. "Here,"
he said, "you do this one."

"Why don't you show me one more time."

"What are you, stupid?"

"Pretty much."

Given his history with Sissyboy Smith, Orin knew this
awful job was just one of those things he would have to get
used to, though he could not shake the memory of a Belmont dealer shot in the head by his rivals. The bullet had
entered his head above one ear, rode around the outside of
his skull and exited above the other ear. Orin had found the
man with a garden hose pressed to the entrance wound,
clear water pouring from the exit wound. He didn't want to
press charges, he said. Just a couple of bandages.

Kelly was waving the gun at Orin again, offering him a
chance to make his bones.

"I'm a vegetarian," said Orin. "This is against my religion."

"Boyd!"

Orin turned and squinted at the doorway, expecting to be
shamed into killing the next baby cow.

Lieutenant Kruger stood there with a clipboard, sunlight
bright behind him. "Got a minute?"

Orin said, "As a matter of fact, I do."

"I thought so."

"Got a smoke?" asked Orin, draping his apron on a hook.

Kruger flipped up his pack of Marlboro Lights, handed
Orin several cigarettes, offered his lighter.

Orin shook him off, stashed the butts in his shirt. They walked outside, away from the hum of the air conditioners, toward a view of the house above them. The Honor Farm pet pig, Stimey, trotted after them, then realized they were not snacking.

"Got a murder?" asked Orin. "Maybe two? You guys talk to Pettibone's people off the Farm?"

"He didn't have any left."

"Visitors?"

Kruger frowned, but he answered. "None in the last three months."

"Damn."

Kruger frowned. "Has George Clarke said anything incriminating to you since the time of occurrence? Any gloating? Maybe a spontaneous admission of guilt."

Orin laughed. "You think George Clarke is capable of pulling off a complicated series of crimes like the one confronting you?"

"Is that what you think I've got?"

"Well, if you don't think that, could we please have our fuck-trailer back."

"Maybe George'll tell me you helped him."

"George is likely to say anything."

"This time, you can't save him."

"This time," said Orin, "I don't want to save him."

Kruger was sweating through his khaki sport coat, staining his underarms. He dropped the small talk and went over the basics of Pettibone's last known conversation, appeared to disbelieve every syllable of it. Finally he closed his clipboard and said, "I know about you. You understand? I've seen everybody's file, from their time on the job and here. And yours is the one that screams scumbag."

WEDNESDAY, JUNE 29, 2:15 P.M.

GRAMPS MCKAY WATCHED ORIN SPILL MORE potatoes than he sacked, and he spit a wad of tobacco to the earthen floor of the produce barn. "God, what a light-weight. They sure don't make 'em like they used to."

"What'd you say, old man?"

"I tell Happy Jack the same thing all the time: Police work prepares men to do absolutely fucking nothing."

Orin, his face red and drenched with sweat, raised his index finger. "And make it look interesting, dangerous, and difficult."

"When I first come on the job—"

The afternoon break whistle sounded long and sweet, and the workers scattered. Gramps harrumphed, swallowed his war story, and left the cool of the barn for the heat of the lawn outside. He sat down alone at a picnic table and opened up a new cigar, stuffed the wrapper in his pocket, stared down at the cornfield below like he was watching a movie.

Orin and Zen Masters stretched out on the warm grass behind the barn, under a birch tree, kicked back to admire the wide, blue Sound and the ever more frantic comings and goings of homicide detectives, interviewing guards, interviewing each other.

Orin pulled the morning newspaper from his back pocket and read to Zen the bare-bones newspaper account of another suicide at the Honor Farm, the second in as many weeks. He pointed in the direction of the main gate and the trailer. "Now, tell me, brother, does that look like a suicide investigation to you?"

"They must have found something they couldn't ignore," said Zen. "They'd have been out of here otherwise." Zen was forty and looked fifty, an emaciated, pockmarked man. Back in the eighties, Zen Masters had been revered for his courage and his class, an elegant executioner. Rooms grew quiet when he entered. Tough guys stepped aside. "They didn't work this hard on the boss's kid."

"Maybe they should have."

"Maybe."

"You know Skip well?" asked Orin.

"I don't know anybody well. And I really don't want to

play this game, okay. It's nothing personal, man, I just got other things I'm working on."

"You're not worried that Dick is linked to Skip?" Orin asked.

"Everything is linked to everything, and never more than now."

Orin was mulling Zen's cryptic testimony when a work detail that included George Clarke and Luther Bailey trooped by the barn, headed for a wood-slat produce truck with "Nassau County Honor Farm" printed all over it. Orin and Zen forgot the deaths for a moment and spent a pleasurable five minutes making fun of the men's efforts to load that truck, their lack of efficiency, attributing it to everything from their parentage to their native intelligence.

When the truck was full, Luther Bailey joined a guard in the cab of the truck and George squeezed into the back with the other vegetables.

"Where are they going?" asked Orin.

"Bunch a stops. The county executive's house. His cousin down the block's house. Couple of developers' offices. The list would make you sick."

"I want that job."

"No you don't. I went once and it damn near wrecked me. We were on Jericho, in traffic, sitting up high so I could see this chick's panties under her skirt, this almost hypnotic triangle of pink. She knew it, too, left it out there in the breeze for me. Worse than thumbscrews."

WEDNESDAY, JUNE 29, 4:45 P.M.

WARDEN BARTHWELL, FINISHED WITH HIS WORK-out, let the overloaded barbell slam to the dirt floor of the pit, enjoying the dull thud of iron he was no longer required to lift. It had been a long hard hazy day on the Farm, with morale noticeably low among the men.

Like a real jail, he thought. Well, good, fuck 'em. Selfish sons of bitches. He found he frequently had to suppress the urge to feel sorry for them, but not today, not when he was hearing from Tommy Kruger that Dick Pettibone might have been murdered.

He stepped behind the bench press to spot for Sally Miles.

"One," she said, raising the barbell off her chest. "Two."

Barthwell had to look away, at Morelli and the other sullen inmate lifters, lest his sexual interest in Sally's pecs became exhibit number one. He knew the Rog could be watching them through his telephoto lens from the solarium or the roof or the woods, burning with ambition and aching for Sally Miles.

Or maybe he was wrapped up in his new obsession: the inmate Orin Boyd.

That afternoon when Rog had arrived for work, he had hunted down Barthwell and presented him with a protocol for new arrivals that was intended to instill discipline and responsibility. Most of the ideas came from ToughLove camps that advertised in the magazines Roger read. He wanted to test some programs on Boyd, no matter that discipline was rarely a problem at the Farm, and Boyd had already been through a real boot camp the U.S. Marine Corps ran.

Roger Smith took negative responses badly, sometimes tearfully. This time, Roger had smiled wearily, as if he were tired of reasoning with a dinosaur. "Fine," he had said. "Forget I brought it up."

WEDNESDAY, JUNE 29, 7:50 P.M.

ORIN STOOD UP IN THE MANSION DINING ROOM, banged his plastic coffee mug on the Formica table, and called for everyone's attention. "Look, fellows," he said, "I don't know about you guys, but I'm scared."

Silence met this confession.

"And pissed. Okay?"

"What are you saying?" asked George.

"I'm saying I think someone on this farm killed Dick Pettibone. And maybe that same fucking scumbag killed Skip Trimble, too." Orin set down his mug, put his hands on his hips, spread his feet six inches, and flexed his neck, ready to lead a veritable lynch mob wherever the evidence indicated.

The majority of his audience resumed their demolition of spaghetti al Kane, the inhalation of needed fluids. This didn't concern them. The minority looked at him in amazement.

Orin had expected this reaction, knowing the police department was very much like a family, in that you were often disappointed, and he was about to ask them to pretend that they had been firemen together, to realize they faced a common enemy.

"Hey, new guy," said Nick. "Two nutjobs offed themselves. Deal with it."

"Without leaving notes? Come *on*. A long-winded son of a bitch like Pettibone?"

"Maybe they had nothing more to say," said Tobin.

"Maybe they knew something they weren't supposed to know. Maybe some of you know it, too. Ever think about that? Let's all think about that." Orin leaned over Artie Tobin's dinner tray. "You locking your door tonight, longhair?"

Tobin looked at Morelli. "I lock my door every night."

Morelli waved a hairy paw at Tobin's plate. *"Mangia,"* Nick said. "The slaughterhouse's freaked him already."

Orin shook his head with dramatic disappointment and moved down the table like a DA pleading a jury. "Come on, Ira. Work with me here. You, Hutchinson, was Skip Trimble really that depressed, that despondent? I wasn't here, so I don't know. Did he ever mention suicide, even once? I gotta tell you boys, the couple of minutes I saw Pettibone, he didn't look like a man at the end of his rope."

Tobin said, "If you knew Dick like we knew Dick, you'd realize what a waste of time this is."

"It's not a waste if someone is killing us off."

"You been here ten minutes," said Dominick Ril. "Don't tell us how to run this gig."

"Carving us out of the herd," Orin said somberly. "Picking us off like flies."

Morelli and others scoffed.

"Humor me, okay. Everybody here's got nothing but time. So who was where last night? Anybody game? Let's beat the dicks at this, and then no one can say nothing about closing this place."

"Barthwell'd never let that happen," said Nick.

Orin spotted Judge Kane leaning on the wall near the kitchen, next to a portrait of a dark-frocked, scowling Kreeling, and he realized that he had never seen the judge in county-issue jeans, that Kane wore either his snow white chef's uniform or tennis whites. As if he weren't really a prisoner, as if he weren't there. Orin suggested they hold a mock grand jury in front of the judge.

"Sounds like fun," said Kane. "Let me know when you come up with a suspect."

"Anybody else?" asked Orin. "What do you say, Zen?"

All eyes swept to the one they feared most. Zen said softly, "Consider me your intelligence division."

"Will you hard-ons stop already," said Morelli. "You're giving me fucking *agita.*"

WEDNESDAY, JUNE 29, 8:30 P.M.

ORIN KNEW THAT KILLING CALVES AND BAGGING produce would not yield up a murderer, that he needed a change of venue, access to records and inmates, and that Captain Smith was not likely to cooperate. He sat on his bed that evening, monitoring his bugs, smoking, thinking of scamming the doctor with truthful I Corps memories, blaming the blood to slink from the slaughterhouse. And then what? They would never give him the gardener's job. Orin had heard at dinner the inside track belonged to Luther Bailey, who yearned to get out from under George's jackboot. And Smith would never let Orin lounge around an office.

Housekeeping was the ticket, he decided, switching Walkman channels.

The pay phone traffic was light that evening and the admin offices quiet, as the majority of official activity remained centered in the conjugal trailer, although what they were working on, no one was saying. He should have bugged the trailer yesterday, when he had the chance, whether he wanted to hear his comrades fuck or not. Rust, he figured, and a touch of the prude.

Then George arrived to shed some light. "They think I whacked that freaking pervert," he said as he barged into Orin's room.

"They told you he was murdered?"

"Not exactly. But they think it's a big deal that he wasn't wearing his glasses. That he had 'em in his shirt pocket. And that his room had clues that mighta meant that he was going out for the night. Like on a date. They said his towel stunk of Old Spice."

"Is that possible here?" asked Orin. "A little R and R?"

George shrugged. "You hear stories now and then. No one ever asked me to go along, so I don't know for sure."

"They probably want to keep it a secret."

"Hey!" said George, offended.

"So Kruger broke your balls?"

"Said if Dick was killed, I was a prime suspect because I was a homophobe, which, let me tell you, damn near led to blows."

Orin blinked and shook his head. "Pettibone was gay?"

"Not that I freaking knew about, or he'd have never got a gander at the Big Guy."

Orin rubbed his face with both hands. "What the fuck is Kruger thinking about?"

George shrugged and said he was tired of thinking, that he was hitting the sack, where he couldn't get into any more trouble. If Orin was smart, he would keep his mouth shut and mind his own business.

Orin disagreed. He walked outside and sat on a lounge

chair by the pool, admiring the dusk, thinking. Nobody swam today, even though the yellow tape came down at four P.M. Nobody played boccie, either. So why were the boccie balls out of the bag on his way back to the dorm that first night, then back in the bag the next day?

Did Kruger clean up, he wondered. Did Smith restore order?

It had been dark when Smith lined up the men to view Pettibone's body, and Orin hadn't noticed. He lit a cigarette and fumed, frustrated by his lack of information, that he was not privy to Kruger's clues.

A mosquito drew blood from his neck and died for its dinner. Orin fieldstripped his smoke and pushed himself off the lounge chair, started down the cobblestone path to the dorm, and stopped short when he saw someone in a golf cart coasting from the rear of the mansion, without headlights on.

The golf cart did not turn left for the command post, instead veered off the paved road into the dark woods, headed for the shore.

Orin grabbed a mountain bike from a rack behind the locker room and followed the cart down the quarter mile dirt path through a forest of black and white oaks, evergreens and maples, gradually lagging behind as the golf cart neared the fences by the service gate.

Orin hid his bike behind the trunk of an oak, worked his way closer on his belly, and was rewarded with a view of Roger Smith unlocking the service gates and hauling two five-gallon gas containers from the rear of the golf cart, through the gates, to his sleek black Iroc. Smith ducked low and funneled the fuel into the tank. When he was finished, he buffed the cover with a rag.

12

THURSDAY, JUNE 30, 7:00 A.M.

LOUIS "PRANK" DINOSTRA SAT AT HIS TERMINAL in the library before breakfast, skipping electronically through the past practices and current excesses of Orin Boyd's financial history. In short order he pulled up the loan records on Orin's car, boat, motorcycle, and house, the new dryer they had bought with a P.C. Richard's card. He found where Judy shopped for groceries. Which school their daughter attended. The veteran's exemption on his real estate taxes. That his mother was long dead, his father missing even longer, that he had managed to drive himself into the assigned-risk pool. That Judy Boyd had undergone a radical hysterectomy two years back.

Prank then carefully analyzed the data, which had always been his particular skill at Intelligence. Prank knew all the scams and their visible symptoms, could spot a trap or peg a fraud in seconds, and for a brief moment of rampant insecurity he hoped the watchers weren't on to him. He remembered that someone had messed with his computer several nights prior, that he could never be sure he wasn't also the target of an invasion.

After an hour of applied analysis, Prank decided that there were two likely possibilities: that except for his wife's substantial salary, this poor schmuck Boyd would be as impoverished as the day was long; or the more obvious conclusion, that Orin Boyd had his loot off the board, literally buried underground.

Prank sat back and wondered if he would be able to do that, sit on a mountain of cash as if it did not exist, continue to drive a crappy old American car and live in a crappy Cape Cod, dress his woman at Sears, and feed his kid at The Ground Round.

Then Prank got down to the dirty work of bits and bytes, swallowing Orin and Judy Boyd's visible money, exhausting their existing credit, ruining any possibility that more would be extended.

THURSDAY, JUNE 30, 11:30 A.M.

ORIN HELD THE DORMITORY PAY PHONE TO HIS ear and stared at Nick Morelli's locked door. It was warm and sticky out that morning, the air oppressive, thick as smoke, holding the persistent odor of barn fast around the mansion. Orin's forearms were spattered with dried chicken blood. "Say that again, slowly," he said.

Judy Boyd said softly, "Your boat sank, sometime last night. Down at the marina. They called me at home this morning. It's a rope going into the water. I called the insurance company, and they said a guy would go by and look at it tomorrow. A couple of weeks from now we'll get a check, less our deductible."

"Which is a grand."

"Sorry. I'm coming tomorrow, remember?"

"It's all I've been able to think about."

"Well, now you have the boat to think about."

"How'd it happen?" said Orin.

"I don't know."

"Do you think you could find out?"

"You want me to dive on the wreck?" she asked.

Orin held his tongue. He had loved that boat—what it stood for, where it had come from—and had been more than content that it was the sole visible benefit of his Belmont success. Standing behind the wheel, legs spread, throttle wide, he could fly. "Ask the marina guy to check it out for me. See if we can't save it. And have him recover my tackle box."

"Anything else?"

"I miss you."

"I miss you, too."

He hung up thinking of the joke about the fisherman who places a personal ad seeking a fun-loving woman with a boat. Send photo of boat.

THURSDAY, JUNE 30, 12:50 P.M.

JUDY BOYD SPENT THE LAST TEN MINUTES OF her lunch break shopping at Genovese. She set her purchases on the counter, started bagging as the young black salesgirl passed over the bar-code eye the shampoo and conditioner, the notepads and loose-leaf binders Dawn would need for sixth grade. Judy handed over her Master-Card, then thumbed through an *Enquirer* while the girl slid the card through a small tan box, crossed her arms, and waited. The little box beeped. The girl handed back the card.

"You're maxed on that," she said. "Got another card?"

"Really?" Judy fumbled inside her purse, handed over her Visa. The box beeped again.

"Sorry," said the girl.

"Something's wrong," Judy told the salesgirl. "Those cards aren't maxed."

"It's not me saying they are."

"You take American Express?" asked Judy.

"Sorry."

Judy felt her throat closing and tears filling her eyes. She abandoned her goods on the counter, walked quickly out to her Taurus, and power-locked the doors, spun her head around to see if she was being followed—for the first time, ever, frightened in broad daylight.

THURSDAY, JUNE 30, 3:50 P.M.

SUNBURNED AND EXHAUSTED FROM HIS AFTERnoon of field work, Orin had showered and dressed in clean denims and was reclining on his bed with his Walkman and a cigarette, watching the local news while alternately listening to dishes being washed in the kitchen, Ira Cohen placing bets with a bookie, and Marion Whithers processing Roger Smith's endless words.

He sat up fast when he saw Senator Cotton on the TV, stepping behind a bank of microphones, accompanied by a striking young black woman. Orin got his Walkman turned off and the TV sound turned up in time to hear Cotton suggest any further questions be directed to his deputy executive assistant, Ms. Sherri Sawchuck.

That's *her,* thought Orin, from outside Leonard's that night, and she wasn't a whore holding back stash. She was legit, a fucking staffer, and they could have been searching her purse for car keys, a beeper, anything. And he wouldn't be here if he had sized up the scene correctly.

"No," Orin said aloud. "That's bullshit." They were kicking her ass when he saw them last. An unjustified assault on a senator would have landed him in Leavenworth.

"The people want full value for their tax dollars," she was saying, "a direct correlation between effort and results. The people are not getting that now, we fear. It costs fortytwo thousand dollars a year to house a prisoner at the Honor Farm, twenty-seven a year in East Meadow. The recidivist rates are—"

Then Roger Smith's voice spilled from the hallway intercom, ordering all prisoners to the dining room for a job counseling seminar, as if the outside world were waiting to embrace these men with love instead of scorn.

Orin shut his appliances off and walked to the mansion with Zen Masters and Bobby Damato. He wanted a seat near a window, where he just might catch a nap away from the palm-slap games and poisonous gas of his brethren. Unfortunately the kitchen staff had already claimed the best seats, so Orin found a table in the middle of the room and put his head down on his arms like a kindergarten kid, took one breath, and gagged. It had been a long time since Orin had suffered a hangover, but he remembered the symptoms, the headache, one's tongue like a Chia Pet. Nick Morelli, slumped at the table ahead of him, was dousing his half-smoked Marlboro in the coffee Ray Fusco had just placed in front of him. Artie Tobin, truly a gentleman of substances, sat next to him, smelling like a fraternity house.

Orin stood up to move away. At that very same moment Captain Smith—who had been shuffling three-by-five file cards but was now about to call for attention—glared at him and shouted, "Where do you think you're going?"

"Nowhere, sir."

"That's exactly why we're having this meeting, because right now, my parrot has a better chance to succeed than you." Captain Smith paused, allowed the ass-kissers a chance to laugh, which they did. "Now, before we get to the meat of the program, I want you men to know that there are goings-on here at the Farm these days we don't much like, besides the suicides. We've got miscounts in the pharmacy, the laundry, movement on the grounds after curfew." He paused again and looked around, made eye-contact with the usual suspects, finishing with Orin.

Orin gave Smith his brain-dead look, stopped just short of drooling, and it occurred to Orin that the only thing he'd really like to do when he got out of jail was go to sea, as his father had done, only his father never came back.

"Music on the grounds after curfew," Smith continued, looking at Luther Bailey. "Possession of pornography."

Someone in the back whispered "extracurricular butt-fucking," and half the crowd laughed.

"Now, we don't want to treat you like babies, but we will if we have to. Some of you prisoners used to unlimited nocturnal wandering are gonna have to break yourselves of the habit, at least for a while. This is a prison farm, not Outward Bound. We've lost two men here recently, let's not forget. Our procedures are being questioned, up and down the line."

"By who?" asked Dom Ril.

"By people who want to sell this place for the fortune it's worth."

Ril said, "Name names."

"I don't see how that's any of your business."

"Then you can forget my possibly constructive suggestion."

Roger Smith could barely conceal his disdain for any suggestion Dominick Ril might have. Ril was just one more crooked cop in a room chock-full of them, men who had disgraced their sworn positions, their families, their brother officers. And then been dumb enough to be caught and convicted, actually sentenced to serve time. Add together the profit from their crimes and you couldn't buy a decent car. Dip-shits, is what Smith was thinking, and everybody in the dining room knew it. Then Nick Morelli began to snore, or rhythmically fart, so Smith switched topics. "Since none of you men will ever do police work again, and since you've also lost your pensions and signed your homes over to defense attorneys, we come to a time where we have to ask the question: How will you live for the rest of your lives?"

George Clarke raised his hand. "I figure I'll hunt down some unsuspecting broad and mooch off her."

"Nice, Clarke. Real nice."

Orin raised his hand. "Question, sir. None of these guys are good at anything legal. Will that present a problem?"

"Suppose you tell us your plans for when you get out, hotshot. How you gonna feed the family?"

Orin considered that no matter his true circumstances, no matter his deal with Trimble, he would never be accepted in the Marine Bureau, that after anything remotely resembling Internal Affairs work, he was as unemployable as the rest of the boys. "Either farming or butchery, I really haven't decided which one I like better yet."

Smith could not mask his anger. "You *like* your jobs here?"

"Love them, sir. Never been happier. It's very manly work. You see the fruits of your labor, instead of jerking off all day, shuffling papers around an office."

"You don't think office work is manly work?"

"It ain't fucking stunt flying, Rog. But it's not as bad as housekeeping."

Roger Smith was by now beet red—this impudent prick from his past, this loser serving time in his jail, still had the gall to publicly humiliate him. "You got it, Boyd," he said, puffing out his chest. "Let's talk housekeeping. Both sessions. Tomorrow you report to Ira for your duties. Prank—you got Boyd's jobs."

"Say what?" yelled Prank, leaping to his feet. "After all this time? 'Cause he's got a big fucking mouth?"

"You're out of here in a couple of days anyway."

"I'm going to Happy Jack."

"You want to stay here six more months?"

Prank stared at Roger Smith for a full twenty seconds, took the time to light a cigarette, quelling some inner monster with mayhem on its mind.

Smith said, "Don't think you can intimidate me, Prank." Prank moved not a muscle. "Wouldn't dream of it."

"Boyd!" yelled Smith.

"Yes, sir?"

"Tomorrow morning—you wear a fucking apron."

THURSDAY, JUNE 30, 5:25 P.M.

DETECTIVE LIEUTENANT KRUGER AND HIS MEN unanimously decided that they had gathered all the available physical evidence and testimony at the scene. Very little of it pointed to murder. They broke down their command post, returned the conjugal trailer to its original condition, ready to turn their attention to other deaths around the county. They sent word up to Captain Smith that Pettibone's room could be cleaned and reused; then, Lieutenant Kruger announced to a gaggle of reporters outside the front gate that they, like everyone else, were awaiting the results of laboratory tests before drawing any conclusions. Until further notice, the untimely death of inmate Richard Pettibone would remain unclassified, which should not be taken to mean suspicious.

"What kind of answer is that?" asked one reporter.

"A safe answer," said Kruger.

"Can you comment on the rumors—"

Out on the water, a foghorn honked.

"I said, can you comment—"

Kruger raised his hands above the crowd like the pope. "Any discussion," he loudly announced, "of a ghost or a curse on Soundview is malicious, irresponsible, and probably an obstruction to the administration of justice."

Then the horde from Homicide dove into their Dodges and departed.

THURSDAY, JUNE 30, 9:30 P.M.

HARMLESS ROBERT WAS TORN BETWEEN THEM, now that he had his own wheels.

Sitting in the dark car, thinking, Helen or Judy? Helen or Judy?

Tough call.

Waiting these last few muggy days and nights on the Sands Point beach road for Boyd's wife to show at the jail had grown tiresome. And of course Robert knew Helen's regular shifts at the diner, so as early as tonight he could know where she lived and be outside in the dark in his car and watch the soft light shine down from her bedroom window. And hope things would progress from there, nature taking her course.

He could practice on Helen, the lost art of dealing with women, a process he had always found so daunting.

Orin Boyd wasn't going anywhere, Robert thought, focusing his binoculars on the fences. The state was holding him right where he could always be found for at least the next three months.

So Robert could come back for Boyd's wife anytime, tomorrow if he wanted to, perhaps with something more to show her than his unendurable sorrow.

Robert finally made up his mind, and his heart beat faster, with love.

Tonight he'd start on Helen Kitsipoulis.

13

DAYBREAK FOUND ZEN MASTERS ON HIS KNEES
by his bed, warding off his dreams, contemplating the ever-
lasting soul of Omar "The Animal" Paison, a rapist, the first
of the seven men he had killed for the citizens of Nassau
County.

Tomorrow it would be child-murderer Robert Jones, Jr.

Then that hostage-taking sex-maniac Derrick Mc-
Ketcham.

Mondays and Tuesdays were set aside for the Worthy
twins, born within minutes of each other and killed within
seconds.

Zen mourned them all, seven bodies for seven days, the
gross sum of his labors. All killed in the line of duty when
he was the outstanding marksman in Emergency Services—
scope jobs, mostly, through windows of opportunity. Head
shots from long range. A source of immediate gratification
and never-ending nightmares.

Zen Masters was in prison, however, because of an
eighth victim, an innocent young housewife and mother

named Dorothy Cuccia he had waxed one morning while piss-drunk, lost in a blackout.

She didn't get her own day of mourning, as he felt this would diminish her memory. He simply thought about her all the time he wasn't thinking of the others, the way she had looked in the crime-scene photographs, impaled on the steering column of her black Honda Civic, her right hand wedged inside her AM/FM cassette player, clutching, he had learned at the trial, a bootleg copy of *Billy Joel's Greatest Hits*.

FRIDAY, JULY 1, 7:30 A.M.

THE EXPANDED—AND MANY THOUGHT EXCESsively punitive—inmate work schedule was announced at breakfast, nearly a doubling of the time spent on chores. Recreation time was cut in half, as were off-grounds educational opportunities. Meals were cut by fifteen minutes. Bed check was moved from eleven P.M. to ten, barely an hour after dark. The summer bake sale, run for the inmates and their families by the ladies from the local Unitarian church, was canceled altogether. Any more untoward excitement, and they could kiss their televisions good-bye. "Everybody got it?" said Jack Barthwell angrily. "Now that we got real prison problems, we're gonna run this place like a real fucking prison."

Gramps McKay was the first inmate to raise his hand. "Warden," he said, "we're already getting the work done right in the time we spend now. Are you telling us to work slower? Corn won't grow no faster, you know. Potatoes got their own particular schedule, too."

Warden Barthwell did not appear to mind the chuckles from the men. "This won't last," he said. "We'll circle this jerk till we get off the front page, then settle back to normal."

Gramps scratched behind his ear. "I do pretty damn good at those bake sales."

"You're the only one," said Barthwell, "except for George."

The guys sitting around George Clarke mussed his hair and poked his ribs while George extolled the virtues of elderly babes.

"What'd the senator want to zing us for?" asked Art Tobin. "Why don't he just trot off to Albany and rob us, like always?"

"Now, now. The senator merely wished to reassure himself that we were meeting our mission."

"Goddamn Sick Dick," said Morelli. "Still jamming us up."

"Hush your mouth, Nick," said Barthwell, "and watch how you speak of the dead, or you'll spend *your* extra time in the hot fucking fields. Maybe if you all hadn't shunned the poor son of a bitch, these measures wouldn't be necessary. Now get to work. And don't anybody talk to me today. I'm pissed at you people."

FRIDAY, JULY 1, 8:10 A.M.

IRA "GENGHIS" COHEN, HEAD OF HOUSEKEEPING, a former street cop in New Cassel, was serving eighteen months on a federal civil rights rap. His conviction was notable in that he was the first Nassau County cop ever convicted of a bias crime. To wit, it had been Ira's lousy luck to be videotaped screaming, "Don't move, spook, or I'll blow your woolly head off," at a black man doing nothing more than following his doctor's advice to jog home from the liquor store he owned.

Ira Cohen was a bleeding-heart liberal lassoed by the left. At least that's what he told Orin, and all in the first five minutes of their acquaintance. Orin stood shivering in the dank basement, nodding dumbly throughout Ira's autobiography. He mumbled something about his own bad luck with soul brothers.

"People of color," Ira corrected him. "After watching

four hundred court-ordered hours of rehabilitative tapes, I'm highly sensitive to racism."

"What's with the hat?"

Ira was wearing a Mets cap backward, with the brim turned up, so he looked like a fugitive from the Bowery Boys.

"Rally cap," said Ira. "Keep the Mets on a roll."

"Right."

Orin was issued his master keys, a push broom, his mop and bucket, a roll of towels, and a can of Pledge and sent forth to roam the mansion, virtually at will, sweeping, dusting, primping, and fussing. Orin used the opportunity to surreptitiously plant the remainder of his bugs where he needed them.

After that he concentrated on the captain's office, where he dissolved four packets of Domino sugar in the captain's Fantastik bottle, screwed on the pump top, set it back on the shelf. He was mulling other booby traps involving Roger's menagerie of house plants on the balcony when he heard footsteps in the hall, a knock at the door.

"Orin?"

It was George, with coffee and doughnuts. "Take five?"

"Where's Luther?"

"I got him washing trucks. Something they call delegating."

"Come in and lock the door," said Orin. "You can help me. I'm doing a little delegating myself."

FRIDAY, JULY 1, 9:15 A.M.

ORIN WAS TIGHTENING DOWN A SWITCHPLATE BEhind Marion's desk when Warden Barthwell arrived on the floor with his jug of holistic juice and his brown bag of fruits under his massive arm, a vital bounce to his step, a broad smile on his face.

"Morning, there, Boyd."

Orin said good morning and followed Barthwell into the

oval office, dusting as he went, opened a window, shook his rag out, admired the dark blue of the early morning Sound. "Is there any more news on Richie Pettibone? It seems already forgotten."

Barthwell studied Orin's face. "You're feeling guilty?"

"You could say that."

Barthwell tossed his sack of chow into a little fridge and plopped behind his desk. "Dick Pettibone was a very weird guy, Orin. His family says that. His doctor says that."

"Really? I thought he was just like all the other mutts."

"Maybe we're both right, eh?"

Orin gave Barthwell's file cabinet a quick shot with the dust rag. "Yes, sir. Thank you, sir."

Orin backed out of the office and pulled his housekeeping cart to the end of the hall. He ducked in a closet and turned on his Walkman, dialed Barthwell. At first he heard nothing, then, with the volume up, he heard the faint sound of push-ups easily accomplished, Barthwell whispering, "one hundred one, one hundred two . . . ."

Friday, July 1, 1:30 P.M.

WARM RAIN FELL ON THE HONOR FARM AS ORIN trudged upstairs to Dr. Robbins's office for a scheduled session, which would spare him an afternoon of window washing. His first conjugal visit with Judy would follow, a county-sponsored romp in the freshly vacated trailer. He knew he should be grateful to his keepers, he knew he should be horny as a toad, and yet he was neither. He had business to conduct with Judy, transactions that would leave him drained.

"Are you feeling any better today?" asked Dr. Robbins as Orin hit the couch.

"I'm in freaking jail, Doc. People in the very same situation are dying. And my tee time has just been moved back two hours."

"Very good," said Doctor Robbins. "Using humor to defuse stress. You are learning."

"Hell, I'm cured."

"You are a violent man, yes?"

"I've had my moments."

"Like this witness you beat . . ."

So Dr. Robbins had actually read his file and was paying close attention. Orin's problems were perhaps more than mere busywork to the aging civil servant, a refreshing possibility, however unlikely.

"I kicked the living shit out of him."

"Because he hurt you?"

Orin posed. "Emotionally?"

"Stop fencing."

"I'm scared, Doc. I'm wondering if I'm anything like Skip or Dick."

"You're not alone, if that's any consolation."

Orin had eavesdropped on that particular couch theme twice already and switched away embarrassed, because he doubted the killer would whine to the shrink about suicide, and because he had learned that one man's pain is another man's mind-numbing drivel.

Dr. Robbins smiled warmly. "We're all of us like Skip and Dick. It doesn't mean we end up killing ourselves."

"But if someone is already predisposed to violence . . ."

"What do you wish to tell me? I sense a well of pain."

Orin closed his eyes and truthfully confessed to the psychiatrist that he had loved to tie nooses as a boy, that he had frequently hanged his rubber Civil War soldiers from elaborate gallows made from Lincoln Logs, that he sometimes flashed on a similar scene from a straw-paper ville near the DMZ.

"Yes," said the doctor quietly. "I see your point."

"Shaky ground, Doc," said Orin. "I already know the knot."

"But the question looms all the larger: Who are you angry at?"

"I don't know. My wife. My father . . . You."

Dr. Robbins said, "Think about it . . . what you've told

me . . . what you're getting ready to tell me, if not today then soon."

Orin stared at his thick hands.

Dr. Robbins stretched his arms above his head slowly, creaking. "You have a conjugal today, yes?"

"Say, that's right."

"Are you anxious, maybe worried about performing?"

"Is that common?"

"What would you suppose?"

"That all depends. On the man. On the woman. How things were before the guy went to jail."

"And what they've been up to in the interim." Doc Robbins stood up and walked gingerly to his window, gazed down upon the serfs who worked the land. "Some men obsess that their women are unfaithful. Some women come here wearing their guilt like shrouds."

"I was hoping for something from Frederick's," said Orin, but the image of Judy kissing her old boss flashed fire through his brain, and he felt his gun at his ear, his failure to pull the trigger, felt again the loss of whatever died that night.

"Some men shut down their desire for sex while in prison," said Robbins, "then find it hard to turn it back on."

"And some guys jerk themselves silly. So what?"

"Have we thought any more about hypnosis?" asked Doc.

"No, we have not."

14

FRIDAY, JULY 1, 5:00 P.M.

JUDY BOYD ARRIVED AT THE HONOR FARM IN THE
black pinstripe suit she preferred for sales meetings, worn
over high-hipped lace panties and a teddy. She parked in
the visitors' lot outside the razor-wire fence, checked her
makeup, got out of her gray Taurus with a PAL gym bag in
her hand, and walked the flowered path to the guard's booth
at the main gate, feeling like a slut checking in for a day-
rate gel-bed romp.

A female guard slid open a small window. "Mrs. Boyd?
I'm Officer Sally Miles."

"I remember," said Judy, "when you picked up Orin."

"Yes. That's right. You okay?" asked Sally.

"I feel like a whore."

"All the wives do, first time at least."

"But they come back?"

"Some of them. I need to know what's in the bag."

Judy unzipped the bag, held it open. "My toiletries. Fresh
underwear."

"No firearms, narcotics, or alcohol?"

"Oh, I do hope we're done with those now."

Sally Miles smiled, opened the gate, pointed to a turquoise double-wide, which could barely be seen through the evergreens. "Follow the path. You'll be fine."

"No strip search?" Judy laughed nervously.

"You're fine," said Sally. "You look beautiful."

Orin was waiting for her on the steps of the trailer, in the shade of a weeping willow, smoking a cigarette, reading the newspaper. He was clean-shaven, his mustache trim, his blond hair mussed in the back as if he had been napping. He stood right up and held her in his arms as if they were slow-dancing, kissing the top of her head.

"I love you," she said. "I keep forgetting how much."

"I love you, too." His lips brushed her earlobe. "The trailer's bugged."

"No," she said as she allowed him to waltz her out of range.

"In the overhead light fixture," he said. "Same kind we use. I don't know if it's permanent, or special just for us."

"Isn't that illegal?"

"Probably only if activated, and maybe not even then."

"I don't believe this." Judy pulled back from him, her eyes filling up. "This feels too much like when we were separated. Do you know what I'm saying? Are we strong enough for this?"

"I'm on a business trip, to a shitty place. It's not like this ain't a pattern in our lives."

Judy leaned her head in the direction of the trailer and asked, "How do we handle this, short of giving them a peep show?"

"We can go in there and fight. Or you can slap me across the face right here."

"I don't want to fight. We fought for years."

Orin held her close again and rubbed her back.

Judy pushed him to arm's length. "I have to tell you, though: While you've been in here, someone ran up humongous bills on our Visa and MasterCard accounts. I called the customer service number and they connected me to their fraud division. They're checking the paper trail, store receipts, whatever. They were very polite and assured me not to worry.

Orin nodded. "Happens all the time."

"Yeah?" said Judy. "Does it? To women whose husbands are in jail undercover? Are all their lives," she said with more emotion than she meant to express, "so violently disrupted. Do they sleep alone and endure snobby neighbors who were once friends? Tell me."

Orin shrugged.

"I think what makes me the maddest is that you look like you're having a good time. I don't think you miss me a bit."

"You're wrong," he said.

"Oh, really? What do you miss about me? Sex once a week? My breath in the morning?"

"Keep it up," said Orin. "Maybe they're getting some of this."

"If you're not at work, you're out on the boat with Dawn, or riding your Harley with those scroungy mutts you call friends."

"What's the matter with that?"

"It doesn't include me."

"Why are you doing this now?" he asked her.

Her back was stiff, her lips drawn. "I don't know."

He stared at her. "Let's walk."

They followed the path thirty yards deeper into the woods, stopped at a small clearing, and sat facing each other on a downed tree trunk, waited to make sure they weren't followed.

"You think I'm in danger, don't you?" she said.

He looked over the top of her head for enemies in the brush.

"Orin?"

"Not if you move to your sister's."

"Again," she said with resignation. Judy and Dawn had gone there the last time, when he was living outside the lines, taking on the powers that shouldn't have been.

"And you should get that haircut and dye-job you've been talking about. And maybe switch cars with one of the reps. I mean, the boat goes down. The charge accounts. There are no accidents."

"In other words the killer's on to you."

"Maybe."

Judy hugged herself and said, "I'm starting to hate this, Orin. The only place I feel safe now is at work."

"You got cash?" he asked.

"I'll hit an ATM tomorrow. And I got your paycheck in the mail, yesterday. Are you aware they're not paying you overtime?"

"No."

"Did you ask?"

"I guess I just assumed."

Judy grimaced.

"How's Dawn like camp?" he asked.

Judy sighed. "She doesn't want to come home, either."

"Now, now."

Judy forced a laugh and kissed him lightly, slung the gym bag over her shoulder, and started back down the path toward the main gate, walking the way she walked when she was not going to be ten minutes early for an appointment. Orin followed her as far as the trailer, then sat on the stoop and lit a cigarette, stared at her pretty ass until she disappeared behind the trees.

He figured if they were watching him, he ought to hang a while; probably no true con ever rushed back from a trailer. You kick back and chew a blade of grass, take all the time you can away from labor, the gaze of the guards.

Other than Sally Miles, and maybe the black guy Oliver Bridges, Orin didn't care much for these guards, and it wasn't professional jealousy. Orin didn't care much for cops, either. But here at the Farm, even with tit jobs and a sweetie like Barthwell running the joint, they acted as if you worked for them, as if they owned you. Each a little Kreeling.

Orin suspected that Roger Smith strongly felt that way, especially at night, when Warden Barthwell went home. Stalking the moors of Kreeling Mansion, lounging on its wide verandas while sampling the treasures of its justly famous wine cellar, deciding the fates of its hirelings and inmates, all that must surely give him great satisfaction. Orin wished he could make himself see Sissyboy as a serial killer, one of those bespectacled nerds who now and then rises from a midwestern cellar to announce a slew of victims. But Orin could only make himself see a prepubescent Roger Smith eating ice cream mixed with spinach and Chinese rice for a dollar, a dollar that Orin then extorted from Sissyboy Smith to ensure a safe walk home.

But the boat, the credit cards. Sissyboy Smith had nothing to do with that.

Which meant either there was a killer on the Farm who wanted him on the defensive, or it was something else entirely, from those years he could barely remember.

Sally Miles, in a golf cart, hit the brakes in front of the trailer, powdered his legs with dust. "Sorry about the wife," she said. "That sort of thing happens all the time."

"It does?"

"Talk to Doc Homo."

Orin raised an eyebrow.

"I saw Judy on her way out. I gave her an opportunity to vent."

"Judy vented?"

Sally winked. "Don't worry, tough guy. Your secret's safe with me."

FRIDAY, JULY 1, 8:45 P.M.

ORIN AND SOME OF THE BOYS WERE STROLLING from the mansion after dinner when rockets exploded in the dark gray sky over the yacht club.

Purple. Red, white, and blue. Yellow flowers bursting into green flowers, bursting into white flowers, topped off with thumps that rattled bones.

Across the fifteen miles of Sound, it appeared that Connecticut was the site of the doomsday launch.

Then Boom. Boom. From the west. Rockets from the east.

Transfixed like children, the inmates spread out on the semicircular lawn in front of the mansion, caught off guard by the opening salvos of Independence Day weekend celebrations, suddenly with fifty miles of incandescent coastline to enjoy.

George ran from the dorm with binoculars, and then everybody took turns watching a raucous party at the yacht club down below, men in tuxedos fox-trotting with women in bikinis.

Orin found Townsend Tripp, with that young black woman—albeit in a dress—standing next to him, disinterested.

He felt an elbow in his ribs. "Please?" asked Zen.

"Where'd we go wrong?" asked Orin, handing over the glasses. "How come we're up here and they're down there, with foxes, in bathing suits?"

"Who said we went wrong?" said George. "Gandhi did a little time. Mandela. Lech Whatever."

It suddenly dawned on Orin that perhaps he was the only one willing to admit that he had gone wrong. Take for instance Nick Morelli, relaxing in the only lawn chair, which had materialized for him from somewhere. Orin tried to remember a more selfish leader anywhere, recalled an incident at a state convention where Nick had received official guests in his suite while enjoying a rubdown from a well-endowed but unlicensed masseuse. Not everyone was amused. Some questioned Nick's judgment for so baldly asking the upstate chiefs, "What kind of masseuse don't polish the rocket?"

"Lovely, is it not?" said Brendan Kane, leaning back on his elbows, next to Orin and Zen.

"I wanted to ask you a question, Judge. You made a steak to go that night. For Pettibone."

"He frequently ate in his room when he was down, Orin. Why not on the lowest night of all?"

"Who brought him the steak?"

"I did."

Then the sky again filled with explosions, and the soft ground rocked beneath their butts. Then someone mentioned the fireworks finale waking the dead, and someone else brought up the ghost, and someone else said, "Don't get Zen started."

Orin closed his eyes and ached at the symbols of freedom, the semblance of normalcy, saw the stark faces of his own ghosts, and yearned for his own hut in his own village. Until a golf cart with its high beams on approached the men, blinding them.

"Hey!"

The headlights flicked off. Captain Smith, elbows resting on the steering wheel, gazed out at the heavens, the wonder-of-it-all. "Damn, but if it don't look like war," Smith said gravely.

Orin and Zen caught each other's eyes, shared the devil's laugh in their hearts.

"Uh, what war was that, Rog?" asked Orin.

"No particular war," said Smith. "I only meant—"

"I'll bet the Rog was with Ronnie Reagan," said Zen, "shoulder-to-shoulder as they liberated Auschwitz."

"With freaking Napoleon," cried George, "at Dunkirk."

Friday, July 1, 10:00 P.M.

ROGER SMITH SMOLDERED ON HIS BALCONY, feeling monstrously inadequate and enormously annoyed. Using a tripod and nightscope, he angrily snapped roll after roll of happy politicians and their bimbos at the yacht club, a joyous mingling of patriotism and patronage. *Click.* A surrogate court judge with the commissioner of public works, who Roger knew generally served as host.

Click. Nice tits on his date. Great teeth when she laughed.

Click. Senator Cotton and a girl in a lovely white thong separated themselves from the crowd and stepped behind the squat stone building. Out of sight, they thought. Invisible, instead of merely transparent.

Click. She opened her clutch while Cotton looked around.

Click. Loaded up a silver shooter, from a plastic bag filled with white. *Click.* Snorted something.

Click. She passed it to the senator. *Click Click Click.* Let Tommy Cotton load up a finger, which he worked onto his teeth and gums. They checked each other for ring-around-the-nostril and slid back to the limelight, smiles frozen on their faces.

Roger Smith, sweating from his armpits and palms, was tempted to tear the film from his camera, frightened of the story he had captured with his lens.

Explosive, he thought. The stuff *Hard Copy* paid big money for.

Maybe even *Geraldo.*

FRIDAY, JULY 1, 11:15 P.M.

HARMLESS ROBERT SAT SUCKING ON HIS MARL-boro in the dented gray Excel, some forty yards down the dead-end street from the Boyd house, thinking, what a week.

First Helen, an unparalleled success.

Now Judy Boyd, hopefully with similar results.

But something was wrong here, he thought. Lights going on and off in different rooms, doors opening and closing. He thought about calling Judy, to hear her voice, and his heart beat faster, dangerously fast. His fingers tightened round the steering wheel, flexed open, so close it was torture, scant yards away.

He started the noisy car, circled the block, and stopped behind the rear of the Boyd house, got an angle on the master bath, its steamy windows.

She was in there now, he thought, scrubbing like hell, wet feet on slick white tile, blinded by shampoo.

The blue light of the television danced on the bedroom window.

He should call her.

Probably scare the hell out of her, as he had out of Helen, when he knocked on her door last night.

Just the thought of it scared him, so he circled the block and was parking again when he saw the red Mustang with black windows pass for the second time. Not driving past the front of the house, not fool enough to make obvious three-point turns at the end of the dead-end street, but coming to a road-test stop at the sign on the corner, looking both ways, then proceeding slowly, like doesn't happen in America anymore, not with Mustangs.

Twenty minutes later the garage door opened and a wet-haired Judy Boyd hauled four large suitcases from the house, loaded them in her car, locked up the house, and drove away.

Where was the child? he wondered. Dawn Marie Boyd. Aged ten.

He flicked his lighter and studied her picture, felt the pressure building in his chest.

15

SATURDAY, JULY 2, 9:15 A.M.

AFTER TEN MINUTES INSIDE HER NEIGHBOR-
hood bank, ten minutes at an exposed desk on a blue-
carpeted platform, watching the young woman pound her
keyboard looking for so much as a penny to the Boyd
family's credit, Judy had every reason in the world to feel
that without her husband around, she was vanishing. She
was sweating through her satin shirt, staring at familiar
tellers behind bulletproof glass, jolly red mobiles adver-
tising mutual funds and municipal bonds and all sorts of
smart things to do with excess money, of which she apparently had none. "Not even my daughter's Christmas
club?"

"Sorry," the clerk said. "Not at this branch."

"You're kidding."

"Bankers don't kid."

Judy knew that. This was not her bank anymore. This
was not her life.

"Would you like to speak to the manager?"

"Please."

The manager was a burly middle-age man with dark eyebrows and a pleasant smile. He assured her he knew her to be a valued, longtime customer of this bank. Judy mentioned the problem with the credit cards. He said he had seen this sort of thing before. If she would give him a moment, he would do a little research.

"Do whatever you have to do to find my money."

He returned in two minutes with coffee and bagels. Judy sat on the edge of her chair, took her coffee black rather than mix packets of sugar and Cremora with shaking hands.

"Mrs. Boyd, are you by any chance experiencing marital difficulties? See, sometimes just before a separation or divorce one party or the other runs up the credit cards or raids the joint accounts. Their lawyers suggest it, to make sure there is cash on hand to pay retainers."

"That's not what happened here," said Judy.

"Let's hope."

SATURDAY, JULY 2, 11:50 A.M.

ORIN WATCHED GEORGE KICK HIS GOLF BALL OUT from behind a weeping willow, then kick it again out to the fairway, swing at it with all his might, and shank it thirty yards back into the woods. George slammed his club into his bag. "This game is too hard. Come on, let's eat."

They sat on a stone bench and pulled out the chicken salad sandwiches the judge had packed in a cooler for them. "Nice, huh?" said George, beaming at his surroundings, taking personal credit for the deep blue of the Sound, the peace of the fields below, as if he had arranged for these accommodations.

"Makes you wonder how Skip could have done it."

"Guy strings himself up, I don't want to know."

"Tough to be the boss's kid. Your fuckups aren't your own."

"You really think that was it?" George stuffed half his sandwich into his mouth and swallowed like a python. "Guys said it was over his wife."

"What was she like?"

"Young. Redhead. Not bad looking. I'd have fucked her," he added needlessly.

"Skip ever talk to you much?"

George wiped his mouth with his sleeve and said, "No more than anybody else. He played tennis with the judge a lot, and shot some stick with whoever. He mostly ran with the geeks."

"What about Sick Dick?"

"Do we have to talk about him?"

"Feeling guilty?"

George frowned and narrowed his already beady eyes. "What do you mean?"

"We throw him out, he does a Virginia Woolf."

"You sound like freaking Kruger."

Orin noticed Brendan Kane strolling elegantly up to the adjacent green, examining a twenty-foot putt. "Skip friendly with Pettibone?" asked Orin.

George wrinkled his brow, thinking hard. "I guess you could say. And Luther and Ira. The fucking geeks. Why?"

"What'd that crowd have in common?"

"Skip and Dick offed themselves. The others should."

The judge missed his birdie, tapped in a four-foot putt for par, then dropped his putter by his golf bag and walked to the bench. Orin tried to imagine him dressed in black robes, pounding a gavel, and failed.

"Mind if I join you?" he said. "The Rog has guests on my court. Playing badminton, in skirts."

"Who's he playing with?" asked Orin.

"I'm pretty sure I saw the county executive before, and he can play anywhere he wants. Tommy Cotton. Real estate agents."

"Why real estate agents?" asked Orin.

"Have you any idea what this place is worth, chopped up and obscenely overdeveloped?"

Orin and George looked around for a moment, taking in the mansion on the crest of the hill just below them, the outbuildings, the vast patchwork of terraced lawns, cobblestone courtyards, and wide fields descending to the beach, and said to the judge simultaneously, "No."

"Mucho bucktares, my amigos," said the judge. "Barthwell or no Barthwell, I suggest we enjoy ourselves while we can."

Saturday, July 2, 2:05 p.m.

"COME IN," SAID NICK. "SHUT THE DOOR. HOW'S that hard-on Boyd looking today?"

Artie Tobin said, "Like his fucking world's collapsing. But then he looked that way when he got here."

Nick grunted, lit a cigar.

Tobin opened the one small window, checked out the gray sky, lit up a smoke. "Goddamn weekends are the worst. I mean, I'd settle for taking my kids to the mall."

"I told you not to think about them. They sure as hell ain't thinking about you."

Tobin took another drag, crushed the cigarette on the sill, and chucked it outside. "So I been thinking, Nick, what'd Prank do with the money?"

Nick sat up on his bed. "Boyd's money?"

"You know. His savings account, his checking, whatever we took. Electronic dollars go somewhere, right?"

"I didn't ask Prank that," said Nick, "and he didn't volunteer, that sneaky prick."

"Ask him, Nicky. In fact, don't ask him, just tell him to zap our thirds into our banks, first thing Monday morning."

Nick was amazed that Prank would even risk the appearance of a double-cross. "We better watch him close. He was never no one to show your back."

Saturday, July 2, 9:45 p.m.

LIGHT RAIN FELL OUTSIDE THE WIDE OPEN CASE-
ment windows that night, soaking fields that needed it. In
the dining room the men were playing cards, bonding
nicely, Orin thought, when word came from the kitchen that
the county medical examiner, based upon Kruger's investigation, had finally classified Pettibone a suicide.

"Yes!" cried George, pounding the table, before realizing
his elation was unseemly compared to the muted reactions
of the other players, the poker faces, so to speak. Nicky,
Artie, and a cop who helped a Mafia guy join the force were
playing for cigarettes with Orin and George, who sat with
his chair turned backward, flicking peanut shells into an
Egyptian urn thrown in 78 A.D.

Orin wondered aloud if Kruger was the joke of the homicide squad, the clown they sent to car crashes with a tape
measure and whisk broom.

"It'll be good to get back to normal," said Nick.

Orin looked over his crappy pair of threes at Nick's dark
face and said, "Normal's pretty good for you, isn't it?"

"What's that mean?"

"Things haven't changed that much for you in here.
You're still the main man."

Nick leaned back in his chair and admired his hand. "I
still got some juice, I'll admit it. Like, right now a guy, say
a small-time village mayor, can slide off a barstool and
climb behind the wheel, and when he hits something solid
and suddenly he's wearing bracelets, who do they call?
Half the fucking time they still call me. And I can sit here
in jail and get him out."

"Ironic," said Orin, "ain't it?"

"Whatever." Nicky caressed his cards and bragged on
about tickets to Jets games, Atlantic City junkets, babes.
"Give a little, get a little. Go along to get along."

"And you honestly don't think our guys were murdered?"

"No, I don't," he said, laying down three queens and sweeping up a pile of cigarettes.

"As far as you're concerned, things are fucking grand."

"What are you getting at, Boyd?"

"You know everybody here, better than anybody else, right? You were their PBA president. You've seen their personnel files. You know the killers and the cutthroats and the liars and the pussies."

"So?"

"So you don't suspect anybody?"

"Sure I do. Skip killed Skip, and Dick killed Dick."

"I guess that's that, then."

"Glad I could help." Nick smiled and nodded. "Another hand?"

"Na," said Orin, "that's all the fun I can take." He threw in his cards, the night's big loser. Even George had won a couple of smokes, which stood for dollars, and George always lost, perhaps because his hand was instantly reflected in his expression, unless he was bluffing, in which case, some whole other set of muscles ruled his face.

"Play again tomorrow?" asked Nick. "Early as we can?"

Art Tobin grinned as if he was in on some kind of joke.

"Sure," said Orin. "There's lots more where that came from. George can tell you."

SATURDAY, JULY 2, 10:30 P.M.

BACK IN HIS WHITE BRICK ROOM, MONITORING the Saturday night Honor Farm vibes, Orin heard mostly doors closing and silence falling as he dialed around the estate. Until the dormitory pay phone rang, and Nick picked up.

"One at two at three," said a woman. "Don't say no, baby. I'm hot."

"I love you," said Nick.

Orin had to admire the old union president, his systems for seeing his needs were met, no matter what. The son of a bitch would corrupt a convent, strong-arm the mother superior. Dopey Tobin would follow blindly. And where did Dominick Ril stand in all this? The little devil had been quiet lately. Because he was stealing back money he felt was rightly his? But if Ril had access to this kind of talent, why wait until Orin was on the Farm? The deed could have been done at long distance. Or was it the judge. Or Zen.

At eleven o'clock there was a brisk knock on Orin's door. Orin called out, "Good night, homey."

Oliver Bridges looked in on him and said, "Let's not forget who's the homeboy here."

At twelve o'clock sharp Orin watched from his window as Oliver Bridges walked down the hill to the gatehouse, to change to his street clothes and drive home. At two o'clock in the morning, with his binoculars strung around his neck, Orin hoisted himself onto the narrow windowsill and slipped out his bedroom window, carefully dropped to the earth.

He hugged the damp stones and scanned the layout. The lights above the command post were on low, triangulating ghostly fog rolling in off the Sound. Heads were moving about in the upstairs offices of the mansion. The golf cart responsible for roving patrol of the grounds was parked near the open kitchen door at the back of the main house, which led Orin to hope the boys were winding down over doughnuts, maybe complaining about Smith. Luther Bailey played a mournful tune on his clarinet, the notes falling through the trees like tears.

Orin stepped from the bushes and strolled directly past the pool to the edge of the woods, not looking back once, as if he owned the place. He quickly found the trail he wanted and worked his way east, up the hill, had not gone a hundred yards through the trees when he heard laughter rising from the other side of a field of corn.

He walked tall amid the chest-high rows, then crawled into the woods, flat on his belly over the wet leaves and pinecones. Past the family cemetery on the bluff. Further east the ground fell away hard toward the marsh, and as

Orin pushed past a thicket of thornbushes, he could see the lights of burning cigarettes far below.

He raised his binoculars and saw that Morelli had climbed over the inner wall and was standing in no-man's-land, drinking a can of beer and sharing a joint with a pretty young woman who was standing on the other side of the chain-link fence. Nick tipped his head back and finished off his Bud, tossed it over the fence. The girl picked it up and put it in a cooler, lobbed him a fresh one, which he basket-caught like Willie Mays. Then Nick dropped his jeans and pressed his tummy hard against the fence, took one more long swig.

SUNDAY, JULY 3, 2:37 A.M.

DAVID TRIMBLE'S STOMACH GROWLED, A RE-minder that he had not eaten well or slept deeply in days, that he was slowly disintegrating. They were now avoiding him at headquarters, mumbling platitudes and ducking out. A valued aide had asked after his emotional health, been demoted, then subsequently returned to his previous rank, all in one painful afternoon. And these were men who owed their positions of power to him.

Dave Trimble had never before dealt with such grief, and it dawned on him that watching others suffer was poor preparation for one's own losses. The pain and humiliation of watching his son's trial now seemed inconsequential.

Trimble had also forgotten how difficult dealing with Orin Boyd could be, how little he cared for the chains of command. It was maddening to be sitting on a damp tree stump in the dark, the police commissioner of a great American county, waiting for news from a lowly patrol-man, maybe the lowest. It helped that Skip was there, behind the fences, not lost among vast fields of stone.

Skip had always hated crowds, and loud noises. David Trimble remembered that. Skip didn't like ball games or bowling alleys. Much preferred to read or listen to music.

He did his homework, his chores; he was honest, compassionate. A wonderful son, with whom he'd had nothing in common. Still had nothing. Off to the right, his man inside scaled the stone wall, dropped to the ground, stepped to the fence.

"Hello, Orin. How's it going? Any luck?"

"Neither of us is as lucky as Nicky right now. He's grabbing himself a windy through the fence, maybe fifty yards away."

"I figured that dumb code meant sex. The other tapes aren't telling me much, either."

"Give them time," said Orin. "We got fish in the water."

Trimble exhaled loudly. "I'm not crazy, then?"

"No. What's happening on the Pettibone case?"

"Kruger liked Bill Masters, if it was murder. Someone doing it for fun. Otherwise, bupkus. He says if we examine each case separately, the conclusions are inescapable."

The wind moved the branches overhead, and they held their breath a moment. "Why Zen Masters?" asked Orin.

"He's the only one whose profile comes close, except of course for yours, and you weren't here when Skip was killed. I think Kruger wishes you were. You really pissed him off."

"George says Dick was a rat from way back. Is that true?"

"Ask Nick Morelli how many cops he jammed up."

"Internal Affairs?" asked Orin.

"A volunteer."

"He ever flop anybody heavy?"

"Not really."

Orin said, "See if you can find out who he hurt while he was here. Have Kruger check Barthwell on that. And ask why he was dressed in clean clothes. I saw him a couple of hours before, and he was scruffy as hell, and he didn't seem to mind. I mean, why clean up to drown yourself?"

"That fits Kruger's original theory of him thinking he was leaving the Farm," said Trimble. "Kinda tough to explain the pocket barbells, though."

"The scientists have all weighed in?"

Trimble said, "No bruises. No drugs. He drowned."

"What did Dick know, and when did he know it," said Orin. "Have Kruger recheck his family for any recent complaints."

"His family didn't visit, and I still don't see how Skip is tied in," said Trimble.

"They were friends, boss," said Orin, "near as I can tell."

Dave Trimble's fingers poked through the fence like claws, as if he were hanging on for balance.

Orin said, "Any idea who bugged the conjugal trailer?"

"None."

"What about my plunging credit rating?"

"I'd guess Dom Ril. And if there's computers involved, he's hooked up with Prank."

"I don't think Ril's got the balls, tell you the truth."

"I'll put the Feds on it, in any event, as soon as you come out." Trimble grinned. "You should also know Tommy Cotton has been working the north shore cocktail circuit, suggesting to all the lockjaw WASPs that the Honor Farm has become an anchor around the police department's neck."

"There's no reason to close the Farm, boss."

"A minority opinion, I'm afraid."

Orin knew this issue was out of Trimble's hands, that Trimble's political superiors might very well sell the Farm without so much as asking his opinion. "How's Tommy Boy's tooth?"

"Turning black . . . like his heart."

They saw the lights of a golf cart approaching on the fence-line road, so they cut their meeting short. Trimble quickly made his way into the woods, while Orin climbed over the inner wall and ran, then belly-crawled back to the bushes outside the dorm, thinking of leeches, brown spiders, the ticks of Long Island. Watch, he thought. He'll get Lyme disease here, and the state retirement doctor will insist it was not job-related, probably some hack like Homo, with an office next to a gas station.

Orin was about to climb in his open window when the side door of the dormitory opened and Zen Masters stepped outside, a man whom Orin recalled had killed at least eight people, a man who had chosen to break curfew dressed in black Gore-Tex.

Zen looked directly at Orin with eyes that were peaceful or drugged. "Hey, what's up?" he said.

"Hey," said Orin. "How's my intelligence division?"

"Dumb as a post, but I'm watching, I'm listening. I couldn't sleep," said Zen.

"Me neither."

"I need the lights of Manhattan."

Orin considered for a moment that Zen might actually be telling the truth. "Doesn't anyone mind our leading these active lives?" he said.

Zen grinned. "Fuck 'em if they can't take a joke."

16

ON SUNDAY MORNING, AFTER THEIR VERY PUBLIC attendance at church, Senator Cotton and his rather dowdy wife of ten years, Paula Crenshaw-Cotton, and their two pretty young daughters took a drive along the Sands Point Peninsula, a rare family outing. Tommy Cotton didn't tell them where they were going or why, suggested only that the innocent children remain silent and pay attention to the palatial homes they were passing, told them some—but not quite all—of the things those people had done to earn those homes.

The kids oohed and aahed on cue while Tommy worked up his inner rage, his jealousy and sense of injustice at the fact that he was not wealthy beyond measure, yet. Then he turned that energy toward a crime-and-punishment speech he would make tomorrow night to a room full of influential businessmen.

He and Townsend Tripp had decided to get tough with crooked cops, those Benedict Arnolds who now enjoyed the serenity of a palatial seaside estate. He would work the pampering angle hard, stand up tough to the PBA. Make it sound as if he were protecting all the honest cops. From pricks like Boyd. And liberals like Trimble. Cops didn't vote anyhow, not like rich conservatives, which the vast majority of families in these neighboring hills were, his true constituency. The senator decided to have someone dig up Orin Boyd's other case, this "old beef" Trimble had mentioned, and use it to embarrass Trimble, show the people the police commissioner was soft on rotten cops. Cotton opened his still-swollen mouth to expound on this plan, and a sharp pain shrieked out of his jaw and bounced around his head, reminding him that his New York City oral surgeon was due back from Israel tomorrow, and he was first in the chair, for at least an extraction, perhaps structural repair.

"You say something?" said Paula Crenshaw-Cotton.

Tommy grunted in the negative, watched the ever-narrowing bumpy road that followed the fences.

They slowed as they passed the main gate, the cobblestone driveway leading like an arrow up to magnificent, now available, Soundview. Tommy turned to face his children. "So what do you think, kids? Is it us, or what?"

SUNDAY, JULY 3, 11:45 A.M.

ORIN WAS THE LAST FALLEN CATHOLIC TO SLINK from the chapel, and he grabbed the monsignor's hand, thanked him for the inspirational sermon, and pulled him back inside. "Remember I told you I was framed?" he said.

"Who could forget?" said O'Rourke.

"They're after my family, too."

"Good Lord."

"Do me a favor, Father. Change Dawn's last name in the camp records to *Kennedy*, just to be safe. And watch her like she's a Kennedy kid."

"I'll defend my turf. You can count on that."

MONDAY, JULY 4, 9:30 A.M.

"SINCE I'M LEAVING THIS WEEK," PRANK DINOS-
tra said to Warden Barthwell, "and you've been so damned
good to me, I thought you ought to know that something
fishy's going on."

Jack Barthwell sat behind his desk enjoying a triple-
overtime holiday, wearing a shredded sweatshirt with a torn
collar, his arms oiled and rippling. Prank wore what he assumed were the last clean work clothes he would ever draw
from the Honor Farm laundry.

"Serious violations?" asked Barthwell. "Or barnyard
bullshit Smith can handle?"

Prank gazed out the window. "I'm not naming names,
you understand."

"That's what put you here in the first place."

"Someone was in the library last week, after hours. They
tried to use my computer."

Barthwell grinned. "It's not exactly your computer."

"While I'm stuck here, it is. Just like no one takes out
Luther's personal basketball. This happened after curfew."

"I imagine a few things went on after curfew that night."

"You're not listening, Warden. I went in the library the
morning after Dickie died, to print out the final draft of my
diary. My security system had been activated."

"Could have been staff," Barthwell offered. "Some of
them are computer literate."

"Like who?"

"Maybe it was the ghost."

Prank made a face that suggested he did not believe in
the supernatural, that human shenanigans were the more
likely explanation.

"I'll look into it. Thanks."

Prank shrugged. "It's your Farm. For now."

Barthwell said, "Look, I really do appreciate your coming in here, and I wish I could reciprocate in kind."

"What do you mean?"

"We've got a problem, Prank." Barthwell opened a

file on his desk and stared at it unhappily. "Your release has been indefinitely delayed. The board has asked to review your case."

Prank regarded Barthwell coolly. "You wouldn't do this to me, would you? I know I was borderline, first time out."

"Truth be told, I want you out of my library, my computer, and probably my payroll records."

"I never messed with payroll, sir, though I did consider docking the fucking Rog."

"Doesn't anybody like him?" asked Barthwell.

"Just his mom."

MONDAY, JULY 4, 2:45 P.M.

"HEY, BOYD!" GRAMPS MCKAY FILLED THE DOOR-way of the empty conference room, pulled his stogie out of his mouth. "Drop the mop. The Rog said to report to the loading dock. I already cleared it with Ira."

"Yassuh, boss. Long's you cleared it with Ira."

Orin stashed his mop and his Walkman in his utility cart, followed Gramps outside and around to the north side of the produce barn. There he joined a work detail comprised of George Clarke and Luther Bailey, under the supervision of Sally Miles.

"Good to have you with us, Orin," said Sally.

Orin bowed and said, "It is I who am honored."

"You got that right," said George. "Faggot upstairs maid."

Orin looked at Luther Bailey. "This is my friend?"

Luther was wearing one of those Jiffy Pop Rasta hats and a look of resignation on his face. "For your sake, I truly hope not."

George had his T-shirt off, lugging a crate up the ramp. Orin shielded his eyes from the sun, smiled up at him. "They let you go topless, big fellow? Folks don't complain?"

"You know," said George, staring down at his flabby

chest and gut, "fuck you. Just . . . fuck you. You ain't no Greek god."

"Hey," said Sally. "One smart-mouth is enough, and she's me."

Orin pitched in, whistling happily, standing aside for George whenever collisions were possible. Then Orin and George wedged themselves among the produce in the rear of the truck, while Luther joined Sally and Vito Kelly in the cab up front. The truck rumbled to life and rolled away from the barn, past the towering mansion, and down the hill to the front gate.

After a brief security check, they were on the road to East Meadow, as free as Honor Farmers got.

Orin nudged him. "You pull strings for me, buddy? I gotta tell you, I'm downright giddy."

"You're the hotshot, remember? Me, I'm nobody. Just a fat-assed, big-titted schmuck."

"What are you talking about?"

George leaned close. "Come on, Orin . . . what'd you get?"

"What are you talking about?"

"In Belmont. The freaking money."

"Don't listen to Ril."

"It's not just Ril; it's everybody. Tell me the truth."

"Not enough to speak of."

"You bought a brand-new boat. A really nice brand-new boat."

"Would you believe I saved up the money for that boat? Would you believe that Judy makes more than I do?"

George made a face that suggested he would not believe either absurdity; so Orin turned his back on his old friend and watched the sun-dappled life of a north shore summer day roll by, free citizens unburdened by investigations— and friendships—going sour.

Two miles south of the Honor Farm property they passed the last of the large estates, and Orin was touched as several Hispanic hedge-clippers along the road doffed their straw hats and made crosses in the direction of the prison truck, one chain gang praying for another.

"The boat sank," said Orin. "Does that help?"

"I never even got a ride on it."

"You big wus."

Ten minutes later the brakes squealed and the shocks groaned as the produce truck bounced over the Alps that pass for speed bumps at East Meadow. The truck stopped at a security booth, then passed through the double fences and the high concrete wall, into the entrance courtyard at the East Meadow jail.

Somewhere above them someone was screaming and slamming metal against metal. From other quarters came laughter at this pain. From the loading dock came two huge corrections officers. They escorted George and Luther and the heavy boxes of frozen veal labeled ADMIN to the forward offices.

Sally Miles told Orin to stay behind, in the fenced yard with the truck. "Don't piss on the produce," she said. "If you're feeling ambitious, you could even unload it."

"Where will you be?"

"On the carpet. Seems someone's made a complaint about me."

"Someone at the Farm?"

Sally nodded sadly. "Anonymous," she said, "which means Roger Smith. Again."

"Why? You won't go to bed with him?"

Sally shuddered. "I won't have a cup of coffee with him, I don't have to."

Sally left, and Orin got to work for her, stacking sackcloth bags of potatoes in a pile on a pallet, working up a good sweat. Sally Miles trusted him enough to leave him alone, he thought suddenly, almost as if she knew he was still on the job. Which meant his cover was blown, or maybe she remembered what he used to be, gave him credit where she figured it was due. Nice woman. Alone and likely to remain so if she kept dating married men.

He stopped for a cigarette and stared up at the barred windows on the tiers above him, the shadows of the faces behind them, wondering how many were personal placements. He tipped his head back, enjoying the patch of sunshine, the heat off the concrete. A greeting rang down from the tier: "Hey, fuck you, pig!"

Orin thought it was nice to be remembered and flipped the boys the bird. A growing chorus of curses rained down. Several lugers launched in his direction fell short on the tarmac.

Orin ducked under the overhang on the loading dock and immediately discovered that he was not alone. Two white cons, one bigger than the other, were messing up his neat pile of potatoes, prodding them with tire irons.

"What's up?" said Orin. "Why you want to do that?"

"We're fucking Muslims," said the biggest con. "We don't eat food that's been handled by pigs."

Without another word they charged, and Orin sidestepped them, tripped one and slapped the other hard on the ear, gathered himself for another rush as he tried to remember a kata suitable for multiple attackers with bludgeons.

"Get him!" they cried out on their second sortie.

Memory served, and Orin ducked and whirled and struck with force, repelled their next sally, then concentrated a series of knee-high kicks on a rapidly shrinking single opponent, the last effort landing on jawbone.

The con still standing gave ground in ever-widening circles, wagging the tire iron, considering retreat.

"You soften that motherfucker up yet?" growled someone else from over Orin's shoulder.

"Not exactly," said the con.

Orin turned around to face the largest, hairiest, black man he had ever seen in his life. The man was staring down at him, his expression eerily deadpan. The fly of his jeans was open, and he spit in his hand and stroked himself, growled, and squinted at Orin. He finally smiled, showing a rack of coffee-stained teeth. "Orin?"

"Your mother'd be absolutely horrified, Maniac. Do you know that?"

Maniac grimaced uneasily and nodded, apologized, wiped off his hand. "I wondered who was whipping on my homeboys. And why did they send us here to poke you? Answer me that. 'Cause I got paid upfront for this job. Kick the blond cop's ass. More when I bring the man your underpants."

"A con?" asked Orin.

Maniac shook his massive head. "That's a negative, dude."

"Interesting." Orin unbuckled his jeans and pulled them off, handed over his labeled briefs, said, "Tell me more, Maniac. Maybe we can sell them some jockstraps."

"Old-timer hack. Says I get a hundred coming and going, do the blond cop on the dock."

Orin pulled up his jeans. "He knew I'd be alone back here?"

Maniac said, "Word."

17

TUESDAY, JULY 5, 10:55 A.M.

THAT MORNING JUDY HAD MANAGED A DEMON-
stration of the new product line and had written the monthly
staff reviews. Two of her trainees wanted raises, one was
pregnant. It came with the turf.

On the wall behind her were the plaques and corporate
proclamations of a sales career well into its second decade.
She was off the street these days, running the show, in
charge of fifteen sales reps and five technicians. Her immediate superiors had always been good enough to treat her
like a man, perhaps because they had met her drunken
police-officer husband at one particularly memorable company picnic.

Nevertheless, that morning they marched right into
Judy's office without knocking, two officers from the home
office accompanied by her branch manager, Bill Marcus,
and a man she did not know, who was introduced as Mr.
Cabarini, from security.

Mr. Cabarini came right to the point. "We have a problem
involving a fraud against the company."

"By one of my people?" Judy had handpicked her sales team; if pressed she could not have named a most likely suspect. She looked from clean-shaven face to clean-shaven face, felt the heat rising in her neck, sweat dribble down her sides, soaking her bra.

"Your expense account reports for the last three months reflect outgo for sixteen sales reps."

"I only have fifteen . . . I don't get it."

"We think you do," said Cabarini.

Never in her life had Judy ever felt so ignorant, so intimidated. "I've worked here a long time, sir, and—"

"Can you tell us who a Mr. R. Smith is?"

She shook her head.

"Interesting. He has the same direct deposit account number as you at your bank."

"That's funny," said Judy. "According to my branch, I don't even *have* an account there."

"Got a check on you?" asked Cabarini.

Judy handed them one from her purse: Cabarini matched the numbers, laid his papers on her desk. Dead solid on.

"Mrs. Boyd, we'd like an explanation."

"Look, right now my husband's working this case against a computer hack who is making our lives miserable. Our credit's been destroyed, our savings—"

Bill Marcus said, "As a courtesy, and because you're one of our top performers for so many years, we feel a short rest is in order, a little counseling. A medical suspension with pay, if you will. And of course you have to return the money. Around nine thousand dollars, so far."

"You men are making a terrible mistake," she said.

"Look, this does not have to be the end of your career. You rest up, you come back good as new, say in six months. Believe me, you'll thank us."

Judy didn't feel like thanking them, felt instead her cheeks flaming and her eyes tearing. She wanted to explain about cops, how sometimes the filth slopped over, but she held her tongue while they stared down at her, impatient with her weakness.

"When," said Cabarini, "do you think you can be out of this office? How long will it take you to pack?"

"You mean by tonight, don't you?"

"Right away, I'm afraid. Company policy."

Judy gazed at her busy wall of fame, her mahogany credenza, estimated the thousands of hours spent to acquire these perks and honors, the minutes to box them and cart them away. "And then you walk me to the door like a criminal?"

"Security helps you load your car."

"I guess it's all in how you look at it," said Judy.

TUESDAY, JULY 5, 4:15 P.M.

VITO KELLY AND SALLY MILES LEFT THE EMployee parking lot of the Honor Farm together in Sally's white Sentra, and she drove up the hill away from the huge stone house and the flat gray tanker-laden Sound. Kelly's car had needed brakes, was supposed to be finished.

Vito Kelly was the senior corrections officer on the Honor Farm, having worked his way up from fence patrol—where one was subjected to the wind and rain and cold of the cliffs—to buildings patrol, then to the command post. He lived out east, in Miller Place, a pretty country town that might as well have been in England. Vito drove only clunkers to work, seventeen of them so far in his twenty-two years on the job.

The mechanic's brother worked the wall at East Meadow, so he cut the guards a discount, actually did the work. You could drive away from his shop with something resembling confidence.

"I hear we're closing down after Christmas," said Vito.

"Oh, yeah? Who starts this rumor, anyway?"

"Senator Sewer, this time."

Sally said nothing, kept her eyes on the winding, tree-lined road, thinking, no room for error.

"What's Happy Jack think?" asked Vito.

"Jack doesn't think out loud. The Rog might hear him. But Jack doesn't know any more than we do. Believe me."

"What do you think about Pettibone?" Vito asked.

Sally took her eyes off the narrow lane to look at Vito. "What am I supposed to think? *You* don't think they're connected, do you?"

Vito shook his head. "I wasn't surprised by Pettibone," he said. "It's just I never figured Skip."

Sally stopped at a blinking yellow light, then turned right along a narrow street lined with white split-rail fences. "You think there's a killer on the Farm?"

Vito said, "I don't know, but anybody else offs themself and they'll for shit-sure close the place. *Newsday* will swear we golfed the poor bastards to death."

"People don't understand. Time in jail is time in jail."

"That's bullshit," said Vito. "These guys had it made. They were street cops or better, some making ninety grand to do bupkus. And they blew it. Now they hang out at a mansion. I find it hard to feel sorry for them."

"I used to. I don't anymore."

"So I've heard."

"What's that mean?"

"You're pretty good friends with that new guy Boyd."

Sally grimaced. "I knew a lot of these guys from court. Orin Boyd just made more arrests than anybody else."

"Just telling you what I hear."

"You're worried about my reputation?"

"We only get one, my mom used to say."

"Vito, everybody already thinks I'm screwing the warden. How much worse can it get?"

"They could think you were screwing a prisoner."

Sally's eyes flashed. "Drive a stake through that one, Vito."

"I already have. Which is why you need to worry."

Sally pulled into the white-pebbled driveway of the Little Fox Hollow Auto Repair Center, which was in what had once been a carriage house for another grand estate. Vito's dented yellow Dodge Dart was parked with other more expensive cars by a row of perfect maples.

Sally waited while Vito went inside, paid for the brake job, waved through the glass for her to go. Then Vito asked to use a phone, said he had to call work. "A nondenial denial on the warden," he said to Roger Smith. "The other one's a negative."

"I owe you."

"What's new?"

TUESDAY, JULY 5, 8:00 P.M.

ROGER SMITH STOOD ON HIS BALCONY, SIPPING A glass of burgundy, stewing in the juices of his thwarted plot. Watching Team Cotton arrive in limousines had him wishing he could run downstairs to greet the man, his hook, his rabbi, the foundation of his career, such as it was. You had to constantly let the man know you were watching his interests, otherwise he took you for granted. Fed you beans. He wanted to tell the senator that Orin Boyd was miserable, friendless, emasculated by his housekeeping chores, begging for mercy; that at night, while Boyd was locked in his room, Roger messed up Barthwell's office, just the little things, enough to indicate a piss-poor work ethic to the warden. He wanted to tell the senator that a whole string of ass-kickings was underway, with so far limited results.

But Happy Jack Barthwell had ordered the Rog to stay in his office and catch up on some federal grant requests. Said that when Smith had learned to just sit at these meetings and listen and learn, maybe they could try again. Of course Roger Smith knew that underneath it all lived the concept that the less Smith knew about the total operation of the Farm, meaning the political side, the less of a threat he was to Barthwell's job.

Fucking deadwood, that's what Barthwell was. A thoroughly corrupt muscle head who had probably shrunk his brain with steroids. Who even remembered the county exec who appointed him? Who fucking cared? Nice guy, sure, but a leader of men? He paid more attention to his high-protein diet than his duty. And he definitely cared more about Sally than he ought to.

Off to his left and way down below, Smith spotted another Honor Farm atrocity, Orin Boyd walking empty-handed, wearing that fucking Walkman, headed to the dorm, and Roger found that particularly galling when conditions in the house had been atrocious lately.

Orin Boyd wasn't in housekeeping because it was easy; yet he did not look like a man being worked to death or humiliated. Bastard looked as if he were on spring break.

Smith yanked out a fresh legal pad and marched out of his always sterile office to the clerical area, began to note whatever deficiencies in cleanliness he could find, what he assumed would be an epic of inefficiency and disregard to duty. There were faint coffee rings on Marion's desk, lint behind the computer. Her wastepaper basket would soon be overflowing. Intolerable conditions abounded in the adjacent bathrooms, the likelihood of fungus growth and bacterial buildup, conditions known to foster disease. Roger Smith got himself madder by the minute, cursing and sweating, began surfing the high terrain on her swivel chair, running his fingers on top of the bookshelf, when the Giordano microphone popped onto the criminally dusty carpet.

WEDNESDAY, JULY 6, 6:00 A.M.

ORIN LAY IN BED, CONSIDERING GOING HOME. There was the matter of his money disappearing. And the boat. Then someone setting him up through the guards for a little rape and pillage. And now Judy, suspended, ready to call *Newsday* on the whole stupid scam. So many fronts, he thought, and so little progress on his real mission, the real reason his summer had turned so chokingly claustrophobic.

Whoever was behind this flypaper diplomacy knew his

way around. And the question remained: Was this person a killer, or was this about Orin's money?

If Orin assumed the deaths were murders, and connected, then the killer was likely someone with little or no alibi for the night of Pettibone's death.

Like Ira, who was alone in his room and said he heard nothing.

Like Zen, out jogging in the dark.

Doc Homo, who never answered to anyone.

George had used the dormitory pay phone several times; other than that, he had had the same opportunity to kill Dick as anyone. No motive, though, other than his hatred of anyone different.

Nick and Artie had said they were together, in their office, going over the betting sheets.

Even Roger Smith had been alone for most of that evening.

The judge was iron-clad, in both cases, if you trusted the Dominicans he was shielding from George.

Orin kept mixing up inmate dossiers in his head, forgetting who was where, on what occasion, trying to match a quirk with a quibble, expecting the answer to spring out at him from nowhere, everywhere. He listened to the quiet pay phone, the quiet offices, noise in the library, like the wind, or the sound of someone crying. He turned on the TV, saw that it was raining from Chicago to Boston. Eighty-five degrees in Boulder, eighty in Kansas City. "Here in the New York metro area we'll have cloudy skies this morning and warm southerly breezes, with heavy rain due later . . ."

Orin had grown fond of the Weather Channel since his imprisonment, the soothing repetition of calm voices with troublesome news, a way to keep in touch with Outside; he could imagine fog in Chicago, sunny skies in San Francisco, a rainy night in Georgia. This was a temporary assignment. There was a world outside he could go back to whenever he wanted. He was not a criminal, nor did he deserve to be punished. Lies, he thought, bordering on statistics.

He put on his Honor Farm sweat suit and snapped off the television set. Zen was waiting for him in the hall, the front of his gray T-shirt already sweaty. Zen poked Orin's gut.

Orin said, "So it's been a while."

"We'll start slow and taper off. Ain't nobody timing us; don't nobody care."

Orin felt a weight rise from his chest as they stepped out of the dorm and took in the Sound—a single sailboat, a tanker anchored miles to the west, gray clouds overhead— then fell into an easy rhythm on the path that led down to the beach.

"So?" said Orin. "Make me intelligent."

"I wish it were that easy," said Zen.

"Funny."

"I wish I could explain it to myself, why I'm sure someone killed those boys."

Too winded to respond in depth, Orin grunted.

"Have you noticed, for instance," said Zen, "that no one swims in the pool anymore?"

"No."

"I noticed Luther had stopped shooting hoops with Ira, so I asked him about it. Luther said it wasn't anything personal, just as long as he stays by himself, any thoughts of suicide will be his own. There's more," said Zen, "but if I say it, I won't see it. Best let it grow wild. Then when we see what we got, we think globally and act locally."

"You'll think globally," said Orin. "I'll act loco."

"To each his own," said Zen. "I just hope the next victim ain't me."

The first mile was the toughest for Orin, his lungs burning, hocking up phlegm, but he caught his pace on the road that passed between the cemetery and the cliff. On their way back down the hill, Zen invited Orin to join him on the mansion roof for something out of the ordinary; and they peeled off across a grassy field for the house and bolted up the narrow servants' stairs to the cupola on the western roof. A startling view of Manhattan awaited them, so close you could almost touch it, shimmering above the treetops of Queens.

Zen slumped below the hand-cut stones and pulled a Bic lighter from his fanny pack, lit a joint, toked up, offered Orin a hit. "Wake and bake?" he said. "Ease the ache?"

Orin said that if he weren't a raving alcoholic, he'd be honored to get ripped with Zen.

"I know the drill—you ain't sober if you're stoned. I clipped this from Tobin's patch."

They sat back a moment, their feet on the ledge of the cupola, Zen holding his hit, Orin fighting off a monster he had thought dead.

Far below, Tobin and Morelli were riding in a golf cart on the road leading down to the beach. Artie Tobin was driving, his ponytail flying behind him like Thor's. Nick had his feet up on the dash, in leather sandals. Surf-casting rods bristled from the back of the cart like antennae.

"What a pisser," said Orin. "Fucking fishing."

"Hunting, too," said Zen as he mimed the act of locking a rifle on high-priority targets, Tobin and Morelli. "Dual hairbags," he said. "Go boom! Boom! . . . Now, that's the way it's done. You sign your fucking work."

WEDNESDAY, JULY 6, 10:00 A.M.

ORIN WAS IN THE LIBRARY, PRETENDING TO DUST the leather volumes in the original house collection, when a hatless Ira Cohen came by to check on him. Orin removed his earphones and said, "This job ain't that bad, you know? Once you get past the woman's work thing."

Ira flinched and looked over his shoulder at the empty doorway. "No wonder Sissyboy hates you."

"You really think he hates me?"

"I'm Jewish. I recognize hate."

Orin nodded, got to work on the blinds.

"Watch the Mets last night?" asked Ira.

Orin put down his feather duster and snapped his fingers. "Ira from Sands Point, on the FAN. It's you, that voice, you're that—"

"—regular guest on the *Mick and The Mad Duck Show.* Yeah. That's me. You didn't know? I used to be Ira from Oceanside, then a bad thing happened."

"Good Lord, a celebrity in our midst."

"I'll bet you want to know how much we get paid?"

"Never crossed my mind."

"They don't even help with the phone bill."

"I'd talk to Doc Robbins, I was you."

Ira laughed and grabbed a rag, pitched in on the blinds, joined Orin in a shower of dust.

"I guess everybody's got their obsessions," Orin said. "Maybe that's why we're here, maybe our mommies didn't tell us we were special often enough. George has his babes, Prank has his diary, Luther's got hoops, Zen has the spirit world."

"What do you have—other than this thing about the suicides?"

"That's it."

WEDNESDAY, JULY 6, 10:45 A.M.

WARDEN BARTHWELL AND CAPTAIN SMITH jogged past the cemetery, shoulder to shoulder on the path, silent but for their labored breaths. Barthwell raised his hands and they stopped, walked with hands on hips. Smith started to say something, but Barthwell interrupted.

"You put it back exactly where it was?" said Barthwell.

"Immediately. To spread disinformation."

"Who?" said Barthwell. "That's what I want to know."

"State Inspectional Services," said Smith. "Gotta be. Right?"

"The suicides?"

"I honestly don't know."

Barthwell shook his head angrily. "It's got to be a guard, then. There's no way to slip in a ringer inmate. These guys were all cops together. They're intermarried like hillbillies."

"We've got a couple new guards lately," offered Smith. "That black guy Bridges."

"I like that black guy Bridges."

"Oh, me too. Don't get me wrong."

"The FBI, maybe?" guessed Barthwell. "That's a goddamn sophisticated bug. I wonder where the listening post is?"

Smith said, "They can hide a repeater somewhere on or near the Farm, and the bastards could be anywhere, or there could simply be an unattended tape recorder. This is really not fair," said Roger. "We run a clean ship here. Top to bottom."

"We think we do, Roger. We think we do." Then Jack Barthwell speculated that Senator Cotton had been on the grounds several times in the last few weeks, that he was no longer an unequivocal friend to the institution.

"We should tell Kruger," said Smith.

Barthwell frowned and said, "Let's just run the jail, Rog. Leave the homicide work to the real cops. Which you are not. Which I am not. You keep this under your hat, you read me? In fact, I suggest we announce tomorrow's big meeting during free time, have our trusted guards watch suspects and see who goes where and does what. If that doesn't turn up anything, we tear the place apart."

"Who do we suspect?" said Roger.

"For now, everybody including your favorite state senator. In fact, let's mention that the son-of-a-bitch is coming tomorrow. That'll sure generate interest. . . . Be nice to know how long the bug was there."

Something Roger Smith was worried about as well. He had always considered the mansion his sanctuary, a reflection of his personality and style. "This is so embarrassing," he said.

"And make up a list of the guards you trust."

18

ORIN SAT ON HIS BED, DESPAIRING OF EVER HEAR-
ing an incriminating utterance, when there was activity outside
the front door of the mansion, Roger Smith and Warden Barthwell together, Barthwell getting ready to leave for the night.

Smith said, "Remember what I said about Boyd liking
Sally."

"Every guy here likes Sally, Rog. Including you. They'd
like her if she looked like a frog, which she don't. Don't
make a big deal of it."

"I'm telling you, he's bad news."

Barthwell grumbled something unintelligible, and Orin
wondered halfheartedly if Roger Smith had also hated Skip
Trimble and Dick Pettibone. Orin tracked Smith's footsteps
as he returned to his office. Then for several minutes it
sounded as if Smith was wiping down his office furniture
and the stubborn streaks would not come out, actually got
worse the harder he worked, and finally the frustration of a
lifetime boiled over in him, and Orin heard a fist slam on
wood and a cry of anguish: "This fucking Fantastik sucks."

Orin switched channels on the Walkman, scanned the bug in the dormitory hallway, heard music, "It's knowing that your door is always open . . ."

He changed channels again, found the bug in the library active. A one-sided phone call from Prank: "So what the fuck happened? What the fuck kind of lawyer are you? People are dying in here. And I'm having nightmares . . . The kind that end badly." The phone clicked off.

Orin ditched the headphones and lit a cigarette, wondering for the umpteenth time if these unexplained deaths were about the real world or the Farm, old wounds or new risks. And how depressing this place was, he thought, this old repository of guilty men and dirty secrets. Orin reminded himself that what these clowns had pleaded out to was often a far cry from what they had done.

Like Prank, rotten from the moment he'd been given the opportunity to profit.

Like most men, Orin figured.

Luther Bailey had forged a good bit of the stolen art to dupe dumb collectors from Boston to Washington. Gramps McKay had more or less executed a heroin dealer. Dominick Ril sold out an entire precinct.

And George Clarke, who seemed to marry every woman he met, was often criminally bad company, but there was worse.

Orin blew a smoke ring and considered the doctor's suggestion he get hypnotized to quit, decided to go for it—and the patch—just before he was released.

He heard the dormitory pay phone ring and snapped up his headphones. Nick picked up immediately, said, "Yo."

"Twenty-two for two," the girl said.

"Cool. Bye."

WEDNESDAY, JULY 6, 9:55 P.M.

CORRECTION OFFICER TERRENCE CANTWELL WAS on dormitory duty that night instead of Oliver Bridges, and

Bridge's relief was no relief for the men: Terry Cantwell was rigid, cruel, an East Meadow regular who had kissed ass and pulled strings to wangle his way onto the substitute schedule, a cranky drunk who hated fence patrol, liked to shut the dorm early and catch up on his rest.

He did not hear Orin Boyd knock softly on Artie Tobin's door, nor did he hear Orin tiptoe down the hall to Nick's room. Orin saw the Do Not Disturb sign hung on the door, knocked anyway, tried the handle. The door was locked, the room unoccupied, unless Morelli was in there dead, which Orin doubted. And Terry Cantwell sure had no idea. Oh, Captain Smith ran a tight fucking ship. You had to give him that.

Orin squeezed out his own bedroom window and joined the soft parade from the dorm. He quickly scaled the dark hill leading to the graveyard, waited like a sniper in the woods near Morelli's love nest. Ten minutes of dead silence in the dark passed before it dawned on him that maybe through overconfidence he had screwed up, that maybe Nicky the moron had a code more sophisticated than A=1, B=2.

Angry at himself, Orin rapidly walked the dark perimeter, hugging the stone wall where possible, deviating only where the underbrush was impassable or the land dropped away into gullies too dangerous to traverse in the dark. They could be back in bed already, he thought. They could be going through his room or following him. He rested a moment with his back against a maple tree and listened to his Walkman, sorry now he hadn't thought to bug his own room. All was quiet in the house, the dorm, the command post, the visitors' center.

He got up, kept moving, slipping on the steep sections.

As he made his way past the cemetery for the second time, he thought of the commissioner, the fool up the hill. He wanted to drop all pretense and yell, "Hey, boss, you see any bimbos come through here? They'd be young and dumb, lots of makeup, no panties, carrying coolers." Trimble would love that. He'd yank Orin, pay him off with a pension, and find someone else to be the departmental crash-test dummy.

Orin climbed over the stone wall and stepped to the chain-link fence. "David," he whispered.

Commissioner Trimble materialized from behind a large bush.

"Remember I asked you to talk to Pettibone's family? To see if they thought they were hearing the truth."

Trimble said, "Of course. Sure. They seemed satisfied by the turn of the investigation. I would have told you otherwise."

"Isn't that kinda odd? That you're satisfied to find out your ex-husband, father, whatever, killed himself?"

"Perhaps they were relieved."

Orin chuckled. "You're a cynical man."

"High praise, coming from you."

"What's Kruger think?"

"Two sad stories connected only by place. He looked at George real hard, he looked at Zen real hard, he looked at Prank. He says we ain't got nothing, kid."

THURSDAY, JULY 7, 9:15 A.M.

HIGH MUCKETY-MUCKS HAD TO BE COMING BE-cause Ira Cohen was wearing a black tuxedo and his Mets cap inside out, and he personally supervised the morning cleaning of the main-floor conference room. He polished crystal nervously while he watched Orin Boyd fill several silver pitchers on the long mahogany table with ice water. "Big meeting today," Ira said, holding up an ashtray to check for spots. "Can't embarrass the boss."

"You're damn right," said Orin. "Who's coming, by the way?"

"That's none of our business, Orin, by the way. One of our duties is to be invisible, while providing impeccable service."

"Gotcha. Kinda like the mob."

Ira smiled, happy to have found, if not a friend, someone he enjoyed working beside. "What I'm saying is they don't usually give me the guest list. Now hurry up there, and get lost. Go play some golf or something until it's time to clean up."

"You don't want me to serve the crumpets?"

"I got ya covered."

Orin frowned. "You don't trust me."

"No one trusts you."

Normally, Orin would have taken offense at a remark like that coming from a man who thought that his personal attire touched the destiny of his favorite sports team. Normally, Orin would have taken that moment to bolt. This time, he pulled a clean rag from his back pocket, and went to work on tiny hand-smudges on the long wooden table.

"That's fine," said Ira. "I'll finish up."

"How'd the Mets do last night?"

Orin might as well have kicked him in the balls. Ira set his can of Pledge on the credenza, stared out the conference room window with visible longing, as if for a missing lover. "Lost."

"Wanna talk about it."

"Not just yet. I'm still thinking of what to say to the Mad Duck. First I gotta get that set in my head."

"You're probably a collector, too?" said Orin. "Am I right? A lot of my friends are out of stocks and into baseball cards."

"I possess certain valuable memorabilia."

"What's the best thing you got? Like a Keith Hernandez jockstrap? My friend got a toilet seat from the Polo Grounds. Signed by the excavation crew."

Ira did not smile, only said wistfully, "The best thing I ever had is gone. Turf from Shea Stadium, the day the sixty-nine Mets clinched. I kept it in a Baggie in my desk at home for years. One day the Baggie is empty, except for a note from my big brother: 'You got ripped off. This shit gave me a headache.' Bastard smoked my championship turf from Shea, and then has the nerve to tell me I got ripped off. He's a doctor now, ashamed to visit me."

"Let me guess, you're the bad son."

"In a very Jewish family."

"Bummer."

Ira nodded out the window. "They're here."

Orin joined Ira at the window, and they watched two stretch limos at the main gate go through the motions of admittance. One of the limos flew an American flag from its antenna.

"Senator Sewer and staff," said Ira. "Pricks on Parade."

"Genghis," said Orin, "such verbal violence. Don't you go backsliding on me."

Thursday, July 7, 9:50 A.M.

ORIN MADE HIMSELF COMFORTABLE IN A THIRD-floor broom closet and waited for the swine to gather at the table he had set, to drink his drool from their water glasses, to spill their secrets into his mikes. The conference room door opened two minutes later, and Orin heard Jack Barthwell say, "No," as if answering a question, not turning down a request.

Then Senator Cotton was saying, "Logistically, this farm can be closed in six weeks, maybe four, if necessary."

"Necessary?" said Barthwell.

"To the common good," said Cotton.

Roger Smith said, "This is a medium-security prison. Shit happens. People get depressed."

"Both of them?" said Tripp. "Give me the odds."

"Cops are always killing themselves," said Smith. "And the ones that do are by and large the ones with nasty secrets."

"Maybe," said Barthwell.

Townsend Tripp coughed. "And then there's that other rather sordid issue."

"Which one is that?" said Barthwell.

"Inmates in love."

"No," said Barthwell.

Tripp said, "Wake up and smell the K-Y."

Barthwell chuckled. "I suppose there's a first time for everything."

"And a last time," said the senator.

"Now," said Tripp, "on to the finances, which look worse by the day, I have to tell you."

Orin smoked a cigarette and listened to Tripp drone on for a while about fixed-cost overruns, excessive dietary expenses, wine lists for visiting dignitaries, good money after bad—all the background noise of political confusion. And what was this fixation with gays, Orin wondered. There was Luther Bailey, alone, as far as Orin knew. Richard Pettibone had been a raging stud. Orin wished he could march into the conference room and throw his shield on the table, start questioning these so-called leaders about their own fucking alibis.

THURSDAY, JULY 7, 10:40 A.M.

PRANK DINOSTRA HAD WASHED THE MORNING gore from his hands and was hard at work on the library computer when his conscience, which he had frequently wrestled but rarely defeated, began to bother him, and his heart beat faster and his palms began to sweat. Because while bouncing around the headquarters' mainframe trying to convert Orin's accrued vacation time to cash, Prank had discovered that Boyd's police salary was off the precinct computer records, but had not been stricken from the total operating budget. Given that Prank was involved in an ongoing criminal conspiracy against Orin Boyd, Prank needed to know where that money went.

Prank punched his best hunch, discovered that an amount identical to Boyd's base salary had been added to the commissioner's special fund on the day Boyd got to the Farm, the day Pettibone died. Prank checked the employee code number, found it was Boyd's reversed. Orin Boyd was still on the payroll.

They knew, he thought. That's what the holdup was on his release. They were letting them dig their own graves. But maybe not. Orin Boyd might, Prank argued to himself, be here to listen for the further confessions of the several men who took seemingly harsh pleas rather too quickly. He might be after Dominick Ril or George Clarke or the judge. Who knew? All of these alternative scenarios made limited sense and in no way affected Prank on a personal level, other than the fact that where once he had been mopping floors and suffering Ira's postgame recaps, he now spent his workdays in a hot and bloody slaughterhouse. What gnawed at him was the suspicion that none of these theories were accurate.

This was about Skip Trimble. Had been from the first. Therefore this was about Prank Dinostra, past, present, and future.

Thursday, July 7, 10:55 a.m.

"I DON'T BELIEVE IT, DOC," SAID WARDEN BARTH-well. "You really think we have another couple?" It was clear the warden was tired of the subject, hoping the doc would back off.

"What goes on in East Meadow?" Orin heard the doc say.

"Forgive me, fellas," said Barthwell, "but the thought of cops swapping spit and bumping dickheads is absurd."

"These men are no longer cops," said the doctor. "Don't forget that. These are men who have been stripped of their psychological and societal armor, reduced to uncivilized prisoners. You should hear them dump their pitiful loads. You'd be driven to vomit, I assure you."

Orin stared at the plaster ceiling, wishing a clearer sense of Skip Trimble would emerge, at least a mold formed by the boundaries Skip had established with others. The victim remained a ghost to Orin, a case file of photographs. Orin also wondered where these assholes were going with this homophobic coffee-klatch. No one was getting raped that he'd heard about, and that was the kind of thing you heard about.

"There are numerous ramifications," said Dr. Robbins. "Psychological, social, legal . . ."

Orin said, "Blah, blah, blah," and switched channels, checked the library, the dormitory pay phone, the conference room, noticed that the television set was off in the guard shack, no one was talking. Maybe that bug was broken, he thought. Or more likely the boys were playing it straight while honored guests were on board. Then a car horn blared at the gate, twice, three times, and a guard said, "Hang on, willya, I'm all alone today."

Orin left the hall closet and hustled over to the dorm to ask George about gate procedures under unusual circumstances. He found the dusty lump that was George asleep under a pinup gallery of the women in his life, women, Orin noticed, whose images had been captured in their prime, not during their brief tour of duty with George, stolen from the albums of their youth. None had actually been taken by George. On the floor next to his bed was a catalogue of Russian brides, with several promising babushkas circled in red crayon. Half a world away, Orin thought, and marked for degradation. George looked old and gray to Orin, his face slack like those of men in intensive care, his nostrils bristling.

Orin was walking back to his own room when he saw Officer Cantwell at the far end of the hallway using a master key to enter Kaminsky's room. Sally Miles and a guard Orin didn't know were crowding out of Genghis Cohen's room on the other side of the hall. Sally saw Orin and motioned him to go back into his room.

Orin closed his door and flew to his window, thinking to wedge his hot-wired Walkman in the mess of ivy above the shutter, noticed just in time the guard posted outside the dorm to observe such maneuvers.

19

THURSDAY, JULY 7, 11:15 A.M.

THE LOCKDOWN HORN BLARED PAINFULLY THREE
times across the wide, terraced fields of the Honor Farm.
Men dropped golf clubs and tennis rackets, dumbbells and
dirty books, and walked directly to their rooms. In accordance with the rules and regulations, they did not talk to
each other, nor did they bunch up; no one so much as ventured a guess as to what might be wrong.

Once in their rooms, they stuck their heads out the windows, neighbors talking to neighbors, passing the word: a
headquarters search team was leaving the mansion, headed
for the dorm. A shakedown of the first magnitude. They
were looking for drugs, booze, knives, objets d'art pilfered
from the mansion, any excuse to bounce the inmates off the
Farm.

George Clarke panicked and threw his smut magazines
out the window, where they were happily collected by Terrence Cantwell.

Dominick Ril honorably burned the nude pictures of his
wife, saved the ones of his girlfriend.

Artie Tobin tossed his last joint out the window and tried to sleep, as he had nothing to worry about and who knew how long this might last.

Long Luther Bailey sat Indian-style on his bed, playing the shark's theme from *Jaws,* until Nick screamed through the walls for Luther to "knock that shit off."

Zen left his room exactly as it always was, stripped bare, and said his prayers, today for a man who had strangled a woman, then raped her, then stumbled into Zen's cross-hairs.

Orin Boyd buried his face in his pillow to regulate his breathing and show them his lazy white-trash ass.

An Officer Marshall knocked politely, opened the door. "Mind if I come in?"

Orin rolled over, rubbed sleep from his eyes, sat up slowly.

"Stand up, please."

Orin complied, and Officer Marshall pulled Orin's pillow off the bed, found nothing underneath.

"What?" said Orin. "Maybe I can help."

THURSDAY, JULY 7, 11:37 A.M.

"GET THE FUCK OUT OF HERE," CRIED ARTIE TO-bin, pulling the sheet off his bed to cover his nakedness. "That's not my Walkman."

Smith held up the expensive listening device. "It's not a Walkman."

"So it's a knockoff. But if I don't own a Walkman, that sure as hell ain't it."

"Cuff him," said Smith. "I'll get to the bottom of this."

"Cuff me?" said Tobin.

"It won't be the first time, now will it?"

Officer Marshall ripped the bedsheet from a stunned Artie Tobin, other guards slapped the handcuffs on, led him from his room, down the hall, Tobin going limp, dragging his bare feet, screaming, "Nick, help . . . Nick . . ."

THURSDAY, JULY 7, 1:50 P.M.

SEVEN GIORDANO MINIMIKES WERE LINED UP like peas on Barthwell's desk blotter, next to his weight-training calendar. Each bug was labeled according to where the search team had found it: Under Command Post Water Cooler, Captain Smith's Curtain Rod, Under Doc Robbins's Couch, The Library, The Conference Room, The Trailer, The Dormitory Pay Phone. The bogus Walkman—labeled "Tobin's Room"—lay next to the bugs.

"It's gotta be the senator," said Barthwell. "Using Artie, through Nick, to find what they need to close the Farm. You suck up to them, Rog. Tell me what you've heard."

"I swear I don't know anything. I love this Farm. I love working for you."

Barthwell fought the impulse to sneer. He walked to his window and said over his shoulder, "You may get my job, Rog, but you won't have it long."

"Stop," said Roger. "How can you say that?"

"Who, then? Because I don't think fucking Artie Tobin knows. Or he'd'a' told us when they were dragging him into the van."

"Maybe he was on a Need-to-Know basis for somebody," said Roger. "Maybe only Nick—"

"You see what I mean, Rog? Artie Tobin don't beat off, Nick Morelli don't know about it. And Tommy Cotton and Nick are gumbas from way back. Now Tommy Cotton wants to close the Farm. Tommy Cotton wants an issue. Nick bugs the joint anytime he fucking pleases," said Barthwell.

Roger slumped in a Queen Anne chair and exhaled loudly. "No," he said. "This isn't happening."

Thursday, July 7, 4:29 p.m.

AS SOON AS THE LOCKDOWN ENDED, THE PRISONERS congregated outside Art Tobin's empty room like Christians at the Tomb.

"What'd he do?" asked Ira.

No one knew.

"Where'd they take him?" asked George.

"East Meadow, I'll bet," said Luther.

"Don't say that," said Nick, grabbing the pay phone.

"East Meadow," said Zen. "Sounds so pastoral . . . Not."

Everybody thought about the real county jail for a moment, the dark tiers, and darker gangs, the ever-present noise and violence, and then everybody looked at Nick. Because if Artie had a problem, Nick probably had a problem, too.

"What?" Nick said as he waited for his call to go through. "What are you hard-ons looking at?"

"What'd they find in his room, Nick?" asked Orin. "A bag of smoke?"

"Get your minds out of the fucking gutter."

"If you say so," said Luther.

Zen patted Nick on the back. "Bummer, dude," he said.

Orin stage-whispered to the others, "I got dibs on Nick's room, you know, if . . ."

"Hey, fuck you, Boyd."

Nick slammed down the phone and paced the dormitory hall from end to end, flexing his fists, shaking his head.

"Call the guardhouse," Dom Ril suggested. He was leaning against the wall near his door, ready to slip inside if things turned ugly. "Those dumb shits'll be more than happy to tell you."

"East Meadow," the guard said a moment later. "General population. Big crackdown the Rog is running."

"Why?" croaked Nick.

"We were kinda hoping you would know."

Nick hung up and stomped for the door. "Sissyboy," he screamed. "You fucking trouser snake!"

Dominick Ril and George Clarke tried to restrain Nick, asking him what was wrong, but Nick broke free and swaggered through the front doors and out onto the brown lawn, followed closely by the inmate posse in their underwear and robes, everyone pleading with him to go to his room and lock the door, don't make things worse.

Then everyone stopped short when they saw Oliver Bridges holding a pump-action shotgun. "Freeze!"

Nick sized up Bridges, started again for the house.

"In a heartbeat, motherfucker," Bridges said coolly, drawing a bead on Nick's head.

"You're next," said Nick softly.

Orin had by then heard quite enough, and he tackled Nick hard from behind, worked a serviceable half nelson under Nick's thick hairy arm and pinned him to the grass. Nick was a wriggling firehose of threats until Roger Smith and his backup materialized over Orin's shoulder. "Bridges," said Smith, "you cuff that son of a bitch."

Gramps McKay pointed a finger at Officer Bridges and said, "Get out of here with that gun before someone gets hurt. And, Roger, take a walk . . . Let him roar, for God's sake."

Nick kept squirming, until he and Orin were face to face, Nick swearing on his children he'd get even, Orin saying it was for his own good, nothing done was permanent.

More backup arrived. Three command post guards cuffed Nick and pulled him to his feet, dragged him toward the mansion.

Roger Smith ordered everyone back to their rooms, yelling, "You haven't heard the last of this . . . this uprising."

"Uprising, my ass," Gramps said. "You'll never learn, will you. You were a fuckup when you got here, and you'll be a fuckup when you leave. All I can say is, thank God you never passed the police exam."

Roger Smith turned red in the face, and he began shouting and shoving and following Gramps back into the dorm, into his room, slamming the door behind them. "Don't you ever challenge my authority!" he screamed. "You'll wind up in solitary with Nick."

"Then it won't be solitary, will it?"

"You insolent old bastard," cried Smith, launching anew into his canned speech about cops gone bad, permissive society, and lenient pantywaist judges.

Gramps sat down on his bed and tried to take it stoically, hoping all the excitement would die down and they could finally get back to farming, saying, "You're absolutely right, Cap. I was out of line. Won't happen again."

Roger Smith crowded the old man, towered over him. "You're out of here tomorrow, McKay. Fuck the rummy priest."

"I said I was sorry. Now, please, Roger, leave me alone. I don't feel so good."

"Leave you alone? Are you giving me orders?"

Gramps coughed, and his breathing grew labored. He waved Smith away. "Do what you want. I gotta lie down."

What Roger Smith wanted to do was keep bitching at a weakling, and he did so, pouring venom over Gramps in buckets, telling him what he really wanted to tell all the others. Gramps's wrinkled face grew paler, sweaty, and he keeled over sideways on the bed and closed his eyes.

"Wake up, you fucking phony. Listen to me."

"Heart," Gramps croaked, hugging himself.

Roger Smith stared down at the strangling old man, finally comprehending the situation. "What should I do?"

"Get help, you fucking idiot. . . ."

Roger Smith ran out into the hall and yelled for a guard to bring oxygen. Some of the inmates heard him, opened their doors against orders. "Get back in your rooms," cried Smith.

"What's the matter now?" asked Orin.

"None of your damn business."

Then Orin looked at Roger Smith in such a way as to produce the spontaneous admission: "Gramps is sick. I called for help."

Orin and Zen rushed past the captain and into the room, saw Gramps on his side on the bed, going pale as the bricks. Without a word they pulled him to the floor. Zen tilted back his head, pulled out Gramps's teeth, covered his mouth with his own, and blew hard, filled the aged lungs with air. Orin compressed the birdlike chest, started the count.

Roger Smith stayed where he was near the door, watching like a paralyzed civilian. Zen and Orin caught a rhythm, kept Gramps warm and filled with air, all the time knowing they were delaying the inevitable, propping up a corpse.

Sixteen minutes later the ambulance arrived, and the medical technicians stabbed him with needles and slapped on the paddles, cranked up the juice, flopped poor Gramps around like a fish until they were sure he had nothing left.

"He's gone," said the tech, patting Zen on the back.

"Ah, no," said Zen, leaning back on his haunches. "Not Gramps."

"Not your fault," said the tech. "You kept him pink. He had every chance to live."

Orin stared up at Roger Smith, willing Smith to look him in the eye.

"I'll get the warden," said Smith.

"And a priest," said Zen.

"And tell Barthwell you killed him," said Orin.

Roger Smith said, "*Excuse* me?"

"Tell him right up front that first you bullied a sick old man, then you panicked, that your fucking incompetence killed him. That way it won't look so bad when we call the district attorney."

Smith looked to Zen for mercy, Zen who was still cradling Gramps's toothless, hairless head in his lap.

"Don't look at me," said Zen. "You fucking killed my friend."

Smith blanched. "You can't say that."

"Everyone's gonna say it." Then Zen turned Gramps's lifeless face toward Smith and pulled open the slack lower jaw, worked it like a puppet's. "You killed me, Sissyboy," Zen mimicked. "You killed me."

20

THREE MEN IN THREE WEEKS, ORIN THOUGHT.

The Honor Farm would be a ghost town by Labor Day.

He was rummaging through Gramps's belongings as soon as the body was rolled away and Captain Roger Smith left the scene unsecured, much as he had the morning Skip Trimble had died. Orin had already found sealed letters to children and grandchildren to be mailed upon his death. A current *Farmer's Almanac*. A family bible. A *New York Times* article about a bum he had blown away. The Medal of Valor and his wedding ring, together in a cheap wooden case. He was filling his pocket with cigars when he heard someone chuckle.

"Didn't take you long," said Prank. "Did it?"

"Long to what?" said Orin.

Prank was leaning in the doorway, smirking at him. "Jump in his grave that fast, brother?"

"Did I miss something? Are we supposed to be friends?"

"At least the rest of us are honest-to-God criminals. You're still on the fucking job."

Orin pulled him by the shirt into Gramps's room and closed the door, searching for an escape clause, a cover-scam. Then suddenly Orin was thinking that if he rode with the flow, he could be home by nightfall, that tomorrow could be the first day of his retirement from a job he had held too long and regarded too little. Or he could strangle Prank Dinostra and toss him out the window. No doubt Detective Kruger would quickly prove he had jumped.

But then Orin might never know who sunk his boat or hacked up his finances. Tough call.

"You're here to find out who killed Skip," Prank declared. "And I want to help."

Orin let him go. "Why?"

"To set things straight with his old man."

Orin looked at Prank closely, took his time lighting a cigarette, said finally, "Fuck me."

"You can't bullshit a bullshitter, Boyd. You only fooled me at first because you seem like you belong here."

"You hurt the boss real bad," said Orin.

"I hurt everybody real bad."

"You hurt me or my people, I'll kill you," said Orin.

"I knew that when I came in here."

Orin closed his eyes and rubbed his face, wondering if the mission was blown, or enhanced, factoring in the high probability that it was Prank Dinostra, known turncoat, who had siphoned his funds and ruined his wife's career.

Prank said, "It was murder from the beginning, man. The only one suicidal on this fucking Farm is me."

"Who?" said Orin.

"The judge and Skip were really weird about each other. Like they had too much history. And if there was one guy on this Farm Skip couldn't stand, it was George fucking Clarke."

"Oh, really?"

Prank smiled warmly. "There's so much you don't know."

Orin and Prank straightened Gramps's room, then made their way up the back stairs to the library, Orin watching the older man's back, remembering a local guide in the central highlands who had led Orin's squad into an ambush, how cold it had been that day, how quiet and lonely it got when the others finally died, how long it took choppers to find him.

Prank spent the next hour giving Orin an overview of what could be done with a terminal, and Orin suddenly felt sorry for crooks still working with guns and knives. With fewer than twelve keystrokes Prank showed Orin how he had figured him out. "They didn't do you no favors," he told Orin. "If I had killed Skippy, you'd be dead now."

"Amateurs, right?"

"They never mean any harm, if it's any consolation."

"Can we get a look at prison records? Personnel records? Telephone logs? Schedules?"

"Your wish is my command."

"Check the phone logs for the day I got here. Outgoing calls between five-thirty and nine P.M. See what kind of activity my arrival caused."

Prank determined that there had been only one outgoing call. Someone had telephoned Dr. Robbins at his home at seven o'clock. They had used the phone in the mansion conference room. The conversation had lasted twelve minutes.

"Check payroll, see if he put in for overtime."

"Why?"

"Don't annoy me, Prank. Just do it."

"Doc Homo's not on the county payroll as an hourly employee."

"He's not doing this for charity."

"He bills each case separately."

Orin's eyebrows rose. "Like an office visit, like we're private patients?"

"I think so."

"Can you check that?"

Prank typed and cursed for a good five minutes, long enough for him to have unlocked Moscow's launch codes. "Nothing for that day," he said at last.

"Tell me about Skip," Orin said. "What was he like?"

"Aloof, smart, maybe a little light in the loafers, compared to the other he-men inmates."

"Seriously? Gay?"

Prank shrugged.

"He took his conjugals for show?"

"He wouldn't be the first that way in here. See Luther."

Orin blinked and shook his head. "Does his father know?"

"Not a chance."

"Maybe you better let me see the famous diary," said Orin.

"Trimble told you, eh? He make me a suspect, too?"

"Absolutely."

Prank stroked a key. "You make up your own mind."

Skip Trimble hung himself in the dorm this morning. At least that's what they're saying. I didn't see the body and I didn't know it had happened until a couple of hours later, at which point I went right to my room and threw up. I had been in the library, asleep at my desk. Luther Bailey told me what actually happened. He was all shook up himself, having found the body. All I could think of was his father, how this would tear his heart out, and I wondered at the size of Skip's anger. That's when my bullshit detector started ringing long and loud. I mean, Skip sometimes acted like a spoiled brat, but he was tough as nails inside. And he was no quitter. His father's seen to that. So now I think maybe somebody killed him, or had him killed, because of his father. Because Skip was not depressed. He was getting happier as the end of his sentence approached. He was even talking about going to medical school. Then I heard they set the time of death as ten o'clock, and everybody had alibis, of course. George was shoveling shit with Luther. Judge Kane was in the kitchen, making lunch. Ril was on Homo's couch. Nick was with Artie in their office. They saw Ira. Dick Pettibone saw Artie. Artie saw Pettibone. Hutchinson and Sutherland were in the infirmary with gastroenteritis. Gramps had a visitor. Comstock and Kelly were mowing the lawn. Field crews were accounted for. Bakers in bed. Who knows what the fucking guards were up to. I tried to call the commissioner, to tell him of my suspicions. Hit the old brick wall. Maybe he figured I would gloat, say something horrible. Can't say as I blame him.

Orin spun away from the screen and faced Prank. "Still think it was murder?"

"Cops kill themselves," said Prank. "Gays kill themselves. Add it together and boom. Maybe he couldn't go back in the closet. Maybe it's a fucking miracle he lasted as long as he did."

Orin put his hands on Prank's shoulders and addressed him as if he were an idiot. "Picture me, won't you, walking into Dave Trimble's office and telling him that."

Prank smiled. "Okay, so I figure you gotta suspect the outright scumbags first: George Clarke, no offense. Dom Ril. Morelli and Tobin, although what they had to gripe about is beyond me, either with the boss or with Skip. Like I said, Judge Kane is intriguing."

"What about Luther Bailey?"

"They were close friends. But Luther's a gentle son of a bitch, you come right down to it."

"What about Dick Pettibone? Any chance he did Skip, then offed himself out of guilt?"

"Not the Dickie I knew."

"What about Zen?"

Prank sat back and shrugged, as if to suggest that Zen was unknowable. Everybody liked Zen. Everybody feared him, too.

Orin said, "He's been freaky lately, don't you think?"

"Everybody's locking their doors lately."

"What's your story?" said Orin. "How'd you crash and burn?"

Prank smiled sadly. "You've heard the official details."

"I'd rather hear the truth."

Prank gave Orin the short version. Two big heads, one on

his neck, one in his pants. "It catches up with a man. Drunk and out-of-town counts."

"Tell me about it."

"Really, the one I miss is my oldest, Brenda. A real pisser, that kid." Prank chuckled warmly. "One time in high school she switched Krazy Glue for Visine, coming home from a concert. The doctors had to use solvents to get her eyelids open. Bren got mad at me for suggesting the Jaws of Life." Prank handed Orin a snapshot from his shirt pocket. "That's just a couple of months later."

"You can hardly tell."

"My son's a sergeant on the Suffolk job. I embarrass him to death."

Prank's life was ruined, and he knew it. He might make amends, but he could never even the score.

Orin asked, "Same guy kill them both?"

Prank grimaced, jerked back to the present. "Maybe."

"You think one of your pals is this bad or this smart?"

"Maybe," Prank repeated.

Orin walked to the window, gazed across the Sound to America, realized he felt the gap, realized that they were missing dinner in the mansion. A chartered fishing boat was chumming for late blues off the jetty, and a wave of homesickness rolled over Orin as his duty stared him straight in the face. "I want to send some urgent, confidential E-mail to the boss."

"No sweat." Prank set his able fingers over the keyboard.

Orin dictated, "Forgive me for not writing more often. Malevolent forces are at work here, in friends and enemies. I sometimes wonder if it's coming from me. Incidentally, I need a face-to-face with the widow tonight."

Prank stopped typing. "You can do that?"

"Oh, yeah."

Prank chuckled softly. "He'll love that 'incidentally' shit."

"Keeps him on his toes."

"That's it?" said Prank.

"We don't have time to make it shorter."

21

THE POLICE COMMISSIONER AND HIS WIDOWED
daughter-in-law made slow progress down the rocky path
in the dark. Orin had been waiting by the outer fence for the
better part of an hour when he heard the scuff of their feet
on the trail. "Over here."

"Sorry we're late," said Trimble as they approached the
chain-link fence.

Orin stepped closer to the fence, to let her see him.

"I heard about Wild Bill," said Trimble, his voice low
and tremulous. "I walked a footpost with Bill McKay, in
Roosevelt, back in sixty-three," said Trimble.

"You talk to Barthwell, about Pettibone?"

"He said Dick never ratted on anybody here, maybe
'cause nobody told him nothing."

"Too bad, 'cause they found the bugs," said Orin. "With
a sweep team, like they knew all about them. They found
your Walkman under Artie Tobin's pillow."

"How'd they know to look?" asked Trimble.

"I was hoping you could find that out. And make sure that

181

Tobin doesn't get hurt over there. He's a clown, but he doesn't deserve to die. And thanks for bringing Maureen to see me, boss. We won't be long, I promise."

Dave Trimble didn't get it at first, that his underling was dismissing him, expecting him to leave that underling alone in the midnight woods with Maureen.

"I want to talk to her alone, if you don't mind."

"I damn well do mind. What's the point?"

"The point is that while I'm working for you, I'm taking hits. My credit's been savaged, my wife got fired—"

"Temporary damage, all easily repaired, once the case is closed. Or would you like me to chance blowing your cover."

"It's okay, Dad," she said. "I'm okay."

Dave Trimble sputtered and blustered, but when he saw that Orin wasn't talking until he left, he turned angrily on his heel and climbed back up through the trees. Maureen Trimble watched until her father-in-law was well out of sight before she turned to face Orin.

"Thank you," said Orin. "He's used to getting his way."

"You don't know the half of it."

Orin suspected that he might. Dave Trimble was not an overly popular commissioner among the rank and file. His officers were pieces in a chess game, moved wherever the Job damn well wanted them. Disgruntled cops who had never met him hated his guts. Orin remembered Belmont cops who brought their own garbage to work and dumped it on the streets.

"Do *you* think someone killed your husband?" said Orin. "Or are we humoring the old man?"

"He's jerking you off, pardon my French. You're just another futile gesture."

Orin grunted. "You and Skip thinking of getting back together, when he got out?"

"We were filing for divorce. Amicably, I might add."

"Really."

"Look, whatever-your-real-name-is, Skip and I were friends who made a terrible mistake. We were gonna undo that mistake and stay friends."

"Why?" asked Orin.

She lowered her eyes and rubbed her knuckles together. "You sound like my shrink."

"You should see *our* depressing son of a bitch."

"Homo, right? Skip hated him."

"Hated?"

"Hated."

"Tell me about the night he got locked up."

She'd made plans, she said, tried to seduce him in a skimpy outfit at the Garden City Hotel. They drank heavily at the bar, then fought. A bouncer intervened. A security guard. Skip whacked the bouncer on the head with an ashtray. Damn near killed him.

"But you loved him?"

"I was flat on my ass when I met Skip. He pulled my face off the mirror, damn near made me a respectable person." Tears rolled down her face, and she curled up into herself and shuddered. Her fingers clawed the fence. Orin wanted suddenly to hold her, more for his comfort than hers. "Why do you think Skip had all these problems?"

She wiped her face on the sleeve of her coat, leaned close enough to the fence that he could smell old cigarettes on her breath. She was thinking and then she was shrugging, unsure. Orin liked this girl, could understand Skip's attraction to her.

"Was Skip gay?" he asked straight out.

She barely hesitated. "Neutered, like. Asexual."

"You seeing anyone now?" asked Orin.

She shook her head.

"Go on up," said Orin. "Tell Dave I gotta talk to him."

The commissioner returned in an avalanche of rocks and leaves.

"She's not all one would have hoped for, I know," said Trimble, "but—"

"Prank busted me, through headquarters' records. That's how I knew to do the E-mail."

"Damn it."

"So now he's helping me. Okay?"

Trimble frowned. "Bad move, Boyd. Let me yank him."

"He wants to pay you back for what he did."

"He wants to twist the knife."

Orin said, "Look, boss, straight out, before this goes any further, any chance Skip was bisexual? I'm hearing—"

Orin might as well have reached through the fence and slapped the old man's face. Trimble lowered his head and said, "Please, don't let them do that to my son. Not until you find me one man who will swear he was . . . involved with Skip."

"You originally accepted the suicide verdict. What made you change your mind?"

"I remembered how much Skip loved life."

"Okay, I'll keep on it. And here," Orin said as he threw the canvas boccie-ball sack over the fence. "Do hair, fibers, spit, blood, semen, the whole nine yards. Suck her dry."

"Why?"

"Just a hunch. And then go home," Orin told him. "Spend some time with your wife."

"Amanda is leaving me. She thinks I blame her."

And she's not the only one, thought Orin, as Trimble leaned his face on the fence. The links cut a Manson-Family cross in his forehead, and Orin remembered seeing similar distance and grief in soldiers who had lost their comrades.

"I'll tell you something, Orin. If Skip did it to kill me, it worked."

Friday, July 8, 9:34 A.M.

ORIN WAS REPLACING DR. ROBBINS'S APPOINT-ment book in his top drawer when the office door opened unexpectedly. Doc Robbins, who was reading his mail, looked up, seemed startled to see Boyd, as if his office miraculously cleaned itself every night.

"Yo, Doc. You look like you just seen a ghost."

The doctor scrunched up his forehead and patted the

pockets of his lab coat absentmindedly. "I thought I left my door locked."

Orin held up the monstrous key ring Ira had entrusted to him. "Housekeeping: we're everywhere and yet we're nowhere. Part of the magic. Know what I mean?"

"Yes, yes, should have known that, I suppose."

"Well, you've got more important things than me on your mind."

Robbins put his mail on his cluttered desk. "Yes, yes. Actually, I do. Shouldn't you be done?"

Orin assumed the pose of penitent confessor. "I am running late this morning. Please don't tell Captain Smith."

"Let me ask you a question, Boyd. What is it with you and Captain Smith?"

"Ancient history. He remembers it better than me."

"Like it was yesterday," said Robbins. "He says as boys you stole his lunch money, that he could not pass you in the hall without his schoolbooks going flying."

Orin sat down on the worn leather couch, leaned his broom against the file cabinet. "Did he mention that he always sat in the front row, kissing ass. That he loved to tell on the other kids. That he picked his nose and ate it."

"He says you and your mates made him eat grotesque combinations of leftover food in the cafeteria. He still can't look at tapioca without gagging. And what exactly is a 'psychological sit-up'?"

Orin shrugged.

"You don't look good, you know that?" said Robbins.

"I really never did," said Orin. "Not on my best days."

"I mean that I see obvious strain in your face this morning, worry lines. You're losing weight."

Orin said, "Maybe you're right, Doc. Maybe this place is wearing me down." He went on at length to explain his view of the Honor Farm as a vortex of disintegration, where an accelerating rate of decay was at work, that he had noticed recently erected buildings were crumbling at a faster rate than the original construction, young cons falling faster than the old ones.

"How was your visit with your wife?"

"We fought."

"So you got your wish, not to be intimate with her."

"Actually, I was ready to jump her bones. But she started running down all of her bullshit problems, finally accused me of having fun here, enjoying my time away from home. That kind of spoiled the mood."

"I imagine it did."

Robbins was looking at him funny, as if he knew Orin had just discovered a stack of fraudulent billings Prank couldn't find in the hard drive, a stack generated by one Dr. Marvin Robbins—the very man who wanted to hypnotize him, and maybe ask him questions that should have been none of his business.

"Is she right?" said Robbins. "Are you really enjoying your time in prison? Because that would indicate to me—"

"I'm not crazy, Doc. I'd still rather be free."

"There is no one here to judge you. No one you respect."

"I miss my daughter," said Orin.

"And your father."

"Drop it, okay, Doc? Too late to fix that flat." Orin stood up from the couch and picked up his cleaning tools.

"I'd still like to talk some more about hypnosis."

"What if you break me of habits I like? What if I can't jerk off anymore? Or I shit my pants when a telephone rings?"

FRIDAY, JULY 8, 10:45 A.M.

NICK MORELLI SAT ON THE EDGE OF THE COT IN his basement cell, trying unsuccessfully to contain his rage and convince Doc Robbins that it was safe to release him.

"Roger Smith doesn't think so," said Doc Robbins. "Roger Smith thinks you might need a transfer. Said you went way across the line yesterday."

"This is crazy," said Nick. "Get me a goddamn telephone."

"Come on, Nick, learn from this."

"What?"

"You feel scared. You feel powerless. You want to strike back. That's what you do to people. That's why they hate you."

Nick coughed and spit in his toilet, glared at Doc Robbins through the bars. His breathing grew loud and labored. "See," said Nick, "I'm calm. Peaceful. Contrite."

"Tell me what Art Tobin had in his room."

"I don't know, goddamnit."

Doc Robbins said, "Then I don't blame you for being concerned."

"What's going on here, Doc? Things used to be so simple."

"I wish I knew."

Friday, July 8, 1:00 P.M.

ORIN PEERED THROUGH THE WINDOW INTO THE chapel, saw Luther Bailey sitting on a stool near the head of the open pine coffin, sketching his old friend's face in death. The M.E. had signed the death certificate, listing the cause as cardiac arrest, sparing the county the cost of investigating the circumstances and an unnecessary autopsy in the case of a witnessed attack. Assistants had prepared the body for interment.

Dave Trimble and Monsignor O'Rourke had arranged for his burial on site, the last place on earth he'd loved.

Barthwell had left the intimate details to Marion Withers after telling her to do whatever she thought was right. Marion had asked Luther to cut Gramps's hair, to drape the chapel windows in purple and black. He had finished his tasks.

Luther did not look up right away when Orin walked in, nor did he seem surprised to see him when he did.

"Nice man," said Orin, nodding at the corpse.

"He grew on you," said Luther, straightening his calf-length, multicolored robes. "Anyway, he grew on me."

Orin walked close to the coffin and looked down on Gramps's sun-damaged face, saw where the lip stitches were already pulling out, good enough for government work.

"What's with the back-to-Africa gig, Luther? I mean, I'm Scotch-Irish, and I don't run around in a kilt."

"Career move," said Luther. "Keeps me in transportation. Working the fields, I'd slap on my do-rag and Joseph robes and stay close by the fence so what they call area residents headed for their yachts could see me good. Some of them seemed to like it, pointing me out to their guests. Then a bunch of liberal bluebloods said it looked like they were filming *Roots* over at Soundview and couldn't more dignified work be found for black inmates, preferably inside? The rest is prison history."

"I like your style."

"You don't know my style."

"Okay."

"I'm what you call a failed role model—hired to fill two categories, suddenly filled three. I mean, I used to give talks at high schools, till they found out I liked men. Sure am glad I answered their recruitment ad."

Out of place on the Farm by way of scale and race and sensibility, Luther was the ultimate outsider, the suspect no one suspected. "You don't socialize much, do you, Luther?"

"In case you haven't noticed, I'm the only homey here."

"Noticed it first thing, now that you mention it. Said to myself, 'Check out the only homey. Wonder what he did.'"

Luther grinned, put aside his sketch pad, said, "Forgery, in the second degree. Among other things."

Orin knew that, just as he knew that Luther gave a decent prison haircut, that he sometimes sketched portraits of the inmates and their visitors for side money, usually adding a suggestion of caricature. Orin had seen a portrait of Nick Morelli that made him look like Napoleon. Ira with big muscles. And the commissioner had shown him one of Skip, in tennis whites. Luther's work-in-progress, his current sketch of Gramps, showed the well-lined face at peace, perhaps in tune with greater mysteries.

"Ever draw for the job?" asked Orin.

"You must be high."

"Ever draw Skip?"

"Man, what the fuck do you care?"

"Just curious."

"You forget, you ain't the man no more. But it's funny, actually," Luther said. "You're the first one to ask me about Skip. Kruger wanted to know why I brushed my teeth so late that morning, had difficulty understanding that after I play my clarinet, my mouth tastes like shit. But no questions about anything important."

"Should they have interviewed you about other things?"

"You should always ask the little people, you want to know what's going on."

Orin took a breath. "Okay. Did you and Skip ever . . ."

Luther fixed Orin with an icy glare. "I never have sex with anyone, Boyd. That's how I stay alive."

"Was he getting it on with someone else?"

"Not that he ever told me."

Orin nodded. "So what would you have told them?"

"What they didn't want to hear. That Skip's real life was his prison. That in many respects he was better off dead."

"You mean that?"

"Ask his father."

"Next time he visits me."

Luther threw back his head and chuckled long and loud, offered his huge palm for Orin to slap.

Orin asked, "Ever draw Pettibone?"

Luther patted his sketch case. "I got him in here somewhere. I'll get you, too, when you least expect it."

"Can I see it? I've been having nightmares," said Orin, "being I was the last one to talk to him. I can't really explain it."

"Nightmares are a common occurrence around here," said Luther as he opened his sketch case, then bent forward and flipped through several sketches. "Here."

The sketch was done in charcoal, a side view of Richard

Pettibone kneeling beside a visitor's table, holding the hands of a woman in a wheelchair.

"You're good," said Orin. "The poor son of a bitch looks truly trapped. That's his wife?"

"The woman he climbed the tree to see."

FRIDAY, JULY 8, 6:30 P.M.

THE BURIAL DETAIL ROGER SMITH COMMANDED had just finished laying the coffin containing Gramps to rest in the Kreeling family cemetery, next to Skip Trimble's still-fresh grave.

Monsignor O'Rourke had said his piece and then walked away with the few children and grandchildren. The rest of the inmates had taken turns tossing earth and flowers into the grave, staring out at the Sound, some in genuine pain. They were getting ready to head back down the hill to dinner, and Orin just thought there ought to be something more, so he clapped his hands together and said so, loudly: "How about you whip out that sidearm of yours and blow off a couple of rounds, Rog. The man was a fucking hero."

"What are you talking about, Boyd?" said Captain Smith. "Get back in line and keep your mouth shut."

"This ain't no fucking bum we're burying here. You guys got that?"

"What do you mean?" said Smith. "We all know that."

Orin pulled a piece of paper from his pocket and began to read aloud. "In 1963 Patrolman William McKay saved two children from the third floor of a burning apartment building. In sixty-seven he killed a bank robber. He got shot himself in seventy-four. Pulled a drowning drunk out of a canal in seventy-nine." Orin looked up at Smith. "I could go on, you know what I'm saying? Do him the honor."

"I can't start blowing off rounds in the middle of Sands Point. What goes up, comes down, remember?"

"And everything that rises," said Zen, "must converge."

Orin began to read again. "In 1983 William McKay suffered a minor heart attack while administering CPR to—"

Smith went chest to chest with Orin, said, "Drop it, now."

Orin looked up from his notes and wrinkled his nose. "Excuse me, Cap, but what the fuck are you wearing?"

Smith took one step backward. "Skin-So-Soft. Why?"

"No . . . Really?"

"As an insect repellent."

"Cut it out and quit kidding."

Captain Smith faced the men. "Detail, dismissed."

Orin turned to George and mumbled something.

"What did you say?" Smith asked.

Dominick Ril waved his hand above his head like a kindergarten snitch. "He called you a perfumed pussy, sir. He said all the wrong people are dying here."

22

THEY REMAINED IN THEIR CELLS WITHOUT
speaking for the better part of an hour, Nick occasionally
glaring through the empty cell between them, Orin lying on
his hard cot, staring at the ceiling, ignoring the psychic
heat. He had cleaned these cells just the other day, never
imagining he might soon be a guest, a lack of foresight for
which he was presently scolding himself. Ira Cohen had the
keys on his master ring. It would have been a small matter
to make dupes.

"You don't know," Nick said finally, "how fucking pissed—"

Orin lifted his head from the wafer-thin pillow. "I was
trying to help, you dopey fuck."

"Maybe," said Nick, shaking his head. "But friend or not,
you get in my way, I mow you down. It's one of my little
quirks."

"One of them?"

"Don't be a fucking wise guy, Boyd. I'm not impressed
with who or what you are."

"Never said you should be. God knows I'm not."

Nick grunted, apparently convinced he had recovered whatever face had been lost on the lawn outside the mansion, a situation where he had been outnumbered, outgunned.

Orin stared up through the bars of his window, past the bottom branches of the yew outside, whistling "Dixie." What he could see of the sky was turning red.

"So what'd you do?" asked Nick.

"Nothing as bad as what you did."

Nick grinned and rolled his finger in a gesture that meant give it up, cut to the chase.

A conspirator's smile creased Orin's face. "Misbehaved at the funeral, basically called Rog a homo."

"In front of the men?"

"Why do it anywhere else?"

Nick rolled his eyes up and frowned, to indicate complicated computations. "Figure they'll try for a week. The Rog is kinda insecure about that stuff."

"I'm past caring, tell you the truth. I'd be better off in East Meadow."

"Now you're really talking crazy." Nick stood up and wrapped his hairy fingers around the bars, yanked hard, to no avail.

"So what happened?" asked Orin. "They find Artie's weed?"

Morelli rested his chin on his shoulder. "That can't be it. They knew all along he had a patch."

"So then what? You know everything that happens here."

Morelli shook his head. "This one, I'm in the dark."

"What were you guys doing the morning Skip died? Maybe it's something like that."

"Jesus Christ, will you drop that shit!"

"Why? What else do I have to do in here? Humor me."

"Okay, are you listening, Boyd? I was taking a shit at the very moment Skip died—a fucking swinger, I'm telling you, a breakfast log I wish I'd photographed. I was listening to Artie making nooky on a nine-hundred number, right outside the bathroom door, and Kruger's got the phone records to prove it."

"And the night Dick drowned?"

"It ain't about those two twisted hard-ons."

"Then we got nothing to worry about."

"Fine," said Nick.

Orin counted to ten, then said, "You think you can fix things for Artie? I mean, East Meadow, man."

Nick never moved. "Right now I'm worried about my-ownself, Boyd, and you should be too."

"What's that mean, Nicky?"

"It means, something about you rubs people wrong. Take it for what it's worth."

A metal door at the end of the hallway opened. Flashlight beams danced on the checkerboard linoleum tiles of the basement floor. Officer Bridges and Warden Barthwell walked toward the row of cells, jangling keys. "Boyd," said Barthwell. "On your feet."

"What about me?" said Nick, his swarthy face pressed against the bars. "I'm sorry, okay, but Roger Smith's a flaming asshole. What would you have done?"

"Maybe tomorrow, Nick," said Barthwell. "Once I get some answers."

"Bring me a phone, goddamn it, I'll get you the answers. You guys got me buried alive."

"Night, Nick," said the warden.

Orin stepped through his open cell door, then lagged back and leaned toward Nick. "Who?" he whispered. "Who can help?"

Nick shook his head and said, "Wheels are spinning for me I don't even know about yet. I'll catch you at break-fast."

"Your call."

Saturday, July 9, 1:55 A.M.

ZEN MASTERS COULDN'T SLEEP AGAIN THAT night, and it wasn't Gramps's dying or the moon or the tides or the ghost he sometimes dreamed about. He was on his knees by the side of his bed, thinking the Worthy Twins were a tough fucking sell. God might have made them, but he sure had to have hated them, at least in life, anytime after their thirteenth birthday. Zen whacked them a month before their seventeenth birthday as they were climbing down a Hempstead fire escape, but not before they had robbed and murdered helpless booth attendants at four central Nassau County gas stations. Jorel and Kalel, their mother had named them, right on their birth certificates. From the crack planet Krypton.

Zen, who had buried them with lead, could still close his eyes and see them fail to fly in Earth's poisonous atmosphere, tumbling over the railing. Once again they were crowding his sleep, confusing the business at hand.

He must not look back. He must look forward. Ready for enemies to pop up like targets at the pistol range. There was no such thing as paranoia, not now, not here.

Zen got off his knees and climbed into bed and lay there sweating and wondering if he had a pretty good idea who was next.

SATURDAY, JULY 9, 7:30 A.M.

"BEFORE YOU LOSERS EAT YOUR BREAKFASTS IN comparative luxury," said Captain Smith, "I want you all to know exactly what happened Thursday, and what will happen any other day we discover a serious breech in rules. The wrongdoer will be apprehended and punished severely. Understand? One strike and you're out."

"What did Tobin do?" asked George.

"That's none of your business."

"I thought you said you'd tell us exactly what happened."

"I never said any such thing."

"When's Nick getting out?" asked Ril. "I'm gonna be awful shorthanded in the office until—"

"When I'm good and fucking ready."

Captain Smith spun on his heel and stalked out on men who clearly felt worse about what had happened to Art Tobin than about the fate of Richard Pettibone or Gramps McKay or Skip Trimble, because they could see themselves locked up in East Meadow and they could not see themselves dead.

Orin didn't have that problem. He sat near a window and picked at his bacon omelette, thinking maybe it was time to bail out and go home. Maybe it was time for Commissioner Trimble to come down off his hill, to say good-bye to his son and move on. Orin felt a nudge at his elbow.

"You're looking green around the gills," said Zen.

"I hate to see cops in trouble."

"We're not cops anymore. And we can lose what we got going here. All of us."

"I'm hip."

"And things can always get worse."

"You like it here, too, don't you?" said Orin.

Zen put down his fork. "Gotta admit, sometimes I feel like I own the place."

Orin wiped up the last of his eggs with his toast. "Has anyone ever gotten out of here, if only for a while?"

Zen stared hard at him, penetrating, not threatening.

Orin said, "Come on man, you hear things."

"Last St. Patty's Day, Tobin was drunk and bragging about him and Nick stepping out and marching in the fucking parade. I didn't pay him any mind." Zen glanced at the kitchen doorway. "Of course, you could ask the man in the robe. He gets in on all the goodies."

"Because I could use a night out," said Orin.

"Be the worst thing for you. Put it out of your mind."

SATURDAY, JULY 9, 11:00 A.M.

"IT'S HIM," SAID ROGER SMITH, AFTER SLAMMING Doc Robbins's office door and throwing himself on the presumably bug-free couch. "Orin Boyd."

"What did he do now?" asked Doc Robbins.

"Everything."

"You're just a little tense, Roger. I told you not to make this place your life, that you need outside interests and—"

"Since he's been here, the place is crumbling like the House of fucking Usher. People die. Crops fail. My house plants are turning brown and my car is running like shit."

"You're exaggerating. Transferring."

"Oh, no," said Roger, waving his finger at the doctor. "I don't fucking think so. Boyd virtually invented the flaming bag of dog shit. That's the way you know it's him. He's laughing at me. All the men are laughing at me."

Doc Robbins smiled calmly at the frantic captain of the guard. "So then do something about it, Roger. Take action."

"I already am . . . I thought."

"Evidently, not enough."

"No," said Roger. "Not by half. The story of my life. But then you know that."

Doc Robbins studied the captain a moment. "If it's any help, Roger, he doesn't feel the least bit of guilt for his crime."

"What do I care what that bastard feels?"

"You're not listening, Roger."

"I'm not?"

"Think about what I've just told you."

Roger gave it a shot, then another, and after a moment slowly nodded, a grin wounding his face. "He's a textbook sociopath, right? Prone to acts of violence. A danger to the other inmates, perhaps, members of the staff?"

"That's the general idea."

"A rotten apple," said Smith. "A—"

"Belongs in East Meadow," said Dr. Robbins, dropping straight to the bottom line. "No doubt about it. But these things take time. Preparation. A paper trail. *Professionalism.*"

Roger sat up and faced Doc Robbins. "I've known him since he's five years old, Doc . . . That motherfucker is no damn good. People don't change; hell, you know that. Get

this started for me, won't you please? For the good of all
concerned."

SATURDAY, JULY 9, 11:50 P.M.

THAT NIGHT ZEN WENT TO BED EARLY, AND HE
dreamed he chased a faceless enemy into a noose, in an an-
tiseptic white dormitory room, much like his own. The
body was then somehow hoisted up by the neck, feet kicking, then still, and then it swung slowly around, and Zen
fully expected to see Skip's gagging face, purple and
swollen.

But the body had Orin's face, and it was laughing at him.

Zen sat up wide awake, quivering and sweating in the
dark, saw by his luminous watch it was almost midnight.

He got out of bed and stripped off his drenched T-shirt,
wiped himself off with a towel, fought back the terror. He
put on clean underwear and went to find Orin, to see what
he was doing.

His hands were shaking as he walked down the hall, and
his heart nearly stopped when he knocked on Orin's door,
hoped against hope for a response.

"Who is it?"

The hallway was deserted when Orin opened the door.

SUNDAY, JULY 10, 10:35 A.M.

ORIN FOUND BRENDAN KANE IN CAPTAIN SMITH'S office, standing on the balcony, lost in thought. "Yo, Judge," said Orin, "good spaghetti last night."

Kane barely turned his head. "Ragu," he said.

"Say what?"

"Though I have twice wed women of Italian extraction, angels who were inordinately proud of their *gravy,* they called it, not *sauce,* made according to Mama's sacred recipe, which is never written down—a little of this, a little of that—I much prefer Ragu, which is what my dear Irish mother served me."

"Mine, too."

Orin lit up one of Gramps's cigars and examined the paperwork on the desk, an analysis of Roger Smith's investments. "Hey, Judge," he said. "Do me a favor. Pick the Rog some dogs."

The judge gave a broker's gracious laugh.

"Let me ask you a question, off the record. Understand you might be able to get me out of here for a night."

"You better watch what you say around here. See Tobin, Art."

"I want to meet my girl outside."

Judge Kane laughed and patted Orin on the back, maybe checking for a wire, maybe not. "Congratulations, Boyd. That's a brand-new record, fastest anybody ever asked, and everybody eventually asks."

Orin watched Kane's face carefully and said, "Skip Trimble told George it could be done."

Kane said, "I believe we've already established George's credibility."

"I'll make it worth your while."

"There is no way out of here, Orin. Just like there aren't any ghosts roaming the grounds at night. Both are lies the men tell themselves for amusement. What you see is what you get. If you don't like this jail, there are others."

"So forget I mentioned it."

The judge cleared his throat. "You know, you are not well thought of in the circles to which I plan to return."

"That's a problem I have, isn't it?"

"Big problem."

SUNDAY, JULY 10, 6:00 P.M.

NICK MORELLI, STILL WEARING SHACKLES, WAS marched into the captain's office by a pair of guards. Nick held his cuffed hands out, and said, "Come on, Rog. Cut me loose and feed me."

"I told you, not yet."

"Why?"

Roger Smith sighed long and loud, and said, "Why?" as if even he were powerless against the wave of violence, the curse that had settled over Soundview. "Why. Why. Why."

"What," said Nick. "What happened?"

Roger folded his hands as if in prayer. "A disaster, Nick. I'm told they have to build Arthur a new butt."

Morelli's heart nearly stopped. "Say that again."

Roger Smith cringed and turned sideways in his chair. "Artie's getting reconstructive surgery on his anus. To save his life. He's in the O.R. now while they haul a surgeon in from the beach."

Nick's cuffed hands fell in front of him, defeated. "He's gonna live?"

"Not that he wants to."

"He was raped?" asked Nick.

"Repeatedly, I'm told. In the infirmary, of all places."

Nick sat down on the couch and buried his head in his chained hands, wondering if the attack was random, or if someone had chosen the low road to settle the score. Roger Smith watched Nick like a dog he didn't know, ready to cry out for help to the guards, at Marion's desk.

"How did this happen?" said Nick, looking up. "How did this fucking happen? *Who* did this, Roger?"

"Don't blame me."

"Tell me the truth, from the beginning."

Roger Smith told Nick that someone had planted bugs around the grounds, so they had naturally held a shake-down. Artie Tobin had had the receiver under his pillow.

Nick sat back and gave a sick laugh. "No fucking way."

"Yes, way."

"You shoulda come to me, Roger. Artie was fucking framed."

Roger studied his chubby hands. "Sad, isn't it? If you're telling the truth."

"I mean, why bug the Farm? We got it made in the shade here. Life has never been more peaceful."

"I don't know why he'd do it, Nick. I don't seem to know anything anymore. Maybe *you* can help there."

While Nicky was allowing that maybe he could poke around a little bit, Roger answered his intercom and was told by Marion that Townsend Tripp was on the line, as well as his mother. "I'll call both of them right back," said

Roger. "And bring me whatever I've got to sign to send Nicky back to the dorm."

"Yes, Captain."

"And find out who keeps smoking in my office."

"Yes, sir."

"Smells like Gramps," said Nick.

"It does not," said Roger.

Townsend Tripp was sure to be searching for tangible evidence of Orin Boyd's suffering, some assurance that he had not entrusted a man's job to a boy. Roger had little to offer him other than escalating plans and fresh recruits. Maybe Nicky could help there as well. Roger was unhandcuffing Nick Morelli and wondering what his mother wanted when a typewritten grocery list climbed out of his fax machine.

SUNDAY, JULY 10, 6:15 P.M.

DOWN THE WIDE HALLWAY, ORIN WAS GETTING comfortable on the company doctor's couch, where he had been unexpectedly called due to a scheduling change. They were reviewing Orin's progress in the intrapersonal relationships arena, vis-à-vis, his little war with Captain Smith. "You'd like to kill him," said Doc Robbins, no doubt thinking of weekend billing rates for psychiatric emergencies.

Orin said, "Slowly. With malice aforethought. After a truckload of pain and suffering."

"That's not healthy."

"Not for him," said Orin, "no."

"Your anger is approaching the uncontrollable," said Robbins.

"I don't know about that, Doc, but this ain't recess or study hall. This is a real jail filled with real bad guys. Roger Smith needs to get over the past, real fast," said Orin, "or I'm gonna have to help him with it."

"Let's talk about why. In detail."

Orin lit a cigar and grinned at the old fraud, and said in his best pain-racked voice, "Okay, here goes," and then he proceeded to tell Dr. Robbins the sad tale of a desperately lonely boy, a story so maudlin, so pathetic, it couldn't possibly be fiction.

SUNDAY, JULY 10, 9:00 P.M.

FREDDY GANDOLFO ARRIVED AT THE VISITORS' center with a box of cigars and a stack of photographs, most of a large Italian family—which included Freddy—enjoying a picnic at Roosevelt Park on Oyster Bay, several others showing Judy Boyd on the front porch of a split-level house, speaking to a woman in a wheelchair who was either holding open a screen door or trying to pull it shut. "Around eleven, she went there," he told his cousin. "You know who that is?" asked Freddy. "I got the address right here."

"Of course I know who it is," said Nick. "You done good, Freddy. Really good. Now you got to do a little bit more."

"Huh?"

"It's time we increased your involvement in our efforts, along with your profits."

Freddy winced. "What are you talking about, cuz? I'm already working twenty-four hours a day on this thing."

Nick looked over at the guard, who would not have noticed if Freddy passed him an Uzi. "Watching, not working," said Nick. "When you work, Freddy, something happens."

MONDAY, JULY 11, 9:30 A.M.

ROGER SMITH COULD NOT BELIEVE HIS EARS. Doc Robbins was actually bailing out on him this morning, arguing for compassion in the Boyd case. "Like I told you, he was *horribly* abused, then bullied, then abandoned," said Robbins. "It's a wonder he's not a mass murderer."

Roger Smith turned from his office window and put down his camera, snarling, "He told you about *my* childhood, you dope. How could you fall for such an obvious ruse?"

Doc Robbins's jaw fell open, and he nodded slowly. "But the suffering seemed almost palpable."

"Well, of course it did. He caused most of it."

Roger dismissed Dr. Robbins abruptly and sat in the stony silence of his sanctuary, fuming. Boyd was beating him at his own game, on his own court, or at least that was how Townsend Tripp had put it when Roger had called him back last night. Roger had stifled a suggestion that they find themselves another errand boy, had instead sworn a bloody oath to redouble his efforts. And now the doc was wavering, or he had been until he realized that Boyd was fucking him, too.

Roger smelled Gramps, in his office, in his clothes, and it made his blood run cold. He grabbed Boyd's file and squared his shoulders and marched down the hall and into the warden's office, where he vehemently restated his case against inmate Orin Boyd.

"Bottom line, Rog," Barthwell said. "What do you want?"

"I want you to transfer that sick puppy to the East Meadow hospital unit. Immediately."

Warden Barthwell put down his forty-five-pound dumbbells and smiled patiently at Roger Smith. "I think we need to try for a little perspective here."

"No more bullshit. No more perspective. Since Boyd has been here, he has waged an insidious campaign against me and my position on this Farm, taking up where he left off with me in school. The men are enjoying it . . . and you are allowing it."

"I thought it was you who took up where school left off."

Roger caught his breath. "I beg your pardon, sir?"

"I thought this was divine retribution, or whatever."

Roger regrouped, threw the file on Barthwell's desk. "Look, there are some confidential transcripts from Boyd's sessions with Homo. He's made physical threats against me, other members of the staff. He's—"

"Listen to me, Roger, and listen good: Enough's enough."

Roger burned inside with all the hate and frustration of a righteous man laid low by idiots. "But . . ."

"Understand, Captain? I'm the warden, and I kinda like that son of a bitch."

24

THE CALL HAD COME IN BEFORE DAWN, THREE
alarms and mutual aid from neighboring departments, two
pumpers and a truck company. The fire was out by nine
o'clock. The bad news found Orin at lunch.

He was driven in a white sheriff's van to his burned down
house by Vito Kelly, Oliver Bridges, and a third man he
didn't know. The guards had been silent on the drive across
the Island to Seaford, offering neither solace nor the consolation of diverting banter. Or maybe they were frightened
he would snap.

Orin's neighbors watched from their curtained windows
as he—wearing handcuffs and leg irons—was helped from
the van.

Orin smelled the wet stink of destruction and stared
through the holes in his home, his heart filled with hate.
The small Cape was nearly gutted, charred from cellar to
roof, one side wall gone except for the chimney. Their personal possessions were strewn inside the house and out,
fouling the lawn and the curb, twisted mountain bikes en-

tangled with Beatles albums. Dawn's Rock'Em Sock'Em Robots. Judy's fur. Dawn's computer.

Just as well they weren't here to see this, Orin thought. A wrecked house was one thing, a father in irons quite another.

Someone had deliberately done this, according to the Nassau County fire marshall, an elderly man in a baseball cap and jumpsuit, still sifting through debris at the rear of the house. He told them a motorcycle had been soaked with an accelerant, jammed between propane tanks, ignited. "You a witness against somebody, or what?" he asked Orin.

"I look like a fucking rat to you?"

The fire marshall shook his head, told the guards to be careful walking around inside, then climbed into his county car and drove away.

"You ready for this?" asked Bridges.

Orin said, "This ain't the first hut I've seen torched."

There was literally nothing left of his childhood. No more pictures of his mother, nor long-lost father, no football trophies, no mementos, no photographs, no history that had not been reduced to ashes. Vietnam was gone—perhaps a silver lining. His old uniforms. His autographed copy of *Dispatches*. The short letter recommending him for the Navy Cross and the long one arguing against it. Poof, as if they had never happened.

They had bought this house with his money, back when cops were paid twenty grand and happy to get it; they could have long ago moved to a bigger house on Judy's salary. Maybe they should have, he thought. Maybe they would now.

He tried to imagine the deed going down, tried to paste a face on the perpetrator. From his past? Or Skip's past? And what of his future, when the case was closed or abandoned? He could never move on without knowing, never let Dawn or Judy from his sight.

The murder investigation was over, he realized. A war he could not afford to lose had begun. And they had already shelled his headquarters, drained his war chest, torched his motorpool, and sunk his fleet. There would be civilian casualties, he knew, innocents tortured, he would—

"Hello? Orin?" A hardscrabble man in ragged work clothes filled the front doorway, looking for a place to knock.

"You an adjuster?" asked Orin. "Because if you are—"

"I'm your father, Orin. Robert Boyd."

Orin's heart skipped as vertigo washed over him.

"I know it's been a long time—"

"Like thirty years," said Orin. "What do you want?"

Vito Kelly's head spun as if he had been slapped. "Show the man a little respect."

Orin gave Vito Kelly a withering glance.

"Not necessary," said Robert Boyd. "I don't deserve any. And, Orin, if you don't want to talk to me, I completely understand. I can leave the way I came."

It was him all right; Orin could see that after his heart started beating again. Still with one foot out the door. Older, more weatherbeaten than ever; a wraith blown away on the lightest of breezes, according to his mother, when she was able to speak of him without losing control, years after he had vanished.

"You know, I almost turned out like you," said Orin. "I was at the airport, had already said my good-byes, which I guess is where we differ, bothering to say good-bye."

"I'll go," said his father. "This was a mistake. I'm sorry, for then, and for now."

"Don't be silly. You just caught me at a bad time," Orin said, holding up his cuffed wrists. "Give me a couple of minutes and I'll have the place shipshape."

Robert Boyd said, "I read you were in jail."

"And you finally felt guilty?"

His father shook his head. "Actually, no."

"Mama said you were a sociopath."

"Run her mouth a little, did she?"

Orin nodded. "A little."

Vito Kelly cleared his throat, took Bridges by the arm, moved out of earshot.

Robert Boyd said, "What I felt, when I read about you, was relieved. I mean, I knew you were a cop. And I had been in jail. No way we could ever get together, right?"

"So now that I'm in prison, you figure we're equals? You figure we pick things up where you walked out."

"Not at all. I was just hoping . . ."

"Yeah," said Orin. "I know what you mean about hoping."

Bridges and Kelly stood out at the curb now, smoking, and Orin considered making a break for it, devoting every last minute of his life to the pursuit of the coward who had burned down his home.

"This is so terrible, Orin. All these things happening to you at once. I was sorta keeping an eye on your place until you got out," said Robert. "Until your wife packed up and left."

Orin blinked, made a show of examining the wreck that was his house, realized his father thought Judy had decided to strike out on her own, preferring an impoverished fresh start to endless shame. "Who else was watching?"

Robert Boyd smiled. "Young guy, your age. Black hair. Red Mustang. Dark windows. Twice that I saw."

"You got a license plate, I hope."

"Never got close enough."

"This guy a cop or a scumbag?"

"There's a difference?" asked his father.

"Goddamn, I am like you. What happened to us way back then?"

Robert coughed and cleared his throat, finally launched into a brief confession of sorts, which he eventually summed up: "I had a drinking problem and stopped. A woman problem and stopped. A travel problem I still got."

"I got a few of your genes, I regret to report."

"I wish I could tell you it was more."

"Hey."

They stepped through the charred back door and walked outside, kicked at loose roof shingles, finally sat at the picnic table, Orin's last sticks of undamaged furniture. Robert Boyd haltingly caught him up on some of the intervening years, told him that later on he had raised another boy, Robert, Jr., fourteen years younger than Orin, who had died in a car crash when he was sixteen, drunk.

"What happened to his mother?" asked Orin.

"Married to somebody else now."

"What do you suppose it is about you?"

"You know, your mother had some quirks as well."

"As I remember it, she was fine until you left. Everything was fine. Of course, I get nostalgic over Vietnam, too, these days."

Orin's father looked around the yard, at the sky. His shoulders heaved.

"You're not dying or anything, are you?" said Orin. "This ain't no last-ditch leap at the gates of heaven."

"I got all the time in the world."

"Good. Because I need your help." Orin took his father's frail wrist and pulled him close over the table. "After they take me away, you double back here."

"You want me to get hold of some friends with a truck? There's stuff you can save in there, with soap and a little elbow grease. I know it all looks like shit right now."

"Forget that crap. I want you to get into the basement somehow. There's a lockbox down there," said Orin. "A big one. Under a tarp under the pool table. Get it and hang on to it for me. Guard it with your life. Just don't try to open it. It's booby-trapped."

"Okay."

Orin sat back and tried to see his own face in his father's, hunting for a link between them, a reason to trust him.

"People can change," said his father, "when they have to."

"I know that, Dad. Because I had to change into you. And then I had to change back."

MONDAY, JULY 11, 4:00 P.M.

SALLY MILES WAS ON DUTY AT THE GATE WHEN they got back from the fire. After a brief security check and the removal of his restraints, she told Orin his wife had called, it was urgent.

"How'd she sound?" he asked Sally.

"Distraught. This has got to be a nightmare for her."

"I suppose."

"And here," she said, handing him a stack of mail. "Mind bringing this up to the boys? We're short tonight."

"Not at all."

Shuffling up the hill to the dorm like a zombie, Orin riffled the mail, finding a confidential letter on PBA stationery addressed to him, a confidential relationship Sally had apparently respected.

He tucked the mail in his shirt and stopped at the dormitory pay phone. Nick Morelli's door was open. Nick was lying on his bed, staring at the ceiling. Orin closed his door, dialed Judy's cellular. "Hey," he said.

"Hey," said Judy. "Is it totaled?"

Orin recalled for her the smoldering clothing, the melted toys and charred appliances, still smelled the ash of their possessions trapped in his clothes, his nostrils, his pores. "I'm sorry, honey."

Judy said nothing for the longest time.

"You'll never guess who dropped by what's left of the house."

"Who?"

"My father . . . God, that sounds weird."

"Wow," said Judy.

"Yeah, wow."

"He thinks you ran out on me when I went to jail."

"You set him straight?"

"Couldn't."

"Great. Are you glad he showed up?"

Orin said he wasn't sure.

"Because I am," said Judy, suddenly crying. "Because maybe he can fill a hole that's been in our family from the beginning. Maybe it's worth the damn house."

"Does Dawn feel the hole?"

"Dawn's fine," Judy said, too quickly, sniffling. "I'm fine."

"Thanks," he said, suddenly thinking that every minute his child was getting older, all of them were devouring their allotted seconds, apart, disconnected. He wanted to swim in the ocean, feel the undertow drag him out. He wanted to go to a Yankee game, with his father and Dawn. He wanted to slice a drive into the drink at Lido, or slap on Harley leather and scare the hell out of a couple of civilians. "Did you find my woman in the wheelchair?" he asked.

"Yes. And she wouldn't say a thing, just begged me to leave and slammed the door in my face."

"You gotta try her again."

"This is a woman who has made up her mind, Orin."

"She doesn't have all the facts."

"Such as?"

He lowered his voice a decibel. "Such as the portrait I got of her holding hands with Mr. Dickie at the visitors' center. If she wants, I can start mailing her husband the wallet-size copies, every day, forever."

"Oh, honey . . ."

"Never mind," he said. "You're right. You get Dawn from camp and go somewhere else, don't even tell me, don't even tell your sister. If they're following you, lose them and stay lost. I'm fucking serious. This is worse than the last time. I got fronts I can't defend."

"Trimble can't help more?" she asked. "I mean—"

"All he can do is make things worse."

"You want me to tell you I'm scared, too?" said Judy.

"I want you to tell me good-bye."

"Be careful, Orin. Just because you're not a con doesn't mean you're not a prisoner."

"I love you," he said.

"I know that."

MONDAY, JULY 11, 5:30 P.M.

ORIN STARED OUT THE LIBRARY WINDOW ACROSS the Sound to the smug Connecticut coastline, his hands clenched, suspecting Prank, and Ril, and Nick, refusing to suspect George, perhaps blindly, wondering if he'd lost his touch, feeling that he already knew everything he needed to know to crack the case, like on one of those game shows. He had only to assemble the private logic behind the public events and punish the guilty.

Forget proving anything in court: this case was no longer headed to court.

Who was watching him, Orin wondered, as he flipped through a mint-condition leather-bound history of Soundview and the Kreeling family, a book commissioned by Thadeus Kreeling IV, grandson of Cyrus. This particular three-pound opus included foldout architectural plans of the house, an original survey map of grounds, and a list of notable guests, including Ring Lardner, W. C. Fields, and Groucho Marx, a list which regrettably ended with a poorly attended fox hunt in 1942. The text was a sanitized version of events over the years at Soundview, obviously written for hire, depicting happy servants attending always gracious family and guests. Life was bountiful and rich until all died peacefully in bed at home, attended by loved ones, except for one son, William, who was lost at sea in 1929.

There it was again, thought Orin, his nightmare and dream tied together. Lost at sea. Like Dad. Only Dad had finally made his way home, which somehow reduced its allure as a destination.

Orin was replacing the bogus family history in the stacks when he found another copy of the same book, this one badly tattered along the spine, its pages dog-eared. Inside, he found its margins were annotated in a tight, feminine script, dark blue ink from a fountain pen, carefully blotted. Several early passages seemed to gleefully indicate the commissioned text was fiction, puffery, that the Kreelings were full-time smugglers during prohibition, that son William had gone down off College Point with a load of Jamaican rum packed in the hold of a family vessel. Smuggling charges were thrice brought against old man Kreeling but never proven, much to the annotator's disappointment.

The younger brother, Sanford Kreeling, did not take ill as advertised, but refused to fill his brother's place at sea, and his father thereafter refused to speak to him, although he and his family were allowed to remain on the grounds. The writer of the alternate version was Sanford's wife, Alice.

The sanitized version said Sanford Kreeling died in his sleep in late 1943. Alice wrote that he hanged himself in the servants' quarters, in the end room.

"There you are," said Prank, rushing into the library. "Man, I just heard about your house—"

Orin raised his hand and said, "I don't want to talk about it. How's our other gig working out?"

Prank dropped the sore subject and straddled his swivel chair, booted up his Tandy. "I found something this afternoon that might mean something."

"What?"

"One bedsheet went to the evidence locker, along with Skip's clothes, the day he died," said Prank. "Two sheets were missing from the laundry count that weekend."

"Yeah?"

"Only time it happened in a year, we lost inventory. You know the Rog."

"Because it was evidence?" said Orin.

"Maybe."

"Or Ira getting set for fucking Banner Day."

"I thought it might be interesting."

Orin patted Prank's shoulder. "It probably would be if either one of us had the brains we were born with. What do you know about this Soundview ghost?"

Prank cocked his head to one side. "I know I ain't seen it." Prank's face showed concern for his new friend's mental health. "Old houses make funny noises, Orin."

"Humor me. Give me the legend."

Prank adopted a working cop's voice and demeanor, almost as if he were someone else: "Soundview's ghost is alleged to be a male white, approximately forty, wanders the grounds, moaning."

"Really."

"Some of the guys have heard crying jags. Some guys say it sounds like gurgling. . . . Zen's the only one who has ever admitted seeing him. But then Zen's not wrapped too fucking tight."

Orin was thinking of the brothers, William and Sanford Kreeling. The good son drowned, the bad one hanged, neither soul at peace. And Dick drowned. And Skip hanged. Someone playing with history, goofing on time.

Orin returned to his chair and reopened the tattered book. He studied the annotated maps, which showed a series of old drywells built across some of the lower terraces and a pair of dotted parallel lines that ran directly from the northeastern base of the house foundation to the cliff above the beach.

"Hey," said Prank. "I'm in the medical billings file now, checking Zen's psychiatric records; only they're not filed under William Masters, with his chest X-rays and urine tests; they're filed under Z. And right behind them there's charges for some kind of steroid or growth hormone."

"Barthwell?"

"I don't know if anyone is seriously sick. There's a whole bunch of records that don't carry patient names, only numbers."

"Homo's a fucking cheat," said Orin, not looking up from the book. "This prison is his own personal Medicaid mill."

MONDAY, JULY 11, 7:38 P.M.

WHILE HIS MATES DINED OVERHEAD, ORIN crawled through the dense belt of shrubs and cobwebs around the mansion, searching unsuccessfully for a clue to those dotted lines he had seen on the map. The air was thick with summer flies, the conversation of inmates, and more questions than he had answers for.

He dusted off his knees and entered the house through the kitchen, went down into the basement. The eastern wall had been paneled, as if someone raised in the suburbs had once planned to finish the place, no matter how massive the house above, and then toss in a wet bar, Islander pennants, rickety stools. On examining the floor along the paneled wall, Orin found evidence of scarring on the concrete, foot traffic approaching one of the panels.

He pried at one side with a screwdriver. The panel popped off, revealing wide wooden doors behind it. Orin set the panel aside and opened the doors, looked inside, and saw the twin rails on which miners' cars had once run clear to the beach, where barges had once off-loaded the coal to heat the mansion. An underground railroad from better days, he realized, blocked ten yards in by a solid concrete wall, which bore a bronze plaque that read: County of Nassau, Ralph Caso, County Executive. Orin stared at the plaque, but what he saw was the only theory he had been able to construct kiss him off like a whore with a habit.

MONDAY, JULY 11, 11:50 P.M.

TOWNSEND TRIPP WAS BEHIND THE WHEEL OF the Beemer. He filled the senator in on his legal research while driving him down Long Beach Road to a midnight meeting in Island Park with Roger Smith. "There have been many attempts to break the prison stipulation over the years, going right back to 1946. The first police commissioner tried to live in Soundview, as I believe the covenant was part of a complicated plea agreement, and thus a benefit he felt belonged to him."

Tommy Cotton folded his *Wall Street Journal* and said out the window wistfully, "Were those the good old days, or what?"

"His scam didn't work. Ours just might. So you tell me."

"It really is all about finesse these days," said Cotton. "The proper application of spin."

"You put me on the preservation committee," said Tripp, "and we're a goddamn lock."

"You took history in college, right?"

"My transcript is a living, breathing document."

Townsend Tripp slowed and pulled the BMW into the parking lot at the Spartacus Diner, found it full.

"Take the handicap slot," said Tommy Cotton. "My fucking jaw is killing me."

Captain Roger Smith was lurking in a half-moon booth in a rear section that was otherwise closed, wearing an ugly purple Nike warm-up and mirrored sunglasses. Over omelettes and toast, which were all the senator could manage these days, they cursed first Roger's inefficiency at delivering punishment, then Jack Barthwell as a bed-wetting liberal, his namby-pamby ways, the fact that the Honor Farm was out of control.

"Bottom line, Roger, you're saying we need to find a way around Barthwell," said the senator.

Roger Smith grunted, his mouth full, as it dawned on him that Cotton was ready to move and he was a part of it. He did not mention that he had been diligently searching for a path around Barthwell since he had arrived at the Farm.

"Jack have any bad habits?" asked Tripp nonchalantly.

"Only the one."

"What's that? Steroids?"

"Sally Miles."

Townsend Tripp leered over the rim of his coffee cup. "No. That's too fucking easy. Mr. Family-Man?"

Roger Smith nodded mournfully, stared at his eggs.

Tripp said, "Human nature is a wonderful thing."

Senator Cotton apparently didn't think it was so wonderful. He growled and said, "I thought Miles didn't screw with married men. That lying *bitch*."

Tripp said, "Obviously something will have to be done."

"Something drastic," said Cotton.

"We shouldn't let them destroy employee morale," suggested Roger Smith. "There are clear-cut rules against affairs with underlings." The bigshots kept nodding happily, so Roger reached into his jogging suit pocket and removed a photograph with the tips of his fingers. "I have a couple of interesting pictures."

Senator Cotton snapped his fingers, took a gander, patted Roger's forearm. "And we know just what to do with them, don't we?"

"You got Barthwell's home address?" asked Tripp.

"Sure."

"House call?" asked Cotton, looking at Tripp. "Tonight?"

"Why let the poor man dangle in the wind?"

The politicians wiped egg off their faces.

"Someone burned down Boyd's house."

"Really?" said Cotton. "What a goddamned shame."

"Doc Robbins thinks he might crack. He's considering a transfer to the psych ward."

"Roger, we've been trying to find the details on his conviction," said Tripp, "and the records are sealed, and the people we can usually reach are dumb on this one. Does that strike you as odd?"

"I don't know. Sometimes the system works. They might be protecting somebody big. They're sure not doing Boyd a favor."

"That's what we figured," said Cotton. "Good. Go home and get some rest."

The bigshots swept out of the diner, leaving Roger Smith to pay the check, which took forever because an old lady with a walker was screaming at the cashier about the Nazi squad car parked in the handicapped spot. Roger left a two-dollar tip near his dirty plate, thinking he would have to watch his back from now on, as if *he* were being videotaped, no more sleeping on the porch, no more Kreeling magnums with dinner, for he knew those two powerful men could turn on him for the slightest of advantages, possibly just for sport. And, of course, now they knew he owned a camera, and a dirty mind, a thought that made his balls twitch. Well, fuck them, he thought. He had shots of them, too, snorting cocaine behind a building like high school dropouts.

At a red light on Sunrise Highway he felt the Iroc running rough again, shifted to neutral and pumped the accelerator to keep the engine turning. He shut off his cop scanner and turned on his radio, to the New York sports channel, so he would know what the guards were talking about tomorrow, so that he would not continue to be the sole supply of fresh funds for the office betting pools.

"Hey, here's Ira from Sands Point, what's on your mind tonight, Ira baby?"

Smith gritted his teeth, pumped his foot, sniffed the air for cigar smoke.

"Same thing as yesterday. The Mets are back in the race, and all I hear about on this station is Steinbrenner."

"The Mets have teased us before."

"Six games back, middle of July. Three-game winning streak. In about a month this town is gonna wake up and find itself in a pennant race. I know it in my heart."

"Everyone needs a dream, Ira. . . . Here's Todd in the Tunnel. . . ."

See? thought Roger. Is that not absolutely insane? Barthwell allows all that country club crap, the close connection to the outside world that perpetuates the Farm's country club reputation. Roger Smith realized that his fingers were clenched around the steering wheel, that he hated Genghis Cohen, as he hated all the cops on the Farm. Even in jail they assumed they were superior to correction personnel, that prison guards carried some defective public-service chromosome that prevented them from performing their service in public. Tommy Cotton was right: they don't fucking get it, that they're being punished. They're all like Boyd. Every last one of them. And they deserved whatever he could give them. It was his sworn duty to fuck these men. The decent citizens of Nassau County deserved no less.

The traffic light changed to green and the Iroc stalled. Behind him a jeep-load of preppies honked and flipped him the bird, called him a Guido as they patched out around him. Roger pulled his off-duty revolver from his ankle holster and laid it on the seat, just in case.

TUESDAY, JULY 12, 10:25 A.M.

JUDY BOYD PARKED HER TAURUS IN THE TREE-lined driveway of the PAL camp, in front of the wide log cabin that housed the infirmary and administration. The three-hour trip from the Island had taken her five, what with stopping every few exits to make sure she wasn't being followed. She threw the trash from her Egg McMuffin into the barrel on the porch, then knocked on the open screen door.

A college-age girl in a blue tie-dyed T-shirt was seated inside at a large metal desk, talking on the phone and reading *The Hobbit.* She hung up, set her paperback aside. "Welcome to Camp O'Rourke," the girl said brightly. "How may I help you?"

Judy explained who she was, that she was there to pick up her daughter.

"Did you call ahead?"

"I didn't have time to call ahead," said Judy. "This is a family emergency."

"What's your daughter's name?"

"Dawn Boyd," said Judy.

The girl turned to her computer screen and tapped keys, frowned at what she saw, tapped some more keys.

"You have her listed as *Dawn Kennedy.* As a security precaution. My husband has a sensitive job."

The girl dramatically slapped her forehead. "Oh, I know who you mean. Dawny. Yeah, sure. She's not here anymore."

"No?"

"Uh-uh," said the girl. "Someone picked her up last night. Yup. She was signed out about one o'clock last night. By her father, it says here."

TUESDAY, JULY 12, 10:50 A.M.

IT WAS QUIET AT THE SLAUGHTERHOUSE THAT morning, the holding pens empty due to a delivery snafu that Nick quickly blamed on Roger Smith not replacing Artie in the office. Thus the regular crew was assigned to weed gardens grown wild since Dick had died. Only Prank was there, napping on a bench, waiting for fresh livestock to arrive, enjoying the air-conditioned otherworldly dark and solitude, when someone punched him hard in the shoulder.

He opened his eyes and covered his crotch. "What?"

"Yo, hard-on!" said Nick Morelli, hovering over him. "I called my bank this morning. You didn't do what I told you to do."

Prank slid back and sat up, looked around the Quonset hut, confused, aware that they were alone. "I told you," said Prank, "that's how you get caught."

"And I told you to let me worry about that."

"Use your head, Nick. Cash out when you walk. Some for you; some for me; some for Art, who's gonna need it."

Nick shook his head. "I don't trust you no more, Prank. I think you've forgotten who butters your bread."

Prank laughed bitterly. "You don't butter shit, Nick. You're not the fucking PBA president anymore. You're an asshole ex-cop in jail. You can't do me any favors. You couldn't even save Artie."

Nick stared down at Prank. "Careful, old man. We both know that's bullshit."

"You went way too fucking far this time, with Boyd."

"Wasn't me that burned his hootch."

"No?" said Prank skeptically.

"Not that I give a fat rat's ass."

"That's cold, Nicky. He didn't deserve it."

"You know, for a guy who supposedly knows everything, you don't know jackshit."

Prank said, "Fine. Whatever. I'm out, you dig? There ain't no million dollars."

"Now, you fucking listen to me, hard-on. You can do what you want, but first I want me and Artie's share of what we already clipped transferred to our own accounts. You just punch your keys and keep your fucking mouth shut."

"Who am I gonna tell?" asked Prank. "Who would believe me?"

"Good point," said Nick.

Only another whack like Boyd would believe him, Prank knew. That was the central problem of his life, an outgrowth of his self-destructive need for attention, Homo had said. A refusal to play second fiddle. Attention that had caused him nothing but woe. He had become another George Clarke, one whose every utterance was taken with salt.

Nick put his foot on the bench, crowding closer. "Don't fuck with me, hard-on. I know everything about you."

"What's that mean?"

Nick winked slowly. "Everything."

Prank stood up and moved away, realized that Stimey was lolling at Nick's feet, stoned on something.

"Imagine this pig is you," said Nick, "and I'll be me, like I always am." Then Nick raised the retractable-bolt gun, showed it to Prank, pressed it into Stimey's shoulder and fired, causing the pig to squeal mightily. "You getting the idea, Prank?" Nick bent over his little buddy, fired again, this time in the flank. The pig moaned in agony, tugging on its leash, rolling in its own blood on the slippery floor. "About what'll happen to you if you fuck with me?"

"Cut it out, Nick. And leave the dumb animal alone."

"You gonna take care of my banking needs, mother-fucker?"

Prank stared down at the wounded pig, sensing more kinship with the animal than with Nick. "Yes."

Nick aimed the gun in Prank's face, then smiled and turned back to his original victim, fired once, twice, in Stimey's temple.

The grateful pig stopped whining.

Nick left Prank alive to clean up.

TUESDAY, JULY 12, 11:05 A.M.

EVEN THOUGH THE TWO POLICE DEPARTMENT properties upstate adjoined each other, they were separated by a minor mountain range, and only loosely encircled by three blacktop country roads. Camp Cope did not advertise its tortured existence with a sign, and Judy simply could not distinguish one unmarked driveway from the next, one dead-end logging road after the other. Her baby had been crying last night, Judy was told by the PAL administrator, when they moved her at one A.M., but Monsignor O'Rourke had managed to calm Dawn down. The good father had simply felt she would be safer in his cabin, at the rehab camp. "Camp Cope," said the woman. "For rehabilitation. Have you heard of it?"

"Why, yes, I believe I have."

If Judy didn't find that damn drunk camp soon, she was going to lose it, actually pull to the side of the road and punch her dashboard. And when she got her hands on that meddlesome priest, she planned to strangle him in front of all his rummy friends.

Judy finally arrived at the Camp Cope parking field a shuddering wreck. She took several moments in her car to compose herself, thinking this was where her husband had found a new start, so to speak, that in spite of other motives at the time, he had dumped his monkey at this woodland retreat.

The front lobby of the white administration cabin was empty of people, but filled with cigar smoke, and Judy pushed through a wooden gate to the rear offices, then stopped short in her tracks.

Dawn was sitting on a couch with the monsignor, smiling, her suitcase by her feet, and they were both surrounded by giggling recoverees in Bermuda shorts, and one of them was saying, "And another time I saw your daddy—"

"Hello?" said Judy. "Any adults here?"

"Why, Mrs. Boyd," said Monsignor O'Rourke. "How good to see you."

"Mommy!"

While Dawn jumped up and hugged Judy fiercely, O'Rourke herded his charges out of the cabin, back to his personal solutions to their problems. Judy squeezed Dawn hard and resisted the urge to scold O'Rourke for telling tales about Dawn's father. Dawn broke free and babbled about what a hero policeman her daddy was, a living legend, the men said.

"Yes, honey," said Judy. "Your father is all of that and more."

26

TUESDAY, JULY 12, 12:15 P.M.

THE NASSAU COUNTY COMMISSIONER OF COR-
rections, Arlen X. Johnson, appeared at the front gate during lunch with an entourage of correction officers in a fleet
of six vehicles. Orin laid aside Alice Kreeling's bitter testimony and watched them coming up the hill from the beach
like invaders, knew that something he had not planned on
was happening, another wild card thrown in the deck.

The alarm rang. An immediate lockdown was ordered
and complied with.

Warden Jack Barthwell, the men were informed over the
loudspeaker, had resigned his command of the Honor Farm
for personal reasons.

Former Captain Roger Smith had been as of 0001 hours
promoted to the rank of warden and was thereby entitled to
the respect and privileges due said rank—as if he hadn't already been taking them.

The limos arrived shortly thereafter, followed by the
news vans.

At two P.M. the inmates were let back out of their rooms

and ordered to turn out on the front lawn to witness a ceremony promoting Roger Smith. Publicity photos had already been taken of Roger with his feet up on the desk, showing he was a regular guy, then saluting the big flag in the courtyard, showing he was a patriot, then gazing across his fields, his sleeves rolled up like a dustbowl farmer. Roger Smith fondly remembered Warden Barthwell for the reporters, as if Barthwell were already dead thirty years and not home trying to figure out what the fuck had happened. The sidebar was planted high and low that Roger Smith, Jack Barthwell's handpicked successor, was simply a man too good to hold back.

State Senator Thomas Cotton—resplendent in a double-breasted navy suit and red power tie—applauded the long-needed changes at Soundview but once again expressed grave doubts about coddling crooked cops. "Look around you, everyone," he said. "Take in the Sound, the sweep of the meadows, the woodland hills above. This magnificent estate ought properly be used to benefit all the residents of New York State, not just dirty detectives and looting lieutenants."

One ink-stained wretch from *Newsday* wanted to know how the senator's jaw was feeling, since all the emergency bridgework. Cotton said he felt as if his head were under construction and the bids had been rigged.

"Did you fire the staffer with the misguided elbow?"

"Hell, no," said Cotton, puffing out his chest. "I promoted him."

Then Cotton and his lackeys dove into the back seats of their official cars and breezed on down to the yacht club for celebratory cocktails.

Roger Smith immediately ordered a second lockdown, then went to his new office and closed the door, where he remained sequestered, cleaning, spraying air freshener, checking for Giordano minimikes.

The prisoners talked to each other from their windows, ready to believe the worst. Rumors flew back and forth along the ivy that afternoon, each weighed and filed. Without Happy Jack, the Farm was closing. Dick Pettibone had been murdered. Skip had been murdered. Artie Tobin was framed. The bugs had been Roger Smith's, used to trap the boss with Sally, who everybody suddenly noticed had not come to work that day, either. Roger Smith got Artie raped. Roger Smith murdered Gramps. The ghost did them all; let God sort it out.

The men with rooms facing south could see their shrimp scampi dinners board one of the county trucks, allegedly to feed the scum in East Meadow. Orin floated the rumor that the Rog was trading their food for cleaning products, on the theory that it was never too early to undermine the boss.

The windows closed and the televisions went on after George Clarke announced that he had heard that after surgery Artie Tobin would have to wear "one of them colo . . . one of them collect-o-matics for the rest of his life."

Zen Masters stayed out of the loop, caring little for the uninformed conjecture of his cohorts. He knew Roger Smith had a limited attention span, that this macho bullshit would not last. And a couple of weeks of real jail wasn't much out of a four-year sentence. Nothing compared to what he deserved.

Nothing like his nightmares.

Last night he had seen a tall black man, like Luther, with a fat white face like Nick's, and he was buried alive. Not calling for help, not struggling, merely lying in his grave among the moldering dead, shivering, waiting for something to happen.

WEDNESDAY, JULY 13, 7:00 A.M.

THEY WERE LET OUT OF THEIR ROOMS FOR CALIS-thenics the next morning, forced by a squad of sullen guards to do push-ups and sit-ups and jumping jacks on the damp front lawn. They were jogging in place in thick fog to the sad bleat of tankers out on the Sound when Warden Roger Smith, wearing what looked like a Russian general's uniform, appeared before them on a white horse, not to speak harshly nor to offer words of encouragement, merely to gloat.

Orin nudged Luther Bailey. "I can't wait to see what you do with this."

"How to make a caricature of a caricature, one wonders?"

Roger Smith stood up in the stirrups and embraced the day. He swatted his steed on its flank and trotted off down the hill toward the beach, as if he were charged by Holy Writ with the defense of the entire coastline.

The sweat-soaked, grass-stained inmates were then quick-marched into the dining room, where they were offered only cold cereal or fruit, coffee, all the orange juice they could swallow, nothing more. Small pockets of conspirators began—with varying levels of commitment—to plan Roger Smith's death.

And the inmates weren't too happy, either.

WEDNESDAY, JULY 13, 7:50 A.M.

ORIN TRIED TO CLEAN THE OVAL OFFICE FIRST, while the new warden was still riding the range. To his great disappointment, he found the lock had been changed, and was then instructed by Marion Whithers that he was no longer required to maintain the premises, that the Rog would do it himself.

"Then how am I supposed to snoop around?" asked Orin.

"You'll think of something."

"And what time do we expect His Highness to return?"

"If there's something you want to do, you'd best do it now."

Orin winked. "Where'd he get the horse?"

"Borrowed from the stables next door, like so much Grey Poupon. Actually, traded for a bottle of port, if I overheard him properly. I had to talk him out of the jodhpurs."

"What's this mean for you?" asked Orin.

"Not a blessed thing. I gave notice as soon as I heard."

"Sorry to hear that."

"A lot of good people have left here in the last few weeks."

Orin put both hands on her desk and looked her in the eye. "I'm not wrong, am I? Thinking those boys were killed."

"I'm not sure anymore," she said. "And I so liked Skip Trimble."

"You think things will settle down?"

Marion pinched her lips together. "No."

Orin wished Marion luck with the rest of her life and shoved his cart down the hall, thinking he needed to talk to Dave Trimble right away, about Dick Pettibone's deposition to the detectives regarding the morning of Skip's death. And he needed to talk to Prank, about a lot of things.

He slipped into Roger's old, now vacant, office and dialed the slaughterhouse, told Barry Comstock that the Rog wanted Prank to respond to the library forthwith, to clean up his fucking mess.

Prank barged into the library ten minutes later, yelling, "What fucking mess?"

Orin told him to calm down, asked him to open the conjugal visits file.

"Why?" asked Prank.

"Starting to think I missed something."

Prank went to work at the screen while Orin stared down from the window at George and Luther Bailey, walking behind lawn mowers at right angles to each other, almost colliding, crosscutting the front lawn to U.S. Open speed.

"Check Nick's activity," said Orin.

A moment later Prank spun around in his chair and announced that Nick Morelli, that once most regular of sexual applicants, had not seen his girlfriend in a month.

"Like since Skip's death?" asked Orin.

"Almost to the day. What's up with that?" said Prank. "I don't see Nick embracing the new celibacy."

"I'll bet he caught a dose from his side piece. The one he meets by the fence."

"A more likely explanation," said Prank, turning back. Orin patted him on the back. "Anything else to tell me?"

"You know what I know."

Orin didn't press the point, so Prank shut off the computer and quickly excused himself, said he wanted to grab a snack before reporting for field work. Who knew when the Rog would knock off the Stalag 17 crap. Orin said he wasn't hungry. He would lag behind to read, and think about ghosts, and contemplate down-to-earth enemies.

WEDNESDAY, JULY 13, 6:30 P.M.

WARDEN SMITH AND NICK MORELLI WERE HUDdled behind the warden's locked door, working the phones, Nick showing off his still formidable reach inside the government, pumping for information the long list of those still willing to gab with a felon. Nick sat on the edge of Smith's desk, calling numbers from memory, rousting allies from their bunkers.

Townsend Tripp didn't know who had bugged the Farm and resented the interruption. "I made calls as soon as I heard," he told Nick. "No one fessed up. Everybody said it sounded like a renegade operation, the kind of thing you and Artie would do."

"Great."

"How's that asshole Boyd doing?"

"Better than my partner."

"Fix that, Nicky. Fast."

"Yeah, yeah."

"And find out," said Tripp, "if you can, the details of his conviction. The boss wants to make an example of him."

"You got no one better placed than me to do that? Sherri-baby can't wiggle her black ass over to headquarters—?"

"Apparently not," said Tripp.

"How do you guys keep winning? That's what I want to know."

"We cheat; just like you always did."

County Executive Gil Otto had no clue who had planted the bugs. "Sorry, Nick. Say, when do you get out? We miss your smiling face around here. Nobody brings in those football tickets anymore."

A deputy chief of detectives promised to look into matters and get back promptly.

Thus it fell to a bitter civilian clerk in the quartermaster section to inform Nick Morelli that the commissioner himself had drawn eight Giordano minimikes, two mobile monitors, and one all-weather recorder with battery pack, on June 26. The equipment had not yet been returned.

Nick laughed good-naturedly and said, "You think he trusts his wife or what?"

"What?" said Roger, tugging Nick's arm. "Who?"

Nick hung up and frowned at Roger Smith. "A squad dick with a wife on the prowl. Nothing to do with this dump."

"Not a police operation, you say. Jesus," said Roger. "Let's think about this."

"What's to think about? One of your hard-on guards is a ringer, and he stuffed the receiver under my buddy's pillow rather than risk getting caught with it."

"Poor Artie," said Smith. "What should I do?"

"Do what you gotta do, Roger, which is maybe nothing, given that none of this happened on your watch. Maybe they were after Barthwell all the time."

"Boy, wouldn't that be nice."

"They got him, right?"

"Yes they did."

Nick left Roger Smith to his worriment and returned to his own office, certain now that Dave Trimble had either planted the bugs himself, while he was grieving all over this dump, or he used a mule. Which explained rather nicely why Boyd's personnel records were sealed even to prying state senators and perhaps why Boyd hadn't once squawked about his disappearing bank accounts.

Unless Prank was in on it, too, from the beginning, and Boyd's bank accounts were always just fine.

Naw, that was crazy, prison paranoia.

Him and Artie had brought the plan to Prank, because of the senator. Nick was reasonably sure of one thing, though: if Boyd was working undercover, Trimble was his only link to the department, even the prison personnel were operating in the dark, a fortuitous twist to a most disagreeable summer. Now he could steer the dopey fuck smack into a wall, or lay the guilt on hostile doorsteps.

Knowledge was power, he thought. Early, exclusive knowledge.

And if Nick had learned one thing from his first fall from grace, it was that when threatened, one should attack immediately, with everything one had.

Nick picked up the phone and dialed upstate. "Hello, Tommy?"

"I'm sorry," said the operator. "The senator's office is closed for the evening. If you care to leave a message . . ."

WEDNESDAY, JULY 13, 11:55 P.M.

ORIN WENT OUT THE WINDOW AFTER OFFICER Bridges signed off that night, made short work of the trip to the fences. Dave Trimble was waiting in the light rain, his thin hair plastered to his scalp. "Glad you could make it," he said. "I'm so sorry about your house."

"Right."

"If you want to pack it in—"

"I do that, I'll never find the torch."

"You may never find him anyway."

"What's up with my boccie bag?"

Trimble smiled. "Some of Pettibone's hair was inside, three good-sized strands. What's it mean?"

"I think Dick let the killer use it like a hood on him, and then the killer played Pin the Dunce in the Deep End. To keep him quiet about something. Put it that way to Kruger. See if it rattles his cage."

"Okay."

"And you've got to head off Tommy Cotton and his buttboy's new rules. Attica's more laid-back now. These midnight strolls could get chancy."

"Not sure I can, right now."

"What do you mean?"

"He's got the high ground on this one."

"But he ain't right."

"Want me to tell him the truth?"

"You do and I quit." Orin knew how these things worked in New York, maybe everywhere; he had often drawn justification for his actions from their lies. To do so once again did not trouble him.

"Let's talk about protection for your wife," said Trimble.

"Don't make me laugh."

"We'll borrow cops from another department."

"There are no other departments. Turn the page."

Dave Trimble bristled, looked both ways, and then lowered his voice. "Fine. Play it your way."

"Look, you either trust me, or you don't."

Trimble held up his palm like a traffic cop. "It's just the waiting . . . and the hating."

"Someone in here has made a hell of an effort to distract me, someone who knows what a fight with me costs."

"Over Skip or Pettibone, which?"

"Probably the same thing. Of course we might never be able to prove it in court. The evidence was discarded weeks ago, the crime scenes polluted by incompetents—"

"Skip didn't kill himself," Trimble said softly, threading his fingers through the fence.

"No. I don't think so."

27

AS ROBERT BOYD CHECKED IN AT THE VISITORS'
center, he gave his son the impression that he was all too
familiar with the routine. And there was none of the terror
across the table so common to first prison visits. "Thanks
for seeing me again, Orin. I know you didn't have to."

"Sure I did. You got my lockbox. Didn't try to open it,
did you, Dad?"

"No."

Orin nodded, looked around. "So, speak," he said.
"What's next for the Boyds?"

Robert lowered his eyes. "Look, I know I can't be your
daddy and I don't deserve to be a friend. I really just want
to know you, to know in my heart that I know you. To help
you in any way I can . . . I guess that's it."

Orin said nothing, aching with loss, thinking that this
man had once bounced him on his knee, played catch with
him, and then walked away for thirty years.

Robert's face was etched with pain and regret for time
squandered and love set aside, things that might have been.

"Did you know I was wounded in Nam?"

Robert said, "No."

"Stepped on a mine and damn near blew my balls off, almost ended the Boyd line, given what we now know."

Tears filled Robert's eyes, and he blew his weathered nose. "Is there anything at all I can do for you or your family? I don't have much money——"

"You still got a boat?"

Dad perked right up. "It's all I got. I live on it."

"Got a phone on it?"

"No."

"Get one. A cellular. So I can reach you when I need to. And, here, take these other instructions. I've decided to give you a second chance." Then Orin abruptly slid back his plastic chair and marched out of the visitors' center, his skin goose-bumped, his vision watery, thinking he definitely had to be out of jail before Dawn met Grandpa, to explain to her how those funny stories he had always told about his dad were still true, but could she please try to forget them or at least not bring them up. He didn't want to relive them and he wouldn't stoop to debate them.

THURSDAY, JULY 14, 10:57 A.M.

THE SENATOR WAS IN HIS ALBANY OFFICE, WEARing tennis whites. He had been packing to leave on a puddle jumper to the East Hampton Airport, planning a long weekend of well-deserved bacchanalia at the Three-Mile Harbor Hotel without his wife and daughters, when the news arrived like a stink bomb that Orin Boyd was a real cop, on a real mission.

"We're sure?" he asked Tripp.

"Yes."

And they had been breaking his balls at every opportunity, Cotton realized. Breaking the law to break his balls. The senator remarked that Nick Morelli ought to have discovered this minor detail sooner. Tripp said nothing, took his lashes.

Senator Cotton gave the development his usual level of due deliberation and decided that he wasn't sure it mattered. Roger Smith and Nick Morelli had done the dirty work. He would say to the first mike thrust in his face that he had known about the mission from the beginning and was therefore a brave and willing participant in the war on crime, as always. The weekend was saved.

He told Tripp the plan.

"You sure?" asked Tripp.

"Sure I'm sure," said Cotton, heading out the door with his suitcase. "Big splash when Boyd goes public."

"We telling the Rog?"

"Apparently no one else has."

THURSDAY, JULY 14, 11:30 A.M.

NICK SAT DOWN IN THE VERY SAME CHAIR THAT Orin had so recently warmed, and he told his cousin Freddy, in no uncertain terms, that Commissioner Trimble was on to them, that he had to go as soon as possible.

"Go?" said Freddy. "As in—"

"Shut your big mouth."

Color drained from Freddy's face. "The police commissioner?"

Nick leaned closer, talked softer. "Yeah the police commissioner. Like tonight. After that we'll think about the wife."

Freddy blinked. "Trimble's wife?"

"Boyd's wife, you fucking moron."

Freddy looked over his shoulder, back and forth. The guards were outside, visible through the bulletproof glass, smoking. "This is fucking nuts. Over a couple of bucks he might have buried?"

"Over the FBI up our ass, over the rest of my sentence

upstate, you fucking hard-on, and maybe a little something for you, like an arson charge."

Freddy sat up straight and hugged himself. "I don't know."

"Yes, you do, Freddy."

"Stop talking like that."

Nick laid his head on the Formica table and moaned. "God is gonna punish me for trusting an asshole like you. I know it."

"This job keeps getting bigger," whined Freddy. "That's the problem."

Nick snorted in exasperation. "Hey, Freddy, you're in for a dime, you're in for a dollar. Or we all spend a nasty stretch in Attica." Nick leaned forward. "The boss, then the babe. *Capisce?*"

"That's if I can find her again," Freddy said. "She's not at her sister's no more. And she ain't got a job to go to."

"Oh, you'll find her again. Don't worry about that. She's in this up to her nipples."

"How?"

"The kid," said Nick.

THURSDAY, JULY 14, 7:00 P.M.

POLICE COMMISSIONER TRIMBLE LEFT HIS TOP-floor office at six o'clock that evening. He was seen by two highway patrol cops as he gassed up his county car behind headquarters, briefly kidded with them about some patrolman's drunken wife mooning County Executive Gil Otto at the PBA Picnic, then wished them safe tours before he climbed back into his Buick and pulled out of the parking lot.

The highway patrol officers, when questioned later, had no idea which way he had turned on Franklin Avenue, however homicide detectives later speculated that he went directly to the Roosevelt Field mall, where he subsequently bought his wife a tennis bracelet, charged to his account at Macy's, at six-forty-five P.M.

From the remaining available evidence, detectives deduced that David Trimble had then returned to his county car in the lot behind Bennigan's, unlocked the door, gotten inside, and fastened his seat belt. He had started the engine, flipped on his Motorola. He had lowered his driver's side window halfway.

He never got the chance to shift the transmission to reverse, however, because then a person or persons unknown had either spilled or sprayed kerosene into the interior of the vehicle and tossed a fully functioning Zippo lighter into the police commissioner's lap.

The Carle Place and Garden City volunteer fire departments responded forthwith to douse the blaze, too late to save the single charred occupant of the vehicle.

THURSDAY, JULY 14, 11:30 P.M.

CHANNEL 12'S CAROL SILVA SAID RESPECTFULLY, ". . . Repeating the top story of the hour, Nassau County Police Commissioner David Trimble is murdered at the Roosevelt Field mall. And Joe has more on the big rain that arrives later tonight."

Judy Boyd shut off the hotel television set and rechecked the chains on her door, reminded herself that this was the Marriott, in the concrete heart of suburban Nassau County. She and Dawn had paid cash in advance for three nights, checked in as Lorrie and Jennifer Rettler, of Westhampton Beach, self-employed.

No one was coming to crash through her door. Gunmen were not waiting in the lobby. Perhaps.

Judy wanted to talk to her husband, to tell him that whatever he was doing at the Farm, it couldn't be worth their marriage, her career. He had to come out. Now. Tonight. There were three thousand cops in Nassau County. Let someone else shoulder the load. A single cop, without kids.

Judy imagined herself telling Orin this, that she couldn't run any further. She then imagined his response, or worse, his lack of a response, pictured the glacial mask he wore when he felt his honor was threatened or his competence questioned.

Dawn reached for the remote and changed channels. "MTV, Mom," she said. "Please. On low."

"Huh?"

"It helps me not to think about Daddy."

"Just not too loud."

". . . repeating this unconfirmed report that another prisoner at the Sands Point Correctional Facility has been seriously injured . . ."

Judy and Dawn rolled out of bed, dressed in black sweat suits, quickly packed up the rest of their clothes. Five minutes later Judy rushed her sleepy daughter past the loud disco, out of the bustling hotel, and into the rain, found her car under a lightpole.

They sat with the doors locked and the windshield wipers swishing, waiting to see if anyone had followed them from the lobby, and it struck Judy that she could be a widow already, Dawn fatherless.

"Where are we going, Mommy?"

"To see Daddy."

Dawn brightened, sat up in her seat. "Really?"

"I think so."

With Commissioner Trimble dead, she figured, they could call in the FBI, real investigators to find real evidence to nail real killers. Who knew what they were truly up against, which nest of hornets they'd disturbed, or if the commissioner's murder had anything at all to do with the Honor Farm.

Twenty minutes later she stared at the high stone wall, trembling, knowing they were far too late for regular hours. A white Volkswagen Golf with darkened windows was the only other car in the lot, parked far away from the gate. She held an umbrella over their heads, and they ran to the gate and waved at the guard in the lighted booth.

Officer Carlson slid open a small glass panel. "Mrs. Boyd? You're way too late," said Carlson.

"It's life and death, officer. Otherwise we wouldn't—"

"The report was false. Everybody is safe in their beds."

"Dawn hasn't seen her father in over a month."

"Sorry, ma'am. We got a new boss here who's a stickler for rules and regulations."

"Roger Smith," Judy said, smiling. "A good friend of the family. We went to high school together."

"So I've heard."

Judy then asked for Officer Miles, was told she'd been demoted and transferred to the East Meadow jail. Then Oliver Bridges poked his head out of the office behind Carlson, listened politely as Judy explained that she had experienced a private medical emergency.

"If it was anybody but her husband, okay," Carlson said to Bridges. "But the Rog'll snap, he hears we cut Boyd a break."

"That ain't right," said Bridges. "What we do for one—"

"Who said anything about right? This is about staying off fence patrol."

"Come on, Carlson, I'll go get him," said Bridges. "Just don't write nothing down."

Thursday, July 14, 11:55 P.M.

"THIS IS AWFULLY NICE OF YOU, BRIDGES," ORIN said as they walked down the dark stone path to the visitors' center.

"Just don't thank me in public, man."

"This isn't a setup, is it? The Rog ain't gonna waste me, trying to escape?"

"The Rog can't ever know about this."

Orin looked at Bridges and cocked one eyebrow, a gesture not entirely lost in the darkness. "Know about what?"

Oliver Bridges pulled open the back door of the visitors' center. "Do what you gotta do quick."

"Hey, Bridges, if they ever find me dead here, don't you believe it was suicide, you hear me. I didn't kill myself at Khe Sanh, I ain't gonna do it here."

Judy and Dawn were waiting at the table, and Orin wished Luther were there to sketch them. He lifted Dawn into his arms and kissed Judy over the top of his child's blond head.

"It's good to see you guys," he said. "How's Monsignor—"

"It's over," Judy said. "The man who sent you is dead."

"I know all about it. The Rog let us watch the news tonight. I'm close," Orin whispered. He set Dawn down and held two fingers an inch apart. "This close."

"Maybe that's why Trimble's dead."

"Hey," he said admiringly, "you're getting good at this."

Judy did not come out of hiding to be praised. She made the universal jerk-me-off gesture and said, "Start calling who you have to call, I'm serious."

"It might not be that simple. My orders went down with my boat, right? Where I was keeping them, so they'd be safe? Dave Trimble's probably went up with his car, where he was keeping them, so they'd be safe."

"How convenient."

"It's not a question of convenience. It's, can we live our lives without looking over our shoulders." Orin's thick neck grew red, and his eyes narrowed. "What, is that why you came in person? You thought I couldn't look you in the eye and say no?"

Judy bit her lower lip and played with the clasp on her purse. "Don't make me laugh."

Orin hugged them both close and whispered final instructions in their ears, then stood up from the table, and signaled Bridges that he was ready to return to the dorm.

The wind blew in warm wet gusts as, tear-streaked, Dawn and Judy made their way from the visitors' center back to her car. The Golf was gone from the parking lot, Judy noted with relief. They got in and locked the doors. Judy picked up the cellular, to call her best single girlfriend, Meryl, to beg for a place to stay, and she prayed that her normally reliable friend was not at that moment barhopping the hotel circuit, or worse, on her back in some strange man's apartment.

THURSDAY, JULY 14, 11:59 P.M.

ANTHONY BELLAPANNUCCI PICKED UP THE PHONE ringing next to his hairy elbow and grunted into the mouthpiece.

"It's me," said his caller. "Nicky."

"We got a lot of fucking Nickys."

"The cop."

"Ex-cop. Long time, no hear."

"I thought that was the way you'd want it."

"Whatever."

"So look—"

"You're not gonna ask me how my father is feeling?"

"I'm sorry. How's your father feeling?"

"Better. Thanks. So why are you calling?"

"I need a couple big jobs done right."

"Trouble getting along with people, Nicky?"

"You could say that."

"When?"

"Yesterday."

"Who?"

Nick gave Anthony the names, starting with Freddy's and ending with Boyd's. "The whole family, okay? I'm all out of choices."

"That's why we're here."

"Call me when it's done."

"Don't go cheap on me now, Nicky. Spring for a fucking newspaper."

FRIDAY, JULY 15, 12:30 A.M.

ORIN AND PRANK PADDED UP THE DIMLY LIT back staircase in their slippers and robes, ducked into the library. Orin pulled a pack of Carlton's from his robe and lit a cigarette.

"Come on, Prank, there's something else you want to tell

me, isn't there? A really dumb, really dangerous thing you did?"

Prank said, "Isn't everything better now?"

"No. Only my money is back."

"Don't let Nick know that."

Orin nodded several times and smiled a satisfied smile, but Prank was not put at ease.

"Look, when we started on you, I didn't know you, I didn't know what you were doing. Tobin, Morelli, and me, we figured to break you, over and under the line, force your wife to the money you're supposed to have hidden."

"And then have a goon fucking rob her?"

"I didn't know about that end." Prank studied his knuckles. "Nick said they didn't do the house. When I heard about it, I confronted him."

"And you believed him?"

"Look, before I was a scumbag, I used to be a decent cop. I can read people."

Every ex-cop Orin knew used to be a "decent cop," a cop's cop, to hear them tell it. None of the rats or thieves ever quit. "You make all the financial moves from here?"

Prank shook his head modestly. "Nick thinks I did, but I know a guy who knows a guy, an expert guide around the newer firewalls. He can spoof his way into IRS records, whatever. Five years ago I could have done some of it. Security's tougher now, and no one is sending me their manuals."

"You should have kept the money, Prank. Once it was back, I knew it was you."

"I didn't know what to do."

"Obviously."

Orin picked up the phone and dialed the main desk at East Meadow. "Yo, dude," he said when a Hispanic-sounding officer answered, gave his name as Corporal Megalito Anduscar, "this is Captain Thompson, over at Parole. How you boys doing? Listen, check your records, you got a slug named Louis Dinostra at the Farm for a week too long now."

"And he is complaining?"

"Very funny, amigo. Just let's not build him a lawsuit with your name on it, *comprende?*"

"What'd you say your name was, gringo?"

"You heard me, Underwear."

"That's Anduscar!"

Orin hung up and looked down at Prank. "So there you go. You're all set."

"You don't trust me anymore, do you?"

"With my wife, I'm gonna trust you . . . the chick you got fired. 'Night, partner. Say your prayers."

Prank remained in the library long after Orin sneaked back to the dorm, thinking about his oldest buddy Davey being torched like a Saigon monk, of his Deadhead daughter Brenda, his surly son the sergeant, thinking that everything he had ever loved had turned to shit. How much of this was his fault? How much could be chalked up to fate? Tears filled his eyes as he stood before his machine, index finger poised above the keyboard. Zen Masters was right, he thought. Eat the blame and let it go. Let all the pain and shame and disappointment go, and do the right thing from that moment on, no matter the cost. That was all that was left to any of them. The dignity of the dying. Thus Prank Dinostra, without remorse or regret, summarily deleted his precious diary, his book of beasts and burdens.

28

FRIDAY, JULY 15, 7:45 A.M.

WARDEN ROGER SMITH WORE TO BREAKFAST THE
official—if hard to look at—dress garb of a Nassau County
warden. The hungry inmates were allowed to fill their trays
from sumptuous steam tables and sit, not eat, until they
had listened to and absorbed several new edicts and policies designed to streamline operations on the Farm. These
bureaucratic bummers included reduced recreation time,
a three-call limit on outgoing calls, and a cutback on conjugals for inmates with disciplinary infractions on their
prison records.

Orin knew that henceforth, if Roger had his way, he
would see little time out of his room, and considered that he
might better finish this case outside the walls. If he could
sit with Lieutenant Kruger and go over all the paperwork,
the two of them might see something together they had
missed while apart. Of course that meant he had to get himself released, legally, and as he had already explained to
Judy—

"And that's just the beginning," said Smith. "The rest will be up to you men."

"Okay, now guys," whispered Ira, "don't nobody else die or they'll yank our TVs."

"And we'll start with your room, wiseass," said Smith. "Then you can listen to your precious little games on a boom box."

Nick stood up, spread his legs, and began to speak without anyone recognizing him. "You know what then, Rog? Fuck this Farm."

Smith cleared wax from his ears and squinted at Nick.

"You heard me," said Nick. "I say we go back to our rooms and don't nobody do nothing until we hear from our lawyers. Let the crops fail and the chickens rot. What the hell do we care?"

Roger Smith said, "You try that, we'll just back up the bus and run you all on over to East Meadow this afternoon."

"What are you talking?" said Orin. "Get a grip, all of you."

"Fuck you, Boyd," cried Smith. "I don't need your help, and I don't care about your goddamn morale."

"Call *Newsday*," someone muttered.

"They hate you pricks. And what are you gonna wave out the windows, fucking tennis rackets? George Clarke, you drop that corn muffin before I have you—"

George froze, dropped the buttered muffin. The rest of the men sat momentarily silent, chastised, picturing their plight the way the outside world might.

Roger Smith poured it on: "And you know what? Someone will slaughter that livestock and pick that corn and bake that bread, rest assured. There's plenty more fuckups where we got you."

"You're kidding yourself, Warden," said Orin. "We're all gonna be outta here just as soon as they can legally cart us away. We're talking Soundview Acres, I'd bet, with duplexes and triplexes—"

"You don't know that," said Smith.

"Either do you."

Roger Smith gathered himself to full height and said, "And now, because Orin and Nick have such big mouths, everyone can go right to work without eating."

The men looked at their plates, then up at Roger. The guards moved in from the corners, shouting, "Let's go, now, move it."

FRIDAY JULY 15, 9:00 A.M.

PRANK DINOSTRA WORE TIGHT-FITTING CIVILIAN clothes four years out of date and carried a suitcase bearing the baggage stickers of Pan Am, Eastern, the Trump Shuttle, and other bankrupt institutions of the late twentieth century. On the other side of the gate, in a shiny black Blazer, his ex-wife sat behind the wheel, apparently not budging.

She had gotten old, he realized, while he was in jail. Life had not begun again for her, as she had fully expected—hell, announced—and bitterness creased her mouth. He climbed into the passenger seat and leaned over to kiss her cheek.

"Don't, Louis. Don't you dare. This is a ride, not a reconciliation."

"I know," he said. "I forgot. I'm sorry."

Joyce Dinostra stepped on the gas and pulled away from the gate, and Prank knew she didn't want to hear that he had changed, that he was sorry; pathetic, she had said last night when his phone call woke her. If she was the first person he thought of for help, he was in big fucking trouble. Take a taxicab. Walk.

Prank had sensed her loneliness and hung on, eventually worn her down, but now, watching her dispiritedly perform this final obligation, he guessed that nothing more would come of their relationship, and that his sentence would never end.

Friday July 15, 9:40 a.m.

THAT MORNING, AS HE WENT ABOUT HIS HOUSE-keeping chores for what he hoped would be the last time, Orin thought about Zen, and George, Nick Morelli, Dom Ril, and Ira, and Luther, Comstock, Kaminsky, the company doctor, and the judge who didn't belong there in the first place. The judge, he thought, and the doctor were two professional men without verifiable alibis. Both plenty smart. Both physical twerps, both expecting to shortly be enjoying comfortable retirements. It didn't make sense. Skip's death in particular had been a crime of passion, Orin believed, perhaps sexual asphyxia, the sort committed by men in their primes.

As Orin carried bags of trash from the house to the Dumpster, he thought of each man's movements on the days in question, each man's possible motives, the range of tall tales they had told. Only one name caused his stomach to flutter, which would be hard to convince a jury amounted to probable cause. Not much of a system, he had to admit. His or theirs.

On one of his return trips from the Dumpster, he noticed Roger Smith's plastic gasoline containers tucked under the back portico again, already filled for another late-night trip to the employee parking lot, a fire hazard if ever Orin saw one.

For safety's sake, and as a police officer on active duty, Orin considered himself honor-bound to pour most of the gas down a storm drain and top the containers off from the garden hose. After all, he thought, walking back into the mansion, who knew better the damage that fire could do.

Friday, July 15, 10:00 a.m.

DOC ROBBINS HAD NO SOONER REMOVED HIS seersucker sport coat and hung it on the hook behind his door than Roger was on him, letting him know the gravy train stopped here if he didn't play ball. The bogus billings, the phony prescriptions, finito. Unethical doctors were a dime a dozen, said Smith. Homo could be replaced.

"Jack Barthwell never threatened me."

"Jack Barthwell's working midnights at East Meadow."

"Fine. Here."

Roger Smith grabbed the updated psychiatric evaluation of Orin Boyd from Doc and ran to his office to read it at once, his face registering pleasure, amusement, excitement, as his eyes embraced phrases like "shows no remorse for his criminal acts," and "a danger to himself and others," and the grand finale: "It would be in the best interest of those prisoners actually attempting to rehabilitate themselves that this disruptive prisoner be assigned a stricter level of incarceration, either at the East Meadow jail, or a state-run facility."

Roger put his feet up on his desk, feeling the way one does after removing a stone from one's shoe. This would take some getting used to, he thought, the perks of power. Because inside these walls he was The Man. The lord of the manor. And the only man he feared was leaving town on a rail.

"Have Orin Boyd come see me, won't you?" he asked Marion.

Friday, July 15, 10:10 A.M.

ORIN LEANED INTO THE INMATE'S CONFERENCE room and fixed Dom Ril with a baleful stare. "Where's Nick?"

"How the fuck should I know?"

"Come on, Dom, you always know everything and never say shit. That's what I like about you."

"You got me wrong this time."

Orin closed the conference room door, took a seat next to Ril's desk in the corner of the bullpen, under a bulletin board covered with flyers for self-help courses and social services. "I don't think so."

"I didn't do anything, you understand?" said Ril. "I don't know why you're here or what you're up to, but I'm clean, a model goddamn inmate. I just want to go home."

"That's all any of us want," said Orin.

"Then stop breaking everybody's balls, okay? Boredom killed those two assholes. They couldn't stand another fucking minute in this madhouse."

"You wouldn't be bored, knowing I was coming after you."

"No."

"So live long and prosper, Dom. But first get lost for ten minutes."

"Say what?" Dom Ril didn't know what Orin would do in those ten minutes, but he knew it would not cover anyone in glory.

"Don't make me ask again."

Dom Ril took a stroll down the hall, and Orin closed the door behind him. In the file cabinet near Nick's desk Orin found the master sheet for the day Skip died, saw that the produce count forms had been filed on time that morning, logged in by Marion before Skip was found dead, before the lockdown.

Orin tore through another drawer and looked at the forms themselves, all signed by Nick Morelli. So now eyewitness testimony and physical evidence supported Nick's alibi, against the chill Orin felt in his gut. Nick had signed these count sheets that morning, some right side up, some upside down. Orin could just picture the fat bastard, his feet up, signing papers without so much as looking at them.

The door opened and Dom Ril stepped back into the office. "Smith's looking for you."

"Oh, goody."

FRIDAY, JULY 15, 10:26 A.M.

IN THE BASEMENT ORIN WROTE THE NOTE HE would send the senator, along with some prints of the photos he and George had stolen from Roger's stash, shots of the great man himself, snorting cocaine from a compact with a fox in a thong behind the yacht club: "Bend over and grab your ankles, Tommy. You're about to take a rocket up your ass. Watch *Newsday*, the *Times*. Assemble your rabbis. Hire lawyers. Explain things at home. Watch it all go up in flames. But look at the bright side, Toot: you might get to serve your sentence on the Honor Farm, where they can always use another cocksucker."

Orin left the note unsigned, dropped pictures and the note into an addressed envelope, then trotted upstairs and slipped it in the outgoing Fed Ex pouch.

"There you are," said Marion. "Roger wants to see you."

"But I don't want to see Roger."

Marion regarded the closed walnut door to the oval office and smiled. "Big bloody club," she said. "Mum's the word."

Orin quickly took the high ground and hid himself in the library, reading *Newsday*, tearing out an article in which Acting Police Commissioner Malone announced that the Honor Farm might be going on the auction block, to allow the property to be "more advantageously exploited. Inmates could expect to be transferred within the next two months, either to facilities upstate or at East Meadow." Orin remembered his mother handing him clippings when he was a boy, mailing them to Vietnam, more or less rearranging the newspaper into the order she thought he should read it. Those clippings were usually prophylactic in nature, regarding alcohol, drugs, guns, and girls. The near occasions of sin. He remembered her ever-present glass of amber scotch, rocks, in the evening, the curl of her cigarette smoke through an American eagle lampshade, how patiently she had waited for his father.

Orin picked up the annotated history of Soundview again, began rereading a section in the back of the book referring to several nighttime rendezvous Alice had made after her husband's death, assignations with a blacksmith lover from a neighboring estate, which for some reason seemed to take place when the tide was out.

Orin looked up from the conclusion of Alice Kreeling's sad tale and examined the photograph above the desk, of Christmas at Soundview, 1940, many Kreelings bundled up and gathered in the courtyard in front of the sundial. Orin hunted for Alice, who should have been about forty-two years old at the time, found her slouching at the right side of the bottom row, with the children, the only one not smiling. She was tiny, he realized, dwarfed by the handsome man in the greatcoat standing behind her, her face a shade darker than the fair-haired Kreelings.

Did any of the others, Orin wondered, know how deeply she despised them and their hypocritical ways, their snooty friends. From the look on her face, she never let them forget it. Three of these kids in the front row were hers. One, a boy, would die of pneumonia before Christmas came again.

The ringing phone startled him back to modern America. He let it ring twice. Then one more ring. Picked it up. Marion Whithers, grown accustomed to either his fondness for overstuffed wing chairs or his interest in the past, had tracked him down to warn him. "They're coming for you, Orin," she said. "I don't know why, but—"

Just then Roger Smith opened the library door, marched over to the desk, and put his finger on the telephone button, cutting Marion off. Orin growled softly, looked from Roger's braided cuff to his epaulet to his pasty white neck.

Oliver Bridges and another guard were with Smith, for backup, hardly visible to Orin through his rage.

"Stand up," said Smith. "Put out your hands."

"Say please."

Warden Smith bristled and said, "Insubordination, eh? We'll just add that to the report."

"What report?" asked Orin. "I'm already in jail, you big Skin-So-Soft sissy."

"The hard way or the easy way, Boyd?"

Orin allowed Roger to slip on the handcuffs. Then Bridges and his assistant marched at Orin's sides as Roger Smith led them down to the basement, and then Smith stood at attention as the guards removed the cuffs and locked Orin in the cell.

"I want a lawyer," Orin said through the bars.

"On a Friday, in July? Get real."

Orin considered for just one moment letting shithead in on the deal, taking the easy way out and perhaps allowing bad people to go unpunished. "I said I need a lawyer, Sissyboy."

"What you need," said the Rog, "is a miracle."

29

"GEORGE, OLD SPORT," SAID ORIN. "THANKS FOR coming right away."

"No one told me you were here till breakfast."

"Doesn't matter. I need you now."

George was on his hands and knees at the narrow, barred window, looking down at Orin. "You need me now," George said. "That's freaking beautiful. This is what you do, isn't it? Follow me around to make corruption cases. For the last six years I've had my own personal detective."

Orin shook his head sadly. "I'm not your personal detective, George. You just happen to show up."

"What are you *doing* here, man?"

"Looking for a murderer."

"Well, it isn't me."

"But you know who it is, don't you?"

George looked over both shoulders and said, "Fuck, no. Will you get that through your thick—"

"Look, I've got an idea," said Orin.

"Like the last time?" George snarled. "I mean, come on,

Orin, my freaking sentence is just about up, and guys here know enough about me to have the DA waiting at the gate. And they don't send you back here twice, you know. That's one of the rules. The second time, you're not an ex-cop, you're an ex-con."

"You don't even want to hear my plan?"

"It ain't gonna matter."

"A phone call, George. That's all."

"The phones are locked down anyway."

Orin walked away from the window, leaned his forehead on the bars of his cell door. "Nicky finally got to you, didn't he?"

"Not just Nick," said George. "Lots of guys have noticed how you've changed."

Orin turned to face his old partner. "Good-bye, George. It's been a real education."

George pushed himself up out of the dirt and dusted off his hands and his knees. "I wish you wouldn't put it like that."

"Tough."

Orin pissed in his coverless toilet, stretched his back and legs, did his push-ups and sit-ups, stared out his window at the base of the bush. Ira Cohen knocked on his cell door a moment later, slid under the bars a tray of hot oatmeal and cold coffee.

Orin said, "I coulda used an omelette. And a carton of Carltons."

"You're lucky you got this. They're having a big meeting about you right now. Fucking Smith is telling everybody you're a Class-A security risk, threatening to call in state inspectors if East Meadow won't take you."

SATURDAY, JULY 16, 11:30 A.M.

TOWNSEND TRIPP SAT IN TOMMY COTTON'S AL-bany office, wondering why he wasn't the boss. He was better educated than Tommy Cotton (Princeton versus Hofstra), better connected to the right sort of people. And yet he lacked the killer instinct, always had, and such being the case was relegated to the sidelines, the backrooms, holding Tommy's coat. The good news was that Tommy Cotton was moving up. And Townsend was gaining invaluable experience and entree, trusted to act on Tommy's behalf at every turn, even opening Tommy's personal mail, which that Saturday morning included the overnight envelope with the devastating photos and unsigned letter.

This had to be a joke, he thought. A very sick joke, calling the senator a cocksucker.

He read the note again, while his party-trained mind ran down the list of plausible spins they might apply to the situation, such as research and development, undercover operations.

What did the sender want? The letter merely threatened. So the bite would come later, when Tommy was sick and tired of living scared. Which meant there was time to counterattack.

Jack Barthwell was the obvious suspect, sure, but who else. Roger Smith didn't have the balls for this move, but that geek might have snapped the photos, like he had snapped Barthwell right out of his job.

Notify the boss and assemble staff, thought Tripp. Assess damage. Practice triage. Simple, impersonal duties to settle his nerves. Be grateful you weren't invited to share in that particular round of lines, the cheap pricks. Townsend Tripp flipped through the Rolodex, called the senator's hotel room in the Hamptons. Busy. Tripp had the hotel operator cut in, was told the phone was off the hook. Tripp left Tommy a message to call back ASAP, lives were at stake. Now pacing behind his desk, Tripp tried the senator's cellular phone, heard a mechanical voice say, "The mobile customer you are trying to reach—"

What else? he wondered, staring at the great seal of the State of New York. How to apply a tourniquet to Tommy's wound? He checked the photos again to reassure himself that his own face was absent from the background. A look at Tommy's wall of fame, the pictures of the famous and infamous hugging the senator, offered little consolation. Tommy Cotton was busted if these threats were carried out. And if Paula Crenshaw-Cotton ever saw the evidence, Tommy could kiss those little girls good-bye, as well.

Tripp considered resigning, effective yesterday. Then he dialed Sherri Sawchuck at her residence hotel, on the theory that the local media would need to be charmingly and massively lied to, thinking she would be annoyed at a call on a rare weekend off.

No answer at the downtown Red Roof; where was she? Sherri had no life outside the business, not in Albany anyway, not that he knew of. Her tribe lived on the Island. She should be home, and she was not.

Did she get an overnight delivery too? he wondered. Was a similar explosive stuffed inside his own screen door at home?

That was to be his first stop, to see if he should even bother to keep on fighting. Then he would go to the airport, try to save his boss. Tommy would owe him everything. Townsend Tripp made a note to fly first class, while he still could.

SATURDAY, JULY 16, 3:55 P.M.

BOBBING ABOUT ON THE FORTY-FOOT BLUE SAIL-boat, far from the eyes of the world, there was no pretending with Sherri. The passion was raw and rocket-fueled. They were equals in contrast, physically inseparable, each using the other to the doorstep of pain and exhaustion. Tommy Cotton loved to watch her work in the galley, naked but for black heels, fixing him umbrella drinks and spicy snacks. Posing for him. Taunting. Coy about her butt. Letting him know she knew how bad he wanted her tits in his mouth, and withholding them.

During the day they sometimes did lines the size of cigarettes and he made her go up on deck when no other boats were around. She would lift her arms to the sun, and her breasts would rise, and his cock would damn near explode. At night, he would take her up against the mast, drilling the darkness and gazing at the stars.

And this was only the beginning, he believed, as he stood at the helm that afternoon, his nose lathered with sunscreen, admiring all he could see.

"Honey," he called down into the galley. "How's about you chop us a chunk?"

"Can you wait till after lunch?"

"I'll make you my lunch."

"Yes, dear."

"And a beer, okay?"

"Sure."

SATURDAY, JULY 16, 4:30 P.M.

A STILL SLIGHTLY AIRSICK TOWNSEND TRIPP GAVE up knocking on the senator's hotel room door and seriously considered the possibility that he had covered up for a bad boss long enough.

One more shot he owed him. No more. One more attempt to give the man a chance to save his professional life.

Tripp found the hotel dock easily enough, at the end of a narrow lane, even found the tender operator, a wizened old man wrapped around a can of Bud and a copy of *Bassmaster.*

"I'm looking for Senator Cotton," said Tripp. "I work for him."

"Doesn't everybody."

"Excuse me?"

The old man took his time lighting a Camel. "My orders say he's not to be disturbed."

"That's ridiculous."

"You work for him, you know he hates to be disturbed."

"This is an emergency."

"They're all emergencies, kid."

Tripp knew he would get nowhere with this East End

dope. When Tommy bought someone, they stayed bought, as a general rule. "Let me ask you this, my good man, my fellow employee, loyal Bonacker, if you will," said Tripp. "His guest for the weekend—any chance she's tall and sexy and black as fucking night?"

The Bud man couldn't help but laugh, showing Tripp a row of crooked teeth. "Son of a bitch," he said. "Maybe you do really work for him, not that that gets you on the boat."

"It doesn't matter," said Tripp. Nothing mattered anymore, not where Tommy Cotton was concerned. Sneaking around on his closest adviser, with her. The nerve of that fucking addict. And, yes, Sherri had won the staff wars, but she had just hitched her wagon to one lame jackass. Townsend Tripp would see to that. He should have seen this coming, he thought. But he would live and he would learn.

Townsend Tripp walked away from the dock that afternoon without another word. He would return to Albany that night and spend a cozy summer Sunday with the senator's files, alone, using this fortuitous headstart to build a life-raft for himself.

30

GEORGE RESTED HIS HAIRY FOREARMS ON THE
handle of his shovel, watching Luther gouge out the corners
of a new grave in the old family cemetery. The hole was already waist-deep, and on Luther that was saying something.
George was thinking that Luther wasn't half bad, that maybe
they ought to be friends. For one thing, Luther had a future
when his sentence was complete. More of a future than
George, what with all those kiss-ass affirmative action programs, and the fact that Luther possessed marketable skills.

"How's your man holding up?" asked Luther, taking a
break, wiping the sweat from his brow.

"Orin's fine," said George. "Why?"

"Because I like him, that's why."

"Don't be thinking that he likes you," said George.

Luther looked past George's knees, at fat white clouds
over the Sound. "I wouldn't dream of it."

"No more than he has to, believe me. Hey, somebody's
got to tell you the freaking truth."

"I hear you turned your back on him."

George's eyes popped open wide, and his hands choked the handle of his unused shovel. "That's a freaking crock of shit. Who had the balls to tell you that?"

"No one said it to me directly, of course. But you know I hear everything here," said Luther. "I'm part of the furniture. And, hey, somebody's got to tell you the freaking truth."

"Now I'm sure I'm not sure what you're talking about."

"Okay, George," said Luther, bending to finish digging the police commissioner's grave, next to the grave Luther had dug for his son. "Forget I mentioned it. What you do is your business."

"Freaking A right."

George glumly dropped his chin to the handle, trying to do just that, trying to forget his confusion, blocking out the consequences.

Nicky had said Orin was a plant, a fucking rat, just like the last time when he swept through Belmont, scarfing up the goodies, keeping the lion's share. George was the patsy, again.

Nick said he didn't understand it, why a cop would work so hard against other cops. Something in his childhood, maybe—the scumbag. So then why was Orin locked in the basement, facing a transfer to Buttfuck U? Or was that just one more trick? He and Orin weren't that freaking close he had to risk the rest of his life; truth be told, they'd hardly seen each other in the last few years. Son of a bitch was pussy-whipped now. Sober. Aloof, like most rich people. He thought he was better than everyone else. And nobody killed nobody, George thought obstinately, watching the wind ruffle the baby grass that covered Skip and Gramps.

He would have known.

SUNDAY, JULY 17, 10:00 A.M.

OFFICER ARNOLD MEYERS WAVED AT THE CHILDren jumping rope on the sidewalk as he turned onto the block.

They did not wave back.

Meyers found the right address and pulled the banged-up marked police car halfway down the driveway, parking it next to the big white house, where he was visible but unobtrusive. He made himself as comfortable as he could on the torn vinyl seat, arranged his Egg McMuffins on the dashboard, stirred sugar into his coffee, and opened his newspaper, figuring he had maybe six hours of abject boredom ahead of him before the police commissioner's widow returned to her home.

She would thank him for minding the place, then dismiss him like a servant, a gofer.

He would return to headquarters, be given another errand, another no-brainer, maybe traffic duty outside a rich kid's birthday party or shopping for office supplies. Last week he and other members of the bow-and-arrow squad used a paddy wagon to deliver a steel-drum band to the Freeport mayor's birthday party.

And all because a month ago a hairbag cop named Orin Boyd could not keep his hands to himself, had to slap around a senator.

Meyers read the article about the funeral, saw who would be there—the giants of the profession—saw no mention of an Officer Meyers on guard duty.

A Mr. Townsend Tripp, speaking for—"the regrettably out-of-town on a well-deserved vacation"—Senator Thomas Cotton, expressed his remorse at the senator's absence from so solemn and momentous an occasion.

Meyers growled and closed the paper. Bastards, all of them, destroying an honorable profession, turning real cops into butlers and roadies, and the brass allowed it, too chickenshit to protest.

He would fuck this job every chance he got for the next twenty years to get even. He was *glad* he hadn't liked Trimble. He didn't like anybody on this job. Pricks.

Meyers grabbed some hand cream and his favorite *Penthouse* from his briefcase, checked his watch, his rearview mirrors, flipped to a letter he particularly enjoyed, from a very naughty babysitter.

SUNDAY, JULY 17, 10:05 A.M.

PRANK DINOSTRA HAD BEEN A FREQUENT VISI-
tor to the police commissioner's house during better days.
They had played cards here, many nights, with everybody
who was anybody: Prank had served as bartender for Skip's
engagement party. Prank had slept in Skip's room on those
boozy occasions when driving would have been criminal.
Now he squatted behind the thick azalea bushes at the rear
of the wide property with his binoculars aimed at the cop in
the driveway, figuring—from the overly pleasured look on
the young cop's face—that he would have ample time to
make his entry and exit unseen. Prank could almost hear the
kid's sergeant later, when the burglary would be discovered
by Amanda Trimble: "What the fuck were you doing all
day, jerking off?"

Prank carded the rear kitchen door, punched in the security code before the bells started ringing.

The tapes Orin had told him about were right where he
knew they would be, in Skip's old room, in a wooden box
under the single bed, along with a set of backup paperwork detailing the entire operation, from Boyd's recruitment to the night before the commissioner's death.
Testament, Prank wondered as he sat on the bed and
scanned the documents, to David Trimble's fierce deter-
mination to protect his own or to his single-minded embrace of denial?

Prank knew well his old friend had been capable of both.

Like most cops.

SUNDAY, JULY 17, 11:30 A.M.

PRANK DINOSTRA REMAINED AT THE REAR OF THE
massive crowd outside the church, among gawking civilians, away from the sea of uniforms and kilts and motorcy-

cles, from Monsignor O'Rourke and his band of angels when they carried out the flag-draped casket. Prank had a cold handgun in his pocket that he shouldn't have had, and he feared being recognized, then either hugged or frisked, then violated.

He need not have worried.

He saw people he knew, and they didn't know him, as if the years inside Soundview had erased him.

He thought he would cry during taps, but he didn't.

The motorcade set out for the Honor Farm and the graveyard on the hill. Prank said his common prayers, the ones he had known all his life, sure they would not be heard. He slipped away from the fringe of the crowd, a man with one last, large thing to do, a man without the time or the heart to return to the Farm to watch his friend's remains join his son's in the ground.

Prank knew which nearby cocktail bars would fill up with blue suits, and he picked for himself one that would not, a sleazy dump at the end of a strip mall in Carle Place, with a neon champagne glass over the dented steel door, one old lady drunk at the far end of the bar. Prank took a seat at the opposite end.

"Don't you look nice," said the barmaid as she waddled over to get his order. "What are you having this afternoon?"

"Something strong . . . overproof rum, and Coke."

"Bad day?"

"I just buried my best friend," said Prank, "and nobody knows it."

The barmaid blinked. "I don't understand."

"Good," he said. "This is not a pretty story."

Prank called Judy Boyd's cellular from the pay phone next to the putrid rest rooms, held his breath while it rang.

"Hello?"

"I'm right around the corner. You ready?" said Prank.

"Born ready," said Judy.

Sunday, July 17, 12:30 p.m.

FREDDY GANDOLFO WAS WEARING HIS WRAP-around mirrored sunglasses and a New Jersey Devils cap, and sitting in a white 1989 Volkswagen Golf, an automobile with New York plates that consisted of some anonymous collection of numbers and letters the state dished out to any hump without the class to personalize. He was considering growing a mustache, maybe a Fu Manchu, anything not to look the way he had at the Roosevelt Field mall the other night.

Cousin Nick had to be pretty impressed, because the real cops were stunned, literally clueless, according to the *Newsday* Freddy held against the steering wheel. Trimble's widow was saying he'd been out a lot lately on a case; she didn't know which one. And police headquarters had no comment on such a case, would neither confirm nor deny that one existed. One of several sidebars rehashed Skip's recent suicide, with a Detective Lieutenant Kruger telling everybody that the events could not possibly be connected. "A great man is gone," he said, "I will not rest until his killer is caught."

Freddy smiled arrogantly behind his dark glasses, in part to ward off the swell of fear flooding his gut that they were at this moment after him like dogs, in part because here was his fifteen minutes of fame, his chance at big money and a fearsome reputation. He checked his target location again, saw in his rearview mirror the front door open. Two women came out to the stoop, one of them Judy Boyd.

Freddy put down the newspaper, pulled off his shades, and took up his binoculars; he swiveled in his seat and watched Judy and her girlfriend, Meryl, trot down the steps of the high-ranch, climb in a black LeBaron convertible.

Freddy started his car and slumped low, ready to slide out behind her, sure she'd be headed east, the direction from which she had come. But Judy and her friend were headed west, and by the time Freddy whipped a U-turn and made it to Glen Cove Road, the bitches were nowhere in . . . Nope, there they were. Southbound.

He trailed the black convertible through heavy traffic onto the southbound Meadowbrook Parkway, past Roosevelt Field, as if to taunt him, finally onto the Southern State Parkway, where they turned east, headed to Suffolk County, and Freddy began to wonder if he wasn't being led on a wild-goose chase.

But that was giving these two bitches an awful lot of credit.

Unless they were driving like this to lose any possible tails, because they were on their way to the money, if any money existed, because, at long last, they needed it.

The redhead driving worked her way south to the water through Bay Shore neighborhoods, turned onto Foster Avenue, and rode it to the end, dropped Judy off at the ticket booth for the ferry to Fire Island Pines.

Boyd had owned a boat, Freddy recalled as he parked the Golf across the street. Before Freddy had sunk the hunk of shit. Which meant Boyd had enjoyed easy access to Fire Island, year-round, if withdrawals were necessary. He could come and go whenever he wanted and no one would be the wiser.

Freddy smelled pay dirt.

He boarded the ferry last, stayed for the duration of the crossing at the opposite end of the high-speed vessel from Judy, hiding behind his crumpled newspaper, wishing he were not wearing tight black polyester slacks and a sleeveless T-shirt that showed off his powerful, colorful arms, dodging probes from nearby males.

Judy was first off the boat onto the wide sunny dock, and she walked briskly down the boardwalk toward the community center, the post office, then turned south, headed for the ocean.

Freddy wondered if she knew he was watching her, if she could feel it the way he could always feel it when the cops were watching him, the way he always knew a day or two before a bust that it was coming. The boardwalk creaked under his feet as he made after her, certain she didn't know he was on to her, because she never once looked back as she strolled past small cottages and the occasional large stone castle, then dropped onto the sandy path that led into a forest, a perfect place for an ambush, if ever Freddy saw one.

Eighty yards into the woods, Freddy could stand it no longer. "Excuse me? Ma'am? Hold up a minute?"

Judy Boyd stopped, slowly turned to face the man who had more than likely burned down her house. "Yes?" she said. "Can I help you? Do I know you?"

Freddy looked back down the narrow trail through the dwarf pines. "Let's just say *I* know *you*."

She tried to memorize what she could see of his face, the way Orin had taught her. "Really?"

"Where's the money, lady?"

"Fuck off."

Freddy's eyes opened wide in primal anger, and it suddenly didn't matter to him anymore that Judy was a woman, a cop's wife, no one talked to Freddy Gandolfo like that. He was thinking of raping her after he smacked her around when her steel-toed hiking boot rose to his crotch, crushing his nuts, dropping him to his knees. He was curling face down into the sand when he felt the barrel of the gun at his neck, then a hand digging his wallet out of his jeans.

"Put your hands behind your back," said a man.

Freddy was terrified and did as he was told, was soon wearing handcuffs, grateful the man standing over him with the gun was a cop, that he would within the hour be chatting with his lawyer, working out a deal. He turned his head to get a look at the cop, felt the snakes in his gut when he observed that the cop riffling his wallet was wearing a black ski mask over his face, like no kind of cop Freddy had ever seen. And Freddy had to pee, really bad.

"What will you do to him?" asked Judy.

"Oh, I'll just explain to Freddy Gandolfo here how I'm gonna be his worst fucking nightmare, short of cousin Nicky, pardon my French."

Freddy brightened. "You know my cousin Nicky?"

"A piece of shit," said Prank. "Let's see that face of yours in the sand."

While Freddy did the ostrich, Prank handed Judy a gym bag filled with the papers and cassette tapes he had burgled from the commissioner's house.

"Thank you," said Judy.

"Tell Orin he was right about me."

"I will," she said. "He loves that."

Prank waited a minute while Judy headed back to the dock, then he marched Freddy Gandolfo through the thick green underbrush at gunpoint to the rear of a dilapidated boathouse, repeatedly jamming the barrel in his back, his head, knocking him off stride.

"You do anything Nicky tells you?" asked Prank. "He tells you suck, you dive and gobble?"

"Stop it. Please. You're scaring me."

Prank grabbed Freddy by the collar and threw him hard against the rotted boards, said, "The scam is over, scumbag. You follow Boyd's wife again and you die. *Capisce?*"

Freddy nodded eagerly, perhaps growing in confidence that he might eventually escape his uncomfortable circumstances.

Prank pulled off Freddy's sunglasses, to get a better read on the man's veracity, and he saw that dumb Freddy's eyebrows were singed nearly bare, the skin above his hook nose raw and blistered.

Prank's brain jumped into overdrive, opening windows on worlds, merging files. And then he knew the who, what, where, and how to it. "Well, I'll be damned," Prank said softly. "Why?"

"Why what?"

"Why Trimble?"

"I burned my face lighting a gas grill, at a tea dance, here on the Island," said Freddy, "and you're not allowed to be picking on me. This is discrimination."

"Hell of a thing, torch an old man."

Prank was considering the complicated logistics of a

civilian hauling Freddy from Fire Island to jail when he heard something. He was turning around, expecting to see Judy Boyd, when the sniper opened fire.

Anthony Bellapannucci stepped from the reeds and stood over the dying men, watching in morbid fascination as their bodies twitched and their blood spilled into the sand.

31

"I HOPE IT'S NOT TOO LATE TO BE CALLING," SAID
Townsend Tripp, knowing that it was never too late at night
to call the people he'd been calling, that they demanded
their intelligence fresh, while it was useful.

"Of course not. What's wrong?"

"The senator has gotten himself in a little jam," said
Tripp, "and I felt it best you know before the public gets
wind of it. I realize you were to have dinner with the senator on Tuesday, and I thought you might want to rethink
those plans."

"What is it," said the import-export lawyer, "drugs or
pussy?"

"Both."

"Feds or local?"

"Could be the CIA, for all I know," said Tripp. "The
goods are real."

"Tommy have a plan?"

"Actually, Tommy doesn't know about this yet, sir. He's
been out of touch this weekend."

"Knee-deep in pussy and drugs, no doubt."

Tripp exhaled as if he actually gave a shit. "Highly likely, I'm sorry to say."

"What are your plans, Townsend?" asked the lawyer.

"Save as many of the faithful as I can, before taking an extended vacation. Hope that when I return one of the faithful remembers my efforts."

"That's smart. Hell, none of this was your fault, right?"

"Perish the thought."

Townsend Tripp said good night and moved one name down the Large Contributor list, punched another number in the descending order of clout, a tobacco lobbyist. Tripp had already alerted the capos and the labor goons, two big-time financiers, one publisher, and one really dangerous United States senator.

Time to get out, he said to them, before the market opens in the morning. Time to put distance between themselves and the loose-cannon senator with personal problems.

Thanks for the heads-up, they all said; you did the right thing.

MONDAY, JULY 18, 10:00 A.M.

DOC ROBBINS ARRIVED AT ORIN'S CELL FOR A regularly scheduled session, apparently not wanting this punitive break to allow any backsliding in therapy or interruption of his cash flow. Orin had figured out this much about the old fraud: sessions did not get skipped, and Homo did not get stiffed.

"How's it going," Doc Robbins asked, pulling up a folding chair outside Orin's cell.

"I need a cigarette. Bad."

Doc Robbins smiled and suggested that this was perhaps the perfect opportunity to beat the filthy habit.

"Hypnosis, you mean? In here?"

"You said you wanted to quit."

"Won't that look like you're churning the account?"

Doc Robbins crossed his legs at the knee and regarded Orin from a different angle. "I think you fear the loss of control."

"Yeah? Really?"

"I think you're afraid I'll learn things about you."

"You're giving yourself an awful lot of credit, Doc. What are you gonna ask me? You gonna ask me about Skip? Or is it Dick you're worried about? Two patients you should have saved, maybe?"

"You're still obsessing, I see."

"Thank God someone is."

Then the hallway door flew open and Warden Smith burst in and stormed to the cell, announcing that any further psychiatric care for Orin Boyd was canceled.

"Are you sure?" asked the doctor. "This might expose us to litigation down the road."

"As of zero-seven hundred hours tomorrow morning you can forget you ever knew him."

"Lots of people have, Doc," said Orin. "Don't feel bad."

Smith said, "I've just told some of the other men that Boyd's to be transferred tomorrow, and you could instantly feel the relief."

MONDAY, JULY 18, 11:00 A.M.

SENATOR THOMAS COTTON SASHAYED INTO HIS Albany offices deeply tanned and dumb as a rock, but he rapidly surmised that something was wrong when he saw the morning mail still piled on the unmanned receptionist's desk, a remarkable dereliction of duty unless the office was operating in the crisis mode (working phone banks, stuffing envelopes, shredding the truth), a situation he couldn't possibly know about given his weekend's privacy requirements.

He leaned into Towny Tripp's office and his heart

stopped beating, for his best friend and most trusted aide had clearly flown the coop, leaving behind an empty desk and ravaged files.

"Uh-oh. I don't fucking like this."

Tommy Cotton staggered to his desk, feeling like a drunk after a blackout, too embarrassed to walk down the hall and ask a peer what had happened in his absence, fearful of adding to the evidence against himself.

It had to be something big, public. But if it was public, someone should have notified him, no matter what his rules were. So maybe that was what the shit-faced tender operator had been blithering about on the ride in from the mooring, looking for a tip for chasing some clown away.

No way. He would have been jumped by the press at the airport, on the steps outside.

This was crazy, he thought, frantically looking about his dark, wood-paneled office for message slips he might have missed, the simple courtesy of a letter of resignation. His head ached and his heart was pounding. He opened his desk drawer and pulled out his jar of spearmint Tums, swallowed three, then he drew his curtains and got down to the protocol for a politician on the ropes.

He called his mentor, the United States senator in Washington, D.C., and not only did he not get through the outer layer of staff, he got chilled by an underling who would not give his name, was told to solve his own problems, that there were nasty sanctions for those who soiled the party.

"I'm out?" asked Cotton.

"And if you're trying to tape us, you fucking rat—"

"I wouldn't think of it. I—"

Click.

Senator Thomas Cotton called the office of a certain well-known financier, who apparently pulled the phone away from an overly protective assistant, and yelled, "Lose my number, schmuck," before slamming down the phone.

"Son of a bitch!" cried Cotton. "Motherfucker!"

Cotton gave up when he actually overheard the tobacco lobbyist instructing his wife to "just hang up on that asshole."

What the fuck was going on?

Fucking Tripp had not only quit without notice and run for the hills, that highbrow sneak had burned all the best bridges behind him. This was insane, that he could be isolated and rendered powerless in a weekend and know nothing of the reason. This was treason of the highest order.

He heard a soft knock on his door, and Sherri Sawchuck, who never left home looking less than pressed, came into his office wearing a navy blue Yale sweat suit, her hair still damp from her shower, which he knew meant she had learned of his problem since he had dropped her off.

"Is it bad?" he said softly. "What did we miss?"

She tossed the couple of pictures Tripp had left her onto his desk. Cotton stared at each one for two minutes, separately, then held them together and gave them twenty seconds more. His head filled with fog.

"Who's the chick?" asked Sherri. "I thought I was the only one you ever—"

"Don't start bitching at me now. Think!" he screamed at her. "You're the Ivy Leaguer. What do I make of this? Huh? Maybe you should order up some plane tickets for me, say five o'clock tonight. I think I need to spend some quiet time this week."

"Me, too?" she asked.

"Better make this a family week. Okay? Nothing personal."

"You know what I think, then, Tommy. I think it's time that I, too, explore opportunities in the private sector."

"Say what?"

"I'm quitting."

"Why?"

"Because I didn't come this far to go down the drain with you. Nothing personal."

Cotton thought fast about how much she knew—

names, dates, and details—and realized a peaceful parting was best for both of them. They might even remain lovers. "Can I still call you," he asked, "when things settle down?"

"I'd rather you didn't."

"Sherri?"

"Sorry, kid."

Tommy Cotton gathered himself and called home. "I'm back," he said cheerfully. "What's up? How are the kids?"

Paula Crenshaw-Cotton matched his phony warmth. "Everything's fine, honey. Did you have a good trip?"

"I've had better."

"That's not what I heard," she said. "I heard this trip included your wildest fantasy."

"What are you talking about?"

"Didn't you get my summons yet, honey, because if you didn't, and you're at the office, hold on for a second so I can have the server—"

"What summons?"

"To court, regarding our separation agreement. I took the liberty of having one drawn up."

"Look," said the senator, "I'm real busy at the moment, Paula. Could we—"

"Hold on a second," she said.

Tommy cut her off angrily, took a deep breath, and pounded his fist on his desk ten times. It was Tripp, doing this to him. His own man. He had to be stopped. So Tommy called the number he had always hoped he would never have to call. "Anthony, my friend," he said. "I need a meeting."

"So I hear. Amazing, isn't it? Tonight at eleven. The usual spot. And, Tommy, let me tell you how sorry he is that you've risked our substantial investment in your career."

"It may not be too late," said Tommy.

"That's good," said Anthony Bellapannucci. "We'll talk."

MONDAY, JULY 18, 3:00 P.M.

ORIN SPENT THAT LONG DAY IN HIS CELL, MISSING his cigarettes and thinking about the murder cases, the linkages he had overlooked, wondering if he should admit to his role. He expected they would debrief him and cut him loose, if they didn't try to blame the police commissioner's death on him. He would go home, settle his own personal scores. He would reconnect with his father, his daughter, hook them up, try to make that relationship work. Buy another boat. Try to keep loving Judy as much as he loved her when they were forced apart. He should feel worse, he thought, having lost another war, gained and lost buddies, like George, who was plainly afraid of Nicky or outsmarted by Nicky, it didn't matter which anymore.

At a little after three o'clock a gaggle of guards walked him in shackles upstairs to make his one official phone call. The entourage passed the doctor's office, which was now getting from Ira the top-to-bottom scrubbing one associated with sudden and permanent turnover.

"Where's Homo?" Orin asked Officer Marshall. "What's going on?"

"He retired," said Marshall.

Orin stopped short, causing a minor pileup of staff. "But I was making such progress."

"Sure you were."

Standing at Marion's desk, Orin held the phone to his ear and dialed with cuffed, shaking hands. The monsignor was out, he was told by the switchboard operator, probably down the road at the rehab camp.

"This is Nassau County Police Officer Orin Boyd—"

"I think you'd better call back when Monsignor O'Rourke is here," the young woman said, and then she hung up—exactly the procedure she had been told to follow.

Without waiting for anyone to tell him he couldn't, Orin quickly dialed Prank at his apartment, and got no answer.

"That's two," said Officer Marshall. "You're only supposed to get one."

"One more, please. This is life and death," said Orin. "And I ain't exactly the hysterical type."

"Sorry."

"Give him one more shot," said Marion.

Marshall nodded at the phone. Orin's hand hovered over the dial as he thought of who to call, who could help, inside the job and out, realized there were damn few left who would vouch for him without a hell of a lot of corroborating evidence. He smiled sadly at Marshall and said, "Geraldo probably gets fifty calls a day from inmates, swearing they were framed, huh?"

"At least."

MONDAY, JULY 18, 7:00 P.M.

ROGER SMITH SET THE DINNER TRAY ON THE floor outside the bars. He pulled up the folding chair and quietly faced the cell as if it were a big-screen TV, as if he expected Orin to get off his cot and beg for his chow. Orin propped himself up on his elbows and stared at Smith for a while, sensing fear from the warden, not the joy he would have expected.

"You know why some of the men are so relieved I'm being shipped out?"

Smith folded his arms across his chest. "Why?"

"Because I'm close to finding the killer."

Smith tipped back his chair and laughed too loud. "You couldn't find a Jew in Crown Heights."

"Where the hell did you get these big balls, Rog? You never had 'em when we were kids. It can't be just these bars, or it shouldn't be."

Roger's face lost a touch of color. "You're all air, Boyd. Just like you were back then."

"I think your memory's cloudy, Sissyboy. You're still

scared to death of me. Take your boots off and smell your feet."

"You fucking cops think you're so special."

"Okay, Rog, name all the movies, television shows, plays, books, comics, or interactive video based on prison guards. In fact, name one."

"*Brubaker.*"

"Do me a favor, don't name another."

"This prison is my little kingdom now. Run by my little book of rules. And they pay me a hundred grand to do it."

"They should lock you up for fraud, because you don't know dick about corrections, about police work, about people. Say in Skip's case, here's what you didn't do, you ass-sucking buff, what any real cop would have done in a heartbeat."

"What?" challenged Roger, standing up so fast he knocked his chair over backward.

"You didn't treat an unattended death like a homicide until proof to the contrary was established. You didn't preserve the scene for detectives. You didn't start a time log. You didn't exclude all persons including police from the scene who did not have an official function to perform. You didn't isolate the witnesses."

Roger Smith seemed to be reviewing what he remembered of his actions that morning, comparing his memories to Orin's charges of malfeasance and nonfeasance. He had yet to mount a defense when Orin said, "You didn't do shit, Roger, except choke."

Roger Smith stared into the cell, sputtering, his eyes unfocused with rage and humiliation. "You know when you were in Vietnam, I rooted for the Cong."

"Lotta people did. Doesn't change the fact you got a killer roaming the grounds, and you won't admit it, much less look for him. You want to be a hero, Sissyboy, here's your chance. You let me out of here now and help me prove those guys were murdered, and you can have all the credit."

Smith turned to leave. "Dream on."

"At least post a guard down here. Your bullshit isolation

scam didn't work at East Meadow, and it ain't gonna work here."

"Are you telling me you're scared?"

Orin said, "I can add injury to insult, Roger. Keep fucking pushing me."

Roger kicked the chair aside and walked to the door. He paused to look back over his star-studded epaulet. "Now who's the sissyboy, eh?"

32

THE HONORABLE THOMAS COTTON PARKED HIS
black BMW in the shadow of the rusty grandstand at Roosevelt Raceway and settled back to wait, thinking of better
days, thinking that when he had first met Anthony's boss
here, the joint had been open for business, a nighttime
place in Nassau to see and be seen. Tony Bellapannucci's
boss had loved the track, the flashy, this-side-of-desperate
crowds, everyone naturally thinking this murderous social
buffoon knew what would happen next, stopping by his
regular table to have the night's card blessed.

Say what you wanted about wiseguys, though. You
could trust them to show for the tough ones. You could trust
them to stand by their own—if they still considered you
their own.

Tommy Cotton realized that he hadn't actually talked to
the boss face-to-face since his election to the Senate, as a
precaution, not a slur, because you never knew who was listening, taking pictures, bribing your friends. He felt certain
Anthony's boss understood, as long as his wishes were

granted. Just as he would now understand their mutual need for damage control.

Nervously looking around the empty parking field, Tommy Cotton knew in his heart the scandal was about to metastasize, go tabloid . . . unless he could find Townsend Tripp and stop his back-channel smear campaign. Sure, he had taken a substantial beating, suffered core and collateral damages, but Tommy Cotton didn't get where he was by ducking confrontation, and he felt that if he could only plug these leaks, he could survive this debacle intact.

And then everyone who had let him down in his midnight hour would pay dearly. He'd torch that tobacco pusher and roast that arrogant Jew, stall his malls with tree-huggers, give the speech of his life for the spotted-snail-whatthe-fuck. And then he'd go home like a real man and whip his fat little wife back in line.

If only it wasn't too late.

Tommy Cotton turned on his interior lights and looked at his Rolex, wondering if the boss was going to be on time, where he might be coming from, the size of the inevitable motorcade, the size of the bodyguards.

When Tommy turned off the light and looked out through the windshield, he saw a single silver Mercedes cruise around the rusty stanchions, shut off its headlights, and stop fifty yards away, like they expected him to get out and walk to them, as a matter of respect.

Tommy Cotton stopped thinking about salvation and started grumbling about the pecking order as he shut off the Beemer and opened his door, and he never heard the man with the piano wire rise up behind him, never quite knew why they were cutting their losses.

TUESDAY, JULY 19, 2:15 A.M.

ORIN DIDN'T HEAR IT SEEPING OVER THE LEDGE, didn't see it dribbling down the ancient bricks and pooling near the drain inside his cell. He smelled it, though, and sat up on his cot thinking of David Trimble, burning down to ashes in his seat belt.

The fumes were thick in his throat. Like fuel oil.

No. Gasoline.

Orin rolled off the cot, put both bare feet in the half-inch puddle. "Cantwell?" he called out.

No answer.

"Hey!"

A lit cigarette flew through the bars of the basement window, landed near the end of Orin's cot, sizzled, flashed a dancing veil of blue across the floor. Orin grabbed the cot, smothered the round.

"Hey, what are you doing? Hey, Cantwell, you fucking lowlife!"

Another cigarette arced into his cell, flared, and died.

Another.

"Help!"

Then Orin heard bushes rustling and footsteps pounding away from his barred window.

"Cantwell! When I get out of here, I'm gonna have you keelhauled! . . . Cantwell!"

TUESDAY, JULY 19, 2:38 A.M.

THE DORMITORY WINDOW CLOSEST TO THE MAN-sion opened wide and a head of thinning red hair poked out, looked both ways. Ira Cohen didn't want to do what he was about to do; in fact, the thought of it absolutely terrified him. He had been awake when he heard Boyd calling for Cantwell, once, twice, three times, in a tone that suggested dire straits. Ira sat up and thought fast about what Zen had been telling him, about working with Boyd in the mansion, his sense that Orin was a good man done wrong, a cop calling for help.

No more standing on the sidelines, wishing and hoping, dreaming of teams he never made, teammates never loved.

Ira knew this was real and he was in it. No excuses. No alibis.

Time to step up and be counted. Time to hit the big shot. More pressure than the World Series, thought Ira, dropping through the ivy to the earth. Because if anyone saw him sneaking about, trying to make a play, there was a chance he could wind up dead. No homecourt edge. No time-outs, baby. No two-minute warning.

TUESDAY, JULY 19, 2:40 A.M.

"CANTWELL!"

"Will you shut the fuck up," Ira stage-whispered through the barred window.

"Ira!" said Orin. "Jesus."

"What's that smell?"

"Someone just tried to torch me, goddamn it. And it's a damn good thing they used Roggie's low-test," said Orin. "You didn't see anybody out there, did you?"

"No. Honest."

Orin worked the angles, figuring the odds, trying like hell to pick a horse he could believe in, made his choice. "I'm still on the job, Genghis. I'm trying to catch Skip's killer."

Ira said, "That damn Zen is always right, isn't he?"

"Pretty much."

"What do you need?"

"I need to get out of here."

"That's what I figured." Ira looked both ways and dropped the cell key through the window bars. Orin caught it, asked Ira if he was ready to do more.

"Such as?"

"Go to my room, pack up my shit, and meet me by the east side door in ten minutes."

"Done."

They heard footsteps echo down the servants' stairs, Officer Cantwell coming back. Orin had time only to unlock the door and hand back the key through the window before Cantwell flopped down on his couch outside the open hallway door.

"That you I heard yelling?" said Cantwell.

"Yes, it was."

"Problem?"

"Oh, a tiny one. Could you come here, please?"

Cantwell grumbled and walked to the cell, flipped on the overhead light. Orin stood near the door, pointed to the wet drain.

Cantwell smelled the gasoline and stepped closer, examined the pool.

"Not exactly the *Exxon Valdez*, I know," said Orin, "but deadly nonetheless."

"Ira can clean it up in the morning."

"It's gasoline, dummy. And those aren't my cigarettes. You guys won't let me have cigarettes, remember?"

Cantwell saw an evening of repose slipping away, and he scratched his head and cursed his luck and leaned forward for a better look just as Orin swung the cell door open, hard into his ruddy face, knocking Cantwell backward, rendering him even more senseless than usual. The clang of metal on bone bounced around the basement, traveled no further.

Orin dragged Cantwell inside the cell and dug through his pockets, his service belt, took his house keys, flashlight, mace, wallet, and folding money, eighty-one bucks. "Cantwell, old buddy," Orin said as he was leaving the basement by the back stairs, "you keep fucking up, you're never gonna be permanent here."

TUESDAY, JULY 19, 2:42 A.M.

ROGER SMITH COULDN'T SLEEP AGAIN, AND IT wasn't all the coffee he had been drinking since he took on this man-size job.

His pajamas were soaked with a chemical sweat, and he wanted a cigarette, even though he did not smoke. Roger turned over in the bed he had slept in since boyhood, and the damp sheets tugged at his feet, and the slats creaked, and his mother called in through his open bedroom door, "Go to sleep, dammit. I can't hear my movie."

"Mom? I need to go to the office."

"Oh, you are just ridiculous."

"I'm going."

She thought about this. "Don't give him the satisfaction, Roggie."

"I have to," said Roger, sitting up, staring through his curtains at the small dark house across the street, where now a young Cuban couple lived, where once a monster was raised.

TUESDAY, JULY 19, 2:49 A.M.

ON THE SECOND FLOOR OF THE QUIET MANSION, Orin crouched outside Warden Smith's office in the dark, gathering his thoughts and energy, frustrated that none of Cantwell's keys did the trick, because Roger Smith trusted no one, with good reason. Because people everywhere just absolutely loved to screw him. So Orin stood up, raised his knee to his chest, and kicked the heavy door off its hinges.

He waited for a reaction from downstairs and heard nothing, then stepped inside the oval office. Roger's World, he thought as he crawled under the locked desk, wedged his feet on one side of the well, his back against the other, took a deep breath and exploded the dowels. He ripped the drawers out with his bare hands, then scanned by moonlight several pages of Roger's personal insurance policy, his Who's Who of Nassau County Swordsmen with Something to Lose—Orin thinking that now was the time to get something on damn near everyone, thinking some of these women were shockingly youthful, others shockingly ugly. The photos he and George had confiscated early on had only told half the story. What was most surprising, but maybe not, was the fact that several had not been taken on or near the Farm—like the one of the assemblyman with those famous bushy eyebrows jamming his tongue down some hooker's throat in front of Madison Square Garden. Roger had stalked his superiors, hunted them with his camera.

Orin took this opportunity to strip to his underwear, feeling no guilt whatsoever as he borrowed a fanny pack, running shoes, and a Gore-Tex suit from the Rog's closet, the suit a purple number with vertical racing stripes.

He rolled up his prison denims, stuffed them in the royal toilet tank. He took the bolt cutters that said on the handle Property of Warden R. Smith, leaned a nine-by-twelve-inch mailing envelope against a chunk of the shattered desk.

TUESDAY, JULY 19, 3:08 A.M.

ROGER'S SHINY IROC COUGHED AND SPUTTERED, died before Roger had a chance to turn it off. He could see the two black faces of the guards in the command post, enjoying his troubles, his fouled injectors, probably laughing about how much he had paid for such a crummy car.

Roger knew he had image problems, dating back to Boyd, which would not easily be corrected. But he had time on his side. And he would grow in his job. Maybe getting all new Honor Farm guards was the answer, men who had not yet been poisoned.

TUESDAY, JULY 19, 3:09 A.M.

THE DOOR WAS OPEN. MORELLI'S DESK ILLUMInated in all its emptiness by the glare of spotlights outside. Orin wasted but a minute going through drawers, finding the electronic pen he had been almost certain would be there—a gift, according to the inscription on its base, from a grateful county. So Nick never signed anything that morning. Because Nick never signed anything at all.

Voices rose from the main stairwell; tired feet scuffed the marble.

Orin closed up the desk and crawled down the hallway to the rear of the house, then tiptoed downstairs and out the back kitchen door, certain at last that it was time to bounce back, time to throw punches in bunches.

"Yo. You looking for me?"

Orin threw himself against the Dumpster, his heart hammering. His eyes grew accustomed to the dark, and he saw a man dressed in black behind the wheel of a golf cart, in the shadows of the eastern portico.

Zen said, "I got your stuff. Where to?"

Orin climbed in next to him. "The Promised Land."

"That's another bus, I think."

Zen hit the accelerator, and they glided silently away from the mansion and up the dark hill.

"Hurry," said Orin, looking back, because the moon was bright and if the hue and cry rose, Orin knew they'd be easy to spot. And Orin needed to be lost in the moneyed hills to the south of the Farm before choppers and dogs joined the hunt.

At the top of a rise they stopped and looked back again at the quiet mansion, and they could see further down a county public-works crew under floodlights, erecting a high wooden security wall between the yacht club and the fences, no doubt to block the privileged from the view of Honor Farm prisoners and staff.

One more day, he would have needed, if the Rog hadn't laid him open to attack. One more day to know why.

They saw the light in a second-floor office go on, and Zen pumped the accelerator and raced headlong for the fences, turned hard left onto the perimeter road. He stopped the cart behind the humming slaughterhouse, pointed to a thick stand of bushes up ahead. "Best route out," he said, "should one be so inclined."

Orin smiled, offered his hand. "Thanks, brother."

"Look, I would have been there sooner for you, but I

wanted to believe they were suicides, because I think of that, too, every day."

"Forget it." Orin handed Zen a scrap of paper, with his father's cellular phone number on it. "You need me, you call."

Zen nodded. "Who?"

Orin shook his head.

"You want him for yourself," said Zen.

"For a lot of people."

"Don't do it," said Zen. "Deliver him up to the law."

"He is the law."

Zen considered this conundrum but a moment. "Too bad for him, then, I guess."

Orin climbed atop the stone wall and checked for the guards' golf cart, then dropped to the roadway and cut a one-yard square from the chain-link fence. He left the monogrammed bolt cutters propped against the fence, then crawled through the hole and held his breath, now the legitimate target of legitimate cops, some of them very good at what they did, as Zen had been.

And Zen was right about the best route to civilization. Not ten yards away was a moonlit path that he followed into a dark tunnel of thick woods, and from there he sprinted across the grassy meadow of the neighboring estate, shining almost white under the moon.

It was all he could do not to laugh out loud.

33

TUESDAY, JULY 19, 3:10 A.M.

ROGER SMITH ARRIVED ON THE SECOND FLOOR
with his pillow and blanket under his arm, angry with
his mother, ready to sleep on his office couch until she
realized things had changed, that he would no longer
accept her badgering to the point where it damaged his
career. He was actually whistling "The Star-Spangled
Banner" at the moment he came face to face with the
obscenity. He said softly, "No," and stepped through
the empty doorframe, turned on the overhead lights,
and stared at his pulverized desk. "What the fuck happened?"

But as soon as he said it, he knew, as soon as he saw
physical damage, smelled the scorched earth of defiance.
He could almost hear secondary fuses burning as he found
the envelope, the batch of color photos he could not recall
sending out to be developed: an aerial shot of him on the
front lawn, holding an expensive bottle of Kreeling wine
by the neck; a glossy portrait of him on his office porch,
picking his nose; one of him gassing up his Iroc in the em-

ployee parking lot from plastic containers that were clearly marked: Property of Nassau County. Gilbert Otto, County Executive.

Roger Smith's heart beat faster while his stomach began to digest itself. His panicked eyes devoured the devastation of his career, his reputation, everything he had built. Roger dove to his knees and frantically dug through the debris that had been his desk, discovered the scrapbook itself was missing, knew in his heart it was over. Warden for a week, thought Roger. And all because of him. Roger righted his chair and slumped in it, wondering how Orin Boyd had managed this assault from his cell, had the office trashed and the photos planted. How did someone in solitary do that?

Roger Smith was flipping through the last of the photos, to learn the full extent of his violation before storming downstairs and making the perpetrator pay, when he came upon a shot of George Clarke. The big idiot was leering over his shoulder at the camera as he pissed on Roger's houseplants.

Smith kicked wood aside until he found his telephone, then called the command post. "Place George Clarke under arrest immediately and come to the basement. If he resists, you blow his fucking brains out."

TUESDAY, JULY 19, 3:17 A.M.

SMITH DESCENDED TO THE BASEMENT TWO steps at a time, framing his opening line, aiming more for Clint Eastwood than Joe Friday, and so naturally he cried out in primal anguish and fear when he saw the cell door ajar, the lumpy Terry Cantwell sleeping on the floor. "Son of shitfuckingcocksucker," he cried. "No. No. No."

Cantwell stirred slightly and moaned.

Roger Smith kicked Cantwell in the ribs and screamed, "I have had just about enough, do you hear me!"

Two guards came running through the doorway, dragging George Clarke, in handcuffs and pajamas, behind them. "What's the matter?" they yelled.

"He's fucking escaped!"

"Who?" asked George.

"Your fucking buddy," cried the Rog. "The motherfucker who took these." Roger Smith mashed a handful of the offending photos into George's face, which caused George to head-butt them out of Roger's hand, which caused the Rog to whack George with his nightstick, knocking him flat on the floor outside the cell.

Roger positioned George's left eyeball an inch from one of the photographs. "Well?" screamed Smith.

Ten seconds passed before George made any response at all, during which time he sadly realized that he had guessed wrong this time, betting with the house, always a mistake with a joker in the deck. George twisted his neck to look up at his jailers.

"That's not me," said George. "My dick is much bigger than that. Someone must have pasted my face onto—"

"Warden?" said one of the guards.

"What?"

"We should probably sound the alarm. Arm the guard and—"

"Do it," cried Roger Smith. "What are you waiting for?"

"Yes, sir."

"He won't get far," Smith sneered to George. "And there ain't a fucking soul out there who will help him."

TUESDAY, JULY 19, 3:40 A.M.

ORIN HAD SPRINTED DIRECTLY SOUTH FROM THE Honor Farm for nearly a mile before encountering so much as a deserted two-lane road, ground he knew would easily be made up by the dogs when they arrived. And in spite of his recent jogs with Zen, his breathing was tortured, his thighs getting heavy.

He had slowed to a trot and was halfway across the meadows of the next estate when behind him he heard the special wail of the siren announcing his departure. He stopped and looked up at the stars, imagining the terror that sound must strike in the hearts of the locals.

Keep on trucking, he told himself. Ten minutes to scramble choppers and dogs meant another mile covered, enlarging their perimeter and diluting their forces. He found a bridle path pockmarked with road apples, which led him to another estate, this one in ruins, and from there he started walking down a paved service road that led to a white-fenced riding ring and dimly lighted, occupied stables.

If he could quickly steal a horse, Orin thought, he might throw off their math and slip their net. He stepped off the road and made his way through the woods, got close enough to smell the horse shit before he saw two men with shotguns, standing just inside the open stable door.

"Shoot to kill," one was saying. "It's the law of the land."

Sirens were howling in the distance as Orin pressed deeper into the trees, heading in another direction. A patrol car was somewhere in the valley below him, ahead of him, with its public address system ordering residents to remain inside, behind locked doors. Orin doubted the men in the stable would obey and expected more of the locals to soon be running about, armed with everything from assault weapons to blunderbusses plucked from mantels.

The first of the choppers beat the trees with its downdraft, probed the canopy with searchlights. Orin checked his watch, knew he had not traveled far enough. His thighs turned to rubber as he followed the chopper further to the south, sticking to the tree cover, looking for a place to break his scent trail, to lose the dogs. Orin didn't actually expect the cops to shoot at him—unless some dipshit rookie like Barney Meyers fucked up—but if they caught him, they'd beat him hard, and the dogs would bite, and the killer would survive to launch additional offensives.

When Orin was out of glucose, oxygen, and every energy source but fear, he spied an ancient barn leaning ten degrees left at the edge of a small cornfield. He stopped and put his hands on his knees, leaned ten degrees left himself. He assumed the barn was abandoned, as its patrician owner no doubt did. Still it was worth a look, for a tractor, or an old car, hell, even a bicycle.

Orin peeked through a broken window, was happy to see a landscaping truck, its rear loaded with mowers and tools. Unfortunately, several bodies littered the floor around the truck in sleeping bags, like cowboys around a campfire.

And the chopper was louder now, doubling back from Northern Boulevard, its searchlight turning night into day at the tree line, now in the cornfield. Orin stepped into the barn as light poured through the holes in the rotted roof.

The men on the floor stirred. One lifted his head. "Yo, dude," he said, "you're early. We start at five."

The elderly Hispanic man was offering him work, Orin realized, until the man also noticed the commotion outside, and then that Orin was not Jose or Alberto. He shined a flashlight up into Orin's face, then smiled as if a prayer had been answered.

"I know you," he said. "You're a detective."

Orin couldn't imagine these fellows had a television set installed out here, but one never knew.

"You let me go once, years ago."

"Oh, yeah?"

Some of the other men woke up grumbling about hassles with cops, then fell happily quiet when they saw they were not being rousted, that their foreman could handle it. "In Belmont," said the man with the flashlight. "I was stealing a bass fiddle for my son—"

". . . And you didn't make the hole in the wall big enough. Yeah, yeah, I remember you. What's happening? How's the family?"

"I have never forgotten your kindness of that night. What can I do for you now, my friend? To repay you."

Orin kneeled next to the old man. "Well, to begin with, things have changed."

TUESDAY, JULY 19, 6:05 A.M.

"WHERE WOULD HE GO?" ASKED ROGER. "HOW does a man just vanish?"

George glared through the bars of his cell and said nothing. Nick Morelli, standing next to Smith, swirled his coffee in his mug and shook his head at George, a signal that this was the wrong time to stand tough for a friend, or the wrong friend. "You don't help the man, how's the man supposed to help you?"

George's face remained a blank, a true reflection of his insider knowledge.

"He's got you pissing on his plants, George. Wise up."

"I'm hungry," said George. "What time is breakfast served down here?"

"He planned this with you," Smith yelled at George. "Don't fucking lie. I know you two were closer than brothers."

"Leave me alone," said George. "You don't know anything."

Roger reached into his briefcase and produced George's book of eligible brides. "I know about this," said the warden. "And I know about mail fraud. And criminal impersonation."

"I never promise 'em nothing . . . and I deliver."

"Are you gonna talk or not?" asked Smith.

"I got nothing to say," George said proudly.

"Then rot."

"Maybe I will."

Smith and Nick turned from the cell and headed for the stairs. "Now, there's a suicide candidate," said Nick. "Maybe you should—"

"We should only be so lucky."

TUESDAY, JULY 19, 8:05 A.M.

ORIN BOYD WAS ON PROSPECT AVENUE IN
stately Garden City—wearing tight green work pants, a
tight Cuervo T-shirt, and a red bandanna 'do rag, with a
screeching jetpack grass-blower strapped to his back—
when Townsend Tripp and Sherri Sawchuck reported Senator Cotton missing, from his Albany office.

"He had a seven-thirty breakfast meeting scheduled for
this morning with one of his biggest supporters," Tripp told
the New York State Police. "He didn't show. He didn't call.
I've been beeping him ever since."

"Has the senator been having any personal problems
lately?" the troopers wanted to know.

"None that we're aware of. Right, Sherri?"

Sherri smiled at her new best friend and ally, Townsend
Tripp, with whom she was steering the senator's office
through rocky waters. "The man has it all."

TUESDAY, JULY 19, 9:50 A.M.

THE TELEVISION NEWS REPORTS SAID THE HONOR
Farm guards had found a hole in the fence, the Nassau
County police dogs had picked up a trail from the hole and
followed it to an abandoned barn.

Area residents were advised to consider the escapee
armed and dangerous and repeatedly given a hot-line number to report any suspicious persons or strange occurrences.

The reporter then stepped in front of this decrepit, listing
barn—as if she had personally tracked the dangerous escapee hither and yon—and called on Acting Police Commissioner Malone to put an end to this "travesty of a prison,
this playpen for crooked cops. . . ."

The anchor began a grave voice-over while they ran aerial views of the Sands Point Peninsula, Mill Neck, Cold
Spring Harbor: "Since their origin, these star-crossed es-

tates along the north shore cliffs have been the setting for many a drama, domestic and otherwise. As best-selling author Nelson DeMille wrote in his elegant novel, *The Gold Coast—*"

Judy shut off the television set, to lower the noise in her head. She and Dawn were holed up in the Freeport Motor Inn that morning, the shade drawn tight against the daylight, making a game of keeping out of sight. There was a miniature coffeemaker in the room and a basket of breadsticks, enough Big Macs from yesterday to hold them till dinnertime, at least.

Judy was on her cellular phone, calling Prank's home number for the tenth time that morning, hearing it ring and ring and ring, because she had read the commissioner's papers and listened to some of the audiotapes and she thought she knew who had killed those men.

TUESDAY, JULY 19, 10:00 A.M.

NICKY HAD BEEN CALLING FREDDY FOR DAYS IT seemed, without success. The story of his life, he thought, picking the wrong partners. Unless Freddy was still tight on Judy Boyd, which could very well lead him into Orin's hands before Anthony Bellapannucci found him, perhaps the most discouraging possibility of all. If Nick knew his cousin, Freddy would sing his fucking lungs out when the torture began.

He dialed Freddy again, let it ring twenty times.

Finally someone picked up. "Stop with the calling, already."

"Who's this?"

"This is the super. Who the hell is this?"

"Freddy's cousin. Let me talk to him."

"Freddy's dead."

"Don't fucking joke."

"Why would I joke? The Suffolk cops just left. They said they found him on Fire Island, with some other dead guy.

But I didn't think Freddy was gay, did you? Man, it just goes to show you—"

Nick hung up, feeling sorry for his aunt but relieved nonetheless.

TUESDAY, JULY 19, 10:37 A.M.

NEW YORK STATE POLICE HOMICIDE DETECTIVES interviewed Senator Cotton's thoroughly mystified wife and children at their home, asked the usual questions, to which they gave the usual answers: When did you last hear from him? Any personal problems? Any idea what he was wearing? Blood type? The name of his doctor? His dentist?

"He's got a million of those these days," said Paula.

"What kind of car was he operating, ma'am?"

"The black Beemer," she said calmly, "which should be relatively easy to find."

"Why?"

"Turn on the Lojack."

"Yeah?"

"Sure. He had one of the first in the state, some kind of pilot program for the bigshots."

TUESDAY, JULY 19, 11:19 A.M.

NASSAU COUNTY HOMICIDE DETECTIVES STOOD chatting casually next to the senator's abandoned BMW, which was still parked behind the Roosevelt Raceway grandstand, its driver's side door coated with drying blood. Uniformed cops were stringing yellow crime-scene tape around the perimeter of the parking lot, while helicopters hovered overhead, making it hard for the squeal man to be heard on his cellular phone, begging headquarters for every available man, woman, and dog, and permission to execute drastic measures.

It was the lead detective's suspicion, he told his mates, that some kind of psycho-political killer had claimed his second high-ranking official in a week. Now, if headquarters didn't want to authorize the overtime to solve these cases, that was another story, but don't anybody come crying to him when somebody smoked the county executive.

34

THE LANDSCAPING TRUCK DRIVEN BY THE OLD man in the maroon jogging suit stopped at a red light a block from the heart of town. In the back of the wood-slat truck were rakes and shovels and mowers, his six regular co-workers—not a green card among them—and Orin Boyd, the very strange gringo cop who had passed out his morning's pay to the others.

When the light changed to green, the truck held one less illegal.

Orin stood in the alley next to the abandoned restaurant and watched the public phone booths outside the Freeport train station for ten minutes before deciding they weren't being watched by someone else.

He was wrong.

He had his quarter poised against the slot when it rang, jolting his heart. Orin glanced about quickly, picked up the receiver. He checked the earpiece for dog shit, placed it to his ear.

"My name is Gerald . . . I've been watching you."

"Not with a gun in your hand, I trust."

"You know your T-shirt shows off your muscles to elegant effect."

"Why thank you, Gerald. Now, do you mind there, my man? I need the line for a very important call."

"Don't hang up," Gerald said breathlessly.

"Why not?"

"Can we meet? Just to talk."

"Not today." Orin hung up and stared out at the long lines of parked cars that had a view of the pay phone, felt sick and sorry for the peeper, probably in a leased Lexus, pulling his pud.

He threw in his change and dialed. One ring and she answered, as if she had been sitting by the phone. "My name is Police Officer Orin Boyd," he said. "You spoke to my wife."

"A lovely woman. What's she doing with you?"

"I'm a lovely man."

"Your picture's all over the television, Officer Boyd . . . of course everybody's taste is different. You probably think I'm a no-good slut for dating Dick."

It was interesting that she called Dick's forays up the tree outside her bathroom dates, but she was the one stuck in the wheelchair. Let her call it what she would. "No opinion," said Orin. "I only met him once."

"He was sweet," she said.

"Thanks for talking to me."

"Like I have a choice."

"Anybody from the police department ever talk to you about that night?"

"No."

"And you couldn't very well volunteer any information."

A pause of five seconds. "My husband thinks things are better."

"They're not?"

"Next question."

"You had a date with Dick that night?"

"Yes."

"Outside the fences?"

"Yes."

"Ever have one before that night?"

"No. That was the first attempt. I had told my husband I was going to watch my sister's kids while she ran an errand or two. Then I drove to the beach, behind the yacht club, and waited and waited in my car for as long as I could. When he didn't show, I figured he had tried and failed, and then when I heard he was dead, I don't know, I kinda figured he killed himself to show me he loved me. So I didn't call the cops."

"He was coming, if it's any consolation. You got that part of it right."

"Somebody really killed him?" she asked.

" 'Fraid so."

A moment's silence passed between them, perhaps for the dead. "Do you have those pictures I need?"

"There never were any pictures."

Orin hung up and scanned the parking lot, for Freeport cops, county cops, state cops, Feds, for Gerald, saw only the sun blazing off the rows of windshields.

He ducked back into the booth and dialed another number.

"State Senator Cotton's office," said the woman. "Sherri Sawchuck speaking."

"This is Marcus McGovern, over at the Suffolk County district attorney's office. Any chance of talking with the boss?"

"Where have you been? The boss is missing, probably dead."

"Bummer for Tommy. Is Stony Tripp there?"

"You mean Mr. Townsend Tripp, don't you? No, I'm sorry, but at the moment he's over at the capitol, being screened to finish the senator's term."

"It'll *take* a real ass to fill that seat."

"I don't find you very funny, sir. What did you say your name was? Mc—"

"Tell him he's wasting his time, if these photographs I'm looking at are real." Orin hung up and walked to the bus stop. He stood before the graffiti-covered Nassau County bus schedule and began the ridiculously difficult procedure of finding a bus that would take him east fast, was about to give up and hail a cab, when a horn honked softly behind him, the friendly toot of a shiny green Jaguar, driven by an older gentleman.

"You're still here," he said through his open window. "That means to me you're thinking about it."

"It?"

"Beginning a friendship."

"It's just that I'm very nervous, Gerald. Do you mind if I sit down?"

Gerald said that he understood mixed emotions and happily moved his briefcase from the front seat to the back. "Please," he said, flipping the lock up. "Climb in. And my name's not really Gerald."

"What a terrible thing," said Orin, "to start our relationship off with a lie."

35

ANTHONY BELLAPANNUCCI PARKED HIS 1979 cherry red Corvette halfway down the block from Meryl Colby's house in Carle Place. He got out directly and walked back to her gate. He wore a trench coat, a white turtleneck, and a gun, and a real Nassau County detective's shield on a chain around his neck, and Meryl made him coffee while he explained how worried he was about Orin Boyd's wife, how urgent it was he—and the police department—find her immediately.

Three minutes later, Anthony was on the car phone to his father. "She don't know dick, Dad. She wasn't told so she couldn't tell. She says Boyd's wife wouldn't stay with anyone she knew anymore, that she wouldn't endanger her friends."

"Which means, what? Motels? Hotels? Airports?"

"I guess."

"Come on home and work the phones."

"I got plans, Pop."

"Sorry."

303

Anthony hung up and slammed his palm on the dashboard. "Goddamn it, I hate working the fucking phones."

TUESDAY, JULY 19, 1:15 P.M.

WARDEN ROGER SMITH REMAINED LOCKED IN the oval office throughout lunch, sitting behind a temporary desk, absorbing flurries of phone blows from a very angry commissioner of corrections. "You with me on this? Your fence is fucking Swiss cheese, Rog."

"Yes, sir."

"You throw the fat-ass house guards out on the perimeter until things quiet down, you hear me?"

"If I could, I'd string Claymore mines."

"And if one more inmate kills himself, or takes a stroll—"

"I hear you. I hear you."

"Don't make me sorry I gave you this job."

"No, sir. I won't."

Roger Smith hung up thinking the corrections commissioner had some set of balls, that he had had absolutely nothing to do with his promotion, that he did what the senator said, just like everybody else did, back when Tommy Cotton was still around.

It frightened him to think that Boyd might have nailed Cotton, but he realized any announced suspicions of this sort would be treated as sour grapes. Anyway, who gave a shit who killed Tommy Cotton. Roger Smith was far more worried about Roger Smith. And the scrapbook from hell.

Just thinking about the book made his stomach clench and his bowels rumble, and he got up and raced to his bathroom, where he should have known sooner that something was seriously amiss, from the way the handle stuck when he tried to flush.

TUESDAY, JULY 19, 1:30 P.M.

TOWNSEND TRIPP REMAINED AT THE SENATOR'S desk throughout the lunch hour, working the phones, feathering his own nest, hoping the senator's body turned up fairly quickly, to accelerate the process of succession. He nibbled at a small chef's salad and played his strong suit, his party's fervent desire for continuity, the status quo, business as usual.

Tripp had already made a political accommodation with Sherri Sawchuck, thinking he might later replace the senator in more ways than one. He had called a string of old Princeton classmates, inviting them on board. Only one thing bothered him, other than the loss of his dear friend Tommy: if Officer Orin Boyd was a truly legitimate undercover operative, why the hell didn't he just walk in the front door of police headquarters, or if he was scared, the back door of *Newsday?*

TUESDAY, JULY 19, 1:35 P.M.

ROGER SMITH OPENED HIS CLOSET DOOR AND suddenly knew the reason no one had spotted a crazy blond man in prison denims running around the north shore.

Orin Boyd had left the Farm in one of Roger's favorite workout suits, the purple number with the black stripes, the one that made him look thin. The cops needed to know that, fast, sour grapes or not. His heart beat faster as he picked up his phone and called the major case squad, boldly asked for the boss, told the man in charge he might have just broken the case.

"How so?"

"Boyd's wearing a purple . . ."

TUESDAY, JULY 19, 3:30 P.M.

". . . JOGGING SUIT WITH BLACK VERTICAL stripes. If you see this suspect, do not attempt to approach or apprehend. Simply note his location and call the major case squad at the headquarters hot-line number, 545—"

Orin switched off the Jaguar's ten-speaker stereo, wondering why it had taken the Roger so long to flush his toilet.

It was cloudy and warm out as Orin parked the Jag across from the run-down boatyard at the end of the canal. He had already dumped the Jag's owner, at his Long Beach condo, the poor man of course highly irate to learn he had picked a dud, calmer when Orin explained that he was commandeering the Jag for official police business, that his wife need not know how they met.

Reggie Swain, the Cove City dockmaster, if you could call him that, stuck his head from a small wooden cottage and took a one-eyed squint at Orin's sharp car, his borrowed yellow golf slacks, and white cashmere sweater. "What do you want?" he asked harshly.

"I'm Robert Boyd's son. He told me to meet him here."

"You look like him. Ever hear that?"

"No."

Swain offered his weathered hand and nodded warmly, as if to say: Robert's boy, done good for himself, damn glad to meet you. "I was only grumpy 'cause I thought you were a fucking developer. Bastards want to make me rich, by, get this, building an aquarium right here next to the big one."

"Condo's built around bowling alleys," said Orin. "That's the next thing you'll see."

"Damn right. Bastards. Your dad's boat's on the end there, you wanna go make yourself comfortable. He left early this morning, himself."

Orin found Dad's twenty-four-foot anonymous white houseboat tied up in the last slip at the end of the ramshackle dock, near rusty bubble-headed gas pumps. He peeled back the gray canvas over the sliding glass door to the living room and stepped aboard, thinking his father's house smelled like Nam, a combination of cigarettes, marsh grass, and gasoline. Pulled the canvas closed, turned on the only floor lamp.

The cellular phone he'd asked his father to buy was on the small fold-down table near the smaller propane stove. Orin dialed Meryl Colby, asked for a status report.

"The cops just left a little while ago. A detective named Louis Mancini."

"Never heard of him. What did he want?"

"You don't know a Louis Mancini? Real cute? Smooth operator?"

"No."

"He said he had a message for Judy. He gave me a number to call if I heard from her."

"Do yourself a favor, Meryl. Lose it."

"Oh, shit."

"What happened with Judy?"

"I dropped her off the other day where she said I should. A couple of hours later she came back for Dawn and left."

"How'd she look?"

"Better. Relieved. She said your friend scared the shit out of the guy on her tail."

"You done good, kid."

"She's *my* friend."

Orin hung up smiling, glad Judy had such a buddy in her life, the kind that didn't ask questions and didn't say no. He had once been that to many people, perhaps too many, but at the moment he could not think of a one who would take his call. So he called Judy.

"We're safe," she assured him.

"Me, too."

"When are you coming in?"

"When it's over."

"Can't it be over now? Let the real cops do it."

"No one can finish this like I *have* to, Judy. Okay?"

Orin heard Dawn call out in the background, "Please, Daddy," and he knew Judy was signaling her to join the chorus.

He said, "Tell Dawn that would mean shirking my duty to my family, something her mother would never do."

"Fine. Forget it."

He gave Judy the next phase of the plan, the address of his father's boatyard, said she'd meet a dockmaster named Reggie who was already a big fan of the family, who would show her to her father-in-law's boat, where she should stay, no matter what.

"How weird does that sound?" said Judy. "Father-in-law."

"Very."

"Orin, I think I know who did it," said Judy. "From reading the reports, and—"

"Who?"

"Dr. Robbins," she said. "I think he might have hypnotized those men into killing themselves."

"We're not talking best care anywhere, I'll give you that."

"You don't think so?"

"No."

"Okay. So what now?"

"Start going through the tapes, find a man using a code when he talks to sexy young women . . ."

The list of her tasks grew longer and, on the surface, more scatter-brained, and Orin sensed that he was losing Judy, so he closed their projected itinerary with a family reunion and a fresh start wherever she wanted to go.

"I don't know where I want to go," she said. "Wherever you go, I guess. Far away."

TUESDAY, JULY 19, 6:15 P.M.

ARTIE TOBIN HAD BEEN RELEASED TO HIS FAMILY, for his own protection, and to heal, if such a thing were possible. He spent his days now in the living room of an older two-story house off Milburn Avenue in Baldwin, three blocks from the bay, a broken man.

Orin parked the Jag on the block behind Tobin's, got out and strolled along the hedge to a driveway without a gate, ducked behind a detached garage. Next door a teenager was grilling burgers, his fat back to Orin, the smoke delicious in Orin's nostrils, making his stomach growl.

Tobin had been home for a week now, Orin figured, sitting on a rubber doughnut, wondering what had gone wrong.

Orin was here to tell him.

He pushed through Tobin's rear bushes into a deserted backyard, quickly climbed a vine-covered trellis to the sill of an open bedroom window, slipped inside. Orin whipped out his cellular phone, dialed the number he read off the phone by the side of the bed. Artie Tobin answered on the second ring.

Orin told him where he was and what he wanted, what he would do if Artie balked. "You bring a weapon upstairs, I swear I'll use it on you."

"I hear you."

"Send the wife and kid to McDonald's, Artie. Don't thank me and don't take no for an answer."

"Right."

Orin could hear Artie pack his family out the door to safety, then limp slowly upstairs in his own house like a man facing a noose. He was paler than Orin remembered, leaning on a cane, wearing a gray sweat suit under a navy robe, his face a mosaic of bruises.

"What do you want?" he asked Orin. "How dare you come to my house."

"Don't apologize, Artie. Don't say, 'I'm sorry, Orin, for sneak-attacking you and your family.'"

"I'm not saying nothing," said Artie. "If you're a real cop, I get a real lawyer."

Orin smiled ruefully. "Well, I really don't know that much about the law, tell you the truth. And I've never been all that real. Maybe that's why I never made sergeant."

"Get out of here."

"You're not that fucking tough, Artie. Even with Nick."

"Fuck Nick and the horse he rode in on."

"Yeah?"

"Yeah."

"Because you covered for him, and then he let you down," said Orin.

Artie sat down slowly in a chair in the corner as his eyes met Orin's gaze. "How did I cover for him?" he asked.

"Oh, you know, when you signed the logbooks for him the morning of Skip's death, using his wonder pen. And then you lied to Lieutenant Kruger—"

Tobin looked ready to faint, leaned on his knees.

"Shall I go on?" asked Orin.

"I'm not testifying, you understand?" said Tobin.

"Why?"

"So Nicky don't burn down *my* fucking house, with me and mine in it. Because I can't go nowhere. Not for two more years." Tobin yanked up the leg of his sweatpants, showed Orin the electronic bracelet.

"Why'd he do it, Artie? That's what I want to know."

Tobin did not react, merely stared into space.

On the wall above him was a plaque—"The Policeman's Prayer"—which went on and on about brave deeds and dark nights, the angels watching, and Orin thought it should have included, *And keep me out of jail, And don't let me be raped.* "When the cops questioned Nick, he said the two of you were in your office, hard at work. Dick Pettibone gave you as an alibi, too. But only you. He was mostly on the third floor, changing the window treatments that morning, a fact duly noted in his memo book. And he never saw Nick, now ain't that strange?"

"Not if you knew Nick."

"Dick figured Nick was lying, but he didn't know why. So he said something, maybe to you."

"Not to me."

"To Nick," Orin prodded.

"Yes. The fucking dope."

"What?"

"Nick told Dick that he was really off the grounds with his girlfriend that morning, copping a blow job. So stupid

Pettibone says he'll forget Nick's white lie for a date out-side of his own."

"Keep going," said Orin. "It's good for the soul."

Tobin sat frozen, perhaps already imaging what Morelli was going to do to him.

So Orin said, "Back of the dorm that night: The walk leads to the kitchen door almost the same way it leads to the pool deck from the front of the dorm. Nick took Dick's glasses off and put the boccie bag on his head. Spun him around, like pin the tail on the jackass."

Tobin did not move or change expression.

Orin said, "Nick had told him about using a coal car down a secret tunnel, with weights, for ballast. Nice touch, I might add, the local color."

"Nick thought so."

Orin nodded, an acceptance of confession, one sinner to the other. Tobin suddenly looked at pictures of his family on the dresser, buried his face in his hands and shuddered.

"Why?" said Orin. "Why Skip?"

Artie composed himself, then looked Orin straight in the eye. "Skip was fucked up, okay. This was half his fault, if not more."

"Yeah?"

"Nick fell asleep on Skip's rubbing table that morning. When he woke up, Skip was giving him a blow job. Nick freaked, strangled him with his bare hands. After that all he could think of was to hang him up in his own room."

"And you had no problem with that?"

"What was I gonna do? It was too fucking late to worry about Skip."

Orin lit a cigarette, thinking.

"What would you have done, Boyd, you wake up and George is knobbing you off?"

Orin said, "Nick got rid of the sheet from his own bed, too, Artie."

"What?"

"This wasn't no one-night stand, and it didn't take place on Skip's rubbing table."

"No?"

"Nick liked his dick sucked, and he didn't care who did it, at least not in there. Problem was, dopey Skippy fell in love."

Artie Tobin lit a cigarette, swallowed two big drags of smoke, threw the butt out the window. Orin suspected he was troubled by the image of Nick—his gumba—with Skip, that way.

"Nick didn't want no love letters from the World, Skip telling everyone who'd listen."

"Damn."

"Hey, Artie, no one knew that upstate district attorney was signing sex-slave contracts and videotaping himself in his nightie and heels. Power corrupts, dude. The weird turn pro."

Artie stared out his window and shook his head.

"Where'd they get you?" Orin asked after a moment.

"The infirmary. Three cons faked migraines. When the orderlies left for lunch, they got better. One of them has HIV, I just heard."

Orin tried not to imagine what Tobin had suffered. "I gotta do us both a big favor now, you dig? Let everyone get on with their lives."

Tobin thought this over, got it, finally nodded his head yes; yes, Nick was out of control, and Artie Tobin represented nothing but a liability. Whatever Orin had in mind was an acceptable solution. "He gets out around Thanksgiving," said Artie.

"I can wait."

36

DUSK DESCENDED OVER SOUNDVIEW AS STAFF recalled from sick leave and summer vacation doubled security patrols on the fences. Additional lighting and generators were trucked in and stanchions were assembled at the far dark corners of the perimeter. The inmates remained confined to their rooms.

Upstairs in the oval office the telephone rang, and Smith flinched so violently he barked his kneecap on the bottom of his cheap, small desk and bit off a nice chunk of tongue. "What? Who is it?"

"Don't you talk to me that way, Roggie. Don't you ever talk to me that way."

Roggie's heart froze. "I'm sorry, Mom. I didn't know it was you. I got an HQ guard on the switchboard who doesn't know what the hell he's doing."

"You shouldn't talk to anyone like that. Didn't your father and I raise you better than that?"

"Yes, Mom. What is it?"

"Are you coming home tonight or not?"

313

"I can't, Mom. Not yet."

"You know something, Roggie, I believe I liked you better before your stupid promotion."

Roger knew things had gone from bad to worse when he got the call from Corrections Command informing him that Orin Boyd was indeed an active NCPD undercover operative, working the murders, that he was the source of the Giordano minimikes.

"No," Roger had said softly into the phone.

"Yes. Records of his mission have been found in Trimble's computer files. No paper to back up any of it, though."

"Uh-huh."

"Of course nobody over there knows why he escaped when he could have just walked out the door. The rumor running around now is that the escape was faked, that Boyd was nailed as a snitch, maybe turned into sausage, right under your nose."

"He could be anywhere," said Roger Smith, "a man like him. Florida. Canada. A million miles away, probably has his money with him, too."

"What money?"

"Oh, there were rumors that he was sitting on a drug score."

"This guy's a hero cop. Wake up and smell the coffee."

"Right . . . I got ya."

"Now, Roger, what do we think this Boyd will say, if and when he should surface? Any chance he might embarrass Corrections? Any chance he might embarrass me?"

"No way," said Roger Smith, "not a chance."

Five minutes later Smith was still lying to his boss when Monsignor O'Rourke barged in unannounced. "Of course he never gave me any indication whatsoever. I would naturally have offered my full cooperation."

"Don't lie, you little scumbag," said O'Rourke, waving a finger that looked like a shilleglagh in Roger's face. "If he's dead, you're fucking next."

TUESDAY, JULY 19, 9:50 P.M.

IT WAS FULLY DARK OUT WHEN THE SECOND VE-
hicle Orin had commandeered that day, a currently mis-
numbered black fiberglass skiff, drifted in rough water
close to the treacherous Sands Point jetty. The boat's owner
was as yet unaware of its participation in the war on crime.

Earlier, just before dusk, Orin and his father had driven
the green Jag to the Huntington Yacht Club, cruised
blithely past uniformed security, and parked, never to return.

They had lugged coolers and fishing poles down to the
marina as if they'd been members since birth. Robert had
selected the skiff, for its maneuverability, draft, and color.
And they had waved at everybody as they left the harbor,
just a father and son going fishing.

Now Orin raised his hand and Dad cut the outboard; they
rolled on white-capped waves and focused on the target
looming above them. Orin had changed into a jet black wet
suit, while Robert wore a yellow slicker, had live bait in his
bucket for verisimilitude.

On the hill above them Soundview was a flood-lit mass
of human activity. The employee parking lot, Orin noticed
through his binoculars, was filled with private cars and a
flotilla of white sheriff's vans. "Jesus," Orin whispered.
"Look at Mr. Roger's neighborhood now."

His father put a hand on his shoulder. "Maybe tonight's a
bad night."

"Tonight's the only night." Orin handed his father the
glasses. "They're all on the fences, I think. Other than the
hit squad Smith's probably got guarding his office."

"Nowhere near where you're going?"

"Every place I've been, actually."

"Damn, I can still remember his father, all red-faced
and sweaty, bellyaching about you doing one thing or another to that snot-nosed little brat. I'd promise to kick the
living shit out of you, and he'd march back home like his

balls were steel balloons. Whatever happened to that putz?"

"Mr. Smith? He died about twenty years ago, I think. Don't ask me how."

"I wasn't gonna."

Orin set his feet wide for balance, bent over, and dragged the lockbox from under the seat, knelt down and spun the combination lock. He flipped open the lid, let out air that was five years stale.

His father said, "I thought that was booby-trapped."

"I lied."

"Whew," said his father, waving away the musty smell. "What the hell's in there?"

Orin pulled out a small pile of twenty-dollar bills and a rag-wrapped Smith & Wesson Chief revolver, his dead partner Kenny Demarco's throw-down weapon, previously fired at hammerhead sharks and streetlights in Roosevelt. Also Kenny's service belt, his handcuffs, blackjack, and some flares. And Orin's last hand grenade, left over from the fun in Southeast Asia.

A wave caught them broadside, almost knocked Orin over.

Dad squinted up at the mansion. "No way to do this by the book?"

"Ain't no book for guys like this."

Robert nodded and started the motor up again and nudged the skiff closer to the jagged shoreline, finally cleared the jetty and hit calmer waters. They trolled slowly past the dark, empty docks of the yacht club, which now sat hunkered down behind a brand-new privacy barrier.

"Further up, Dad, where the bluff is steepest."

"It's already too shallow here. You're gonna have to wade in. How long till high tide?" Dad asked, though he knew. "How long until that tunnel fills back up?"

"Four hours, maybe a little bit more."

"Don't mess with Mother Nature."

Orin strapped on Kenny's service belt, checked his tools. "I'm hip."

"I'll be right here waiting."

"I know."

They shook hands awkwardly as the boat rocked, then Orin lowered the anchor over the side and followed the weight into the water.

TUESDAY, JULY 19, 10:55 P.M.

NICK MORELLI SAT FROZEN ON HIS BED, WATCH-ing the local news, frantic that there was nothing on Orin Boyd being dead, alive, whatever; at least he'd know how to play things.

Anthony Bellapannucci was very good at what he did, so Nick had that going for him. Of course, it was gonna cost him every penny he had, but there are just some things a man's gotta have.

A different reporter appeared on his screen, a young red-head in a yellow blazer. She was walking on a beach near an abandoned boathouse, talking about two men found murdered on Fire Island, one of them his cousin.

Nick got up and switched channels, hunting for Boyd.

TUESDAY, JULY 19, 10:58 P.M.

KNEE-DEEP IN THE SUCKING MARSH, ORIN WAS flashing on rice paddies and the land mine he once rode to treetop heights. Flat on his belly in the muck, he remembered mustering out in jolly San Fran, 1969, the streets full of music and magicians, a scrawny chick named Johnatha who gave him orange sunshine LSD and told him darkly that his first name was an anagram of *noir*, his last rhymed with *void*. Good piece of ass, old Johnatha. Probably on some school board somewhere rural now, like Oregon . . . Focus, he told himself sternly. Alice Kreeling had written that the tunnel opening could be found by lining up the boathouse chimney with the tallest spire of Falaise; follow that line along the base of the cliff, he could almost hear her say.

Orin wondered if the muck had smelled half this bad fifty years ago and how far the cliff had receded, buffeted by fifty years of nor'easters. Orin trusted Alice, felt that he could almost hear her voice—rather, he realized, the voice was Marion's, slightly English. Saying, onward, young man. Onward.

Orin reached the base of the kudzu-coated cliff and hugged the earth behind a clump of bushes, listening for the guards, for dogs, wondering if they had expanded their perimeter, hung sonobuoys outside the wire. Then onward in the dark, toward Falaise, he moved on all fours, until his gloved right hand pressed clean through some rotten boards, and he tumbled headfirst into the chamber.

TUESDAY, JULY 19, 11:07 P.M.

IN THE MANSION ROGER SMITH WAS STILL HARD at work on his official report explaining Orin's escape from incarceration, his rationale for command decisions that, under a different light—say federal statutes—might appear discriminatory, small-minded, and cruel.

Tough on crime and criminals, he thought, was the way to portray himself. A hard man cleaning up a long-festering mess that had been brought on by lax discipline. (See photo evidence.) Or he could blame the missing senator for mucking things up. A jurisdictional mishap, again beyond his control.

If the cops had been smart, they would have notified him of the undercover investigation in the first place.

He could have helped. Him and Orin went way back, don't you know.

A failure of communication, was what it was, nothing more. And the failure had not been his.

He was willing to move on, if the police department was, if Orin Boyd could ever forgive him.

The Honor Farm was at last secure, Roger told himself, the players in this sordid drama gone from the field. He could actually survive this rocky start.

Then Roger Smith caught his own reflection in the mirror, and he saw a large man trapped behind a little desk, and he knew he was going down like a stone.

TUESDAY, JULY 19, 11:08 P.M.

JUDY AND DAWN SAT HUDDLED TOGETHER IN THE dimly lit galley of Robert's houseboat, Judy using an earphone to listen to the pile of Honor Farm surveillance tapes, fast-forwarding through mountains of drivel, stopping to search for someone talking in codes, stopping to hear her husband talking to George.

How strange it felt to sit in her father-in-law's home, without ever having met the man, with no idea of his motives, his hopes. On the wall near a shelf of books was a yellow Post-It, with the phone number of a woman named Helen Kitsipoulis written down, wrapped in a heart, of all things. What did that mean about Orin's daddy? she wondered. Dawn's grandfather, the pirate she had always asked questions about.

Dawn wasn't asking any questions now, Judy realized. Dawn was waiting to speak to her father before she made up her mind about any grandfather that just showed up when the house burned down.

"Come on, baby," Judy said, shutting off the recorder. "Let's try to sleep. Mommy has to wake up in a little while."

They climbed into the bunk Orin had briefly occupied only hours earlier. Judy set the alarm clock, placed it on the floor.

"Mommy, when will we see Daddy?"

"As soon as his job is finished. Go to sleep."

"Mommy?"

"Yes?"

"Did Daddy really whip a whole drug gang by himself?"

Judy hugged her daughter tight and whispered in her ear. "He might have mentioned something like that."

TUESDAY, JULY 19, 11:10 P.M.

ORIN SPAT OUT SPLINTERS AND MOSS, FOUND NO other physical damage had been suffered during his fall into the old smuggler's tunnel. It was not likely he had made so much noise that someone topside would notice, but he listened to make sure, and it was then he heard the rats.

He switched on his penlight and saw them crawling on each other around the rotted base of the airshaft up ahead, three-pounders, some of them, and his stomach wrenched. The snap of a flare sent them scurrying into cracks in the rotted wood, for now.

Orin judged the water he was sitting in to be four inches deep, giving him some eighteen inches more to play with before the Sound reflooded the tunnel and sealed off his escape route.

He stuck his head up out of the jagged hole and tied one end of his rope to the base of the shrub near the opening, tied the other end around his waist, lit a second flare for the rats, and inched forward. He felt the water growing higher, above his hips, under his arms, and he realized that his calculations were faulty, that the base had been dug at a much lower level near the shaft, and he had far less time to come and go from the Farm than he previously thought. Maybe an hour. Maybe less. Above him now was the blackness of the vertical shaft, and he could see by the sputtering flare the bottom iron rungs he would use to assist his ascent through the cobwebs and gloom of fifty years.

As he stood up inside the shaft, he caught his foot on what felt like a branch, reached back to pry it free, knew right away it was part of a human skeleton, long buried in the muck. Perhaps one of the original workers on the secret project, a death never reported.

Orin held his penlight in his mouth, tipped his head back, and started climbing up the rusty rungs. He heard the rats close in below him.

37

JERRY COLANGELO HAD SEEN RIGHT AWAY THE
message from the cops, about wanting to speak to whoever
was on duty when that woman and her daughter checked
out of the Freeport Motor Inn yesterday.

Which was him, Jerry, he told Detective Louis Mancini
straight out. Lady and her kid packed up and left about
four-thirty in the afternoon.

"How do you know what time it was?"

"She came in and asked if I knew the bay in Suffolk
County. Some small marina in Copiague. Boat City, I think.
Something like that. I told her I knew Reynolds Channel,
west, that I was a Island Park boy, born and raised."

"What kind of car?"

Colangelo handed Anthony a copy of Judy's registration
form, including the make, color, and plates of her Ford Taurus.

"Luggage?"

"Four suitcases."

"She use the phone?"

"No."

322

"You notice if she had any visitors? Like a blond guy of fifty, maybe?"

"Can't say as I did. Not that I looked. Most of our guests prefer privacy to service, know what I mean? Joey Buttfuck stayed here, am I right?"

Anthony figured he was just eleven hours behind them now, and closing fast. "Right," he said. "And dumb Joey got caught."

WEDNESDAY, JULY 20, 12:25 A.M.

THE DORMITORY PAY PHONE RANG AS IF IT COULD see him, as if it knew he was standing there. "Anthony?" whispered Nick. "Is that you?"

"One at two at three," said the wildest of his women.

Nick thought a moment, then said, "Are you fucking crazy?"

"I'm hot."

Five seconds crawled by, Nick's heart pounding so hard he could hear it, blood rushing from his brain to his groin, weighing the two-for-one odds of scoring a blow job when the fence guard was doubled, pissing off Sissyboy so early in his reign.

He'd have fifteen minutes, he figured, not the usual thirty. Maybe half the regular guards would let him slide anyway, if things went awry. Decent odds.

"One at two at three," she repeated.

"I'll try," he said.

"I'm hot."

WEDNESDAY, JULY 20, 1:08 A.M.

ORIN FOLLOWED THE THIN CONE OF LIGHT UP THE iron ladder through the cliff to the top rung. Two feet above that last rung was a metal ceiling, the top of the shaft. Orin twisted the brass handle at one side and raised the trapdoor two inches, sucked down the fresh air of the graveyard, and listened as if his life depended on it.

No homecoming committee was waiting for him in the cemetery, or if they were, they were very, very good. He gave them a minute more to prove it, then crawled out of the shaft, and locked the bogus headstone for E. H. Kreeling open in the vertical position. He stretched out flat on damp grass that needed cutting, stared up through the trees at the stars, listening. When his breathing returned to normal, he ventured on all fours to a spot behind an old grave that gave him cover and a view of the house down below. He checked his watch and settled down to wait, almost giddy, the old cemetery just another base camp in the long list of such addresses in his life.

WEDNESDAY, JULY 20, 1:26 A.M.

DAWN COULDN'T SLEEP, AND JUDY COULDN'T either. Maybe it was the waves slapping the houseboat. Maybe it was the mosquitoes buzzing the window screens. Or the fish smell trapped in the bed sheets.

Dawn turned on the little black-and-white television, and Judy got out of bed and stepped through the sliding doors onto the dock.

A million stars filled the sky now. A big fat moon was setting to the west. The wind was quiet. Homeless people notice these things, she thought. Frightened people.

Judy heard fat tires slow-crunching gravel on the other side of the canal and pressed close against the houseboat. She leaned back inside and whispered for Dawn to shut off the set.

"But, Mom."

"Do it, now," Judy snarled.

Dawn did as she was told, then jumped back into bed and under her blankets.

Judy spotted a shiny red Corvette casing the big boats tied

up on the other side of the canal. The red Corvette was running silent, deep, no headlamps. The driver had a flashlight he poked intermittently from his window, like some kind of lazy burglar scanning his targets. But how many lazy burglars drove classic cars? Unless that was stolen, too. Something, she knew, was odd about this situation. The light was shining on cars, not boats. She stepped back into the houseboat. "Get up, honey," she said. "We're leaving right now."

"Where are we going?"

"I don't know yet. Just put a jacket on."

"Over my underwear?"

"Yes, honey. Don't argue."

Judy knew in her soul the red Corvette sliding among the other boats like an oil slick was looking for her and her baby, her Taurus. As safe as you thought you could be, you were wrong. Havens crumbled as fast as they were discovered. These kinds of people never played fair, and they never went away.

"Ready?" she asked her terrified child.

"Ready."

Dawn stepped through the sliding doors to the unsteady gangplank, waited.

Judy snapped up the tapes and the tape recorder and the files and her keys and the cellular phone, grabbed the heart-wrapped number for Helen off the wall. Arms loaded, she took one last look around. She was forgetting something, she was sure.

"Mom, there's a car at the end of the block."

"I'm coming."

Judy stepped outside, locked the sliding glass door behind them. Bent over like thieves, they padded down the dock in their slippers.

WEDNESDAY, JULY 20, 1:47 A.M.

TERRY CANTWELL WAS PROWLING THE PERIMEter in a golf cart, with a swollen eye, a walkie-talkie, and a riot gun, thinking that Warden Smith was a total fucking jerk, thinking, Who could blame Boyd for busting out?

Of all the guys on the Farm, Boyd had seemed about the least likely to stir up shit, long as you didn't provoke him, which Smith did. And that was when everyone thought he was a convict. The man had appeared willing to pay his freight, right up until he booked. Based on his years at East Meadow, Cantwell knew they persecuted who they persecuted; usually wasn't no rhyme or reason as to why, unless it was outright political revenge, which sometimes happened.

None of which mattered now, since the cops had just identified the bodies on Fire Island, and Monsignor O'Rourke was on all the television stations, broadcasting an all-clear message to Boyd, a plea from the acting police commissioner to surface, to undergo debriefing.

Sissyboy, Boyd had called Smith, to his pasty white face. You had to like that. Cantwell was half-smiling through his pain as he glided down the perimeter road, past the old cemetery, glad to be still on the Farm at all.

Damn, he thought. Prank was dead. At that moment thirty bucks an hour to breathe fresh air and patrol the fence line seemed fair. Retire at fifty-five on a New York State pension. Move down south, where it was worth something.

WEDNESDAY, JULY 20, 1:49 A.M.

ANTHONY BELLAPANNUCCI BROKE THE FEEBLE lock on the houseboat's sliding door with his crowbar and stepped aboard, gun drawn, ready for anything. He swept the small cabin for targets, male, female, animal, his finger taut on the trigger.

Gone, he realized. But their smell was still in the air, if this was the right place, and son-of-a-fucking-bitch it was, by the letters he found addressed to Mr. Robert Boyd on the wooden wire-spool that served as a cocktail table.

How close had he been? Ten minutes?

He felt the bed. Maybe five minutes?

This had to be a coincidence, them leaving as he was coming.

No way they knew he was after them. He was a pro; they were rank amateurs, chicks, for Christ's sake. They would return, probably with a sack of chow. This job was as good as done.

Anthony Bellapannucci went outside and settled back in his Vette to wait, feeling satisfied and useful.

WEDNESDAY, JULY 20, 1:55 A.M.

ORIN SQUATTED IN THE CLUSTER OF THORN bushes behind the cemetery and watched Nick Morelli through binoculars, lumbering his way up the path like a bear. Thirty yards away he was, then twenty, looking back down at the dark house, sticking to the shadows, then literally tiptoeing past the graveyard gate.

Ten yards away, he was, and puffing up the path like a steam engine, going to meet his girl whether it killed him or not.

Two yards. One.

There are moments, Orin realized, when we have at our mercy the fate of another human being. He had worked for this moment, worked himself up for this moment. There was the black hair on the back of Nick's thick skull and there was nothing else in the world.

Nick crumpled heavily under the lash of the blackjack, and Orin was quickly on his knees in the long wet grass, tying the rope around Nick's fat waist.

WEDNESDAY, JULY 20, 1:56 A.M.

"I WANT A HEAD COUNT," ROGER SMITH SAID TO Officer Marshall. "Now. Something's bugging me. Something's wrong."

"He's gone, boss. Put it behind you."

"Head count."

"Right, boss."

Roger paced the balcony, a general besieged, sure disaster loomed, the way it had every single day of his regime. Then his radio crackled, barked the bad news: "Nick Morelli's out of his room."

"No."

"Probably getting his horn blown."

"I don't care if he's screwing the Queen of England. Hit the alarm. And have somebody ready my horse."

WEDNESDAY, JULY 20, 1:59 A.M.

EVEN FROM DOWN ON THE MARSH, WITH THE waves slapping behind him and the wind whipping up, Robert Boyd could hear the whoop of the siren and see the guards with flashlights pouring out of the command post, heading up the hill, down the hill, for the fence, for the slaughterhouse.

It was a good thing he'd anticipated this. A good thing his son had brought him along.

Robert stood up in the black skiff and picked up the fishing rod, set his feet wide like he was in for a fight. He took a deep breath and started reeling as hard and as fast as he could, yanking the loosened pin from the spoon of the hand grenade he had not ten minutes earlier wedged underneath the yacht club's brand-new wall.

Six, he counted to himself. Five. Four.

The explosion was all he could have hoped for, if a little bit early, reverberating off the old stone boathouse as it summarily flattened a center section of the brand-new wall.

Up on the hill, in the house and the dorm and in the fields and on the lawns, all eyes turned to the sea.

WEDNESDAY, JULY 20, 2:00 A.M.

THE RATS SCATTERED AS ORIN PLAYED OUT ROPE, lowering Nick's thick body through the old rum-runner's shaft, bouncing him off the iron rungs with all the care a temp shows the merchandise when the boss isn't looking.

Faster, he thought. His plan only worked underground, in a tunnel forgotten for fifty years.

Orin heard the grenade explode and froze, fearing the worst, that he'd lost his father just as he'd found him. But then it struck him that the sound had come from the west and not directly below the bluff, where the boat was hidden.

No time to think about it anyway. Speed was everything now. Orin let the rope run through his hands, half a second, heard a splash, felt slack. He took a last fast look around the dark, quiet graveyard, a quiver running through his heart. He was going back, he knew, for better or worse, to a place he had never left. Orin closed the trapdoor and followed Nick down to the base of the shaft.

The rats knew better now, and they stayed clear as Orin cuffed Nick's lifeless wrists to the bottom rung. Then Orin wedged a flare into the wall above Nick and crouched in the rising water, staring at his mud-covered hapless foe, waiting, not debating.

WEDNESDAY, JULY 20, 2:08 A.M.

THE BATTLE FOR SOUNDVIEW YACHT CLUB WAS over in fifteen noisy minutes. After the smoke cleared, Roger Smith rode down to the club on his white horse and declared the scene badly damaged but secured. Honor Farm guards counted twenty-eight bullet holes in the wood, countless chinks in the ancient stone. No one was injured, and Nick Morelli's corpse was not found among the rubble.

The fence line, the warden was informed by Vito Kelly, was secure.

"No holes?"

"Not a one."

"And my bolt cutters?"

"In your office."

"Excellent."

"So now what?" asked Officer Marshall. "Drag the Sound?"

"Not funny, Marshall. Not helpful."

"Sorry, sir."

Roger stroked his mount's neck and stared up the hill. "He's still in here. You know that, Vito? I'll bet we caught on to him just in time. In fact, I'll stake my fucking career on it."

"You could be right, Rog."

"Marshall, you get those fucking bastards out of bed."

Marshall frowned. "Why do that, sir?"

"Because we're locking them in the basement. And then we're combing every inch of this fucking Farm with dogs."

WEDNESDAY, JULY 20, 2:19 A.M.

"YOUR DATE HAD TO CANCEL SO I CAME."

Nick shook off the pain and the cross-eyed funk, blinked in the glare of the flashlight, rattled his chains, saw the bones in the water, and blanched.

"Jesus Christ, man. Jesus Christ!"

Nick tried to scramble, felt his restraints and began to comprehend his situation. He cried out loudly, once, twice, saw that Orin didn't mind, shut his mouth.

"This is what you do to people, Nick. Not that much fucking fun, is it?"

"Oh, my fucking God."

"You might just want to watch your language, Nick, in case all that stuff they taught us in catechism was true."

"What are you talking about?"

"Now, now, let's not get hysterical."

Nick threw back his head and got hysterical, screaming again for help, calling down curses and oaths.

"Soundproof, from Prohibition days," said Orin. "Save your breath."

Nick gave it one more shot, then settled back sullenly, finally asked Orin what this vigilante stunt was all about.

"Crimes against humanity, my man," said Orin. "Let's take a stroll down memory lane."

"You rat bastard, you Internal Affairs fucking scumbag."

"Homicide, Nick. Not a morals beef."

In the limited light it was only the two of them, and Nick didn't waste time denying things. "Who'd believe a fucking hard-on like you?" he said.

"Who cares? is a better question."

"What?"

"They'd believe Skip was your buttboy."

Nick struggled wildly against his cuffs, kicking mud at Orin. "Nobody," he screamed, "and I mean nobody, gets away with that."

Orin checked his watch and said, "I'd stay for more of this lame performance, Nick, but, well, you know time and tide wait for no man."

"Boyd! That shit with Skip—who told you that? Fucking Tobin? Or was it Pettibone?"

"High tide in an hour, Nick. Don't think I'm coming back, 'cause I'm not."

"Huh?"

"We're in a storage tunnel under the family crypt, under Skip, and his father. The Kreelings used it to smuggle rum during Prohibition. I learned about it in a book. *Comprende* 'book'?"

"What the fuck do I care?"

"Well, Nick, because they could only use it at dead low tide, which it was about an hour ago." Orin directed the flashlight beam at the waterline six feet above them on the muck-packed wall of the air shaft. "So figure you got about twenty minutes, before the Sound comes pouring in."

"You don't have the balls."

"Sure I do."

Nick stared into Orin's face. "You do, don't you?"

"I got no choice, Nick. You're fucking cancer. Don't waste your time hoping I'll come back. Use it to pray."

"Come on, hard-on. What's a house between brothers?"

"My only brother died in a car crash, Nick, when he was sixteen years old. Please don't dishonor his memory."

Nick shook his head in amazement. "You know what, Boyd? I'll confess."

Orin knew that not even the new and nastier New York State could give Nick what he deserved. Not that Orin believed in capital punishment. Orin didn't trust the state to rake leaves.

"How about that?" said Nick. "Ought to make you quite a hero."

"You overestimate our importance, Nick. I'll see you in hell."

Then Orin backed away quickly and, falling often, half-crawled, half-waded through the rising high water in the tunnel, and came up at last in the outfall chamber, under a canopy of stars.

Behind him, Nick was begging, cursing.

Above him sounds of chaos filled the night, the whoop of an angry chopper. Sirens were howling as fire trucks raced down the hill on Sound Road. Orin climbed out against the inflowing water and got busy sealing the tunnel, replacing the wooden hatch, the reeds and dead grass—thinking that if he ever had to move his Belmont money, Nick could watch it here. Then, bent over at the waist, he raced through the marsh grass, thinking of nothing in the world but land mines.

His father was waiting for him at the wheel of the hidden black skiff, smart enough not to ask any questions.

Orin pushed the skiff out of the reeds and into waist-deep water before he scurried over the gunwale and fell flat on his back on the deck.

"You okay?" asked his father as he tugged the engine to life, then throttled back, in his element.

"Like taking out the trash, Dad."

Robert steered them due north with one hand and used the other to help peel Orin out of his wet suit. A pack of dogs were suddenly barking as they sped away from the marsh, the hills, and the bedlam above them.

The Sound got rough further out, and the skiff bounced across whitecaps that rattled their teeth and bones. Robert stayed on course, aiming for the blinking red lights on the LILCO stacks.

After ten minutes they slowed to a sensible speed and switched on their running lights. Robert turned his back to the wind, cupped his hands, and lit a cigarette, a signal Orin remembered from his childhood: the toughest part was over. He looked around and saw that quite miraculously they were two crooked harbors east from the prison, just a father and son out for blues.

38

Wednesday, July 20, 5:17 A.M.

ANTHONY BELLAPANNUCCI FLOPPED DOWN HARD on his king-size water bed, bouncing his wife wide awake.

Angela Bellapannucci groaned dramatically, to let him know. "Home so early?" she said unhappily.

Anthony tucked his shoulder holster under the silky purple pillow and told Angela that his temporary employer had fucking skipped out on him, in a very public way.

"Hanh?"

"No shit. My Dad called, while I'm staking out the houseboat. The asshole I'm working for escaped from jail last night. Left me hanging in the fucking wind."

"Yeah?"

"No hole in the fence this time, I hear."

"Hanh?"

"Maybe he pole-vaulted the sucker," suggested Anthony.

"Whatever."

"They don't know how he fucking did it, but he's gone."

"Uh-huh."

"Badabing-badaboom; I fold my tent and head for the

crib. No pay, no play, you dig? . . . Sweetie? Hey! Don't play dead, Angela. I said, Hey!"

WEDNESDAY, JULY 20, 7:37 A.M.

"HELEN KITSIPOULIS," SAID ROBERT, "THIS IS MY son, Orin Boyd, the cop."

Helen lowered her glasses and looked Orin over warily. Next to her in the booth Dawn was grinning and Judy looked ready to bawl, right there in public. "I'm gonna want to see a badge," said Helen, "and a recent ID card."

"*Helen—,*" scolded Robert.

Helen laughed warmly and shook Orin's hand, and said any kin of Robert's was doubly welcome at the Spartacus Diner, for whatever that was worth. Then she stood up and put her arm around Robert's bony shoulder and said, "And this is *your* granddaughter, Dawn, and *your* daughter-in-law, Judy. They came to my apartment in the middle of the night."

Robert grabbed Helen's hand and stared wordlessly down at his son's little family, while they gave him the once-over as well, doing a very nice job of hiding their disappointment.

"Hello, Dad," said Judy.

"Hi, Grandpa," said Dawn.

"Ladies."

Helen went to get coffee while the men slid into the booth. Orin lit a cigarette and watched the sun blaze through the red nautical curtains while his father rambled on nervously to the girls, trying to explain himself without scaring them off. Helen returned with coffee and suggested they order before they fell asleep sitting up.

Orin didn't feel like eating. He felt like drinking. Hard. Driving his boat. Hard. Riding his Harley. Harder. His father's cellular phone rang. Robert answered and handed it to Orin.

It was Zen. "Did you hear about Prank?"

"No."

"On television since last night, bro. They found him shot dead on Fire Island, with Nicky's cousin Freddy Gandolfo. Make sense to you?"

"Yeah," said Orin. "Sure. Prank died in the line of duty. He signed his work. When you get out, we can hunt his shooter down."

"If the cops don't have him yet."

"Hey," said Orin. "We are the cops."

Zen said after a moment, "I suppose it gives one something to live for."

"I'll call you, brother," Orin said, and hung up, handed Robert the phone.

He really would call Zen in a day or so, after he had eaten and slept and made love to Judy several times.

He would also call Brenda Dinostra, and tell her how much her father had loved her; then he would visit the son, the big-deal sergeant, and tell him how his father had died.

Orin looked at Judy and realized how close he had come to losing her, losing everything.

Then Orin stared at his own father and felt his mother's disapproval, kept smiling at his old man anyway, so he wouldn't cry in front of Dawn.

"What?" said Dad. "You eating or not?"

"Hang on a sec. I almost forgot somebody."

Orin waved off their protests and ducked out into the lobby, where he saw that all the local papers were running his departmental photo next to Nick's, explaining the difference below the fold. He dug a quarter from his pocket and leaned against the cigarette machine, dialed up the Honor Farm.

Twelve unanswered rings put him to wondering if Dad's grenade had damaged the phone lines; then at last a young woman picked up and said, "Nassau County Correctional Facility at Sands Point, Roberta Quinlan speaking."

"Let me speak to the Rog, won't you please. This is Police Officer Orin Boyd."

Marion Whither's overwhelmed replacement explained

that Warden Roger Smith didn't work there anymore, that he had been forcibly removed from command during the night, after he had herded all the innocent prisoners into four basement cells and let dogs run wild on the grounds. "Someone named Barthwell is coming to replace him." Roberta added that she hoped the new warden was as nice as the prisoners she had already met. "And what a gorgeous place to work," she cooed. "Like something out of a fairy tale. . . . And today, on my lunch break, this guy George is gonna show me where Gatsby slept."

POCKET BOOKS HARDCOVER
PROUDLY PRESENTS

LADIES OF THE NIGHT

John Westermann

**Coming Soon in Hardcover
from Pocket Books**

**Turn the page for a preview of
Ladies of the Night. . . .**

Thursday, Oct. 24

It was Thursday night, at the height of the silly season.

Deputy Nassau County executive Elizabeth Lucido stood at one end of the bunting-covered dais, wishing she was almost any place else. Elizabeth was thirty-five, with conservative curves on a tall frame, her brown hair swept back in a braid. She wore a navy business suit with white pantyhose, and gold appropriate to her position. Her party, the Republican Party, had just needlessly introduced its current slate to its biggest contributors. The male white pols arrayed to her left were waving at the oft-fleeced faithful, graciously accepting their applause.

Twelve-year veteran county executive Martin Daly was to head the ticket again.

A red-white-and-blue banner overhead proclaimed that Daly had the Experience to Make Changes. It had been Martin Daly's own idea, this novel strategy: suggesting to the populace that he was the candidate best able to make long-desired changes, simply by changing himself.

Martin Daly's problem was, it wasn't working. Though he was only fifty years of age, approaching his prime to hear him tell it, people were getting sick of him.

Democratic Party challenger Jackson Hind was running neck and neck with Daly, never mind that his party hadn't won a big race in Nassau in thirty years—largely due to the opposition of a remarkable political machine, currently owned and operated by its legendary chairman, Seymour Cammeroli. (Should a female Dem have appeared in her kindergarten play, she will be labeled by Seymour a known thespian; male liberals were said to favor homogenius rule. Heads were switched on photos with local pariahs like Joey Buttafuocco and Alphonse D'Amato.)

Seymour Cammeroli had mashed his face between her breasts when Elizabeth had first entered the steakhouse, then whispered up at her diamond earring, "You mark my words. This fucking clown could blow it for everyone."

"This fucking clown" meant Martin Daly, of course, a tall, arrogant man with salt-and-pepper hair and lines in his face that cried yachtsman. Last year Daly had grown so full of himself he had announced for the governor's race, much to the dismay of Seymour Cammeroli, who needed him at home. The ill-considered effort had fizzled, and Daly had quietly withdrawn, saying, alas, his loyalty remained with the taxpayers of Nassau County.

At that moment the big Mick phony appeared to be fighting back tears as he waved at his supporters. His second wife, Kymberly Scallia-Daly, stood next to him, looking drunk and disheveled, as usual. Next to her, his twenty-five-year-old son, Marty Junior, slouched as if the applause embarrassed him. The painfully thin district attorney, Arthur Prefect, and his cluster of minor potentates fanned out from there.

Elizabeth Lucido figured she could ruin half of them, knowing what she knew of their sorry lives, their sordid hobbies, their endless ambition for the free lunch; and yet legions of developers, tobacco lawyers, and health insurance executives stood behind thousand-dollar chicken dinners, cheering these bums as if they were truly the people's servants. It was a system that used to enrage Elizabeth when she was fresh from Columbia Law; she had worked so hard and sacrificed so much only to earn the opportunity to sell her soul. Now she made allowances for twists in logic and decorum. Maturity, she called it. Something in the water. Everybody knew the unexplainable happened with remarkable frequency on Long Island: bimbos shot wives, nut-jobs riddled commuter trains, mild-looking predators stalked kids, and planes fell from the sky; nothing you could do but clean up.

A three-piece band struck up "Happy Days Are Here Again," and Elizabeth decided that she'd had all the maturity she could stand. She nudged her immediate neighbor on the dais. "You think he'll need me for anything else?" she said through a frosty smile.

The burly white cop with the slick-shaved head said "No" through his own phony grin. "Nothing I can think of, nothing that couldn't wait until morning. Or next freaking year."

Lieutenant Robert Rankel was grumpily enduring a rough divorce, with twins away at separate private colleges. He had been Daly's bodyguard and driver for at least ten years, and normally he could sit through anything. These days his patience seemed stretched. "Getting tired of this horseshit, Bob?"

"Wouldn't matter if I was. Have you any idea what textbooks go for these days? Not to mention spring break in London for two. Good Lord, have times changed. Spoiled brats."

Elizabeth knew Rankel would likely be out until dawn on a night like this, piloting Martin and Kym around the circuit, in those leather-knuckles driving gloves Martin so liked him to wear, fetching drinks and holding coats, discouraging dissent in their immediate area, pretty light work for the ninety-eight grand Rankel had made last year. An essential expense, Martin called it, allowing him to move among his people without fear.

A crock of donkey shit, Police Commissioner Frank Murphy had called it, but the spending item passed anyway, because an expenditure like that wasn't Frank Murphy's call.

Elizabeth had seen the newly appointed police commissioner earlier, at the bar, hoisting Scotch on the rocks and telling war stories, pressing his own pounds of flesh. Elizabeth considered the sandy-haired Murphy a class act among these bad suits; one of the few officials she knew who so far had maintained a degree of independence from the party, with principals beyond "What's in it for me?" Murphy had left the restaurant scant minutes after police bagpipers had wailed Martin Daly's arrival, well before the fifty–fifty raffle, a slight that would not be ignored. They were down in her book to have lunch next week at a cozy Long Beach nook where they would stare at each other over wine, and leave feeling good about the world.

"I'm out of here, then," Elizabeth said to Rankel. "I've got an early start tomorrow. Make my apologies."

"I only wish I could go with you."

While the back-slappers high-fived and belly-bumped the ticket, Elizabeth slipped away from the dais and made her way to the front door. She found her claim check in her pocket along with a business card a young committeeman had pressed on her during the cocktail hour.

Outside the evening air smelled of grilled steaks and rain.

"Honda Prelude," she said to the car-park girl, imagining the chaos facing the poor kid later, when all those drunk public officials left at once. "Taurus," they would bark in unison, "black, four-door with a TV antenna. "Of course, many wouldn't know their official plate numbers, and who could blame them? They parked in numbered spaces outside their municipal office buildings; this problem arose only at off-site fund-raisers, and everybody eventually got matched up, usually by whipping out their cell phones and calling their secretaries at home.

Elizabeth had refused a company car, as a matter of style, and because she suspected more than a few hid eavesdropping devices. She waved to the pickets who lined the sidewalk opposite the restaurant, some holding signs, wearing gas masks, mugging for the mini-cams. A couple even waved back. DALY STARVES ELDERLY, read one big sign. THE MORAL MAJORITY IS NEITHER.

The car-park girl whipped the black Honda Prelude to a halt at Elizabeth's feet as the demonstrators chanted, "Daly dyes his hair."

"They're right, you know," Elizabeth said as she handed over a five-dollar bill. "About the hair."

The car-park girl regarded the demonstrators. "Who's Daly?"

"Nobody special."

"Thanks for the tip."

Elizabeth locked her doors and rolled away from the hoopla, exhausted at the end of a long day during a long campaign—all for the hearts and minds of the few eligible voters who still troubled themselves to turn out. All that money they had spent, for a dozen years now, and the car-park girl had never heard of Martin Daly.

Elizabeth's heart beat faster.

She considered the possibility that she and Jackson Hind had a chance to personally orchestrate the collapse of the last great political machine in America.

And that, she thought, was why this particular *abo-gado* had gone political in the first place.

Her redbrick ranch on a cramped side street in New Hyde Park was dark when she pulled into the driveway. Elizabeth wondered if she had forgotten to set her timer lights. That would be like her, during a hot race, dropping the details of her life in favor of Martin's agenda.

Across the street, Miss Wentzel was at her living room window, peeking through the blinds, keeping her eye on the neighborhood, watching over her fellow spinster; you never knew these days, what with drugs and AIDS and guns.

Elizabeth waved and Miss Wentzel waved back.

Elizabeth lugged three policy manuals and her briefcase into the house. She kicked off her heels, dropped her books on the kitchen counter, checked her answering machine. There was a message from her mother, reminding her to take her vitamins, suggesting a brunch date for Sunday, her treat. As if Elizabeth had a spare Sunday in October, as if she wouldn't be walking a swing district. There was a plea from her administrative assistant to remember her breakfast meeting at the Marriott with the mortgage bankers. A short message from Jackson Hind, who seemed to be calling from a bar: "Why aren't you home yet? I can't stand thinking of you among those swine."

She slumped on the living room couch, put her feet up on the cocktail table, next to the phone. The thought of calling her mother drained her. Better to call Mom tomorrow, with cheer in her voice. Probably the same was true for Jackson. And it didn't hurt that he was aching for her. Not one bit.

These were days to be savored, not rushed. She would have kept a journal, had she not feared it falling into enemy hands. More than once she had imagined herself facing District Attorney Prefect's star-chamber grand jury, being perp-walked from the courthouse to the outhouse.

She had battled back the fear.

The world was bigger than Nassau County, warmer than New York.

Jackson had taught her that.

Then Elizabeth heard his signature knock, and a smile creased her face. She padded to the door in her stockinged feet and stood on tiptoes. Through the beveled glass she saw the back of his head, and she knew he was making sure he had not been followed.

Friday, Oct. 25

Good God, he hated beepers. If this was progress, thought Police Commissioner Frank Murphy, leave him most emphatically out.

Murphy apologized to his immediate—and largely elderly—neighbors and slid from his usual pew. He had been baptized in this old brick church in Fairhaven, educated in its school during the prosperous years on Long Island, when almost everyone lived in a new house, worked for a defense company, and bowled on Friday nights. And then the cold war had ended, and Fairchild and Hazeltine and Grumman began shrinking and dying. The best jobs were suddenly government jobs, and those were hard to come by. People moved away, or made do with less. Frank Murphy remembered when mass was said in Latin, when there was still a place called Limbo.

He had prayed that Friday morning for his wife's

continued happiness, and he had prayed for his younger brother Wally, as always. He had prayed for the poor and the sick. Now he prayed this persistent beeping was not bad news, the coin of his realm.

At the rear of the church he dipped his fingers in holy water, turned, kneeled, and made the sign of the cross, then stepped through the wide, heavy doors into the light. He unlocked his gray Crown Victoria and climbed behind the wheel, yanked his car phone off the dashboard.

Captain Jake "The Snack" Posner picked up the hot line on one ring, a civil service record of some sort. "Commissioner Murphy's office," he said.

Jake Posner ran the Favor Bank and Rumor Mill: He always knew who owed whom, who was screwing whom, who was drinking too much, or misbehaving when they did, intelligence that could usually wait until after nine o'clock.

Murphy grumped, "Can't a man visit his Maker without you—"

"Elizabeth Lucido is missing or was kidnapped, Frank. Sometime last night. From her house, it looks like. Artie Prefect is already on his way."

"To make matters worse," said Murphy.

"He answers his pages right away."

"I can't believe he didn't have a closing or something."

Once a third-rate probate lawyer, Artie Prefect was now the district attorney of Nassau County, largely because he was the malleable husband of Chairman Cammeroli's moustachioed sister Rose. He more than doubled his public salary doing real estate, wills and divorces for the faithful. Arthur Prefect knew he was detested and enjoyed it. His attendance was subtraction by addition at any type of scene.

"You got Elizabeth's address?" asked Jake.

"Huh?"

"Well, of course you do."

Murphy stared through his windshield at the church and grimaced. "And people say children are cruel."

"Now you know, Frank. Now you know."

"I hear you."

"What was once an isolated tragedy might have just become an epidemic, if, God forbid, we don't find that Elizabeth is dog-sitting for a neighbor or something."

"Say again?" said Murphy.

"Two big-shot Republican broads, Frank. Poof. Gone. From their houses. And if they ain't safe, nobody is. And this on the heels of a very shitty summer."

Jake was right. That summer, Frank Murphy's first as police commissioner, Nassau County had suffered a crime wave of almost biblical proportions. First the movie-plex stickup dominated the news, then a bloody drive-by in New Cassell. A German visitor to the waterfront was raped in the galley of a trawler.

Then, in early September, Mrs. Babs Whitcomb III, the pretty young wife of the famous philanthropist, and the outspoken leader of the Republican Women's Caucus, disappeared without a trace from her Old Westbury estate.

That case remained open, at a stone-cold dead end.

"I'm on the way," said Murphy. "Maybe I can beat the press there."

Nassau County homicide detectives Maude Fleming and Rocky Blair caught the squeal, on the last of their grave-yard shifts, just hours from a long weekend off. They saw the early arrivals standing on Elizabeth Lucido's front stoop as Rocky parked their unmarked black Plymouth outside the jumble of emergency vehicles.

Rocky was a blue-blazered hulk, a thirty-year-old weight lifter with a flat-top haircut. He said, "Looks like no sleep today, eh?"

Maude Fleming didn't answer as she shoved open the passenger's door and climbed out. She was forty, openly gay, with swimmer's shoulders, going on her seventh year in homicide. Maude dressed like a CEO for her gruesome duties, this clear dawn in a gray pinstriped suit and black pumps. She and Rocky shared a barber.

District Attorney Prefect pulled in behind them, tapped his horn lightly, and saluted.

Rocky said, "Oh, great."

"Just remember," Maude told him over the roof of their car. "We didn't fucking do it."

"Innocent as lambs, we are," said Rocky.

Maude and Rocky had things rolling in no time, the first duties at a crime scene.

Maude got rid of the spectators, then set the truly needed workers to their tasks: the photographs, the sketches, the search for fingerprints, witnesses, the painstaking collection of clothing and carpet fibers, hair, semen, and blood. Maude was playing this case as a homicide until someone proved to her otherwise, because this one looked too familiar to the one unsolved case on her résumé: Mrs. Babs Whitcomb III.

As always, Maude would supervise the gathering of evidence and the questioning of witnesses, and Rocky would leg out her theories, a system that worked for them, credit shared equally.

She made him smarter and he made her tougher. He didn't care who she slept with, and she didn't care that he lacked the facility to stifle first impressions, that he sometimes said the dumbest things.

Her own particular skill was to focus clearly on gruesome situations, to see—and understand the significance of—details others overlooked because they were squeamish or frightened, or lacked her imagination.